To Heal a Wounded Rogue

previously published as **Fortune's Flower**

by

MARY ELLEN BOYD

ISBN-13: 978-1-7376781-3-7
ISBN 10: 1-7376781-3-6

Once again, I am compelled to thank
the members of the
Minneapolis Writer's Workshop
for all the things they taught
me over so many years.

Some of the members are gone now
but I remember them fondly.
I would not have learned
enough to even consider releasing
my books to the public were it not
for their generosity, sharing so
much of what they knew with myself
and with all the other members
fortunate enough
to have found this valuable
group.

So to Herb, who said,
"Mary, who ever told you writing was easy?"
and Rex and Mary and
Marjorie and Ivan,
all of whom are gone now,
and to the current members
who continue their legacy:

Thank you so much.

1

_1809_

The clattering knock jolted Verbena out of precious sleep. She threw on her old robe, hearing a few more threads rip in the thin fabric, and hurried out from the small room in which she slept, just beyond the kitchen. Hopefully she would reach the door before whoever it was woke her father. He had come home drunk again last night, and fought her when she tried to put him to bed. The last thing she needed was a repeat.

She pushed her curly pale, sleep-mussed hair out of her eyes, the better to see. The house was barely light, only differences in shadows marked the furniture, but she knew it too well to need a candle, and there was no time, anyway. The pounding began again. Verbena flipped the bar and jerked the door open. "What is it?" she hissed in a whisper before her tired eyes focused on the person standing outside. "Oh! Why—"

She surprised herself by even recognizing the woman. Agnes, her sister's thin, pinch-mouthed, grey-haired maid, whom Verbena had seen only a few times when Edeline dropped in for one of her rare visits. What business would Agnes have here at this hour? No one of wealth got up this early. Edeline had certainly forgotten how by this time, she had been married into wealth and luxury for six years, and Agnes would hardly come on her own.

So who had sent Edeline's maid? And why? Verbena's heart skipped a beat as drowsiness gave way to the first stabs of panic. "Edeline?"

Agnes looked down at Verbena's robe with distaste. The rip must have been obvious even though the light was poor, just a bare slit on the horizon that marked the night's end. Verbena felt her cheeks heat as she caught herself comparing their two garments, her tatty robe and the woman's maid's uniform, crisply pressed even at this young hour of the day. It was as if Agnes knew that everything in Verbena's wardrobe was equally poor. After all, the Barnes were no longer comfortable enough, their house an aging façade, the whitewash worn away, the windows cracked, not something easy to hide.

A painful reminder of what once was, the days before the government started passing the laws that separated land, dividing the countryside between those who owned it and those who lived and worked on it.

And the small landholders began losing what little they had. Landholders like her family.

"Here," Agnes said shortly as she shoved a note on fine paper into Verbena's hand. "I was to bring this to you. Now I have done my duty." She ran her scornful gaze once more over Verbena's figure, then turned and stalked away.

Verbena shut the door quietly behind Agnes, watching her melt into the first faint promise of a summer's dawn, and sat down at the heavy bench by the door. She swiped again at the loose blonde locks that blocked her view and saw her name written in bold letters on the folded linen paper. Her bed pulled at her, the day's work lay in front of her like an unending road, washing all her father's clothes from this last voyage, cooking for him and the other four children, baking bread, helping the girls sweep and scrub the floor, and all the other chores they did to keep the house going. This letter from her sister delivered at such an odd time could only be bad, bad news. She had not even known Edeline and her husband were back in the small town of Thernbury. Verbena braced herself and broke the thick seal.

The rich paper crinkled under her hands as she smoothed it flat on her knee, the words a black sprawl on the paleness of the paper. Verbena held the letter closer, squinting at the words, wishing she dared light a candle, but candles cast light and smelled. Her father's room was too close, a straight line from the front door into what had once been the back parlor, before the children all came. She could never predict what would wake him, and waking him right now was the very thing she wanted most to avoid.

Edeline's childish handwriting was done in large round, hurried letters in thick black ink. She angled the paper until the letters took shape. *"Help me, Verbena. Come to Thernwood Place immediately"* – the last word had been underlined – *"and I will explain."* There was a postscript in smaller letters, as if it had been added with only a moment to spare. *"Don't let anyone here see you come. Go the gazebo. I will watch for you. <u>It is important</u>."* She had underlined the last three words so hard the quill had nearly gone through the paper.

Edeline had always been inclined to the dramatic. It was hard to take this message seriously, but it sounded like she was truly panicked. It had been so long since her last letter, and now this strange missive with the equally strange delivery.

There had to be a powerful reason for Edeline go to all this effort, sending a maid before the sun was up. A chill went up Verbena's spine that had nothing to do with the cool summer night. Edeline asking her for help? What did she think Verbena could do, whatever the problem? Edeline was married to Andrew Thern of Thernwood Manor. The Therns owned most of the land around the village, which meant they had most of the money, too.

Verbena longed for some of that money, ached for it, some nights when she was too tired to sleep she even wept for it. Money solved everything. With money, they could buy food and not have to depend on the tiny patch of garden behind the house, they could pay for the fences the government kept demanding. With money, she could send the boys off to school. How Julius would love that!

With money she would not have the humiliation of depending on her sister's remembering to send a little something so Verbena could buy food or clothes or shoes for the children.

Verbena held the letter to her chest, fretting anxiously. Go now, at this unbelievable time of the morning, with the sun not even up? Something must be desperately wrong in the Thern's house, if Edeline required her to sneak a visit to the gazebo, and at such a ridiculous hour.

A thump came from across the hall, followed by a curse. Her father was awake.

Verbena jumped to her feet in the small square entryway, her fingers curling tightly against the fine paper. No doubt Agnes's knocking had finally penetrated his drunken haze. He was going to be in a foul temper. He had been so terribly drunk when he got home last night, his first day back in town. Thomas Barnes never wasted much time catching up from the months of enforced sobriety at sea.

His door bumped open and he stumbled out, holding onto the stairway's solid wall as he stared around. She did not need light to know his eyes would be red and bloodshot, or to see the veins the last six years of drink were painting on his nose. The odor of whiskey washed out with him. He was not a tall man, but the muscles he carried from all his work at sea made him look bigger. His dark blonde hair stood up in a thick shock of speckled grey, an unlikely halo. Verbena stood quietly, hoping he would not notice her. The shadows were fainter than they had been mere moments ago.

At the end of the stairway wall, Barnes made the right turn toward the dining room with almost military precision and she heard him collide with the table, its heavy legs scraping along the wood floor. He belched a shocking word out of his mouth. He was doing it again, going outside to take care of his business. He had a chamber pot in his room, but seldom used it.

The back door creaked open before she could make the dash through the dining room and the kitchen into her room, and he stumbled in again. She followed his path by the scraping of his feet. When he came into sight his eyes were no more focused than when he first appeared, fixed straight ahead, blank and unseeing, a narrow sliver of reflection. By some oddity of drunkenness, this time he missed all the furniture on his way back to his room, walking as if pulled on a string, placing each foot carefully on the floor in slow motion. He made the same precise turn as he passed by a second time, what remained of his attention fixed on that bedroom door. He went down the hall with no major damage, and the door slammed shut.

When she heard his body flop on the bed, the still-sturdy frame complaining, a quiet sound through the heavy door, Verbena made her decision. Married or not, Edeline was still her sister. If she wanted help, it was up to Verbena to provide it. Edeline had, after all, done her duty in providing funds for her siblings. Where would they have been if not for her? Verbena hurried across the worn wooden floor to her room, avoiding by long practice the places where it creaked, moving so fast her robe filled with air like a curtain in the wind.

Once inside, her own door shut tight against any stray sound, Verbena threw off her robe and nightgown and grabbed the closest dress from the peg. In the half-light, she could not tell which gown it was, but it hardly mattered. None were any better than the others, and she was going to be running through the woods to get there.

She pulled her mother's silver-handled brush, a treasure she carefully hid from her father, through her hair, and tied a ribbon tightly, hoping it would stay in place through the woods. One more moment to pull on her boots. They were well made, another hand-down from her mother, high-topped and low-heeled, perfect for a run through the woods. As quietly as possible, ever-mindful of her father's too-recent waking, she crept back through the kitchen. Everything was becoming visible now, even into the dining room where she could see the long table, the bench that always got in the way, their father's large flat-backed chair. Verbena eased the kitchen door open, slipped out, and hurried down the path.

When she reached the Thern's fence at the forest's edge, Verbena stopped at the wooden guardian, a silent 'no trespassing' warning. She paused and looked around as she put her first foot on the fence, but no one jumped out, no dogs howled a warning, so she swung herself over the top and landed on the other side with a swirl of skirts.

Then she took off, racing along the stony track that ran parallel to the sweeping drive toward the wide, gracious doorway of Thernwood Manor, holding up her skirt to speed her way, dodging the branches that draped over the neglected, unkempt path, more visible with the hints of pink and yellow creeping over the horizon and tinting the leaves, each exposed color a reminder of how little time she had, the risk she took.

Part way there, she stopped to catch her breath and ease the cramp in her side. It had been too long since she had run so hard. This spot was the perfect place for a rest, her special place, and it was so long since she had been here. In the days before the fence's barricade, she had always found an excuse to rest on the old log that had fallen along the path some time in the past and was taking its time going back to the earth. She was out of sight of her own house, and of the Therns' large mansion, from anyone who might see her.

No one had ever caught her here except *him*. Damon Thern, Edeline's dark-haired, dark-eyed brother-in-law. It was a memory Verbena had never shared with anyone.

He certainly would never recall the event, assuming she ever even saw him again. It was her memory. She had been carrying a large basket of her mother's bread to several tenant farmers of the Therns who struggled daily to survive on their small rented patches of land. As every other time, Verbena had taken the usual shortcut through the Thern woods. Her mother insisted she dress up as if making a call upon a valued friend when making the deliveries. "You will show them the same respect you do those above you," was her mother's motto.

Such extravagance of attire had never made sense to Verbena. It smacked too much of emphasizing what they had that the others did not. When she had tried to argue with Mother, she had gotten a disappointed stare, as if she had said something so crushing that her mother had been too wounded to speak. So she had been wearing a blue sprigged muslin gown with a lace ribbon that tied under her breasts. She had pushed off her hat and it hung down her back, but even now, in the crispness of the summer morning, Verbena could remember the warmth of that day. Her hair had been freshly styled, her half-boots neatly polished, the perfect young lady except for being alone in the woods.

That day might have been one of many, just one more trip like so many other trips she had made in better days, but for him. She had rounded this same bend, the basket getting heavier and heavier, when a tree root snagged her ankle and she had tumbled into the small clearing. The basket went flying as she threw out her hands to catch herself. Her palms stung when she landed.

A sound, a resonant rumble, came from very close by.

Startled, Verbena had looked up from her ignominious position on the ground. And looked up. And looked further up.

Damon had been there on the small trail she used, sitting like a prince on his steed. A blush heated her cheeks. She knew him from their village church, where his family had their own pew right at the front, knew his name, even his moniker. Damon the Demon, for his wildness. He was the most handsome man she had ever seen, curly dark hair visible even under his tall hat, mysterious near-black eyes, and taller than usual on his huge chestnut horse, towering over her where she sat on the path.

He dismounted with smooth grace and hurried over to her. She sat up quickly, brushed off her abraded palms before he reached her, and hoped nothing was bleeding. He reached her before she could tell.

"Are you hurt?" he had asked in a deep voice that raised the soft hairs on her arms and sent shivers down her spine. He hardly seemed to be living down to his reputation.

A gloved hand appeared in front of her face. "No, I thank you," she had answered, and her voice had been breathless. It might even have become so from the fall.

Damon crouched down beside her, seeming to take pity on her strained neck, and watched her, those dark eyes following her movement. She had never seen him up so close. His hair was as black as a raven's wing, and the curls looked as soft as her baby sister's hair. She had been tempted to reach out and touch them to see if she was right. Her brothers hated curly hair, although her mother said they would outgrow it. Did Damon's waves embarrass him?

While she was staring at him, he noticed her hands. "You are injured." He had taken both her hands and turned them over, looking at them with a frown. He released one hand, but kept hold on the other. She remembered the surprise as he pulled out a white handkerchief and pressed it against the very area that stung the most as if it mattered not at all that her hand was dirty as well.

He took the handkerchief away, and it was spotted with red. "You see? You are bleeding." He put the cloth on her palm again.

"Then it just started. I was not bleeding when I looked." Calling that brief glance 'looking' was a vast exaggeration, she knew.

Damon raised one dark brow and said nothing.

She felt another flush of red creep up her cheeks. She must look like a ripe apple. "Clearly I am now."

He wrapped the handkerchief around her hand and tied it in a neat knot across the top. "Do not take this off until you get home." He settled back on his heels and frowned. "I hardly expected to see a young woman wandering about the woods alone. Do your parents know that you are out?"

"I'm known in the village. No one would hurt me." Verbena

remembered how she had met his gaze bravely despite the quivering inside.

"I would not be so certain of that." He had looked at her again, more carefully, but nothing in his gaze made her uncomfortable.

"They know I bring bread, and many of them need it." And then Verbena had seen the basket sitting on its side. "Oh, no! The bread! How many are lost?" She scrambled to her feet, pretending not to notice the large hand that again appeared at the edge of her vision, and hurried over to the basket.

Somehow he managed to beat her there. "Just one, I think, will have to be left for the birds." He picked the basket up, but made no effort to give it to her, just stood there holding it. "Lucky birds. These smell delicious. And to think I had no breakfast this morning. My stomach is scolding me soundly right now." His dark eyes had twinkled at her across that over-sized basket.

Prior to that, she would never have thought such dark eyes could twinkle. But they certainly could, and did. At least his had. A gentle smile curved his lips, and for the first time she had noticed the shape of his mouth. It fit his face, she thought, firm, thin upper lip, slightly fuller lower. She wondered what it would feel like, just to touch, and another new, forbidden thought came, to kiss. The woods had suddenly seemed quiet, as if all the birds were holding their breath just as she was.

Verbena's heart had pounded, the only sound her ears heard. She did not know what to do, or if she wanted to do anything but savor this slice of time when Damon Thern looked at her and saw her. But then her mother's voice had seemed to come out of nowhere. *You will take these loaves to the neighboring farms.* Was the voice a divine nudge, saving her from herself?

It had been insistent, that quiet echo of her mind, pulling her away from her foolish daydreams, dreams of a girl poised on the edge of womanhood. The mundane world came back, the birds chattered in annoyance at being interrupted. She had reached for the basket, and after a brief delay he let go. He gestured at her hands. "You should wash those off as soon as possible. I have heard that is the best way to avoid infection. Perhaps you should go back to your house and take care of your scrapes first?" His eyes were still gentle. "I would be happy to escort you."

"Thank you, no," she said, but she had not backed away. "You have been most kind, but I must get these to the other farms."

"But you will wash your hands thoroughly and get all the dirt off?" His face went soft with worry when usually it was imposing, all sharp edges, a strong face to go with his strong body.

So she had promised, and then she had gathered all her courage and asked a question that had flown around the village for weeks. "Is it true that you will be putting more fences up?"

Damon said nothing for a moment, his face suddenly shaded. All the softness of a moment ago was gone. A muscle flexed in his jaw. She could still feel the slight chill that had washed over her. He was a Thern. Everyone knew the fences were going up at their instigation. In a burst of unexpected courage, she had said, "Because of all these fences, farmers and hunters around the village have been threatened with arrest for going into lands they have used for centuries."

"You are slightly misinformed." His voice had turned as stiff as his posture. "We have nothing to do with the decision to fence the land. It is a government order, and everywhere you go, everyone is doing the same thing. It has been going on for years and I fear there will be no stopping it."

She said nothing, just absorbed his words. This was happening everywhere?

He sighed. "As long as you have heard this much, and since you are clearly curious, I should tell you I have heard Parliament is working on still more Enclosure Acts. The fences are expensive for everyone. One hopes they will tire of passing these laws soon." Damon said it with finality, and she knew their conversation had come to an end.

"What about your cloth?" Verbena had looked down at her bandaged hand, the best she could gesture while clutching the basket. A design in blue in the white fabric had caught her eye, letters she could not make out then.

"Keep it. I have so many, I won't even miss it." He was probably even telling the truth. Why would he want it anyway, now that it was bloodstained and dirty?

Funny she had not thought of that handkerchief in years, but now, standing in that small glen, she remembered exactly where it was. She had washed it as clean as she could, and saved it, thinking some day she might be able to give it back, have one more chance to talk to him, to see if they could recapture those moments past when they stood, however briefly, on level ground. She could hardly have used it, not with the embroidered initials, the blue DT that had caught her eye. The day had never come when she could talk to him, remind him, and return it, but she had kept it.

That had almost been the end of the memory. There had only been a moment left together, when Damon touched a finger to the brim of his hat, gave a graceful bow, mounted, and turned the horse, trotting down the path where he soon vanished behind the thick curtain of green. He must have kept her trespassing secret because no one ever came to order her to stay off the wood path.

How prophetic he had been. By the time the Enclosure Acts had hit the Barnes and their small bit of land, land that had housed a cow, a pig and several sheep, and they found out the fees for the fences that they were forced to erect, her mother had been dead, her father had begun his drinking bouts, and money had been far too scarce. The Therns had closed off the last of the common lands, cutting everyone, including them, from the grazing areas the entire village had enjoyed as far back as anyone's tales went. Not just grazing disappeared, so did the calves and kids and piglets that arrived regularly from the neighbors' animals that shared the once-open fields.

Her family still had a tiny bit of land left that had not yet had to be sold to pay for the fence, enough for a small garden and some chickens, and they had the house, but for how long?

Verbena did not know why that one moment of her life had

stuck with her. She must have been all of fifteen then, seven years ago, and he was already a grown man. He must be over thirty now.

Her breath was back now, the stitch was gone. That memory was such a silly thing and there was no more excuse to linger. She started running again but her recollections kept her pounding feet company, only those and the startled rustle of bird's wings.

She had been so lost in her thoughts that when the track curved around the last stand of trees, she was startled to find she was already there. Thernwood stood before her in all its immense glory, magnificent even before the sun was fully up, dark brick, white window frames, and pillars marching like white statues, muted in the dark. Verbena grabbed a trunk to stop herself from bursting into the manicured lawn that surrounded the whole house. She saw the drive ahead leading to broad entrance, then curving toward the stables, pale worn double lines left by carriage wheels. She did not know where the gazebo was, but it could not be that hard to find.

Verbena stayed in the trees, following their shield as she circled behind the house, wondering how Edeline would see her. She'd never been so close to the mansion before. One did not come uninvited.

Although Edeline's letter classified as an invitation of sorts. From the furtive way her sister had summoned her, Verbena suspected the Therns would not see it the same way.

The windows on the lower level were covered, drapes drawn tight in an odd summer defense against the cool air, as were most of the windows on the next floor. One of the curtains on the main floor twitched, a tiny gap opening between the panels, leaking a swath of light. Verbena backed further into the trees.

She slipped between the trunks, looking for the Thern's gazebo. It would have been most helpful if Edeline had sketched a map. A rush of color to her left, a jolt in the fading greyness of dawn's arrival, scared her, and she jumped, tripping over a root and falling against a tree.

It was Edeline, fully dressed, running toward her. Her soft

brown hair had been pulled up on her head, but it was coming loose, pins no doubt raining onto the lawn. Verbena saw a curl slip loose and tumble down to her sister's shoulder, but Edeline did not seem to notice, instead pointed frantically in a muddled direction, her arm a pale wave flapping back and forth, and kept running, her gown wrapping around her legs and impeding her progress. Verbena kept pace, staying within the trees' scant protection.

When they got out of sight of the house, Edeline stopped, wrapping an arm around a trunk for support and gulping for air. Verbena eased through the trees and joined her.

Edeline put a hand to her chest, her deep breaths pushing against it. Her words came rapidly, but still hushed. "Come quickly, before someone sees us!" Her blue eyes were wide and glazed. "We have to hurry. Someone might have heard me slip out." Her face had lines that had never been there before, and her skin was pale and grey. She grabbed Verbena's arm and pulled her along through the edge of the trees. She was shaking, her hand almost vibrating on Verbena's arm.

Verbena glanced at the mansion appearing and disappearing through the stand of trees as she followed her sister. "What is it? Why did you send the note?"

"Not here," Edeline whispered in a rush. "The gazebo. No one will see us there." She led the way around the sheds tucked behind the mansion, another layer of protection keeping them shielded from the house. Rosebushes past their first blooming tried to snag their gowns.

The gazebo appeared, nestled in the center of a man-made glade where the rosebushes had been trained over an arched opening of ornate metal. Small trees surrounded the many-sided little white building, and flowers circled its base in splotches of fluffy light colors, giving only hints of their true hues. Glass panes were covered with ivy working its way up the sides and over the top, a heavy tracery of dark leaves layered one upon another, lifting with the breeze. It must be beautiful in the daytime.

Verbena looked back at the path they had taken. She never would have had the courage to venture this far into the Thern's property, she never would have found the gazebo on her own. Thank goodness Edeline had seen her from the upper window.

If that watcher was Edeline. She had come out rather quickly for having been on the second floor.

Edeline slid the latch and waved Verbena inside. Sheltered by the trees and the vines, even in the dusky half-light the gazebo felt like a place apart. The white stone walls and floor gave an eerie glow, amplifying the coming day.

Flowers scented the room, blending like a delicate perfume. Roses, wallflower, sweet peas, violets and lavender, all delicate in the early morning, made their presence known from the other side of the white walls. It was a room for lovers, for good news and restful moments, not for the dread that filled it now.

Edeline dropped down on one of the fancy white wooden benches that lined the wall, and sighed, her face a pale moon. "We're safe. At least for a little while." Something thrummed through her voice, a tension barely held in check.

Verbena glanced out the door, but nothing changed, nothing moved. They were hidden for the moment. She turned back to her sister. "Edeline, what is going on? Why are you so frightened? Tell me, what is it?"

Just that quickly, Edeline buried her face in and burst into tears, loud, noisy sobs breaking through the need for quiet, as if some inner anguish could no longer be contained. "Oh, Verbena! Andrew is dead . . . and I am pregnant."

2

Verbena gasped. All her irritation at her sister evaporated like dew. "Oh, no! Oh, Edeline, I am so sorry," she said, feeling the emptiness of her words. She hurried over to the bench and sank down beside her sister, pulling Edeline against herself and holding her just like she did the younger children. Sorry. What a pitiful thing to say. "What happened? How?"

Edeline looked at Verbena with streaming eyes, the tears making glowing silver tracks down her cheeks. Words poured out. "He was my heart, my only protection, and he is gone. I'm all alone. He has been sick off and on for weeks, months, that is why we came out to the country, and I hoped, I prayed, he would get better, but I knew it was bad, I knew it was so very bad." Her sobs echoed in the gazebo, so loudly that Verbena did not dare trust the glass windows to hold the sound in, not even with the layer of ivy.

"Hush, oh, Edeline, you must hush. Someone will surely hear you." She tightened her arms and wished for the right words. "When did it happen?"

"This night. An hour ago."

Verbena held her gasp. An hour. "What can I do? Tell me."

Edeline lifted her head and Verbena could see the anger in her eyes beneath the sadness. "You think . . . my life is charmed . . . don't you?" The sentence was broken by the shudders that shook her as she tried to control herself. "If you only knew . . . what my life has been like! If I had known. If only I had known before! I am a prisoner. I feared the butler would catch Agnes, early though it is, and tell Madame Thern. They would not give me another maid and she was all I had, the only way I could get word to you." Her hands clenched on Verbena's arms.

"A butler can't outrank you."

Edeline took a gasping breath, and Verbena let her go. "You think not? I assure you, it is true. It has been horrible! My life is a misery! They hate me, they always have. I was never good enough for their son. I should not say this, I should never speak so, but Andrew did not see. They were too clever for him. He always saw the good in people. I tried to I tell him what they were doing, but he would not believe me. I know they wanted him to send me off." Her face softened with some memory. "He never understood their hints, never heard their insults. All I had was that he was my husband and they could not change that. With him gone, I am lost!"

Verbena was very afraid her sister might just be right about Andrew. She knew which one she would trust with the immense wealth and property the Therns had to protect. Andrew was the dreamer, Damon the doer. In Andrew's hands, the land might very well fall into disrepair while he sat in his study and read his books, or spent money finding rare tomes to add to his collection. She had seen him several times over the years reading books by the river, a dreamy expression on his face, as if there was no one else in the world but himself.

"I have to leave quickly," Edeline said, the words tumbling over each other. "I have to find somewhere safe, somewhere they would never think to look. They can't know yet, I have been so careful, but the minute they find out they will take my baby away! He is the heir. They will never let me raise him."

"Surely not!" Verbena gasped. "You are the mother. They have no right!"

"Oh, Verbena. You have no idea. It was bad enough in the early days, there was Father's land and Mother's graciousness and charm. The house was in better shape then, so we Barnes were at least respectable. When the Enclosure Acts were passed and they put up the fence around their land and Father had to sell off land to pay for our own fences, and I heard that you had to sell the animals" – her words came out faster and faster – "Oh, the laughter. I heard them talking when they did not know I was around."

Frantic fingers clutched at Verbena's arms. "Never, ever think that you can cross the lines of class, Verbena. It is not possible. We have our place and they have theirs. I was a fool to think that Andrew's love would protect me." Sobs shook her slender frame again. "Even the servants were treated better than me, at least they knew their place. They never listened to me, never once, and no one insisted they do so. Why would they listen to me? I'm one of them, masquerading as the mistress of the house. Orders come from someone superior. They mocked me on a daily basis. I could give the cook the dinner menu, and something else entirely showed up on the table." She hiccupped but the words kept coming. "I could never prove that Madame Thern was behind it, but she was, I know she was!"

Edeline wiped a hand across her face, spreading her tears across cheeks blotched with weeping. "They are all grieving inside the house, not because Andrew is dead, but because it is not me lying there cold! I must stay for the funeral, I do – *did* love Andrew despite everything, but the very minute I can get away, I'm leaving, and do not think you can talk me out of it. They will not even bother to look for me – as long as they do not find out about the baby." She gripped Verbena's arms so tight Verbena knew it would leave bruises. "No matter what, they must never know about the baby. I can't let him be raised by *them*."

Despite Edeline's grief, irritation poked at Verbena. "You forget something. Like you said, this child is the heir. Can you not see what that means? All that Andrew has – had goes to it. That changes everything. You are safe now. You are its mother."

"Have you heard nothing I said? If I can't hire my own maid, what about hiring a nanny? Do you think they would ask my opinion? They would hire whoever they wanted." Edeline's tears dried. She took another swipe at her cheeks to wipe the lingering trails of wetness off. "I don't care what he has, or what he will inherit. You do not know these people. You do not know this society. You either belong or you do not, and we – you, me, all of us, do not. We are a laughingstock to them. These people do nothing but gossip, dance all night and go to the theater. I could tolerate it if that was the worst, but it is not."

She shook her head as if trying to block an image in her mind. "I have seen people in the richest of clothes shoo away little beggar children in rags. I have seen people fall down on the street of hunger and all the well-dressed people of the *ton* just walk around them. Their only reaction is to complain that the riff-raff are allowed out among respectable people. Not just the Therns, although they have done the same. Everyone acts like this. It is just the way things are done."

Edeline's hands clutched at her bodice as if to pull it off. "My modiste can't come to the front door to deliver my gowns. When you go to dinner, you are not allowed to look at the footmen who wait on you. And woe betide you if you stop to visit with a maid! I watch them and I know they would treat Julius that way, and Matthew." Her voice trembled again. "And you, and the girls. I want my child to be kind, I want him to be a man respected by his neighbors, and not because of what he has. I can't let him become one of them."

Verbena had seen some of this on the occasions when the Therns came into town. She had seen them ignore the townspeople at church, but she had never thought of Julius or Matthew being treated like that. Damon had talked to her on the path. There had been no distance until she mentioned those hated Enclosure Acts. Perhaps he had not thought of her as of another, lesser class.

Her mother's insistence on her dressing her best might have spared her from being a victim of snobbery.

Somehow, though, such behavior did not quite fit the man. But what did she know, after just one brief conversation?

She had to try one more time to get her sister to think. She knew, if Edeline had forgotten, just how hard life was without money, and just what her sister was throwing away. "You can teach him better." Edeline seemed to assume this child would be a boy, and Verbena found herself following her sister's example. "Perhaps that is your purpose, to make him better than the class to which he belongs."

The look Edeline gave her seared her skin. "That is a large assignment for a child, don't you think? I don't believe that is my responsibility as a mother, to force my child to remake the world. I just want him to be happy, and to learn fairness, and that he can't do in this class. No. I will take him away and I will give him the life that will make him happy. We were happy as children. I will see to it that he is, as well."

Verbena thought of Lizabeth and Annabelle. Were they happy? She was not at all sure she wanted to ask. Whatever Edeline had gone through with the Therns, she had forgotten much about life with the less privileged. Even before the hard times had hit, their life was not as gilded as her sister wanted to remember, though Verbena knew she would not be able to convince her otherwise.

Edeline was carrying the heir to whatever money the Therns had, and Verbena could only assume that was quite a bit. She wanted to leave that all behind. Verbena could only hope when Edeline's mind cleared, she would go back and demand the child's due.

She wondered how they would survive, how she would provide for her brothers and sisters, without Edeline's gifts, and felt guilty that the thought had even slid through her mind. Andrew was dead. "Where will you go?"

"I promise I have been thinking on nothing else for days, from the moment Andrew got worse." Edeline gave a hiccup of a last sob. "You must help me find somewhere."

The request irritated Verbena. Why did everyone expect her to make things right? And then the solution popped up, so obvious she was amazed neither of them had thought of it instantly. "I have it! How perfect! Mother's sister. Remember Aunt Mabel? She lives near Bath, and she married a wealthy man in trade. She writes from time to time. I don't know if you knew, but she is widowed now." She bit her lip. "You will have to find a way to get there. We will need money. Can you get some?"

Edeline seemed to sit straighter. "I don't know. Maybe. I can't ask anyone here at Thernwood, that is a certainty. Andrew handled all the finances. I might have a bit of money left, but I have no idea how much. I have not gotten any allowance for – I don't remember when. Andrew was sick, I could not think of money." Her eyes filled again. She cleared her throat fiercely.

The gazebo was quiet for another minute. Edeline looked down and tugged at a bit of rose-colored lace, murmuring absently, "I will have to get some black gowns made. Somehow. I can no longer go about in what I have." She gave a shudder, grabbed Verbena's arms again, and held on. "Do not tell anyone that I'm increasing, not the children, not even Father. Especially not Father. You will write Aunt Mabel for me, won't you? I may not have much time. Can you, oh please, will you help me escape? Promise me!"

Looking in Edeline's moist blue eyes, Verbena stifled a sigh. It was a mistake, but this was her sister. She would defend her family from everything. And everyone. "I promise." She could only hope they were not making a terrible mistake.

The sisters parted at the garden arch. Verbena watched Edeline's figure disappear around the sheds, walking back to a house that terrified her.

Edeline's foolish plan was one more burden to carry, and the children needed their breakfast. Thomas Barnes was undoubtedly up by now, and he was going to be angry. His first rising had alarmed her already, warning that last night's drinking was wearing off. How the man could drink himself into a stupor and still wake early in the morning, she did not know. Verbena straightened her shoulders and took a deep breath. She had been gone far too long as it was. She turned the opposite way, and slipped back into the woods.

THE SUN still hid beneath the horizon, leaving him in enough darkness to keep anyone from seeing the tears on his cheeks.

Andrew was dead. He, Damon Theodore Thern, was the heir now. As often as he had worried what his brother the dreamer would do with the family estate, he never wanted the responsibility himself. Especially not at the expense of Andrew's life.

Damon took a step wrong and his leg buckled. He grabbed a branch just in time to keep himself from doing a facer into the mat of rotting leaves from last autumn. The doctor had warned him, when he refused to let the man saw off his leg, that it would never be normal.

He had made the right decision. If he had to hang onto branches or lean on a cane for the rest of his life, he would do it on his own two feet. He had not gone back to London yet. It was one thing to be so confident when alone, it was another when surrounded by former friends and new acquaintances.

His leg stopped throbbing, and Damon forced himself to start walking again. He wanted to reach the little clearing. He had not made it there, not yet, but he would this time. He needed to visit the place of that memory, needed to go back to where he had last seen her. Her memory had helped him through the worst times before, maybe it would again.

For the last grim years, the face he had seen, the face that had kept him company when the nights were dark and the battle waited only for sunrise to resume with smoke, blood, screams, and the smell of death, was a girl with curly hair the color of sunshine and eyes like summer leaves, carrying a basket nearly as big as she was.

He had left the village only days after that meeting, not knowing what an impact that single encounter would have. His grandmother, his mother's mother, had left him property, a medium-sized house three villages away from Thernwood complete with land and livestock, horses and sheep and cows. Damon visited it once when he reached his majority, assured himself that everything was well, checked the village for comely maids, and went on to London, where he found his share of mistresses, slept as late as he wanted, attended balls, and raced on the trails of Hyde Park.

He had hired a man of affairs for that nearly-forgotten inheritance, who lived there year-round and watched over the place as if it were his own. Strange that he had never gone back to the little village and his own land.

Damon shook his head at the man he had been, and at the high price he had paid. Shortly after that visit to Thernwood and in the foolishness of youth, he had leapt at the chance to go to war just to get away from a life that had become ever more stifling and pointless, joined the army, an officer because of his wealth and birth, and sailed away to France and the battlefield.

That was when the dreams had started. At first it had confused him, that the face he saw was not that of any of his mistresses, but of a girl he had only seen once, standing on a woody path, holding a basket of bread that perfumed the air with its warm, yeasty scent. He even thought, sometimes, after a battle when the odors on the air were blood and death, that he still smelled her bread.

He learned to live for those dreams, had put the smiles he wanted to see on her face, anything to get a respite from the nightmare that surrounded him in the day. When the bullet had torn through his leg and sent him home, Damon chose to go, not to his London house nor to his grandmother's gift, but here, to Thernwood, the place where his dreams had given him peace. Oddly enough, the dreams stopped then.

For several months as his body fought the infection and the fever, he stared at the walls in his bedchamber. Somewhere inside he had held onto too much youth and health to succumb and as weeks passed, the wounds found a way to heal as much as they could. Life awakened outside his window with the spring, bringing with it the need to find her. He learned to walk again, struggled to keep his balance as he reawakened his familiarity with the land, spent days wandering these very woods.

Of course the fences demanded by the Enclosure Acts were up. Every rock that went into the stone fences, every pole that fit into every slot in the wood on the forest fences, every wooden gate meant no one was allowed through, that she could not follow this path, his only link to her. Only the most audacious tenants would dare cross the barriers of wood and stone now, but she had not been dressed as one of them.

He had never asked her name, had just assumed from her attire, and from the responsibility she apparently felt toward others who might be hungry, that she had to be of the landed gentry.

The family had not thrown a house party since he arrived, the one thing that would draw in all the gentry from miles around. Andrew had been sick. Such a thing would not happen now. This path and the small clearing was the only link he had to her, a foolish idea, but he could go and stand there and remember.

EDELINE CREPT back into the big house as quietly as she had left, but despite her care Agnes waited for her by the servants' door, reproach etched on her face. "The family wishes to see you in Andrew's room. *They* are mourning."

Her tone was as haughty as a queen's. Dread dripped down Edeline's spine like blood as she followed her maid up the dim stairs.

Even when she still had a place in the house, Edeline thought, before last night, she had never dared to censure Agnes. The maid's wages came from the estate, and Edeline knew, had known all along, that every word she herself uttered got back to Madam Thern.

She had been foolish to have entrusted the letter to Agnes, but she dared not get anyone else involved. If it had not been Agnes it would have been another of the maids, and they all owed their loyalty to the Therns. The *other* Therns, never her, despite her marriage. She had not exaggerated when she told Verbena so.

Edeline followed her mother-in-law's maid up the stairs. Her steps slowed as they neared Andrew's room. A few servants were still up, drifting past like quiet ghosts, weeping softly when out of sight of the family as they did the endless petty chores the Therns demanded. It never occurred to them that servants needed sleep, and Edeline wished she had the authority to demand consideration for their workers.

She could not even get consideration for herself. Still, it would be nice to see if such a kindness would soften the servants toward herself. Not that it would change her mind about leaving.

Agnes made no effort to be polite. Her lip curled. "Let us hope you manage to stay where you belong this time." And she stalked off.

Edeline supposed the woman's open effrontery said it all. She looked at the faint light washing past the door's edge. No doubt worse waited inside, but she would not have to endure it much longer. Taking courage from that thought, she eased the door open just far enough to slip in.

Red-rimmed and accusing eyes glared at her from three matching faces, Andrew's mother and sisters. She did not know where his father and brother were. Facing three was more than enough.

Where the boys were split between light and dark, Andrew a pale, gentle blonde with his father's blue eyes, Damon vivid dark with the snapping black eyes of his mother, the two girls were the blend, both brunette, one blue-eyed like their father, the other dark like Imogene. Catherine and Margaret turned away.

That left her alone, in a matter of speaking, to face Madam Thern.

Imogene Thern rose slowly, her face like a storm building, darker and darker, the atmosphere around her matching her coloring, menace pummeling at her until Edeline could barely breathe. The air itself was thick, whether with grief or loathing, Edeline could not tell. "What a thoughtless girl you are. At last I can speak my mind, now that my son is gone. I have been waiting for this chance."

For your son to die? Edeline wanted to ask, but she bit her tongue and sidled toward the bed, keeping a wary eye on her mother-in-law, trying to ignore the ugly words battering her.

"You never deserved him, you with your commonness, your lack of breeding. You showed it again now, with your husband lying here dead and you out doing who knows what. Dallying with one of the stableboys, most likely. Your husband not even in his grave!"

Andrew lay so still, his face like wax in that strange washed-out color that proclaimed to everyone that life was gone, hope was gone. His hair was still damp from the wet cloth she had wiped over his forehead again and again, hoping the coolness would put the fever's fire out. His lips, though, were dry, all evidence of her last kisses when she begged him to stay, to kiss her back, to whisper her name one more time, withered now.

Cruel words battered her but Edeline stopped listening, all her attention on the shell of her husband. His hands were so still, the skin lying loose as if the very bones underneath had shriveled. She could not bring herself to touch those hands, not when they would not curl absently around her as they had when he was reading and she would slide in next to him. He had held her hand then, still reading, not even taking his attention from the page but knowing she was there and more content because of it. His lips had curved each time, just a little, a smile hovering there until he had finished and could put the book aside and take her up on her invitation, even if it was just a kiss before rolling over and sliding into sleep.

He had usually been too tired to do anything more. It was no wonder it had taken him these six years to plant a child in her womb.

He died not knowing his heir was on the way. She had known even then, known without knowing, that death had hovered too close. It would have been one more burden for him to carry into death, that she would be raising their child without him.

So she had kept her silence but now, just for a moment, she wished he had known.

"Well?" Mrs. Thern snapped, the word sharp and close by, making Edeline jump and whirl around. A hand struck her face hard enough that the sound was sharp as a gunshot in the room. Edeline clapped a palm over the stinging cheek and stared, jolted back to reality, at her mother-in-law.

"You— you— " Mrs. Thern sputtered, struggling for words, then tried again. "You commoner! Look around you!" She waved a hand at the room. Edeline did not bother to so much as move her eyes. "You don't belong here, you never did."

She was becoming redundant, Edeline thought dimly, repeating the same insults. But Mrs. Thern was not nearly done. "Andrew died as a refined person should, in his bed, with his true family at his side."

Unlike a certain high-placed and very married lord who had recently been found dead in a popular brothel, Edeline thought, and wished she dared say it to Mrs. Thern, remind the woman of the cracks in her precious Society. She also wished she dared remind Mrs. Thern just who had nursed Andrew for the endless aching weeks of his final illness.

"How typical of your common origins, that he died and you survived."

Common origins. She remembered, finally, what she had said to Verbena only moments ago. Freedom was nearly at hand. A spark flared inside Edeline, and she fanned it, let it build. "But I heard you say many a time, every time a servant made a mistake, that the common people died so easily." She actually waved a hand toward the door, surprised that any part of her body had the audacity to move. "You said how very fortunate that was, so a new, better crop could take their place."

She lowered her hand one inch at a time, watching Mrs. Thern for the first signs of another impending attack, verbal or physical, although she had no idea what she would do in response. "And if you will remember, I'm his wife, his true family in God's eyes, and I was at his side every minute he was sick. I sat with him in the carriage when we took the trip down here at your insistence."

"You did not stay at his side long, though," Mrs. Thern sniped back.

"I was beside him until his very last breath," Edeline returned, but her voice was drowned out.

"Mother," Margaret cut in with quelling tones. It was not in character for either of the girls to stand against their mother, probably since they agreed with her all the time, but Edeline was grateful for even this small rebellion from her sister-in-law. "Don't start again. You have made your point. There are more important things to do at the moment than bother with her."

Now *that* sounded more like Margaret.

Love, her love for Andrew and his for her, made Edeline take one final stand. This burst of courage, or daring, or shock, did not have to be for long. "I went to the gazebo to weep in private. God knows, I get none here." She sat down on the bed and glared at them. "This is our bedroom, Andrew's and mine. Since you disapprove of my going out to find privacy, I will order you all to find yours elsewhere. While Andrew is with me, this room still belongs to us, and you have no place here. You have said your good-byes for the nonce, now I ask you to leave."

Her mother-in-law found her voice again. "Just wait until my son is buried." It came out a snarl, but the three women amazed Edeline by turning away and walking out of the door.

They had one final unspoken say when the door slammed shut, the sound echoing through the house.

Edeline sagged, her rebellion slipping away as though draining through a crack in the floor, and placed a hand on low on her belly, protecting her secret. She turned to her husband's still face and made him a vow, silently, in case there were ears at the door. *Andrew, I will protect our child. If it is the last thing I do, I will keep our baby safe from them.*

She sat in the hard chair beside the bed and stared at his face for a long time as the sun came up and filled the room.

THE PATH SHOWED CLEARLY, TOO CLEARLY. THE SUN WAS NEARLY UP.

It was a nasty thing to be around her father when he was craving liquor, and she had left the children sleeping in the house. Verbena knew she could not protect her younger brothers and sisters from all of it, but she promised herself long ago that she would do her best to shield them from as much as she could. She picked up her skirts and started running.

Her special place in the woods came up quickly. Why was it the coming back was always faster than the getting there, she wondered distantly, and suddenly skidded to a stop so quickly she nearly fell.

Damon stood in the middle of the path, his back to her, a stark, unmoving figure blocking her way. Tall as ever, his shoulders broad, his hair dark, he dominated the small clearing even without a horse to lift him above other mortals. The sun must have cleared the horizon, for a glow touched his hair. Or else it was her imagination, the effect he had always had on her. That giddy fifteen-year-old was back, her breath catching in her throat.

He turned at the sound of her stumbling steps, his gaze unfixed, his face washed out with grief, stark and unavoidable, palpable on the air. His blue coat was uneven on his shoulders, as if he'd thrown it on when he left the house, and he wore no cravat. Verbena stood awkwardly, not knowing what to do next, half expecting him to throw her off his land.

"Who are you? Did you not see the fence? This is protected land." His voice was rough. After Edeline's grief, she knew with complete certainty that the sharpness was not directed toward her.

Verbena did not have time to answer. She saw the instant recognition hit. His sad, red-rimmed eyes suddenly focused on her and they widened, his black gaze piercing the years. He took a sharp breath, and a strange sound pierced the air. "It is you?" His voice was gravely and harsh, he cleared his throat and tried again. "You are the girl I met on this very path with the basket of bread, are you not? After all these years, it is you."

***

THE GIRL NODDED, and he saw in her eyes that she knew exactly the day he referred to. She could not know, however, why he remembered that day, or what seeing her on this path, in that exact spot, was doing to him.

She was here, real after all those ephemeral dreams, on his side of that same fence. He did not dare blink for fear he was wrong and she would vanish like all the other dreams of the night. His feet were stuck to the ground or they would have let him move to her, his hands were frozen at his side or he would have reached for her. He could only stare and take note of the other changes.

Not so young any longer but still as appealing, as fresh as the summer morn, curling hair of sun-gold, eyes of leaf-green. Her lithesome body had grown no taller, but it was womanly now, all girlishness gone, and round in the right places. Her face was still slender, her skin flushed and glowing, pink cheeks, rose-petal lips.

He could hardly do what his dream-self would have done, kiss those lips, pull her into his arms and hold her, just to feel her heart beat, feel her breath against his chest. He fixed his gaze on her, absorbing her face into his mind, this new face of her grown into woman.

Her eyes narrowed, but she could not know that he had learned to read men in the seconds before the battle began, learned to know which of them could hold the line, and which were in danger of breaking and running and needed a sharp word and a forceful presence.

Or a distraction. "We have never been formally introduced. I am Damon Thern. May I ask your name?"

She hesitated, and Damon held his breath. She did not answer and his heightened senses knew she was still poised to run.

"So we have a mystery here." He hoped his smile would soften his tone and avoid sending her into panicked flight. He moved over and leaned against a tree to hide the weakness that had flared in his wounded leg. His leg was not up to a chase.

Fear clouded her green eyes. Damon had seen that same expression, eyes clouded with fear, on his sister-in-law far too many times of late. He clapped a hand to his forehead. "You are Edeline's sister. How stupid of me. I should have noticed it immediately."

Her breathing sped up, her eyes fixed wide like a trapped deer's.

"Edeline sent for you, did she not?" He saw the answer in her face, more fear behind her green eyes. "I should have expected that. Of course she would want her family with her at a time like – this." Damon cleared his throat before he embarrassed himself further. How odd, he thought with a start, that Edeline had never even mentioned her. "*Now* may I have your name?" Edeline had never said anything about her family. Nor had Andrew – he shoved aside the slash of pain. "We are in-laws. Of a sort."

She bit her lip. He could see her brain working behind her eyes. With a sigh of resignation, she said, "Verbena."

Verbena. The healing flower. Damon gave a shallow bow, the best he could do. If he did not sit soon, he would fall on his face.

There was a downed tree not far away. He waved to it now.

"Please, come sit with me. Just for a moment or two," he added when he saw the 'no' start in her eyes. "We are practically related, and I know next to nothing about you. Where are you in the family?" Damon smiled at her, his best smile, the one that had garnered him all the mistresses any man could want.

He tucked her hand into his arm without letting her decide and turned her toward the tree, hoping she would not notice how heavily he was leaning on her. She was so much shorter than he that his elbow nearly rested on her shoulder. He looked down onto her pale, white-gold curls and wished he dared touch them to see if they were as soft as they appeared.

"I'm second. She is the eldest, as you might expect." Verbena looked up at him, her gaze direct. "I shall save you the wondering. I am two and twenty." She said it without any obvious embarrassment and went along with him, walking smoothly over the grass. He could hardly seat her properly, waiting until she was settled before sitting down himself as a gentleman should. No, he dropped down onto that ancient, dead tree trunk just in time, and let the air in his lungs out with a groan of pain and relief.

Verbena sat down slowly, perching on the edge of the trunk as if ready to jump up and bolt. She startled him when her hand touched his arm, as soft as a butterfly, there and gone, no longer than a blink. "Are you ill?"

He sighed. It was so far from being a secret, how could she not have heard? She seemed genuinely concerned. "I was wounded in the war. I thought the word had blanketed the village."

Verbena looked at him more closely. In the rising sun she could see the lines of pain around his mouth, the dark circles under his eyes, and the grey tinge beneath his tanned skin. He was thinner than before, too. The coat was not loose from hurry, it was simply loose. "No, I had not heard. I do not have the luxury of making calls and listening to gossip."

"No?" He tilted his head as he asked the question, teasing, disbelieving.

"No." She was talking to Damon once more. Verbena could hardly believe it. He was sitting close enough on the tree trunk that if she dared, she could touch him again. She still felt his warmth on her fingertips. If only she did not have to measure her words so closely.

He was even more handsome up close, despite the marks pain and sadness had left on him. Age had given his face character. His shoulders were just as wide as she remembered, though she could see his arms were thinner, leaving the sleeves draped over bones. He was wearing the new trousers, not breeches, and one leg looked twisted under the woven fabric. Even Julius had more muscles than Damon Thern did now. She remembered the coat that had stretched taut seven years ago and made her heart flutter at his blatant strength. Her overloaded basket of fresh bread had been nothing to him then. She wondered if he could even hold it now.

He cleared his throat. "So. How many of you are there? Edeline says noth – " he seemed to catch himself. "Your sister is quiet about her family."

She hesitated while she thought. Anyone in the village could tell him what he wanted to know. "We are six all together, four girls, and my brothers are in the middle."

"And your parents?"

"My mother is dead. She died the year Edeline married Andrew." After all these years, her mother's death was still sore. They had not just lost their mother. Their father might as well have died with her, he was so changed.

Verbena suspected her sister had told no one about her mother's death. Edeline had not made it to the funeral, and they all had struggled with resentment at how she had ignored them in their time of grief. Now Verbena knew why. If the tale she had just heard was true, even a portion of it, Edeline's asking for a trip back to this town, indeed any reminder of who she was and how little the family had would have left her open to more abuse and mockery.

At least Edeline had loved Andrew. That was a consolation.

The lines around Damon's eyes deepened, the flash of humor she had seen disappearing as grief settled on him again, the heavy weight pulling his shoulders down. "I am indeed sorry. I might have known Edeline's mother was dead, but I'm ashamed to admit I did not remember it." His brows went down. "What are their ages? And remember," the smile of a moment ago crept back, "I can find out easily enough, now that I know who you are."

"The boys are seventeen and fourteen."

"And the girls?"

"Eight and seven."

"Four, in addition to yourself." She could not read his face. "Is there a nanny or nurse to help?"

She choked on a laugh. Or was it a scoff? "No." It was light enough he had to be able to see how old her gown was. No one who could afford a nanny would dare wear this gown. Not even in the dark.

"No help? You are raising them?" He read something in that sound, based on the next question. "You no doubt do much of the work your mother would have done?"

What could she say to that? He remembered the basket of bread she was carrying to feed others. How little he knew! "Yes."

A deep scowl across the brow matched the tightness around his mouth. "And your sister has kept you all a secret this whole time."

With long practice Verbena defended Edeline. She was going to be doing a lot more of that in the future, she realized. "You have not been here this whole time. I do not know if we are a secret to the rest of your family. Or your staff."

"True. You said you were two and twenty? Is your father still alive?"

"Yes."

"I'm certain he is grateful to have such a diligent daughter."

Verbena turned her head from that prying gaze. She could walk away, he could not pursue her, but for some reason she did not want to do that to him. "My father is often not home."

He sighed, the vibration running along the trunk, and shook his head.

Verbena felt the strange compulsion to defend her father. "He is a sailor."

"You live nearby." It was not a question.

"Yes."

"In the village?" He looked at her again, one eyebrow raised.

"Just outside. We have a small bit of land."

Damon nodded. "I did remember Andrew married a local girl." His voice broke near the end, and he went very still.

Verbena could not ignore the grief that sat on him. Thern or not, he suffered as Edeline did, and she could not let it go unremarked. "I am sorry for the loss of your brother."

He nodded. They both were quiet for a moment, as if neither knew what to say after that. Finally he said, "I never wanted to be heir."

But he was not the heir now if Edeline carried a boy, and he did not know it. Could not know it. She spoke carefully. "It is a heavy responsibility."

Damon nodded again. She thought she saw a sheen of moisture on his eyes. He turned away. Looking at him, Verbena wondered that he could belong to the same family Edeline had told her about. This one, at least, could still feel. Perhaps . . . perhaps he could see reason. He would need to.

She gathered her courage. "Since you have been away for a while, you may not know all that has happened. Your tenants might not be as tractable as they once were. Resentment is rising, and a number have moved away. Life is not easy here anymore." The tenants would not be shy with their bitterness.

He seemed to read her mind. "Ah, yes. I remember from the last time. I have noticed the fences. They make walking about much more difficult."

Verbena highly doubted he needed to walk much. Or that he

even could. She had this chance and she would not lose it. "It is more than that." Words rushed out, pushed by the injustice she struggled with every day. "So many lost all grazing for their stock with the Enclosure Acts. Every year it seems Parliament passes more of them, keeping all of us off lands that we once were able to use at will. People are starving in your village, on your land!"

Damon's head jerked back as if slapped. "I know of no starving villagers. And these laws have a purpose. At first the benefits were not obvious, but it is a brilliant way to manage our flocks and herds. How are we to control our breeding if our cattle and our sheep are allowed to mix with the villagers' animals? Or try to cross pollinate our new varieties of wheat and rye if your plants mix with ours? We are already seeing the results. The sheep we are producing out of the controlled breeding are fatter, and more healthy. The wheat experiments are even better than expected."

"Experiments?" It came out as a whisper. His word had hit like a blow, callous and unfeeling, stealing the breath from her lungs. She cleared her throat and tried for more volume without success. "This is all an experiment? Fencing off lands, forcing everyone who owns anything to put up fences they neither needed nor wanted? How dare you say this is for our ultimate good?"

She glared at him. Strength came back into her voice. "Tell that to your tenants who can no longer keep their sheep or their cattle because they have nowhere to graze them. What ultimate good is it for them? Try to convince them that someday it will help when they leave for London, hoping for work. I don't see the good, now or later, when we can no longer feed our families."

The words kept rolling out. "It got especially bad when the common grounds were fenced. They had belonged to everyone! Those were the fields for all the villagers' sheep and cows to graze. Before you pushed us off those grounds, before you found it so important to lay your claim on them, people could eat and clothe their families. We had milk and meat, we all shared our breeding stock with each other. Everyone could have a new lamb or calf, these awful breeding messes you are so eager to eliminate. Now we have the added cost of fencing our own properties – well, people are starving for the cost of a fence because those who passed those laws found it . . . *expedient* for themselves."

Damon raised a hand to stop her. Only her need to take another breath made her comply. "You seem inordinately well informed."

Her hands clenched, hiding in the folds of her skirt. "I would be the veriest idiot if I could not see what was before my own eyes. I don't have the option of running away to London to hide. I live here every day, I see what happens. We Barnes have little land left, yet I have to find a way to pay for our own fences."

He seemed to sit straighter. "I did not run away, nor do I hide. If you feel I owe you an apology for laws I had nothing to do with, then I certainly will apologize. For my whole class, if that will help. Perhaps there was a better way of managing the land. There is – there was – nothing I could do to prevent the passage of so many laws, but they are working. And if others are affected badly, I'm truly sorry." He looked off into the woods, but his eyes were haunted. "I can't fix everything." His voice was so soft she barely heard the last sentence.

He had been in the war. She had heard some tales of the horrors Napoleon had thrust on the Continent. He had seen them, lived them, and suffered.

But it was still hard to absolve him of blame for her problems when he was so determined to defend the cause. She let out a deep breath, trying to release the anger that bubbled up every time she thought of their struggle. She did not want to take it out on him – exactly. Someone, certainly, but not him. After all, he had not even been here, as he said. He had been in the war. He had undoubtedly seen worse horrors than the starving villages that surrounded them.

Damon's father had been here, though. His mother, his haughty sisters, his dreaming brother who could not see what was in front of his face.

A bird suddenly chirped from nearby, and Verbena jumped to

her feet. "I have to go. I have breakfast to prepare before my brothers go to work."

The sun painted the leaves with color. She was in for it when she got back. Please let Father still be asleep, she prayed quickly, but suspected that prayer, like so many in the past few years, would go unanswered.

He grabbed her arm before she could run, and struggled upright. "Your brothers work? What do they do?"

"Whatever work they can get. We do not have the luxury of servants. We all contribute whatever we can." She tried to ignore his hand, warm on her arm, holding her in place, and his chest so close to her, where she could see every breath he took. Through the fine fabric of his shirt, she saw the dusting of chest hair, making her heart go fluttery, and causing a curious melting in her knees. She stiffened them, and forced herself to look away from the temptation in front of her.

"You all contribute." His eyes narrowed as he quoted her words. "Why do I think none contribute as much as you? It is barely dawn, yet you have already been out to minister to your sister's needs, and now you are racing home to feed the others. What else do you do for them? Do you clean for them? Wash their clothes? Raise them? You sound like little more than a servant." His eyes burned down.

"It is not Edeline's fault," she blurted. "She has been in London. She is married – well, she was. She had her own – " Verbena caught herself before she said 'problems.' "Family to take care of. I was already an adult, if I did not take care of my brothers and sisters, undoubtedly I would have had a family of my own to care for."

"You said your mother died soon after Andrew and Edeline wed. They were married for six years, so if you are twenty and two now, you were sixteen when it happened?" He sounded disgusted, furious, but his hold on her arm was still gentle. Firm, but gentle. "You have borne that responsibility all this time." He shook his head as he looked down at her. "Fine. Go take care of your family." He smiled. "You are not alone anymore."

Verbena stared at him, appalled. Edeline would be back at the Barnes' family home at any time, at least briefly, and soon her pregnancy would show. *Not alone any more.* Just when she needed him to ignore her most.

She turned and ran down the path.

4

She was too late. Her father was waiting when she slipped into the kitchen. He still wore the same stained clothes he had been in earlier, the heavy brown breeches that sagged about his knees, his collarless shirt blotched with stains that spoke of ale and soup that had missed his mouth. The wrinkles from sleeping fully dressed did little to hide the signs of hard wear. "There is nothing cooking! Did you not think of us while you went out to enjoy yourself?" He closed on her, his voice a soft, ominous hiss. The lingering odor of whiskey brushed her nose. "What have you been doing? Who did you go out to meet? Did I raise a whore?"

Whore? Verbena lost her breath in shock. She backed up, missing the door, and thumped against the wall. The look on his face frightened her, black with rage, his eyes bloodshot. He had been angry so many times, but this promised worse. "Edeline sent a letter for me early this morning," she said, words rushing out, trying desperately to reach beneath the remnants of drink. "Andrew is dead."

He stopped just out of arm's reach, a blessed distance of safety, his red-rimmed eyes wide and appalled, suddenly comprehending. "You are certain?"

"Oh, yes, very certain. She asked me to meet her at the Thern's. She told me herself." Verbena stayed where she was, at the edge of the door, all the while knowing that she could not run and leave the other children to their father's abuse. Her heart banged an uneven rhythm against her ribs.

Thomas squinted at her. "When did this happen?"

"Some time during the night. I don't know exactly when."

He spat on the floor. Verbena tried to hide her revulsion. "She never did remember us before, when she had all that lovely money. No doubt she'll not get any now, childless as she is."

Verbena forced herself not to react. She had never told their father about the funds her sister had sent. Small as the gifts had been, they were vital and she could not let Thomas know about them. Her father always managed to sail off to sea just before the tavern's bill came due. If not the tavern, the leather maker would present a bill for a new belt or the cobbler would ask payment for new shoes that Thomas decided in secret were absolutely necessary, and she would have to find some way to pay them. Between the coins she managed to hide from his wages and Edeline's small gifts, they had managed.

Without that help, Verbena did not know what she would do.

Anger crept back into Thomas's eyes, and was turned on Verbena, burning her with its heat. "She *would* be barren, the thankless girl. She had no children to waste that lovely dosh on, but she could never even spare a coin for us. Well, she better not be thinking she can come back here, not after ignoring us all these years."

Verbena managed to keep her face still, but a tremor skittered over her spine like water on a hot griddle. When, oh when, was Father going back to sea? If they were lucky – which they seldom were – he would be off soon. It had better be before Edeline managed her escape, or things would get very difficult.

A brooding look came into his eyes, something that always worried Verbena because it preceded some scheme to get money out of the Therns. Thomas Barnes might rant about the Therns owing them because of their tenuous relationship through Edeline, but he was hardly stupid enough to show up at the door and make demands.

Or not before now.

"Edeline may have forgotten her family, but you are attractive enough, if a bit on the short side. The brother-in-law, that rakehell Damon—" Thomas narrowed his eyes at her until they became reddish slits, like the devil in the pictures she had seen back when she had time to read books. He leered at her. "He is still unmarried, you know. The story is that he was wounded in the war. You could do worse." His gaze hardened. "What's more, you won't forget your family like she did. Yes, that is a good idea. You marry the younger brother, and you be sure to take care of us."

She would not stand there and have her father measure her worth in cash. She shoved down the slash of anger, and risked moving. He said nothing as she walked over to the kitchen fire, but she felt his gaze on her. Verbena grabbed a ladle hanging over the bucket and scooped water to dump into the empty pot hanging from a hook, then pushed the long rod over the fire. The stillness from across the room made her skin prickle. She took the poker and jabbed at the coals, hidden under the ashes last night to keep them warm and glowing. A few more pokes, harder than necessary, at the smoking logs, a handy substitute for her father, some shavings for fuel, and the fire sputtered to life.

Thomas finally moved, his booted feet clumping across the floor. "Make yourself useful and get some food for your brothers and sisters. It's all you are good for now. At least until you figure out how to make Damon marry you." He barked a single mocking laugh that finished with a rolling belch and leaked alcohol and onions into the room.

The door rattled shut behind him. *All you are good for.* Cooking, cleaning, like a servant, just as Damon had said moments ago. Solving their problems, finding a way to pay the bills, feed the children – and keep Edeline's secret. If only she could have a respite, just a few weeks off from the weight on her shoulders.

Money problems loomed very big today, bringing the companion, guilt. Guilt at coveting what her sister had, guilt at having to steal money from her father's wages every time he came back from the sea. Guilt at lying about those little gifts Edeline had sent out of her own allowance from time to time. Guilt or not, she had to do a familiar chore. She did not know how long she had before her father returned. Verbena shoved the poker back and raced for his room.

It never took long after his arrival for him to undo all her hard work. The room was a mess, the bed a mound of tangled covers, and clothes had been left where they fell. The tang of whiskey hung over everything, and she was certain she would find flasks dripping the last of their contents when the time came to clean.

Much to her surprise and relief, he had made the hurried search easy for her. The old leather money pouch sat in plain sight on the dresser, lumpy with wages he had not managed to spend yet. She pulled at the knot, her ears turned toward the kitchen door, and the string finally gave. Coins lay in a jumble, large silver coins, smaller gold ones. It was always a risk, taking enough to keep them fed, to pay the pub and buy the essential clothes and food they could no longer provide for themselves, and yet not let him realize.

She took several of the small gold coins and one large silver one, wishing she dared take more, tied the pouch back up and ran for her room. She had a small box, easily hidden, the perfect place to stow her plunder. The coins jingled as she dropped them in, a soft sound but there was no one nearby to hear.

Verbena hurried back to the kitchen and glanced out the window. Her father was nowhere in sight. Maybe the children would be able to eat in peace. She picked a log from the diminishing pile beside the fireplace. She would have to remind the boys to get more somewhere. None of the available trees were on their land anymore.

Oh, for the days when they could take an axe and a saw and head openly into the woods, to cut down at will. But those days were gone. She looked out the window at the garden and the small plot of land they still owned. She remembered the huge log Damon had rested on. That would supply them enough wood for months, but they dared not take it.

The water bubbled softly from the pot, and Verbena scooped out some oatmeal and dumped it in. Thumps came from overhead, the boys, from the weight of feet on the floor. She stirred the oats and covered the pot, counting time by the creaking of the floor board overhead.

Perhaps if the table was fully set and the meal ready, she could forestall another of her father's rages. Verbena made short work of setting the table, bowls and cups and spoons ready for what they did have to eat before hurrying back to finish the gruel.

She was just about to uncover the pot of fully set oatmeal when Julius walked into the dining room, dressed but still sleep-rumpled, his wavy hair not combed, and a hint of the beard that would grow someday on his face. He shared her coloring, with soft, wavy blonde hair, but blue eyes instead of her own green. He was not tall, but she still had to look up to him. "Good morning, Bena," he said absent-mindedly, raising his gaze up from the book in his hands just long enough to notice her and avoid running into the table. "The bread is gone. I forgot to tell you last night. Matthew and I finished it off. We were hungry."

"Oh, dear," she groaned, making light of their hunger with a mock swing at his shoulder, which he ducked with long practice. "You two will just have to stop growing. For now, it is just porridge for breakfast." She dropped her voice. "If you want something to eat later, you could start by pulling some turnips. They are probably ripe enough." Small, but sweeter, and they would be a nice treat. "And please, not a word of complaint."

He stopped and actually looked at her, his book marked by a finger tucked in the page. He must have felt something in the air because he mouthed, "Father?" Their eyes met in a moment of mutual understanding. "Sorry. I will not have time now, but if you can wait, I can dig them this evening and you can cook them tomorrow." He turned his attention back to the book, caught the bench leg with his foot by some sense she never possessed, and sat down, all without taking his eyes off the pages.

There was no milk for drinking, none for pouring over the porridge. She filled up Julius's bowl and poured water into his mug. He dug in without more than a glance, but he swallowed hard to get the porridge down, and Verbena winced. In a few more weeks there would be berries to sweeten it, but not yet.

He looked up at her, taking a moment to focus from his reading. "I will be working at the Holman's today, weeding their bean patch. Old man Holman told me I could bring home one basket of early beans. That will help a little, will it not?" His eyes held thoughts of far away as he marked his place in the book with a finger, grasping last precious minutes of reading before his day of hard, menial work began. Verbena prayed days like this did not presage the rest of his life, wasting his clever mind. If only Edeline could see him now, desperate for knowledge and reduced to pulling weeds. This was the life she would have for her own child?

"Yes, that is good," she said, pushing the words past a tight throat. It was not good, really, not good at all, not for Julius. He should be studying to be a solicitor, or a doctor, something to stretch that studious mind. "Julius, are you hap – "

Her question was cut off by the sound of more footsteps coming down the steps from the upper floor. Matthew burst into the dining room like an awkward colt, tripping over the bench leg and catching himself against the table, knocking his shin with a groan.

Verbena glanced down at his leg, evaluating the scrape as minor, but reminding her of yet another chore. His pantaloons were outgrown, the buttons that should fasten from the knee down to the ankle dangled useless on a few strands of thread several inches away from the holes, and Verbena knew from experience that at his age, just turned fourteen, he would start going through them faster than she could make them. She would have to find Julius's outgrown ones and adapt any that still had wear left somehow to Matthew's slightly longer legs.

Matthew saw her and a bright smile lit his green eyes, nearly a match for her own. "Bena! What are we going to eat? The bread is gone." He pushed a lock of brown hair back. "I need my hair cut before Sunday."

"I know," she said. "Wash your hair some time before bed, and I will take care of it this evening. Don't plan anything for later. It will be a busy night for you. I need you to help your brother pull turnips before it gets dark."

Turnips and beans.

"I'm to help the farrier today. He says he will teach me the trade if I learn quickly enough." Matthew flashed another carefree smile, far too cheerful this early, dropped down on the bench seat, and grabbed his bowl and spoon. He made only a single face at the meal before taking steady bites, barely stopping to swallow.

"I thought I told you no slop! Does nothing I say pass your ears? I want meat," Thomas growled from behind, startling her by his silent entry and putting her thoughts into harsh words. The boys went utterly silent, not even the spoons made a sound. Verbena did not dare turn around. Her father's voice went up, "Surely we can sacrifice a chicken more often."

Verbena counted to ten.

Thomas glared at the bowls sitting steaming with hot oatmeal and then at her, with cold eyes. "You think I slave on a ship to have you cook me gruel?"

From where she stood, Verbena caught a glimpse of her sisters. On the stairs, Lizabeth stood quiet in the shadows, as still as a statue. Above her, Annabelle's bare foot hung just over the edge of the last visible step. Her toes were curled tightly, and Verbena knew if she saw Annabelle's face, it would be somber and far too old for her tender age.

Father did not sense them, thank goodness. She could only hope neither boy would look their direction. Julius would not give anything away, not deliberately, but Matthew's face was too mobile, too quick. Right now he stared at his oatmeal rather than risk meeting his father's eyes. Thomas went on, oblivious to his sons' distress. "Your mother always managed on the wages I earned, yet you can't cook a single chicken for me now."

She wanted to yell at him that he drank his wages before they went to his children. That the whiskey he still breathed into the air needed to be paid for, that his eldest daughter helped far more than he did.

He always forgot, when he was drinking, that back then, those days he liked to remember when Mother managed so easily, they had the run of the countryside, hills to graze their sheep, and room for a pig. Sailing was another way to forget that privately owned land had to be marked and fenced, the expense hanging over their head until it could no longer be avoided.

Yes, they had a few chickens, but she rationed every hen as carefully as she could because eggs went further than the meat, mixed in griddle cakes, nutbreads, and muffins and whatever other baked foods Verbena could mix up to pad their empty stomachs.

Thomas looked down at the table, and for the first time, Verbena realized his anger was even beyond what she thought. "You will have to find something else to feed me." His eyes narrowed at her, mean little taunting slits.

"I'll send one of the girls out for eggs, then." She hoped the hens were laying well. She hated to waste eggs for her father's breakfast, because she wanted to use them for supper. Placating him was more important right now, if it would spare chickens, and the children.

The girls were still hiding on the stairs.

Thomas moved around the table, walking in slow, menacing steps that sent a chill up her spine. She felt the wall on her back. Behind him, she saw Julius's face set into angry lines. She shook her head slightly, hoping he saw and would obey. He remained seated, a good sign.

In a movement so fast her mind did not recognize it until too late, putting all his anger and lingering drunkenness into it, he flipped Matthew's bowl off the table. The bowl hurtled straight at her, spewing hot porridge. Verbena jerked aside too late. Porridge sprayed across her gown, sticking to her face, her hair, her arm, and the bowl clattered to the floor.

Julius leapt to his feet. "Don't you dare treat her like that!"

"Julius, no!" Verbena tripped over her skirt as she lurched out of her father's reach, his hands coming at her like claws, aimed for her throat. One shoe came down on a glob of porridge, scooting her foot from under her.

She landed hard on the floor, pain burning her hip. A new, vicious jolt tore through her midsection, slamming the breath out of her lungs with a single cry. Father's boot, she realized through the haze of fire in her ribs and the din of screaming and hoarse shouts.

"I'll butcher my own meat!" Thomas stormed out of the room, through the kitchen, and out the back door. Verbena heard the 'snick' of the axe coming out of the stump. She needed those chickens, especially her favorite, who was the best laying hen they ever had. They nearly lived on her eggs alone. She could not let him start slaughtering indiscriminately. In this state, he might not stop until they were all butchered.

The boys came rushing over, the girls were screaming in the stairway. "Hush!" Julius called to them in a voice deeper than she had heard before. He knelt down beside her. "Are you hurt?"

Behind him, Matthew crouched as well, his eyes pools of green distress. "Father kicked you," he whispered.

"Don't let him . . . start killing . . . chickens," Verbena gasped around the stab of pain when she inhaled. She held out a hand, pointing toward the small shed with the one arm that still worked. Julius grasped her hand and pulled without thinking, a hard yank. "Stop him before—" she got out on the yelp of pain, but she was on her feet.

Clamping an arm over the spot that hurt, she stumbled toward the kitchen door. It still stood open. Matthew pushed past her on his way out as he rushed to obey. He probably did not hit her that hard, but her vision went fully black for a moment, and she hung onto the porch pillar.

"Verbena?" Julius held Father's musket.

"No, Julius! Not that way. . . Put that back!" Her fingers caught his sleeve.

Julius actually glared at her. "I am not going to wound him, but I can scare him away. I promise I won't shoot him by accident." With a gentle pull, he freed her fingers, and took the porch steps in a single bound. This was not the boy who lived through his books. He was standing on the brink of manhood, and it had been hard-won.

Verbena's ribs burned and every breath made her muscles shake. Her body was cold, so cold. Dear God, keep them safe, she prayed quickly, and hoped the Almighty deigned to listen to someone as small as herself.

A wet hiccup caught from behind caught her attention. "Verbena?" She turned carefully. Lizbeth's usually happy face was blotched with red from crying. Verbena would normally rush over and gather her little sister close, but she could not move just then. "What is it?"

"Was Father trying to kill you?" Lizabeth's hazel eyes were huge. Behind her, Annabelle had her thumb in her mouth, something she had not done for a year or more, and the tears on her cheeks reflected the morning sun that crept past the porch awning.

"Oh, baby," Verbena crooned, not knowing which of the girls she was talking to. "He's just hungry." Another excuse piled on so many years of excuses.

"Julius and Matthew are hungry, too," Lizabeth snapped, the red blotches on her face growing into hot anger. "And they don't throw their food, or hit you."

"Father is bigger. He needs more food." It was a pitiful try, and Lizabeth was smart enough to see right through it.

Shouting came from the coop. "Stay here!" She pointed Lizabeth back into the house. "No matter what you hear, you and Annabelle are to stay in the house. No matter what." One glare, as fierce as she could make it, but she dared not wait any longer, the voices were getting worse.

Matthew shrieked, "No, Father, no!"

And the musket boomed.

The girls' screams started again. "Stay!" Verbena snapped over her shoulder, and forced her legs down the stairs and across the yard. Chickens scattered from behind the stable, squawking and flapping, their fat bodies getting in her way like a small swarm of awkward giant bees. She flapped at them with one arm as her other arm clutched that burning spot in her side, but she could not stop.

She rounded the old stable corner right into a brawl of arms and elbows. Something hard slammed into the side of her face. She reeled off and pitched to the side. Images flashed, Father and Julius fighting over the gun, the barrel pointing straight up in the air, a puff of smoke coming from its end, Matthew grabbing at the musket's hot barrel and leaping back, everyone seeming to get taller and farther away. Her body impacted, seeming to bounce and roll, her limbs loose, floating above her as if disconnected, her arms could not work to make the awful movement stop, her whole midsection went cold, and the world went dark.

5

AT THE SHARP CRACK THAT BROKE THE MORNING QUIET, DAMON pulled the horse up. Shouts followed that single gunshot, and then the screaming of children.

Sounds that had no place in a fresh English morning.

He followed the panicked cries, pushing the horse along the fence to the gate and through.

The house around which the cries emanated needed paint and probably more: two full stories and a small attic, a gabled roof that looked as if it leaked, a side portico that sagged.

He heard another scream coming from behind the house, back of a weathered shed that may once have been a stable but that now housed chickens. As he rode up the short drive he could smell the birds before he saw them.

He rounded the corner of the shed and hauled on the reins just in time to prevent his stallion from trodding on a familiar yellow gown dotted with pink. Two little barefoot girls hung onto each other, their screams getting louder with every breath.

A burly man and a tall blonde boy, almost of age to be a man himself, both grappling over a gun pointed straight in the air, froze in place. They all seemed to notice his horse at the same moment. Blessed silence fell from the girls.

Damon wished he had brought his own weapon. "What is the meaning of this?" The words seared the air in the voice that had kept his entire battalion under control. He swung from the horse and leaned down by Verbena's body, his bad leg at an awkward angle, one eye on the ugly scene in front of him.

There was no blood, at least none Damon could see. The horse stood rock-still, *he* was the one who trembled. He reached for Verbena's neck, hoping, praying for the pulse. At first he did not feel it, his hand was shaking and his own heart beat too loud. He took another breath, closed his eyes for the merest moment, and there it was, strong and steady.

"It is a good thing she is still alive," he snarled as he stood and walked with measured steps toward the duo, neither one ready to relinquish the weapon. "Give that to me." He grabbed the long gun by the still-hot barrel and jerked it free. The boy backed away, glaring between him and the burly man equally.

With the gun safely away from the pair of idiots, he switched his own glare between the two. "One of you had better have an explanation."

"We did not shoot her." That from the boy. "She came around the corner and ran into us and fainted."

As explanations went, that one was sadly lacking. "Explain the bruise on the side of her face." The two miscreants looked down at her as if he had said something remarkable. He would find out the rest once Verbena was awake and out of danger. "You," he pointed at the older man. "Pick her up and carry her into the house." At least that would keep the man away from the gun.

A chicken flapped down to the ground from somewhere overhead and landed near Verbena's slack hand. The man swore as he slapped at another one that followed it. No doubt the flock had taken refuge on the roof of the little shed at his side.

Red rushed up the man's face, and his lip curled. "An' who might you be, that you think you can come onto private property and start giving orders? This is my family, and I will take care of them as I see fit."

This was Mr. Barnes? This flushed and threatening man was Verbena's and Edeline's father? Damon glared at him with disgust. "I can't see that you are caring for them any too well. Pick up your daughter, sir, and get her into the house!"

The blonde boy's brows were still furrowed in a glare. His face was blotched red, from exertion or embarrassment, it was impossible to tell, and a sleeve hung torn from the shoulder of a shirt that had seen better days. Damon remembered with a flash of sympathy being that age, big enough to try, but not big enough to succeed. As long as the boy did not make any sudden moves, he could be ignored.

Damon kept his attention on the burly man. He was going to be trouble. "I am Damon Thern."

Mr. Barnes' face went still, his eyes surprised for the space of a blink before a cold measuring look crept into them. "One of them, are ye? A Lord High Thern. I see what you are doing," he sneered. "You come onto my land giving orders. This is not France, Mr. High and Mighty Officer, and we are not your troops. Right now this property still belongs to the Barnes and you are the one trespassing!"

"I did not come as an officer," Damon said with asperity. "I came to help, but now that you bring it up, if I choose, I could have you clapped in irons on any charge I wish. I'll not ask you again, sir, pick up your daughter and get her into the house!" Damon's very fingertips tingled with restrained rage.

With a muttered curse, Barnes crouched down and picked Verbena up. She hung limp in his arms. The tall, blonde boy glared at Damon again, and followed the father. The young girls, who had been clinging to each other and hiccupping softly, the final remnants of their screams, looked at him fearfully, turned on their collective heels and raced after their father, their bare feet pattering against the hard-packed earth.

To think, their father and brother had just been fighting over a loaded gun, yet he, who had only come to help, was the greater of two evils.

The big gun, the source of this misery, felt like a familiar friend. His horse, like the trained beast that he was, had stayed close enough that Damon could just reach out and catch the reins. He kept the musket in his hand and turned to follow the family around the small shed. Verbena's stillness scared him. A young male voice from behind surprised him.

"Thank you for stopping to help."

Damon spun around, catching himself before he fell.

It was a dark-haired boy. His eyes peered over the horse's back. "I'm Matthew, and my brother is Julius."

By the time they reached the house, Damon thought he might know all he needed about Verbena. He started walking, and sure enough, the boy fell in step on the other side of the horse.

"I hope Verbena will be all right," Matthew went on in a rush, pouring out his dread in time to their footfalls, echoing Damon's fears. "I would not normally say anything, I don't talk about my family much," – Damon bit his cheek to keep the inappropriate smile in check – "but Father kicked her because she cooked porridge for breakfast."

The urge to smile vanished. Damon picked up the pace. Verbena could not be left alone with the father this boy described.

"She kept holding her side. We need a doctor to look at her, too, but we – " Matthew flushed, but once he had started it seemed he could not stop, all his anxieties coming out in a rush, only remembering to hush his voice lest someone hear him, "we can't afford to send for him. I don't think he is very good, anyway. That is what Verbena says all the time." In a belated realization, Matthew suddenly asked as they reached the side porch, "Did you not say your name was Thern? Are you related to the Therns who own the village?"

His voice had gone wary. Damon put his hand on the slight shoulder and said, "Yes. Yes, I am. I'm glad to meet you, Matthew, but sorry for the circumstances." He looped the reins over the shaky porch railing, grabbed the equally shaky post and climbed the steps. The door creaked open before he reached it, pushed from inside by Mr. Barnes. The door's hinges caught, shrilly complaining, as Barnes gave a vicious shove for that last inch, and crowded Damon toward the porch edge. Those hinges needed to be oiled at least, possibly replaced, but the man did not seem to notice the sounds.

"Who said you could come in?" Barnes filled the doorway. "You don't own this place." Stale whiskey puffed out with every word.

"Are you not even worried about your daughter, Barnes?" Damon's anger, fueled by Matthew's confession, was barely held under leash, and Barnes had to feel it. He shifted his grip on the gun, and looked at the man. He did not move beyond that one shift, but he did not have to, he knew Barnes could tell that so much as a single wrong threat and he would swing.

"Fine. Just remember whose house this is." Barnes stormed off into the house.

Damon stepped over the threshold into a kitchen. Iron pots and pans hung on hooks along the fireplace wall. He got a quick impression of cupboards, but Barnes had moved further into the house. Damon followed the sound of the man's footsteps through a dining room with a long, scuffed table, the dings and chips proclaiming hard use. Benches ran along the table's sides, a large functional dark wood chair sat at the table's far end.

On the floor lay a cracked bowl, and drying splotches of oatmeal. His jaw clenched harder. Verbena did not deserve this. None of the children did.

A second door led out of the dining room and into a hallway. Stairs came down from the next floor on his left, and the front door with its tiny vestibule was on his right. Beyond the stairs the hall led to another room, but that door was closed.

Damon looked at the room directly in front of him. Most likely that was the parlor, from the wide doorway with double doors that hung unevenly out of their frame and clearly had not been moved for some time. There was no one to invite him in but he entered anyway, and got a quick impression of old furniture still kept clean, small tables with oil lamps on them, one with a cracked glass chimney. Chairs, an old wingback whose fabric upholstery showed wear, the colors faded from sunlight, the others of solid wood, flat backs and seats without a pillow to soften them, and last, a tired settee to his right where Verbena lay still and limp, the two little girls standing close.

At least her father had not dropped her on the floor.

"It was an accident," Barnes said, with a quick gaze toward his daughter. The stale scent of whisky drifted past again, stronger inside than on the porch. Damon dismissed him. Father or not, he would be of no help.

One ruffle of Verbena's yellow gown slid off the edge of the settee. He had not seen any movement to make it shift. Damon's gaze did a swift examination of her pale face, still and expression-less against a pillow.

Everything about her was still. He was used to wounds that gushed blood, or strangely angled broken bones, but a woman so motionless, so pale? He did not know where to start. With the father standing so close, so intimidating, clearly no one would say more than he had managed to learn from Matthew.

Barnes might have caused even more damage taking her to the house. Broken bones should not be moved, Damon knew, but she could hardly have been left outside in the dirt by the shed, and he could no longer manage a woman even as slight as her.

"Someone bring a bowl of water and a cloth." He looked around at the anxious faces. Matthew nodded a couple quick bobs of the head, and slipped out, keeping a distance from his father.

A pair of big blue eyes in a sweet young face, one of the young sisters, stared solemnly at him from the farthest end of the settee where Verbena's head lay. "Is she breathing?" Damon asked the girl.

The little girl nodded and leaned over the arm, easing closer to her sister's body, not taking her eyes from him. She was afraid, but not panicked.

Verbena's father *kicked* her. Damon shook his head. Had this sort of thing happened before? His hands tightened into fists, the one holding the gun could feel imprints of the carving press into his fingers, and forced himself to relax. One of the straight-backed chairs stood nearby. He grabbed it, walked around the settee, and thumped it down by Verbena's side.

"Send for Doctor Horton," he said as he sat down, not knowing exactly which of the bodies in the room he was addressing. Damon leaned the gun against the settee between himself and Verbena. If anyone wanted to get at it, they would have to go through him. Wounded leg or not, he knew he could, would, defend her.

"We never call the doctor. The man is a thief. I would not let Horton work on my horse. He won't leave his house without a coin in hand first."

Matthew appeared in the doorway, his hands full of a dripping bowl and cloth, and cleared his throat. Damon recognized the signal, remembered the boy's comment. *We can't afford to send for him.* The family could worry about their pride when Verbena was well.

"I will stand the cost." Damon tried to look Barnes in the eye, but the man's gaze would not stay in one place for any length of time, darting around the room as if following a frantic mouse.

Matthew came the rest of the way in with the bowl. Damon set it on the floor in easy reach. *I don't think he's very good, anyway.* Verbena's words, supposedly. A handy excuse to avoid telling children they could not afford a doctor.

He squeezed the cloth out and set it on Verbena's bruised face, but she did not move. Alarm rang inside like a physical bell. He had heard of cases where people never woke up. "Go for the doctor, Barnes! We need him here now!" Damon felt the man's onrushing sobriety, and knew he was in that period when alcohol felt as necessary as the next breath. He would be useless in a moment. Better to get Barnes out of the house and deal with the children alone. Maybe, with their father gone, the children would be as talkative as Matthew had been.

In his dreams, Damon had never imagined her living in terror and abuse.

"Fine." Barnes barked the word. "Pay for him. You will see. He is a crook."

"Take my horse, man, and get the doctor. And know this – " Barnes looked at him with a hopeful excitement tingeing his face, his hands clenching and unclenching. "I care not if you sleep in the tavern after that, but believe me when I say if I do not see the doctor here in this house within – " he glanced around and found the nearest clock, noting the time. "Twenty minutes, I will have the magistrate clap you in irons and forget about you. Are we quite clear?"

Barnes nodded frantically, and licked his lips as if already tasting the drink he craved.

"Go!"

Damon hoped Barnes believed his threats. He had meant every word of them.

6

She was in bed. Why did she not feel like moving, she who was always first to rise? Another moment and she would get up. There was never enough time to lie abed.

A shadow passed over her. Verbena turned to see who it was. Sudden pain brought a gasp. "Oh!" Her head throbbed and one cheek felt hot and tight. The light seeping through her small window burned her eyes.

"Here. Let me help you," a familiar voice said, and her sister's face appeared, blocking the sun for a moment. Edeline slid an arm around Verbena's shoulder. "Damon sent for the doctor and for me. We're still waiting for the doctor. I'm so glad you are awake. We were beginning to worry." She eased Verbena higher on her small bed. It was not comfortable, and Verbena bit back a moan.

She settled against the headboard. "My ribs . . . hurt. Is anyone else injured? What happened? How long have I been asleep?" Moving had started a new pain right . . . there. She held one hand to that sharp stab in her side, but it did not help. Her face seemed puffy around the sore cheek, the words had come out slurred.

"Everyone is well." Edeline sat down in the small chair by the side of the bed.

Her sister wore a dark blue dress, probably the best she could do until the modiste was able to get her new wardrobe finished.

Wardrobe! Memory returned in full, mourning and Andrew's death – and Thomas's rage and the gun. Sudden fear chilled Verbena, and the angry words of the fight came back. It was not safe for Edeline to be here right now! "Where is Father?" she blurted out, and tried to sit up. The pain doubled, making her gasp. She sank back and tried to catch her breath.

"Damon says there is a ship sailing soon. He promises to get Father a position on it." Edeline's face drooped. "Oh, Verbena. I had no idea it was this bad. Julius said Father kicked you. I am so sorry. I have been so selfish." Her voice was thick with shame and sadness. "Here I complained to you about my situation and you are living with violence and beatings. I'm so terribly sorry. You must think me the most callous person." Edeline brought one of Verbena's cold, chapped hands to her cheek.

The tender gesture closed Verbena's throat. She wished she could hug her sister, ease her self-reproach. Her voice thick, she said, "Oh, Edeline! Not at all! This has never happened before. Truly. Most of the time Father is gone."

"And you are alone. That is supposed to make me feel better?" Edeline leaned forward, a picture of grief in her dark gown and her sad face.

"You sent us letters. And money. We always knew you thought of us." Verbena tightened her hand on her sisters. "I promise you, Father has never kicked me before. How thoughtful of Damon to send for you even if you found things at their worst."

"He was very angry."

"Father? Or Damon?" Verbena heard her own familiarity and corrected herself, "I mean, Mr. Thern?"

"Father certainly is angry, but I was speaking of Damon." Edeline gave her a strange look. "You were given leave to use his Christian name?"

'I was just repeating you." A sharp pain stabbed her side again and Verbena winced. "The idea to send Father back to sea was very good." In fact, it was better than good, it was the best of all possibilities. How remarkable that Damon – Mr. Thern, she must remember that – even thought of getting her father out of the way.

She set a hand carefully on the sore spot on her side again. It did not help. If Da – Mr. Thern had been anywhere near Thomas this morning, there was no way the drunkenness could be hidden. How embarrassing. And confusing. "How did Mr. Thern get involved?

"He was riding past, he said, and heard a commotion."

Commotion. That might mean anything, and since she had rushed out at the gunshot and remembered only turning the corner of the shed, anything could have happened after that. Commotion. Verbena felt red rush up her face. This was far beyond embarrassing. She did not know how she would ever face him again.

He would undoubtedly keep himself far, far away. His hinted promise of the morning whispered through her memory. *You are not alone any more.* She had not wanted his interest, but to have it end like this! Really, she told herself, nothing had changed. She did not know him before, she would not know him now. Verbena looked up at her sister. "How long can you stay?"

Instead of answering, Edeline pressed something cool and wet on Verbena's cheek.

"What is that for?" It would certainly not cool the blush.

"You have a nasty bruise here, and it is swollen." Edeline's eyes lit up. "Not that I'm glad you got hurt, but the timing is just too perfect. We can plot and plan all we need."

That did not answer her first question but from the other side of the door whispers interrupted them. "Come in, girls," Edeline called, giving Verbena a wink. "They will come in anyway, better to know where they are."

Lizabeth leaned over the foot of the bed, while Annabelle hovered just out of sight. Verbena did not feel up to much movement, and only knew of her presence by Edeline looking at something beyond the door. "You are awake. We were so scared. Damon made us leave when the doctor came. He said to stay out while you slept, but I heard Edeline talking, and I just knew you had to be awake. I like him. He is very nice."

This was all quite odd. Damon sending Father off on a ship, Edeline sent for to comfort her, and now the little girls were charmed by him. Why was Damon being so gracious to her family? Verbena forced herself to relax. "He has indeed been good to us today, has he not?"

"He yelled at Father and I thought he might beat Father. He's handsome, don't you think so?" Lizabeth looked so very serious.

Verbena had to bite the inside of her cheek to hide the smile that threatened. "Handsome is as handsome does."

"Everybody always says that," Lizabeth scoffed, "but I don't think it is true. Trudy's brother is not nice at all, but all the girls still think he is handsome."

"Maybe they don't know the things about him that you know," Edeline said.

"Maybe. I know Trudy tells me things special, 'cause she is my most dearest friend."

Annabelle suddenly appeared by Verbena's side. She poked Verbena's shoulder, leaned over and whispered, "Bena? Bena?"

When Verbena turned with care toward Annabelle, her sister's brown hair shielded her little face. She leaned in close to Verbena, until she was all dark blue eyes and tangled hair, and whispered, "Who is the lady?" Down by her waist, about at the level of the bed, her small index finger pointed toward Edeline.

Verbena did not look at her older sister. She did not want to see the hurt in her eyes. If Annabelle did not know Edeline at all, what about Lizabeth, who was only slightly older? She had been natural, all lively and talkative, because nothing much stopped Lizabeth. That did not mean she knew her eldest sister. Edeline's contact had been mainly through letters. Verbena did not want to put a number to the rare times Edeline had managed to actually stay long enough for tea. She now had a better idea of how difficult finding even those infrequent visits had been.

"Remember, Annabelle? That lady is your oldest sister. Her name is Edeline."

Annabelle shook her head. "No. You are my oldest sister. My other oldest sister is Lizabeth."

Verbena's heart ached on Edeline's behalf. "You were a tiny baby when Edeline got married. She has been living in London, which is a very far away place. But this was originally her home."

She realized she had Lizabeth's attention, too. With her usual openness, Lizabeth turned to Edeline. "Is that true? Are you really my sister, too?"

In a soggy, wavering voice, Edeline said, "Yes. I really am your oldest sister."

"How come you never came to visit us?"

"Lizabeth!" Verbena thought she had taught the children better manners. Such a question was simply rude. "She has come on occasion." Her mind counted in spite of herself. Twice? Three times?

"No, no, it is quite all right, Verbena." Edeline's eyes were covered with a sudden sheen of tears. "Lizabeth, it is a long story, one I will share with you another day, but not today."

The clearing of a throat from the doorway was a welcome distraction. "My apologies." Damon sounded stiff and formal. It seemed wrong to put him in the awkward position of guest after all his efforts – and expense – on their behalf.

Verbena turned to face him, her head pounding at the movement. The blush of embarrassment had faded, but she felt her face heat again, and not just from the strangeness of a man in her room. No, she owed Damon so much for what he had done today, and she had no idea what she could ever do to repay him. "Please," she said. "Do come in."

He crossed the room. Two steps and he was there, tall as ever, imposing in her small bedroom. He was dressed as darkly as Edeline, but even had he not been, his mourning marked his face as it had done hours ago.

"Thank you for – " she started.

"How are you feeling?"

They both managed an awkward laugh. He waved a hand toward Verbena. "Please."

That little laugh cooled her face, and somehow, his mourning attire put her troubles in a different light. "Thank you for all you have done. We are so very much in your debt. And to bring Edeline, it is most kind and I am grateful."

"I did not do it for your gratitude." His mouth curved in a faint smile. He was so elegant in his rich suit, while she was in the same worn, sprigged day gown of this morning's chance meeting, much the worse for wear after what had happened.

Verbena covered the sore cheek with her hand, and hoped it did not look as bad as it felt. Tangled hair brushed her fingers. What a mess she must be! She did not have enough hands to cover every imperfection, so she instead plucked at the thin blanket that covered her to her waist. It, like her gown, had lost most of the color it once had, and was now a muddy grey. The whole room was small and sorry, as battered as her poor, aching body. "I'm sorry you had to see us at such a disadvantage." Just like that, the blush was back, her face seemed hot as a lit candle.

Damon sobered. "I would not have you feel embarrassed. I am only glad I was around to help." He looked past her, and a new smile, cheerful and teasing, bloomed on his face. "Hello, young ladies. I hope you are no longer afraid of me. I did not mean to frighten you when I first arrived."

Verbena turned enough to see Lizabeth and Annabelle. Lizabeth, as usual, spoke up. "I was not afraid of you."

That was too much for Annabelle. Verbena watched her youngest sister puff up like a banty hen as she turned to Lizabeth. "Yes, you were. You cried and ran away."

"I did not run away from him!" Lizabeth leaned forward in her usual fight-starting pose. "I was running after Verbena. I was worried about her."

This was all news for Verbena. She had told the girls to stay in the house. Clearly they had not obeyed. There must be another story behind that.

Her imposing guest took matters into his own hands before she could intervene. "It was very good of both of you to follow your sister. I was worried about her, too."

Annabelle actually took one step forward, and actually pulled on his pant leg. "Thank you for helping Bena."

He smiled down at her with his charming smile. "You are most welcome, little one."

"I'm Annabelle."

He bowed to her, something not easy to manage in such a small room with so many guests. "I am delighted to make your acquaintance."

Annabelle giggled.

Verbena's eyes widened as she watched the byplay. Even her swollen eye seemed to open, she felt the skin pull.

There was one matter that needed to be addressed. Not having been awake and aware during the . . . commotion that Damon had been exposed to, she did not know how bad it became, but she could imagine. Verbena straightened her shoulders as best she could and forced herself to meet Damon's gaze. "I must apologize for my father."

His dark eyes were warm. He even kept his smile in place. "I have not asked for an apology, nor will I."

If he could overlook her father, she would have to work at overlooking his family. It took real effort not to look at her sister, much as she wanted to see Edeline's face. This was not the behavior from a Thern she had been led to expect.

Damon had been away from his family's influence for some time. Now that he was back among them, now that he was the new heir – or so he thought – it might not be so easy to hold to his new opinions.

She would wait and see.

7

Just before the noon meal, Verbena stood at the front door, one arm cradled against the pain in her side and the pressure from the doctor's tight bindings. Her attention was split between Damon and squat Mr. Dibble, the village carpenter, dressed for work in his worn apron, his leather bag of tools draped over one bulky shoulder. Mr. Dibble always reminded Verbena of a bull, and the resemblance was all the more pronounced today standing next to Damon's tall leanness.

"G'day, Miss Verbena. Gud ta see ya." Mr. Dibble's eyes were narrow, and he looked from her to Damon and back again.

"Mr. Dibble?" Verbena felt her own eyes narrow as she turned her attention to his companion. How could he expose their situation to anyone?

"I can explain, if I may?" Damon's face was all innocence. He removed his tall hat, ran a hand over his dark hair, and tucked the hat under one arm. He gave a slight bow. "Miss Barnes. If you forgive me my impertinence, I noticed when I came to visit your family" – a polite way of discussing the scene he had been thrust into – "that your parlor doors were broken. I did not think it good for you to be fighting with them, not in your condition." He quickly corrected himself. "Or rather, with your injury."

Damon stepped aside and gestured toward Mr. Dibble. "I believe you are acquainted. He agreed to come and fix them." That move seemed to put Damon closer to the entryway.

"I got the time, miss." Mr. Dibble smiled his broken-toothed smile. "I brung all me tools. I can get it fixed in two shakes. All I needs is a good look."

Mr. Dibble did not have the manners Damon had, and started walking, right toward the door and through, leaving Verbena no alternative but to step aside. "Which ones be they?" He scanned the foyer, a totally unnecessary analysis in Verbena's opinion, with the parlor doors leaning like drunken men. "Oh, I see. If it be worn wood, I can fix it. If the hinges be broken, ye'll be needin the black-smith, but let me take a look before we go callin someone else to come stick his nose in."

He crossed the small opening and, head cocked to one side, looked at the gap where the door hinges were pulling away from the jamb. "Yessir, Mr. Thern, it be the wood fer sure. I best be off for some new wood from me shop."

"Verbena?" Damon spoke so softly that had they been any farther apart she would not have heard. "Perhaps you should sit down." He took her arm and walked her into the parlor, where he seated her on the settee with as much elegance as if she was a duchess.

He sat on the large ladder-back chair at her side and examined her face. She wondered how she looked in the bright daylight. In the small hand mirror in the dimness of her room, aside from the growing bruise, she had looked pale. With such bright light pouring in on her, Verbena imagined she must look half-dead.

There was nothing threatening in his actions, but her sister's secret weighed on her, and surely must show in her face, one more thing to make her look dreadful.

"I understand the doctor has been here. I apologize if you view all this as presumptuous," Damon said in a calm but firm voice. "I assure you I only wish to help. Edeline is part of my family, you are her family and this is my privilege."

"Edeline might be family – of a sort, but we are not. Not really." The words were not easy, but they had to be said. They had an audience, after all. She had to keep herself from turning to look at Mr. Dibble as he measured the doors. She wanted those doors fixed and Damon's offer, however presumptuous, was a terrible temptation. "I am grateful for the doctor. But this – truly, I would be most uncomfortable accepting such an expensive gift from you."

He leaned forward and spoke so softly Verbena could hardly hear him. His chocolate eyes were so close that she found herself staring at them, unable to so much as blink. "Do you always argue like this? It truly is a gift. Think of it as helping your brothers and sisters, if you must. I recall you taking me to task once about not paying better attention to the welfare of the villagers. Dibble needs work, I can provide him with that."

He did not wait for her to respond, but rose to his feet with that slow painful movement that must be galling for a man who used to be as active as he once was. She found she had a new appreciation for what his injury cost him. In a few days her injury would be a thing of the past and her life would be normal once again.

Not that normal was a good thing, but at least she knew what it would bring.

Her gaze followed him. Her neck hurt looking up so far, so she made to rise herself.

"Do not bestir yourself, Miss Barnes."

Miss Barnes? A moment ago she was Verbena. But then she saw Mr. Dibble had gone very still. No doubt everyone in the village would want to know why Damon had hired him. And when the village gossip mongers heard he had been hired, not for Thernwood, but rather to work on the Barnes' house – well, hopefully they would all remember the family connection. Damon's formality would at least hold the worst of the rumors at bay.

Damon gave her another formal bow and walked toward the front door, taking Mr. Dibble with him. Verbena heard them talking.

"I best fix the whole frame, I'm thinkin, and more than this door. I noticed the front door was headin for this same problem. Cain't have another door go fallin off."

The list of things that needed fixing would grow like the weeds in spring.

Unfortunately, the list might be, if anything, too conservative. The two men closed the outer door behind them, but their words floated through the open window.

"Will you need help getting the wood here?"

"Naw. I got me own wagon, cain't hardly do me work without it, now could I? Me bein a carpenter an all, I kin patch it up much as it needs an keep it runnin. This village would hardly survive without me help."

Verbena felt a smile curve her mouth as she listened to Dibble brag. The Therns might own the land, but without simple workers like the village carpenter, even the big houses would soon be in as bad shape as her own.

It was rather a nice leveler.

THREE HOURS LATER, over the sound of Mr. Dibble's hammer, a rhythmic rattle finally drew Verbena's attention.

She turned away from the kitchen table, where she sat on the bench washing dishes in her biggest pot so she could rest while she worked. Her hands were getting chapped, and they stung from the lye and the hot water. "Oh, who can that be?" she muttered as she dabbed her hands on her apron, then slipped it off as she hurried over to the door.

Damon stood there again, the second time in one day. Years when he was only a young girl's memory and now he seemed to be as ever-present as weeds in spring.

"Mr. Thern. What a surprise." She heard the touch of dryness in her own voice. She somehow was not as astonished as she should be. "Did you forget something here?"

He removed his hat, tucking it under his arm, and that was the only thing he might have left behind. Although if he had, she would have noticed it sitting abandoned right away. A woman stood at his side, dark hair well dusted with grey peeking out from under her worn bonnet. Round from birthing many children, all now grown and married, she was dressed in a blue gingham gown, carrying a basket over her arm. A wooden scrub brush poked its bristly head out of the top.

Mrs. Downs. Verbena knew her name, but had never had any dealings with her. Her father's flaws were a constant source of embarrassment. Paying visits was unthinkable.

She turned back to Damon. It was bad enough the village would learn the inside of the house was in as bad shape as the outside. She could only imagine what salacious news this new visitor would bring back to spread. She raised her brows and waited for an explanation.

"I noticed you have not been following the doctor's advice. I asked around the village, and Mrs. Downs came highly recommended. She is known as a hard worker, and a good cook. I want to be able to tell the doctor that you are being careful, and cared for. I do not wish either of us to incur his wrath." A smile lurked around his mouth, and his dark eyes were dancing with their own humor.

He took a step closer to the door. Verbena looked at Mrs. Downs' smiling face, and smothered her sigh. "Please come in," she said, but she knew they would come in regardless.

"I hear you were hurt. You look pale, my dear. What a pity that we ain't had a chance to become acquainted before now. And your sister so newly widowed. Poor dear. So young to be a widow."

As Mrs. Downs spoke, she set down her basket, removed her bonnet, hung it on one of the pegs, pulled out her apron and started tying it. *Goodness*, Verbena thought, *this one is not wasting any time, either.* She did not want to admit it, but part of her gave a sigh of relief. That spot on her side had been hurting more than she dared admit, and the work would not wait. The children all had their own chores. Matthew was catching fish for supper, Julius was pulling weeds at the Holman's, and the girls were feeding the chickens and cleaning the coop.

Now she could concentrate on the tasks that did not require any lifting or scrubbing. Like mending Matthew's pantaloons, and trying to alter one of Julius's to fit. That she could do without pain.

She felt Damon's eyes on her. Much as she wanted to blurt out her gratitude, she could not bring herself to look at him yet. She had to make sure her embarrassment would not show first.

Was Edeline wrong about the Therns?

Mrs. Downs looked around the kitchen. "I see you been doing the dishes. You jest forget about that. Don't you be worryin about a thing. I can do all the heavy work. A broken rib, now, that is a bad thing. Especially for someone as tiny as you. Why, I wager even breathing hurts. An you have no padding on them bones of yours. I remember catching my heel in my skirt hem an takin a tumble down some stairs an landin hard once. But I'm so much stronger than you, an even then I had a bit of paddin. Even so, I was bruised for days, let me tell you."

Damon stood off to the side, that same smile on his face, his eyes never wavering away from here. Not even with Mr. Dibble banging away on the door frame.

Mrs. Downs rubbed her hands together. "Now you just show me where your laundry is. Soon's I'm done with the dishes, I'll get on that. I'm a wonder with the scrub board, let me tell you. I can get a whole week worth of laundry done in no time. Course, it is just my man an me now, what with all the children grown up. You should have seen the smile on his face when Mr. Thern here said how much he'd pay me for just a little bit of work that I can do in my sleep."

Her bright brown eyes pinned Verbena. How she wished she dared turn to Damon right now and give him a glare! Yes, she was grateful, but anyone would know at a glance, or a minute's listen, that if there was anything the village did not know yet about the Barnes, this woman would ferret it out. And her ability to keep any secrets at all seemed nonexistent.

"You jest scat now, an leave me be to work."

In spite of her misgivings, Verbena had to smile. She suspected if Damon had not taken her arm and started leading her out, Mrs. Downs would have pushed her out herself.

So she collected her bonnet and let Damon walk her past Mr. Dibble and out the front door. Strange, to feel a visitor in her own house. She normally used the back door, out the kitchen, just because it was shortest to the chicken coop.

But Damon took her out her front door. And down the rocky path toward the small woods that separated them from the village. At least he was not taking her toward Thernwood. His hand rested on hers where it was linked through his elbow.

Verbena did not know what to do, other than keep walking. She looked down at her chapped, red hand where it rested on his rich blue coat. She curled her fingers, hoping to hide them, and stayed at his side. It was a clear, sunny day, not too warm for a walk.

Matthew's pantaloons could wait a little longer. It really was a lovely day, and she did not remember ever going for a stroll without having to get somewhere.

The birds sang in the trees around them as if they too enjoyed the sun. The air was fresh, not sticky as it could get on really hot days, but light, easy to breathe. She smelled a hint of bread baking, drifting toward them on the breeze. It blended with the delicate scents of trees and blooming things. And Damon, as he warmed with the exertion.

He drew them both to a stop. "So. Am I improving myself a little bit in your eyes?"

She felt his head dip to see her face around the bonnet's brim. She looked back, into those expressive dark eyes. "I do not know why you are doing this for us, but I'm grateful. You don't realize what a help this is."

He sighed. "Oh, but I think I do. I am not doing this for your gratitude, although I'm glad it will help you."

He started walking again, with his hitched gait. "In the war, many women followed their husbands. We had women around the camp all the time. I watched them work. It never ended, washing and cooking, even caring for the children, although there was not much of that in my regiment. But I did see it. Women even followed their husbands onto the battlefield rather than stay behind, waiting and worrying."

He took another breath, deep, as if bracing himself and Verbena waited. They walked a few more steps before he spoke again. "You remind me of them. Hard-working and utterly loyal to those you love. You would follow your husband into the battle, I believe."

She stumbled, but he caught her arm and steadied her until she found her balance and they could resume their walk.

He looked down at her again. "You are an admirable woman, Miss Verbena."

They had reached the end of the drive, where it split to go to the village or around to Thernwood. He halted in the shade of a great oak and stared off toward the first houses that marked the village. "You were right about most of my class. Before I spoke with you, I knew nothing about the people who live here. I assumed they did well. The houses all appeared clean, the shops were not boarded. I had no idea where they got their business, or who had the coin to pay them. I might excuse myself because I was ill, but I do not have that excuse now."

Verbena recalled their conversation by the log, the same one that seemed to have made such an impression on him. Two people at least in the village had reason to be glad she had called him out on his lapses. "I'm not totally without guilt myself. I seldom go into the village. There just is not time for any casual calls, and when I do go, it is to pay the bills my father incurs."

He shook his head. "You at least do that much. Your criticism of my class was deserved. I am not them, nor am I blind to what goes on."

In his own house? But she could not ask.

"I promise, I will monitor my inheritance better than my brother did."

"Or your father?" She could not believe the words came out.

He frowned at her, and seemed to draw away even though her hand was still held in his elbow. "I can't speak for my father. The village is surviving, so clearly he does watch over them."

Verbena had no response to that. Maybe Mr. Thern did care for the village. They paid rents, after all. The Barnes, however, owned their small bit, and were outside the Thern's purview.

Verbena wished she could take her sharp words back. Anything she said might make it harder for Edeline, but somehow she did not think Damon would tell tales on her. She had the sudden wish to draw out his smile again. "I apologize. That was cruel of me. I do not know your family, and have no business speaking ill of them."

He accepted it with a quick nod. "Will you at least absolve me of being careless and thoughtless?"

She found a smile, and hoped it looked genuine. "You are doing very well. The villagers will spread the stories of your care far and wide."

"And you?" His gaze sharpened.

"I have no one to tell. Other than the children, of course."

He gave a quick squeeze on her arm where it rested on his. "Do you absolve me of being thoughtless?"

From the intensity in his eyes, Verbena knew it mattered. "Yes, I do absolve you. You are doing very well. You will be a wonderful landlord, I'm certain."

"How am I doing as person? Not a useless fribble?"

Her smile was certainly genuine now. "Not at all a useless fribble."

"Good. At least I have redeemed myself in other respects

because I fear I have pushed myself too far and now I must bring you back to your house."

"Lean on me, if you need to. I'm stronger than I look."

"And injured yourself. But yes, I do know how strong you are." They started back, his steps halting and slow, but his color was still good and if he had pain, he did not show it. At least not in his face.

He was stronger than he looked, too, she thought, and wished she dared gaze at him, look and take more of the measure of this man.

But propriety intervened. And loyalty, just as he had said a moment ago, held her back.

8

VERBENA HEARD THE CHURCH BELL TOLLING THE DEATH KNELL FOR Andrew as she walked carefully down the dusty village street. She was late, but at least she had taken care of one errand. The letter to Aunt Mabel was on its way. The children had stayed at home. None had attire presentable enough for a funeral, especially not with so many of the wealthy down from London.

Edeline needed support. That meant at least one of the Barnes had to make an appearance. She was the only one who could. And that simply because she fit into Mother's old clothes, one of which, while not a mourning gown, was black and would pass.

Despite the swelling around her ribs from Father's kick, Verbena had managed to get into Mother's gown and shoes. Her hair, however, had been beyond her. Even though it was pinned up, she had done an awkward job and did not have much faith that the pins would stay. Maybe the bonnet would help.

So here she was, scurrying to the church to let Edeline see she was not alone. Someone shuffled up behind her, and Verbena stepped sideways. A man strode boldly up the stone stairs and grabbed the big bronze handles. Verbena hurried after him, and managed to slip through before they shut.

As if in sympathy, the bell tolled exactly as the door thumped closed. The long mournful peal sent shivers down her spine. It was somehow different from the pealing that happened every Sunday, this one slow and chilling.

Verbena did not even know if their plan for Edeline's escape was still in force. Ever since Damon had driven Edeline back to Thernwood in the majestic family carriage, they had not seen her, nor had there been word. To be sure, it had been scarcely two days, and she knew the Therns house had been filled with visitors.

The sensibilities and restrictions from London on who could and could not attend funerals had not reached their little town, and the church was filled to capacity. It was easy to see who were villagers. The men wore coarse woolens and must be stifling in the stuffy heat of the church. The local women wore linens and chintz in every color of the rainbow, and their hats drooped from long use. Here and there, a man's rough nankeen-clad leg poked out into the aisle. Candles flickered in the sconces on the wall, and the good silver candlesticks that came out only on special occasions were placed on either side of Andrew's coffin. The black velvet pall covering the coffin draped down to the floor, forming a puddle of death there.

Toward the front were the London guests. Somewhere the Therns must be held in affection, for so many to come and even attend the funeral.

Silk rustled its distinctive sound, and taffeta shimmered in the blend of stained glass sunlight and the softer glow from the candles. Bonnets were everywhere. Straw and silk, ruffled and bowed, and as pristine as the day they were made. Today all were distinguished by the sign of mourning. Black bows and ribbons and ruffles peeking from underneath, everyone had at least done something to show respect for the occasion.

Verbena tried to be inconspicuous as she looked around for a place to sit. She did not see Edeline before she was allowed to squeeze through a row, and it was worse after she got seated. One of the local farmers sat on one side, smelling slightly of cow. The village milliner sat on the other side, a painfully thin woman, and taller than most of the men in the town. Her husband barely came up to her shoulder, but they seemed happy enough.

Verbena could not see around the bodies in front of her, let alone spot Edeline, and she wished – not for the first time – for a little more height. As she gingerly leaned against the firm support of the pew's back, she had to accept that the whole painful journey to town was a wasted effort. Edeline would never know she had even come. The church was filled with people desperate for something to overhear – and spread.

Just like their hired housekeeper. Mrs. Downs was full of gossip and delighted to pass every bit of it along. They had already been updated on all manner of the Thern's private affairs.

As the congregation shuffled into silence, Verbena heard the woman's voice again. "The Thern's high and mighty friends have come all the way from London," Mrs. Downs had gushed the first time she came, after Damon had left and the two were getting better acquainted. "There's all manner of the fancy here. I hear tell our plain Mr. Thern got himself a title when he was in London. He is a baronet, that he is. That's why he 'as been gone so long this last time. That makes him a 'sir' now, an I suspect he'll be making the most of it. So our *Sir* Edward Thern," she stressed the title with a strange pride, "wanted to move the funeral to London, but there is a family cemetery in the churchyard here, an they decided it was not seemly to bring the body all the way back down to town."

Thank goodness for a family cemetery, Verbena had thought then, and the thought returned with force. Had the Therns gone to London to bury Andrew, they would have dragged Edeline, the new widow, with them as a matter of course and any hope of escape would have been at least most difficult, at worst, impossible.

Now the Therns had the weight of a title on their side. A baronet, which was some small comfort. A duke or an earl would have been too much to fight.

The bell's tolling faded into silence and the vicar took his place in the pulpit.

Verbena tried to concentrate as the parson droned on about Andrew's righteous life and the joys that awaited him on his resurrection, but she kept hoping for at least a glimpse of her sister. Sitting in the back as she was with no way to see what was happening in the front rows, she cared little about Andrew's eternal fate.

Her mind stubbornly stuck on her sister's welfare. Had she fainted, or gotten sick, or any one of a dozen things a pregnant woman might do to give herself away? If Mrs. Downs was right, and the big house was filled with guests, hiding her condition was going to be an hour by hour, minute by minute fright.

The congregation rose. The first few rows milled about, and Verbena watched them split into two groups. The men followed the coffin, but the women went out a different door, not down the aisle. Big burly footmen surrounded the women in their fancy expensive garb and ushered them through the opposite door, normally used on the hottest days to provide ventilation. Verbena tried to see around the mass of people between them and find her sister somewhere in that group, but it was hopeless.

She had hesitated too long. Someone behind her pushed, and Verbena gasped. The pain eased before the person could shove again. She exited with her pew, moving down the aisle toward the main doors.

Ah, well. She had done her best, but now had driven herself too far, and she needed to rest.

A hairpin fell onto the ground in front of her as she stepped outside into the sunlight. Verbena left it there. Her hair was falling down, as she expected, yet another reason to slip away.

The bulk of the crowd turned right toward the village proper, the shops and houses, and Verbena turned left with the stragglers.

IF HE HAD NOT BEEN SO tall, he would not have even seen her in the crowd. Damon stopped at the top of the stairs and watched Verbena walk away. She looked right and left, but thankfully she did not turn and look up. He had to force himself to stay in place.

As soon as Andrew's consignment was over, he intended to pay the Barnes a visit.

He had more than one reason for checking up on them. All was not well with Edeline, either. The two women must have met the day Andrew died for more than sisterly comfort, and he would very much like to know what that was.

He had a plan for Verbena. More a wish, actually. If he had designed a woman for himself, it would have been her.

Maybe he *had* designed her, in the blood and dirt and death of the war, kept her face as the ideal to which all other woman must compare. But what was she *really* like? He had seen what she wanted him to see, but something was going on under the surface.

THE DOOR WAS FLUNG OPEN. Matthew burst inside, hardly the proper decorum for such a somber day. "Verbena went to the funeral this morning," he said to someone behind him.

Verbena swung her legs down to the floor, eased herself upright, and winced sharply at that harsh, quick pain around her ribs. Matthew's report would hardly be news to Mrs. Downs, and instead Damon's rich voice rolled through the air. "I am very glad to hear it. Thank you for letting me come see how she is doing for myself."

Lizabeth and Annabelle leapt to their feet in such unison it seemed they had practiced the move, and dashed past the settee and out the parlor doors.

Her biggest fear, that Damon would continue his inexplicable interest in the family, was coming to pass. In the midst of his constant watch, she and Edeline were supposed to plot a workable escape plan?

"Damon! Damon!" the girls warbled, with complete disregard to his status as heir to a Title. "You came back!"

His chuckle was just as warm as his voice. Verbena suddenly realized she had never heard him laugh before. How hard was it to put on a smiling face on the day of his brother's funeral?

"I need to speak to your sister," he said, and the footsteps came closer, his measured and hesitant, favoring the leg, the girls' light, almost dancing across the floor.

And there he was, dressed for mourning in his black silk coat and black cravat, bowing before her, picking up her hand and kissing it. His skin still showed signs of his slow recovery, and the lingering paleness seemed stark and jarring against the somber colors of grief. His near-black hair with its rich waves, a match for his garments, was almost close enough to touch. He looked up at her through the dark strands and for a moment everything else slipped away and all she could see were his eyes, like midnight pools.

Verbena fought the urge to snatch her hand back. His lips were warm, she felt his breath brush her skin. His hand under hers was strong, capable, with power she wished she could depend on, a power that might easily turn against her family.

"How are your parents?" she asked. Such a common question, a standard, meaningless courtesy, but she really needed to know. Edeline had to be able to slip away. And she herself needed a moment to gather her scattered thoughts after that startling gesture. It was even harder to regain her composure with his ebony eyes fixed on her.

"They are as well as can be expected, thank you." He finally let go of her hand.

"And how is Edeline?" She hoped he blamed her breathlessness on her injury.

Damon pulled the ladderback chair over close and seated himself, which worried her. She did not think she could hide all her thoughts with him so near. His face sobered, lines appearing that she had not seen before. "She is taking it hard. We are all thinking of going back to London. My father thinks my mother and the girls need to be occupied, rather than stay here with the memories. The family will leave with the guests."

The girls. His sisters. Verbena had heard about them. "Is Edeline going along?"

He pulled back, surprise on his face. "Of course! Where else would she be?"

Verbena's heart turned over. "Would it not be better for Edeline to stay here, where she has family?"

He scowled at her, the sad lines on his face becoming angry ones. "Here? You mean, in this house?"

"*We* are her family and this *was* her house before she wed," Verbena said with asperity. "And there is no reason she should not be allowed to work. Won't that help? Keep her mind busy?" Really, how did the rich take their mind off their troubles?

He shook his head, as if to a silly child. "She does not need to wear herself out. You don't see her, hiding in the gazebo, weeping, wandering the grounds. No, London would be better."

London would also send Edeline in the wrong direction, away from Aunt Mabel's home and security. Money was going to be tight as it was. A longer journey and it might not happen. "This area has happy memories for her. Perhaps she is revisiting places where they fell in love."

He folded his arms and frowned down at her. Even seated, he was large, and worse, he had a truly impressive frown. "Brooding is not good, surely you can see that. Besides, Mother needs her around. Edeline is the last link to Andrew."

The last link to Andrew? He could not have heard that from his mother! "Don't Edeline's feelings matter? If she needs to wander, does she not have the right? I would certainly not forbid her from time to herself."

The frown remained. "Of course, she does, and I'm not forbidding her time alone. I am just saying she and Mother can comfort each other."

Verbena had to look away, for fear he would see her irritation.

"I never thought of a mother-in-law as being closer than one's birth family."

"You have never been married. When two women share love for the same man, it can bind them together."

"Or they can compete over him." She could not stop her runaway tongue, and the words were out.

Damon gave her a funny look. "You have a sour view of marriage." His dark eyes narrowed. "I hope when you marry, you will find it in your heart to accept your mother-in-law. After all, she loved your husband first."

She had to lighten the mood, before they really started to fight. "I have no prospects. I come with a family – it tends to drive men away."

The frown faded. "You have not met the right man until now. I agree your father is a dampening influence, but he can be managed. It just takes a firm hand, someone who has seen worse than him." The corner of his mouth twitched. A smile? That could hardly be.

She could not manage a smile in return, and did not even try. "Where will I find someone like that in a small village like this?" Verbena realized she was plucking at her gown. Unlike Damon, she had wasted no time changing her garment. This one was old, it would not stand up to her nervous fingers. She forced them still.

The smile became real, spreading to his eyes, dancing with humor. "You never know – he might be closer than you think."

She could not imagine who he had in mind. Perhaps there were male guests at Thernwood whose parents would not object to a daughter-in-law with siblings, a drunken father and no dowry. She already knew what the Therns' feelings were on that matter.

He leaned back, and the smile faded. "Now, you and I both know where you were today. I saw you leaving the church. Did Mrs. Downs know where you were going?"

Verbena felt her eyes narrow. "You must not blame her!"

"No? And why not?" He was still, his dark eyes hiding some secret even while he seemed to be searching for hers.

Why had she not thought someone else would get in trouble? Of course everyone – meaning Damon – *must* understand. "She had nothing to do with my going. The decision was all mine. And I'm nearly well. It is just a bruise, after all."

"Who told you that? We can't be certain, of course, no one can, but the doctor told me he thought you might have cracked a rib. I hired help for you so you could heal, not risk your health further." His voice had grown tighter as he spoke, as though leashed by force of will.

A cracked rib? "I did not know that, did I?" She would not apologize for attending the funeral. "Edeline is my sister, who would dare keep me from going?"

He blew out a breath, and his head drooped. "I would not have prevented you. In fact, I would have sent a carriage for you rather than have you walk all that way."

"All what way? A walk to the church, that I make every Sunday? " Verbena's heart thumped in her chest so hard she feared he would hear it. His nearness, his persistence, and the need to talk to her sister turned into a boiling brew inside. For a moment she thought she might get sick.

She wanted to trust him so much! The worry about her sister's flight, about when or even *if* it would happen, had been growing ever since Edeline left the house. Verbena watched his face. The fixed doors, a housekeeper, an offer, albeit late, for a carriage ride to the funeral. Could she ask him for one small favor? "Will you please let Edeline know that I did go to the funeral today?" She could only hope her sister understood what she dared not send through a messenger. "I do not want her to think she was there alone."

"She was not alone." The smile vanished from mouth and eyes. "She had all of us. We grieved with her."

Verbena decided not to argue that. More and more, she suspected he did not see what his mother did to Edeline. "But she did not have *me*. I'm her sister, and she did not even know I came."

He looked thoughtful. "I think you are right, she should know. Yes, I will tell her."

"When she is alone," Verbena insisted. "With no one around." Aloneness would be easier on her sister, keep the mockers from mocking and the eavesdroppers from hearing.

"Oh, come, Verbena. If I did not know better, I would think you believe she is ashamed of you."

"Edeline is not ashamed of me! But I can't say the same for the others who are there."

"Our guests?" His brows came down, and his eyes seemed to look into the distance – or the past, memories of words he had heard.

"I know our family does not measure up to your guests. It is better for her if no one hears our name. I don't want her to be questioned. I don't want to leave her open to scrutiny or talking behind her back. More than is already done, that is." And perhaps Edeline would think of some way to get word back so Verbena would know whether or not their escape plan was still in force. "Don't tell me you have not heard the way they talk of us. I won't believe you. I know what our own village says about Father, and they remember when things were different. Please, let Edeline be spared that."

"Fine." He slapped his black gloves against his leg, a soft snap of sound.

Verbena looked at him and wished she could see into his mind. Into his heart. He had given his word, but he was a Thern and she had to remember that. He did not seem The Enemy, not like the rest of his family, but a wrong word would be all it might take. Someone could well guess their secret and the child would be lost as Andrew's family swallowed it up, drilling into it the haughty stiffness that was their signature.

Giving it a life of wealth and privilege that Edeline had determined was its downfall. How much did happiness cost and what was its currency? Verbena knew full well the cost of poverty and it was very expensive indeed.

But it was Edeline's child, and Edeline's decision. There was so little time for a rescue, and her hopes were fading. Verbena knew she had provided all the help and assurance that she could, particularly in the shape she was in, battered and weak yet.

The silence had grown long, she thought. He must have thought so as well. He gave a bow and took his leave.

Verbena watched him as long as she could. The door shut with a firm thump, and she winced. She may have just made things worse, but what else could she do?

9

DAMON SLOWED THE HORSE AS HE NEARED THE FRONT DOOR AND saw the groom. With all the guests up from London for the funeral, the house had lost all semblance of privacy.

Verbena had been right about that, he could admit to himself. He would have to find a way to get Edeline out of the house. He knew how his father felt about the Barnes, and sadly could understand it in part. Mr. Barnes was a problem, an embarrassment to his whole family. The house servants would know of him. They had been hired from the village. Servants were not supposed to fraternize with the guests, but if someone asked a servant a direct question they expected to get a direct answer. Edeline was a major topic of conversation about the house now, most of it unfavorable. He had heard enough to know. Being so close to her home and family, secrets were hard to keep hidden. Edward's sentiments might very well be echoed elsewhere.

"Sir? May I take your horse?" The groom spoke hesitantly. What a shame they had a title now. It had changed everything, from the demeanor of the servants to the behavior of the guests.

"Certainly." He dismounted and tossed the reins to the man and stood at the bottom of the stairs, dreading going inside to find

Edeline and pry her from the clutches of his mother and the guests.

The guests. Those awful guests who wanted pretty stories of the war, all cleaned up and brushed off, valor and excitement but no blood or gore, no stench of the dying. Parents of girls wanted to thrust their daughters at him. They probably would have chosen someone else – anyone else – when he was only a second son with the smaller portion of wealth and land and a crippled leg, but to be an Honorable, with a title, albeit a small one, and the sole heir to all his father's wealth made him only too appealing.

Sole heir.

He started up the portico stairs slowly, hoping no one had seen him and would come bustling out to cheer him up. Mother, in particular, wanted him at her side all the time, introducing him to all the young daughters of people he was certain she had scarcely met before, young girls who simpered and giggled despite the solemnity in the house, and smiled at him across the dinner table.

Of course, all the table linens were now black, and so quickly dyed that it tended to come off on fingers, and occasionally faces.

No one came outside this time. Taking advantage of a precious few moments of peace, Damon walked over to the railing and stared across the lawn toward the trees that separated their massive spread from the Barnes' small patch of land. He let the grief swamp him. He was tired of death, tired of grieving in public. He wanted time alone to mourn in peace.

A houseful of women panting after him, and the one woman he wanted seemed oblivious to his attempts at courtship. One walk, he had managed one walk with her, and that one far too short. He had rescued her and her brothers, paid for the doctor, hired a woman to do the hardest chores so she could rest, fixed her doors, found a ship for the father, now sailing away toward Africa and the Far East to collect fabrics and spices for the burgeoning colonies of America. Barnes would be out of their lives for months, and return with wages.

Compared to the twittering, giggling birds inside, she was the only one who was real. He had seen too much to settle for anything less. A wife whose only interests were shopping and clothes would be intolerable. He could see Verbena managing a house of servants easily. After her brothers and sisters, servants would be a relief. They could not talk back. She knew cooking and cleaning and sewing and illness and injury. She knew how to make do with nothing, he longed to drape her in pearls and velvet.

The large door behind him opened. He turned around. "Father." He had known Andrew took after their father, but now, seeing him, the resemblance was a physical pain. Tall, slender, sandy brown hair tending toward blonde now with the distinguished traces of grey, and Andrew's blue eyes. He himself favored their Welsh mother, with her dark hair and equally dark eyes. In spite of their differences, he and Andrew had always gotten along well, and he missed him so badly that each heartbeat was like the stab of a knife. Even when he was a continent away, he had always known Andrew was waiting for his infrequent letters, and that gave him endless comfort.

Edward Thern walked over to the railing and clutched the stone tightly, his knuckles going white. The two men stood, staring out over the land. Then his father sighed, deep and heartfelt. "I shall never get over missing Andrew."

"Neither shall I," Damon returned, surprised but moved at this unusual communication. "It seems I can't get away from the memories."

Edward turned to face him. "I can hardly wait to get to London. I intend to leave on the heels of the guests, before the grief becomes overwhelming for our women. Your mother and sisters are equally eager to go. There is too much sadness in this house, and memories. London is just the distraction we need."

Verbena's message pricked him. "You know Edeline's sister is injured. Her father did the damage."

"That man!" Edward's lips curled in disdain. "Had I known what Barnes would turn out to be, I would never have allowed Andrew to marry into such a family. I would have locked him up to keep him away from *them*." The last word curdled, as if the very speaking of it was spoiled.

Damon had seen parts of Mr. Barnes his father could only guess at, but it irked him to hear those children, and Verbena, lumped together with their father.

"They were not of our class, not ever," Father went on, staring out across the spread of green in front of them. "Barnes had inherited land, although scarcely an impressive piece. He had both a flock and a small herd of cows, but he was dependent on the common land for grazing. *Our* land, as I reminded Andrew again and again. He did not seem to understand the class divisions. I thought I had taught him better than that. And Andrew – " an involuntary smile tugged at his mouth. "Your brother, for all his dreaming ways, had a core of iron. He would have that woman and none other. Rather than cut him off, which would have caused unwelcome comment, I gave in."

He shook his head in a soft gesture. "Thank goodness she was pretty, soft-spoken, well-mannered, which came as a surprise." He blew out a hard breath, as if the air in his lungs was tainted. "If only she had contracted the fever and died instead of Andrew. It would spare us the possibility of *that man*," he fairly spat the words, "showing up uninvited someday."

Sudden, sickening rage welled up, burning through his bones, making his hands tingle. Damon glared at his father. "I can't believe I heard that. I have seen people die of fever, of bullets, of sword cuts, of knife wounds, of festering infection – shall I continue? I would never wish death on anyone!"

His father looked at him blankly for a moment, as if wondering what he had said that prompted the outburst. Finally he blinked. "Oh, don't be absurd. You take everything so seriously. Come now, son. Don't tell me if you could make a deal with God and trade your sister-in-law for your brother, you would turn that down? You scarcely know the girl. Be honest with me. Tell me you would rather have her in the family than him."

The question came as a jolt. The rage washed away. "I don't

have that choice." Now that the thought was there, he could not brush it aside. What would he do? Could he honestly say he would turn down the chance to have Andrew alive and well before him?

Damon looked at his father, looked at the white around his lips, the ashen skin, the high color on the cheeks left over from his emotions while everything else remained drained. Father was just speaking from grief, lancing the pain. Damon had seen and heard worse during the battles when friends died, alive one moment, dead the next, leaving the survivors to turn their grief – and guns – on anything that moved.

"She will remarry someday, and someone else can deal with the man." Edward shook his head. "For right now, however, it is unfortunate that her family lives so close. So far no one has seen them, they have not had the audacity to come onto the property."

Ah, but one of them had had enough audacity. One of them had been on the property, but that secret was safe.

Father looked over at him, his eyes suddenly shrewd. "You have been off in France. I know I must make allowances for war's effect, but don't think I have not noticed you have been spending time in that house, worrying over that family instead of your own. They are suffering from a situation of their own making. I give you the same warning I gave Andrew: the other children are not welcome." His eyes narrowed into cold slits. "You will not be following in your brother's steps. This house is full of young women who are suitable. You will pick from such as them. Is that understood?"

Damon refused to react. He did not plan to discuss his intentions. He had to convince Verbena first and she might be the bigger challenge. He simply said, "I would rather feel sympathy for those children than scorn them. I have a feeling Edeline wants to stay here and help her family."

Father made an ugly snort of sound. "She only wants what will embarrass us. If it would humiliate us if she stays here, she will want to stay. If it would be more embarrassing to go to London, she will go. Common folk are totally unaware of proper behaviors. It is a constant indignity. All one has to do is spend a night at the theater or the opera to see what the lower classes are like. And Edeline comes from that class." He clapped a hand on Damon's shoulder, and leaned close, speaking softly and quickly as if he feared being overheard. "Watch. She will find a way to embarrass us."

He understood better why Verbena had insisted on her greeting being given in privacy. He might have been accidentally accurate in telling her she was ashamed of who she was. A drunkard's daughter living in a crumbling house. Strange that she did not seem eager for a way out. He could not believe she had not had a single offer of marriage in all these years. Edeline had taken her chance and married Andrew, but then, his father said Barnes had not been a drunkard at the time.

Damon saw again Verbena with the basket of bread those long years ago, young and carefree. Barnes' drinking must have started later, after Edeline's wedding, because if the man had been in this state, Edward would never permitted the marriage, Andrew's stubbornness or not.

She only wants what will embarrass us. He did not know Edeline, that was true. Underneath his father's wild, grieving words, there might well be experience. He himself had not seen Edeline in Society, he did not know what she was like there.

He would have to watch, particularly now, after Father's warning. "I should go inside. I'm certain I was seen and I can hardly hide much longer."

"Go, then. Lord knows, I am not much company right now, myself." Edward turned away.

There was nothing else to do but square his shoulders and face the horde of women, find Edeline and give her Verbena's message.

He moved toward the large sitting room, behind which he thought he heard the murmur of voices. Bracing himself, he pushed the door open and walked through.

He had never seen a room so oppressive, so determinedly in mourning. It seemed everyone had come prepared for the occasion. Several wore black gowns, and everyone had some evidence of sympathetic mourning, black gloves, black scarves, capes and rings, earrings and necklaces of jet, the only proper mourning jewelry. Around the room, eyes turned toward him, people anxious for a disruption in the gloom.

The hole Andrew's death left suddenly opened in front of Damon, endless years without his brother, his own grief a black maw threatening to consume him with guilt. Every inheritance, Thernwood, the London house, this new, unexpected title that he would someday receive, all because Andrew had died.

He bowed to the group. "Thank you all for coming. Your presence is a comfort." He scanned the room quickly, and saw his quarry sitting against the wall behind the small circle of chairs that held his mother and sisters. She looked very much like she wanted to cry. Again.

She did not look like a woman who meant to embarrass anyone. Instead, she looked exactly like what she was, a new widow far too young for her grief. He knew of very few who faced her loss with such impressive dignity.

As Damon crossed the room, nodding at the many greetings, he noted the contrast between the sisters. Even in mourning, Verbena' sunlit hair would have been a beacon, while Edeline's brunette tresses nearly blended with her black cap. Despite her fairness, Verbena's skin had the richer color, speaking of time working outside, and energy.

That might be unfair, Damon scolded himself. Edeline had just lost her husband. Of course she would be pale, or perhaps it was just the contrast with the dark circles under her red-rimmed eyes that her skin seemed washed out.

As he drew nearer he saw more differences between the two. Differences that were more than skin deep. Verbena would hardly hide behind others, grieving or not. She would not sit to be waited on, but would find something to do.

He bent and kissed his mother and sisters, then turned to Edeline, and held out his hand. "My dear sister, if you would be so kind, I would beg a moment of your time."

At first, Edeline did not move. He wondered if she had even heard him. Maybe movement itself was beyond her at this moment. With an odd jerk, she suddenly reached out her hand and set it on his bent arm, clenching it with a convulsive grip. "Thank you," she said, her voice soft and thin. "I have not had time with you since . . ." her voice trailed off.

They made it out of the room without being stopped, Edeline's pale face and black gown providing more of a deterrent than even a regiment of armed guards. Her grief was like a living thing. It was hard to believe his father's words. She did not seem capable of planning the humiliation of anyone.

The railing was empty. Damon wondered where his father had gone. He glanced down at Edeline. "May I take you to the gazebo? We should have a measure of privacy there, and I think the air would do you good."

There was a brief hesitation as if she doubted his intentions, then she said in that subdued way of hers, "Yes, that would be very nice." He could not imagine Verbena being so submissive, and fought back a smile at the thought.

They walked across the stoned drive, roughed by all the carriages and horses' hooves. Just beyond the false wall formed by the hedges came the real attraction, a sunlit glade so perfectly created it looked as though it had grown there without assistance of any kind.

Rosebushes teased by the sun made the border, a thorny barrier for a small building in the glade's center. The flowers at the gazebo's base were in full bloom, reds and pinks, yellows and blues, whose names he had never known, a display almost garish for a house of mourning. The ivy growing over the little building helped subdue the white stone walls that otherwise might hurt the eyes in the sun's glare.

It was romantic, even he could feel it. The only problem was that he had brought the wrong woman here, and a whole room of gossiping guests had seen him escort Edeline out. He thought of Verbena and her trek through the woods those short days ago. She must love all things natural and growing. He wished he could see her as she strolled around this tranquil place.

The gazebo was already occupied. A woman stood with her back to them, one hand tapping a slender finger against her cheek, the other clenched down at her side.

"Excuse me, madam?"

The woman inside jumped and whirled around. She appeared genuinely surprised. "I am sorry. I did not expect to be disturbed."

Damon nodded once. "I apologize, but my sister-in-law needs a respite from all the guests, kind though they are. If we may take your place here?"

The woman smiled, and it lit up her face. She was tall and voluptuous, hair so black it was nearly blue piled on her head in thick curls, tendrils left dangling on either side of her face, a face that needed no attention drawn to it. High cheekbones, large dark eyes hinting at mysteries waiting to be discovered, a sculptured nose, a chin firm but not stubborn, round breasts puffing over the top of her bodice, deep cleavage. The loose skirt could not hide the tiny waist beneath. If Damon had not found his heart engaged, he might – and probably once would – have found that smile intriguing and irresistible, those eyes mesmerizing, that waist tempting. But in the last few days, he had seen genuineness, and he knew in an instant's warning that this smile was practiced. It reached her face, but her eyes were untouched.

She bent over and picked up a sheaf of music and a summer wrap. He did not have to touch the wrap to know how soft it would be. She would hold it out to a man, asking him to help arrange it over her shoulders. She would flirt at balls, making her captive sweat that her favors were straying, allow men of unsavory reputation bring her plates of food and glasses of wine, forget dances promised and go onto the floor with another, leaving her victim standing snubbed on the side with the wallflowers.

He had done that once when young and foolish. Never again. Now he wanted a woman who would look straight at him, speak her mind, protect who she loved.

He bowed politely, then stepped aside as she passed through the door. "Madam."

She gave him a sidelong look from beneath long, dark eyelashes. "Sir Damon."

This one would be a dangerous enemy. He waited for her to sashay out of the glade before he turned to Edeline, who had moved to the side, pretending to enjoy the roses. "I have a message from your sister. She insisted I talk to you in privacy. She wanted you to know that she did go to the funeral. I don't think she should have gone and I told her so, but she *would* be there. She said no one would have stopped her."

"I wish . . ." Edeline's voice was still soft, and it shook with tears held under tight leash. "I wish I could have seen her."

"I saw her at the very end, but she was on her way home. Which was for the best." He caught the edge that had crept into his voice just thinking of Verbena's foolishness.

Edeline smiled. A small one, but for just a moment her grief had lifted. "Yes, she is very strong-willed." The smile faded. "She has had to be."

Damon waved toward the empty gazebo. "You look like you could use privacy. Stay here as long as you wish. I will wait in the clearing, just in case anyone decided to follow us."

He ushered her inside, gave a bow, then turned and walked out the gazebo, but did not go far.

10

EDELINE KNEW FULL WELL WHY HER SISTER WANTED THE MESSAGE TO be given in privacy. She had had about all she could take of the Thern's guests. They did not have to say anything to her face. It all had been said in open rooms with the doors left wide open, and when they knew she was nearby.

"At least they will be rid of Andrew's wife." "Have you heard she lived in this very village?" "I was shown her house. You should see it! It is falling to pieces!" "And she had no dowry, either!" "Of course she had none. With that house!" "And her father! Have you heard about the man? He is a *drunk*! The entire village is ashamed of him."

No, she did not want to be in this family any longer. She rested her hand on her belly and thought of the child hiding inside, then realized what she had done and pulled it away. The only one to see was Damon, and she did not know where he was standing at the moment.

But that touch reminded her why she had to go and soon. Their child, nestled inside. Life would be so much harder without Andrew's money, but she expected nothing from the Therns anyway.

Well, nothing from the *other* Therns. Damon thus far had been different. She did not know how he fit in. He looked so much like his mother. She shivered. Might that unpleasant a nature be hiding beneath his courteous words?

Edeline shook her head at her thoughts. She had seen enough of the Therns, more than enough, and of all of them. Damon included.

Verbena had showed up at the funeral. It could only mean one thing. Her sister was still ready to try and help her escape.

No one in the house had mentioned to her how – or even if – the Therns planned to leave for London. Leave or stay, if she was going to get away, she had to do it soon. If she had to guess what her in-laws planned for her, it would be to find her a little place far away from their hallowed section of London and forget about her. Alone in London, severed from Andrew's house and Andrew's money, that would be just like them.

Thank goodness they did not know she was pregnant.

She had to get word back to Verbena, and Damon seemed to be her only chance, although trusting him any further brought its own risk. She had seen him talking with his father on the portico and she knew what her father-in-law thought of her. Or was he still her father-in-law? She rubbed her forehead with the back of her hand, trying to soothe the ache that just would not go away.

They could hardly plan unless she and Verbena had a chance to talk. Alone. Edeline stepped to the gazebo door, only to see her brother-in-law standing a short distance away, his hand braced against the trunk of a tree. She should have remembered his weak leg and sent him back, somewhere he could sit down and rest.

She saw his gaze sharpen when she appeared at the door. Damon had left her by herself, but he had been watching.

"Edeline." His long legs ate up the short distance, even with his uneven steps. "Do you wish to go back to the house?" Despite their vigilance, his eyes held their own sadness.

At last, this was the very opening she wanted. She had to push down the flash of sympathy at those eyes. "No. I can't be around so many people any more. I want to go to my family's house and check on Verbena. Maybe their troubles will take my mind off my own."

"I was just there," he said smoothly. "I can tell you whatever you wish to know."

"I need to see them." Sudden irritation stiffened her resolve. "It has been two days since I had a chance to talk to any of them. As you yourself said, I did not even see Verbena at the funeral."

Damon sighed and nodded. "Very well. I can see that the worry is not doing you any good."

Edeline turned and walked out of the clearing, not even letting herself look behind lest he take that as a second thought and change his mind.

***

VERBENA WAS in the parlor when they arrived. Her sewing basket sat on the floor by her feet. She was busily stitching a pair of pantaloons that, at a guess, were being altered for Matthew. Edeline still could not get used to how tall the two boys were getting. And the little girls – maybe after the baby was born, Aunt Mabel would let them all come to Bath for a visit.

Edeline knelt by the settee and took her hand, using the opportunity to kiss Verbena's cheek and whisper, "We need a moment."

Verbena met her eyes and gave a faint nod. Edeline asked in a normal voice, "How are your bindings?" She lifted her eyebrows. "As long as I'm here, why don't I check them?"

Verbena's eyes twinkled. "Oh, would you? They pinch something awful. I am not at all certain they are doing any good. I wish I could just remove them altogether, but I can't get them off by myself."

"They are not supposed to come off," Damon interjected from the doorway, his deep voice surprising them both. "You will not disobey the doctor, is that understood?"

Verbena felt heat rush up her cheeks. She would not have

spoken so freely about removing anything, even bindings of which he was well aware, had she realized he stood close enough to hear. She wrinkled her nose at her sister, and Edeline tried not to grin.

"They should at least be checked." Verbena flushed, but she winked at Edeline. "Don't you think?"

"Of course." Edeline looked expectantly up at their guest. "I apologize for deserting you, but would you mind very much if we step out for a moment?"

Damon gave an elegant bow. "I will wait for you here, if I may."

They slipped past him and through the house into Verbena's room arm in arm. Damon watched them go, a small furrow between his eyes.

Verbena pulled the door shut, and whispered, "I think he suspects something."

"Off with your gown. Where are the clean wraps?" Edeline hissed. "Let's get this done. I don't know how long we dare delay. Hold still." She set to work untying the gown's ribbons quickly. "Have you heard back from Aunt Mabel?"

"No," Verbena whispered back, her voice so faint there was no worry about being overheard. "I only sent the letter today before the funeral. There has scarcely been time to get a response. But I am certain she will welcome you. She was always so tolerant with us children, and she does write from time to time."

Edeline started on the wrapping knot. "Goodness, it is tight. No wonder you felt pinched." She looked up from her efforts. "I have been thinking. I believe they will try to bar me from Andrew's house. If I were so much as to head that direction even to get clothes, I think I would be followed, just to be sure I'm not trying to arrive before them. I think my only choice is to leave early and go straight to Aunt Mabel's. I can hardly ask for one of their carriages, either, in case they try to find out from the coachman where we went, so there must be another way."

"The mail coach," Verbena said slowly.

Edeline's fingers froze on the ribbons. "Oh, please, anything else. Mail coaches are notorious. They get robbed regularly, they're uncomfortable, and they carry only members of the lower classes."

"We *are* the lower classes, Edeline," Verbena hissed tersely. "It is not ideal, I know, but they are cheap and fast, and right now, that is the only option we have."

"The stage is cheaper. Why can I not just go by stage?" Edeline's voice raised.

"Hush! Do you want Damon to hear? The stage is too slow."

Edeline sank down on the bed. Her face seemed paler than a moment ago, or perhaps it was just the way the light came through the curtains. "Once I get away, I should be safe enough. They don't know about the babe."

Verbena thought about that. She would definitely rather have her sister in a stage than a mail coach, but preference was no longer an option. "You look pale. We might be able to pass it off as grief, but what if someone guesses about the child? I think speed is of the essence now. The faster the trip, the sooner you will be at Aunt Mabel's. And the fastest way is by mail coach."

"You are right." Edeline stood again and started back on the knot. "Again. But how will we pay for even that? The mail is more expensive." The knot finally gave. Verbena raised her arms and let Edeline begin unwrapping. "I should have remembered my allowance, but Andrew was so sick, I did not even think of asking for it. I only wanted him – " her voice broke and she dabbed at her eyes with the end of the wrapping.

"We need ten pounds for the ticket," Verbena said, whispering fast and tactfully letting her sister regain her composure, "unless we pay half here and leave the remainder for Aunt Mabel to pay, which seems mercenary since we are depending on her for so much already. None of which she even knows about yet."

Edeline cleared her throat. "I might have ten pounds left from my last allowance. If I have to go through Andrew's coat pockets, I will." The words had a determination Verbena had been waiting for. Her sister was ready. Ten pounds was all that stood between her and freedom.

"Get up early. The mail coach is first come, first served."

VERBENA GAVE Edeline a cautious hug and watched Damon lead her sister out the front door, whisking her back to Thernwood. Now that their plans were in the works, one tension had been replaced by another.

Ten pounds. At five pence a mile, if they paid the whole fare, that would leave nothing for Edeline, not even the expected tip for the guard. They had decided not to count on Aunt Mabel's having the cash for the rest of the fare. Their aunt might not even be there to pay any remainder. It was summer, the height of the Season. She could very well be in London. As long as someone was there to open the house, even a skeleton staff, Edeline would have a place to stay, and that was what mattered.

Edeline had better be right about Andrew's family, that they would be only too glad to see the back of her, Verbena thought. She also had better be right that no one had guessed about the baby. That was the real threat. If the Therns guessed, no matter what they thought of Edeline, they would want that child for themselves. It, not Damon, was the heir.

She still thought her sister was being a fool. To sacrifice security for a hand to mouth existence? But if her sister *was* right and they would take the child away?

How much would they dare?

In the interest of secrecy, she would manage the food for Edeline. Thank goodness for Mrs. Downs' generous cooking. There would be bread, and maybe even some cheese. A clean cloth to wrap them in, and an old reticule as a basket.

Matthew arrived with his usual enthusiasm, kicking the back door open, startling her. Verbena turned away from the front door. There was nothing else to see now, anyway.

"I got all the eggs," he called, and she heard the basket thump on the table. "And I bought us some cream." The metal milk bucket rang as it took its place next to the eggs. Everything he did made twice as much noise as when the other children did it. She arrived in the kitchen just as he called, "I suppose we need butter." He added, in a more moderate voice, "Oh, sorry, Bena, I did not see you there."

"I was just saying goodbye to Edeline. She was visiting. Yes, if you could churn some butter, I would appreciate it very much," she answered, and gave him a quick peck on his cheek as a thank-you. Soon he would be too adult for such displays. Even now, she had to go on tip-toe to reach.

"Damon told me they were going back to London soon," Matthew said as he picked the bucket of cream up again, thumping it soundly against the side of the table as he did. "So Edeline won't be around any longer." He scraped at a spot of something on his pants with his free hand. "I thought she might stay here. We can use the help."

"True." Verbena was surprised. What prompted that idea? Edeline was practically a stranger to him, too, not just the girls.

"If Edeline were here, she could do some of the cooking, and then Damon would not have to hire someone."

"I know. But it is most kind of him to do so much for us."

Matthew stopped at the back door and looked at Verbena with a new wisdom in his eyes. "I wonder why he is doing so much. I like him, but no one else there has paid any attention to us ever."

"True." There did not seem to be anything else to say. Verbena welcomed the sound of light feet pattering along the hard-packed path toward the back door. Familiar young voices giggled.

"She will be so surprised. I want to tell her first." That was Annabelle, sounding happy.

"No! I'm the oldest. It is my turn." Whatever news Annabelle wanted to spill, Lizabeth was ready to spoil it. Things were back to normal. "You always get to go first."

Which was a blatant lie, Verbena thought, but it was the privilege of older ones to think the younger ones got spoiled. Edeline had done the same to her years ago when life was simple and the biggest problem was who came first.

"No, I do not either!"

There was a cluster at the doorway between him going out and them coming in. A new argument was about to start, so Verbena intervened. She met them at the door as Matthew moved along the porch toward the churn at the corner of the house.

"We made money," Lizabeth called, her voice increasing volume as she skidded to a stop in front of Verbena and held out a very dirty hand. The front of her dress was caked with mud. In her palm rested three coins, as dirty as her hand.

Verbena smiled, and hoped the dirt would come out of the dress. "How did you manage that?"

Annabelle wailed, "It was my turn!" She seemed to have stopped in the perfect place in the kitchen that allowed her voice to carry, through the hallway, no doubt up the stairs, certainly into the parlor, until Verbena thought her ears were ringing.

"Baby," Lizabeth scoffed.

"I am not!" The wails redoubled.

"Girls! Hush! We do not do this where anyone can hear." Verbena wanted to do her own screaming, wished for the simple days when she could hold both girls and rock them quiet. For an appalling moment, when Annabelle kept crying and Lizabeth taunted her with silent faces, when Matthew's churning rhythm paused and she knew something distracted him and he might not remember to start churning again, she wanted help in the person of Damon to come.

She was so alone right now, so burdened with decisions to make, children to care for, Edeline to get away, the Therns to worry about, and Damon himself one last worry, so handsome, so strong, and so perplexing.

EDELINE WALKED into Thernwood with Damon right behind her. Adams met them at the front door, his usual sour expression firmly in place. "Madam, you are wanted in Sir Edward's office. He is waiting for you there."

Damon stepped up to her side. "What is it?"

Edeline looked between the two men. Damon was frowning, but she saw an angry spark in his eyes. Edward Thern wanted to speak to her? Damon knew – or suspected – what it was and did not like it. Her already uneasy stomach tightened and for a moment she thought she might be sick.

Adams was as impassive as ever. "I would hardly know, sir. It is not my place to ask questions. I was merely told to give the message."

Damon looked down at her. He was so much taller than Andrew – her heart blocked her lungs and for a moment she could not breathe. *Andrew.* Would she always have this awful emptiness every time she thought of him?

But Damon was speaking. "We should not keep Father waiting." He did not move either, just looked down at her with that same spark in his eyes. "I do not know why my father is waiting for you, but I fear I should probably apologize beforehand. I know my family has said some harsh things about you, or at the very least has not stopped the worst of the gossip, and for that I apologize. It is beneath us."

The ache in Edeline's chest grew worse. She could not turn. Just one more breath, one moment before she had to walk into that room and find out – what? "I thank you for that." She managed to wave a hand in the direction of his father's office. "We should not keep him waiting."

Damon gave a brief nod and ushered her ahead of him.

They entered the room in near silence, their footsteps muffled by the rich Turkish carpet. The deep green curtains were pulled over the windows, the room dim except for a lampstand burning to one side of the massive desk of carved dark wood. That desk, Edeline always thought, had been purchased strictly for the

purpose of intimidation, a purpose it served well just now. Whatever he wanted to discuss, it could not be good news.

For a moment, she did not think anyone was there. A shadow
moved by the draperies. Edward Thern was standing there, all in
black, just a darker color in the dimness. He did not invite her to
sit. As her eyes adjusted, she could see his face.

"Edeline." A coldness surrounded him, a coldness that
proclaimed his standing was not out of courtesy but rather to
avoid giving the impression that this meeting would take any of
his precious time.

The only warmth in the room came from the man at her side.

"My wife," Edward said, in the same cold tone, "and I have
discussed this and we have decided it is best if you go back to your
family and recover. We feel the pace of London is too much for
you. It is not unheard of for widows to find a place to take time to
grieve. No one will think anything of it if you do not come back
with us.'

For the space of a breath, she wondered if she had heard right.
A buzz started in her ears. Edeline's heart gave a little leap of
happiness. How funny, that this opportunity would drop into her
very lap like this!

"Sit," Damon's voice said, and she sat. Let him think she needed
to. Better to sit than to dance.

A laugh built in her chest around the sorrow that had become a
part of her, and she swallowed hard to keep it inside. All the planning she and Verbena had done! All their plots, Verbena coming to
the funeral to try to catch her, making excuses to talk alone in
Verbena's room – and all that time she was going to be left here
unattended to plan her escape!

Damon was silent at her side. She wondered what he was
thinking. Such a pretty apology when they first arrived at Thernwood, and yet here he said nothing. But she heard his breathing,
harsh and rough, as if he was angry.

"I have sent for Agnes. You can show her what to pack."
Edward picked a paper off his desk.

She was dismissed. Edeline stood. Sounds eased through her euphoria, the rustling of the paper in Edward's hands, the chirping of a bird outside his window, footsteps coming down the hallway.

One last battle to fight with Agnes and she would be rid of the woman forever. Her head lifted as the weight of years slipped away. No more Agnes, no more insults from Catherine and Margaret, no more cutting remarks from her mother-in-law.

She was finally free.

It came at an appalling cost, but she was free. From now on she would only be around people who loved her. She would make certain of that.

Just a few more minutes, Edeline told herself, just a few more minutes and it would be over.

11

DAMON SHUT HIS FATHER'S OFFICE DOOR QUIETLY BEHIND EDELINE, although every muscle inside screamed for action. He stared at the dark wood in front of him.

He had to find a way to fix this. Verbena had tried to explain the gulf between his family and the rest of the village but he had not understood the true nature of it. He had been too long in the war, where men had a chance to be judged on their own merits.

But now Verbena's sister was being sent away humiliated, and almost penniless. He knew the kind of money his family possessed. Edeline, who should have been able to make a swath through the bachelors and widowers of London and take her pick, would go back to her childhood home with little more than the clothes she had brought along.

He turned around and looked at his father. Who was this man he had known and loved all his life? Had this snobbery been there all the time?

Edward's eyebrows raised. He still held the paper he had been pretending to read. "Yes, son? You might as well speak, it is written all over your face. You think me the most callous of men, cruel and brutal. You think I should have let her come with us to London."

"Yes, Father." Damon's hands clenched, he felt the tension all the way up his arms. "Yes, I do. All your words about what an embarrassment she was – I thought them the words of grief. You *meant* them."

"Of course I did." Edward sat down behind his impressive desk, the movement smooth and relaxed, as if proclaiming how completely untroubled his conscience was. He set the paper down. "She is no longer a part of our family. Andrew is dead, all ties between us are severed. So I did what I have longed to do for six long years. I sent her back to her family."

"You and I both know that is not how it works. As Andrew's widow, she gets all that was his. She is a wealthy woman now."

A smug smile curved his father's mouth. "Well now, son, that is where you are wrong. Andrew had nothing."

A laugh of disbelief bubbled out of Damon's throat. "Don't be ridiculous! He could not have had *nothing*. I know how much money we have. I know our very wealth is why we received our title. Of course Andrew had money. And that goes to Edeline."

Edward shook his head. "No. Heir or not, I knew him well enough to know he could not manage this estate."

Damon braced a hand against the bookshelf for support. "What difference does that make for his widow? We are responsible for her future wellbeing. At least until she remarries. We owe Andrew that much."

Edward leaned back in his chair, looking smug and satisfied. "She is only entitled to what remained of Andrew's last allowance. And that was already disbursed. Andrew left no will, nothing to provide for her."

Damon could feel the blood pound in his head. He repeated, "No will? How is that possible? He knew he was ill for some time. I don't believe he would have done nothing to plan for Edeline. He *loved* her." Damon looked at his father, so unconcerned, and an ugly thought formed. "Father, what have you done?"

Edward's eyebrows raised. "I? I have done nothing. Do you really think I could be so heartless as to ignore my dearest son, my own firstborn, his dying wishes?" He leaned forward, his hands half-extended as if in a plea. "I am not ashamed to say that I did not approve of Andrew's choice of a wife. I never will consider her to have been his equal. And it is true that Andrew had been ill for a time. Your mother and I had much on our minds. You were near death. Andrew had been sick before and had always pulled through. We had no reason to think he would not recover again. It was only the last few weeks that we realized this time was different. Do you think I was worried about any *will?*"

He let out a weary sigh. "It truly saddens me to know you could even think I would be capable of destroying a will left by my son. Even if it was to take care of *her.*" Then he straightened. His voice grew strong again. "Anyway, it is not like she will be destitute. She does have family. Her own family. They have land, and a house. It is highly unlikely she will starve."

Verbena had tried to tell him how little his family knew about what happened outside their own world. It was one thing to hear it from her, quite another to hear it from his own father. "Do you ever wonder how *anyone* in the village finds enough to eat? They pay their rents, but they no longer have use of the village green. We own that, remember? And we fenced it off. That means Edeline's family can't use it either. Do you ever wonder what happened to the cows, the sheep and goats that used to graze there? I promise you, Father, if Edeline is to live with her brothers and sisters – which is totally unnecessary – her family will need whatever income she brings to them."

Edward's face flushed with anger. "Now you are going to make me responsible for the whole family? Just how many people am I supposed to fund?"

Bad enough that Verbena's sister was being thrown out of the family house. But thrown out with nothing? "She was your daughter-in-law! We most certainly have a responsibility to her!" Why could his father not see that? "I'm not saying we must pay everyone in the household, but we have a responsibility to *her.* She gets an allowance. Andrew's allowance. At the very least."

His father just looked at him as if he were speaking a foreign language. "I have already explained that Andrew had nothing of his own. Perhaps it is for the best that it will go to you instead of him. I thought I would have time to teach him before I was gone. That was my plan, to slowly ease him into his responsibilities. God knows, I had tried over the years, but he had absolutely no aptitude for it. And even after he wed, he was off in a world of his own much of the time. I sent for him over and over again, scheduled meetings with our estate manager, but half of them he forgot – so he said. Much as I loved my son, I never understood him."

"*I* did, though," Damon said, shoving down his anger. "I understood him. And I understand, partly, what you mean. He did not comprehend numbers, he told me. Letters came easily to him, but numbers never made sense. When we were on the schoolroom together, I tried myself to teach him. Much of the time I did his assignments for him because he was so frustrated. He would have needed an honest manager, one he could trust not to cheat him, but he *did* value his inheritance. I listened to him, you see. You *talked* to him, I *listened* to him. Perhaps that is the problem."

Edward slapped a hand on the desk. The sound cracked in the air. "Talk or listen, it would have made no difference. He needed to learn, and he had not. So I kept him on an allowance."

"Which is Edeline's allowance now. You can *not* leave her without funds. As Andrew's widow, she is entitled to whatever income he had at the time of his death. And I refuse – " Damon took the few steps up to his father's desk and leaned into it. He felt his hands curl into fists against the hard wood. "I *refuse* to believe Andrew had nothing."

Edward raised one eyebrow and leaned back in his chair. He seemed to pull himself together with effort. "I don't care if you believe it or not, Damon, it is true. Perhaps if they had had children, your brother might have seen fit to take more interest, but it had not happened, and so I had to keep him on a very tight leash. There might be last quarter's allowance, although as I said, I doubt it, but there certainly is nothing else."

Damon's eyes narrowed. His throat was almost too tight to speak, as if his anger had him by the neck instead of his father. He could not let Edeline go back to her sister destitute, much less remain that way. He leaned closer to his father and said with deliberation, "Then I will give her something from my own income. Don't forget, I have money of my own."

His father's eyes went wide, and he shot up from his chair. The wheels whirred on the carpet and the chair slammed against the wall. "You most certainly will not! You might as well set her up as your mistress— and that will never do!"

Damon straightened up from the desk. The two men were about a height. It would not be easy to force his father to do anything. In fact, it might be impossible, and he might well have to dig into his own funds to give Edeline anything.

So be it. If he had to support her, then he would. For Andrew, he could do no less and live with himself. Damon folded his arms over his chest, and met his father's furious gaze straight on. "I fail to see why sending your own son's widow away with at least *something* should be such a problem for you. She was Andrew's wife."

"Don't remind me," his father growled. "That was not my choice, I assure you."

"Father. Enough." Damon took a deep breath. "How much did you pay him annually? One thousand pounds? Two?"

"Not that it is any of your concern, but I paid him one thousand a year. Enough to keep him solvent but not enough to let him get himself into trouble.'

Damon nodded. "One thousand pounds." He might as well start there. "That is due Edeline, you know that."

"No, it is not. I already told you, she is no longer part of our family."

Damon pretended he had not heard. "So one thousand a year is two hundred fifty pounds quarterly. I will take your draft over today, and wait while you write it."

"Don't think you can bully me." Edward's voice was cold.

"Fine. I can afford two hundred fifty pounds. Just remember I gave you the opportunity to handle this honorably and quell any gossip that might leak out." He turned and started across the room with a firm stride. If his father let him go and he wound up being the sole support of Edeline, then he would. The room was quiet except his father's rough breaths and the soft thump of his own heels on the carpet. Damon reached for the door handle.

"Damon! Stop!"

Damon turned, but kept his hand on the brass knob. "Yes, Father?"

"I only paid Andrew that much because there were two of them. He had a wife to support, and stables. The stables are gone. She has no need of them. If it will prevent you from being the cause of nasty gossip, I agree to give her two hundred fifty pounds a year. That will be twenty pounds a month."

Damon did the calculations in his head. If all went as he planned, he could be married to Verbena soon. Life was much less expensive in this village than in London, and he could take steps even now to make it more so. An excellent idea came to him. He could not think of a single shopkeeper in Thernbury who would dare refuse.

Could the Barnes survive on twenty pounds a month until, well, until whatever happened between Verbena and himself, if they had no other expenses? Based on the condition of their house and what he had seen of their food, they had been surviving on much less.

He walked back to the matching chairs that faced the desk and lowered himself. As if he had all the time in the world, Damon rested his elbows on the chair arms, and linked his fingers. "Why don't you write out the first installment? Twenty pounds. That will hardly inconvenience you. I can bring it over. Remember, you have just tossed Edeline out of London's society, where she might have had a chance of finding a reputable husband, and removing any link to you."

Edward spluttered and blustered, but he pulled the chair back from the wall, sat down with audible displeasure, jerked open his drawer and pulled out a heavy sheet of paper. As he dipped the quill into the inkwell that sat on his desk, his head jerked back up. "Don't push me further, Damon. Monthly installments. I will not pay her a year's allowance at a time. Do you want her father to get his hands on it?"

Damon went still. Much as he hated to admit it, his father had a point. He gave a single nod. "Agreed."

Edward shoved the signed bank draft over. "Here! I hope you are satisfied."

"Thank you, Father." Damon rose, took the paper and read it, then turned and walked to the door, stopping to look back. "Just remember as you write out each new installment, if you don't want to do it for her, tell yourself you are doing it for Andrew."

Before he could pull the door open, Edward barked, "One might think you wanted that woman for yourself."

"I assure you, Father, I do not want her." Damon opened the door and walked out. No, he did not want his brother's widow. He intended to do his best to marry her sister.

<hr>

VERBENA STOOD next to Edeline in the tiny vestibule and watched the first trunk be unloaded from the carriage by two strapping male servants. Not footmen, as they did not wear the Thern blue uniform laden with frogs and epaulets on the outer coat, and grey stripes down the legs. Probably groomsmen from the stable, with their bulky boots, loose, rough trousers, shirts that had seen better days, and a handkerchief tied around the neck in place of a cravat. Another servant, this one wearing the uniform, sat on the carriage holding the reins with a bored expression on his face.

The front door that Damon had paid to have fixed stood open, making it easy for them to bring in her sister's belongings.

They had let Edeline go in the carriage, a surprising bit of courtesy. The Therns could easily have sent her here on a farm cart. Verbena thought of Marie Antoinette, being carried through the streets on a tumbrel. At least Edeline would still have her head when it was all over.

Verbena counted the trunks. Three. Modern styles being what they were, gowns took up much less space than those of their grandparents' day. Assuming it was just clothing in them and not sentimental treasures, Edeline should be able to make it through this pregnancy with enough to wear.

"I know this has caught us all off guard." Edeline reached out for Verbena's hand, and they both held on tight. "Where did you think to put me?"

That was the question, Verbena thought. They were already packed two to a bed. Except for herself, but she slept in the small room off the kitchen. The two upstairs bedrooms with their slanted ceilings did not have much usable space. Did Edeline remember? "I could ask the boys if they would take Father's room, but much as I hate to say it, I don't expect them to. That would be the most convenient, if the boys would move down into his room, and the girls could remain in their own room and you could have the boys' bedroom."

Edeline started shaking her head before Verbena even finished. "Don't put them out. We don't know how long Father will be away. I really think his room should be open when he comes back."

Neither mentioned the faint tinge of vomit and drink that no amount of scrubbing had managed to completely remove.

Verbena was only too familiar with the house's failings. The house was going to be a shock to someone who had become used to the elegance of the Thern's residences. The boxy little rooms with their worn furniture, the faded paint inside and out, the peeling wallpaper and sagging porches. The chimney had not begun falling down in bits yet, but that day was coming and she did not know what she would do when it did. At least the roof had not sprung a leak.

Edeline's face showed none of that. For the first time since Verbena had seen her that awful morning, her sister's eyes were at peace.

She turned back to the scene outside. The third trunk was being unloaded from the carriage roof. They were running out of time.

"There is another possibility." The men picked up the first trunk and started up the walk. "My bed is small, so if we all have to share, I thought Annabella could sleep with me. You don't mind sleeping with Lizabeth in her bed?"

"I will sleep wherever you put me. It won't be for long. Just until we hear from Aunt Mabel."

The first trunk neared the door, and Verbena stepped aside to make room. Giving the two men her sweetest smile, she said, "If you would be so good, could you carry the trunks up the stairs and leave them outside the door on the left?"

The men nodded. The one in front said gruffly, "Sir Damon said we was to put them anywheres we was told."

"Thank him for us."

The man nodded, and heavy boots clomped up the steep steps. The trunk landed with a hard *thump*. With four children in the house that kind of sound was so familiar Verbena did not even wince, but Edeline did. "I hope that did not mar the floor."

Verbena gave her sister a rueful smile. "There is nothing that can be done to this floor that has not already happened."

The men came back down. The sounds repeated themselves, heavy footfalls carrying the weight up, the deep *thump* as the trunk was set down, and the clump of boots as the men went back out for the last trip.

Verbena could no longer restrain her curiosity. "What did they say when they threw you out? How bad was it?"

Edeline did not meet her eyes. "Sir Edward was actually very polite."

Verbena scowled at her sister, annoyed that Edeline would not meet her eyes and her best scowl was going unappreciated. "Hmph. At least they let you take your clothes. They might have tossed you out with only what you had on your back! That would not have surprised me at all."

"Oh, Verbena. You exaggerate. I don't mind, actually. It makes everything else so much easier." But she still did not meet Verbena's eyes. The most painful of insults could be couched in the most courteous of words.

"True." And the convenience *was* true, but that did not help. Every time she thought of Edeline being told to go, and how the Therns hauled her belongings out, knowing the house was full of London Society who almost certainly guessed what was going on, Verbena burned. She forced herself to take a soothing breath, propped her hands on her hips and watched the last trunk start its journey.

This time the sounds from overhead were a bit alarming, scrapes and screeches, a rather jarring crash, and a loud word not normally used in front of women. Both of them turned to stare up the steps. One of the men came down limping.

Verbena looked for blood. "Are you injured?"

"Tain't as bad as a kick from a horse, ma'am." The man tried to smile.

"I'm so sorry you got hurt. I hope it feels better soon."

Edeline smiled sweetly at the two men. "Thank you. This was very kind."

"Yer welcome," the other servant muttered, his ears turning red, and eased himself around her.

The carriage rumbled back down the drive and away. As the last sounds faded, Edeline turned to Verbena. Her smile lit her face. "I'm free now. Free to do whatever I want. I don't need to weigh my every word any more. And I'm going to take my time to plan the rest of my escape before I have to leave."

"Don't take too much time. You know gossip in the village. If anyone so much as guesses that you are with child, news will be up to Thernwood and then off to London as fast as the horse can go. If you are right about them, they will be back to claim the baby. I don't suppose they gave you any of Andrew's money before sending you off?"

Edeline turned away. "Not yet."

"I did not think they would." Not the parents, at any rate. But Damon, how could he go along with this? She pushed the hurt aside. "Let us begin unpacking. We can leave some of the fancier gowns, and take out the ones that will be most practical.

Edeline hesitated, and her eyes picked up a moist sheen. "Yes. That will be fine. It is only for a few days, after all. You are right, soon enough I will leave as well."

They looked at each other for a moment. "Oh, Edeline, it has been wonderful having you around again. I shall miss you."

The water in Edeline's eyes threatened to spill over. "I know. But perhaps you can all come visit. The children would love to see Bath."

Edeline fumbled for a handkerchief, while Verbena used the skirt of her apron. The children could come in at any moment. It would hardly do to be caught weeping.

"Let's get the room set up for you," Verbena said when she knew her voice would be steady.

They started up the stairs, and saw the three trunks that blocked their way, one tucked tight to the next, neatly barricading both bedroom doors – and the latches were facing in. Somehow she and Edeline were going to have to pull them apart just to get them open!

A giggle prompted by despair threatened. It was either laugh or cry. "My goodness! How are we going to unpack these?'

Edeline looked at the wedged trunks and back to her sister. Verbena saw her lips start to twitch. They both studied the hallway, never very wide, and started to laugh.

THE TABLE WAS CROWDED with all four children and herself and Edeline. Edeline had been given Father's chair and did not seem at all uncomfortable to be sitting there. But then, Father had not been drinking the last time she ate with the family, and Mother was still alive.

Verbena watered the fish soup and added some turnips to stretch it for an extra mouth. She had also baked an extra loaf of bread, a good choice as it was the only part of the meal Edeline was interested in. At least there was fresh butter for the thick warm slices.

Perhaps the smell of fish in the house was not the best choice of a first meal together, considering the state of her sister's stomach. Undoubtedly, at Thernwood the kitchen was so far away that any cooking smells would never reach the family. Verbena wished she could cook something that would not bother Edeline but meal choices were always limited, and fish were free. They had the added benefit that catching them was more a treat for the boys than a chore.

The table was oddly quiet. Not even the boys, who still had memories of their oldest sister, seemed to know what to say. Her heart ached for Edeline. Those six years away had created a gulf it would take time to fill in. None of the children knew yet that they would not have that time. Not for a while, at any rate.

It did not help the mood around the table that the two of them were hiding such an enormous secret from the others. There was also the other burden of what to do with Edeline's clothes. She would of course bring along as many as possible, but three such huge trunks' worth? Perhaps they could be stowed away in the attic with Mother's old gowns. Once the babe was born, Edeline could decide what to do with them.

They had decided to tell the children Edeline was going to stay with friends. That explanation would hardly excite comment in the village, and would erase any tracks for the curious, should there be any, to follow.

But they would not say anything until it was time for her to go.

The knock at the front door started all of them.

"I'll get it," Matthew shouted, and fled the table. Verbena rose after him, only to stop at hearing his greeting.

"Oh! Hello, Damon. We did not expect you. Did you come to see Edeline? She is here now, you know."

"Yes, I do know," came Damon's warm voice, utterly devoid of any hint of triumph or hostility. "I came to see her. Is she available?"

Verbena hurried out into the hallway. "Matthew, you can go back to your dinner. I will take care of this." She patted him on the shoulder, and squeezed around him. "Everything will be fine."

And what a lie that was! She stood in the entryway to keep Damon from coming in. Her heart pounded at the sight of him. She did not know whether it was excitement, an emotion she was beginning to associate with him, or dread at what this might mean for Edeline.

He had certainly dressed for an occasion. A fashion plate of the well-clad man, his black coat and burgundy vest over his white shirt, the snowy cravat tied in an intricate bow. His black pantaloons were clean, and his boots had only the faintest hint of the dust from his jaunt over. He held a tall hat under one arm, drawing attention to the black armband.

In spite of his obvious mourning state, what a catch he must be to the Thern's guests!

Verbena had to force herself not to reach up and smooth her hair. Her sleeves were pushed up from cooking. She hastily pulled them down, only to notice a fresh stain on one. She rolled it back up and pretended she merely meant to adjust them. "To what do we owe the honor of this visit?"

He bowed. "I have come with good news. I convinced my father to agree to continue Edeline's allowance. I have the first monthly payment."

"Monthly payment?" Verbena stared up at him. Money. Money to ship Edeline's trunks. Maybe even enough to pay for a room at an inn during the trip and still have some left over for meals so she would not have to depend on whatever Verbena could package for her? Money so Edeline would not be a burden to Aunt Mabel. And monthly! "You actually got him to agree?"

He smiled down at her. The soft evening breeze ruffled the waves in his dark hair. "Yes, Verbena. I got him to agree."

"Did you have to hold a revolver to his head?" She wished she could take the words back.

Other than the smile that faded, he did not react to her insult and that made her feel worse. "No. I did not. I realize you are not happy with my father right now, but he is not a bad man."

"I apologize." She had the oddest urge to touch him, to soothe the sting away. "It was unworthy of me. But you are right, we are not happy with him at the moment. This whole thing was cruel, from beginning to end."

"I can't disagree with you. I believe there is a history between our two parents. I don't know what it is, and it little matters now, but he did do the right thing by your sister. In the end." Damon glanced beyond her. "*Now* may I be allowed to see your sister and give her the news and the bank draft?"

Verbena smiled. Her whole body felt light. "Yes. Yes, I think she would very much like to know."

She had a new thought. She caught Damon's sleeve before she realized what she had done. Damon trapped her hand. His eyes held her gaze, something new and unexpected simmering in them. A warm flush that had nothing to do with the summer night washed over her. They both seemed to remember where their hands were at the same moment, but he took his time pulling his away. She struggled to recall what she meant to say. "Their town-house, where she and Andrew lived? I assume your parents took that away, as well?"

"My father claims the house never belonged to Andrew. He said," Damon seemed to catch himself. "Well, that is neither here nor there, but the house was not theirs. It still remains with my father. So, no, I'm sorry. I fear she will not be able to move back."

"It never belonged to Andrew?" How strange. "I have no doubt it is filled with precious items, probably gifts Andrew bought her. Is she ever going to get any of those back?"

Damon ran a hand over his hair. "I don't know. I am truly sorry. I did not even think to ask. I will see to it that she gets at least some of her possessions." He sighed again. "The rest goes to the heir, which is now me."

Verbena tried not to react.

He did not seem to notice anything wrong. "I still have my own place in London so my father may see no rush on resolving the situation with Andrew's. I will ask Edeline to give me a list of what she wants. Certainly there will be clothes. I will have them packed up and shipped here. But as I say, I don't know when that will be."

"I – we are very grateful."

He cleared his throat, although it did not seem to be clouded. "I had hoped to stay here, but I must now get back to London myself. I have business of my own that has waited far too long already. I don't how long it will take."

"This is most kind of you. I know we have been a terrible burden on you. I don't know . . ." she floundered to a stop. *Will you ever come back?* She hoped the question was not written on her face as she looked up at him, trying to hold his face in her mind, his eyes like dark pools that seemed to pull her in, his hair with its rich waves that tempted her to touch, a face of such masculine beauty with the strong nose, high cheekbones, and firm chin.

She stepped back so he could enter.

DAMON LET OUT A BREATH. He still felt her hand on his sleeve. "Verbena. I will be back. I promise."

He had hoped to stay longer, but it was not possible.

Courtship was indeed a difficult business.

He touched his pocket to make sure the draft his father had written was still safely there, and followed Verbena into the house.

12

Damon left his bedroom for breakfast at eight the next morning. The house was quiet, thank goodness. He was tired of guests. He was tired of the *ton* gossip that accompanied every meal. And of the young women who wanted to flirt. Or insisted he hold their thread when they tried to embroider. Or begged him to tell them what every flower in the garden was. What did he know about flowers?

Except verbena. He knew that one. And its namesake. Or was the flower *her* namesake?

He started down the long stairway to the main floor. Maybe he would actually make it through one meal without being interrupted.

The big dining room was nearly empty for the first time in four days, not counting the two footmen. Food already sat on the sideboard, bacon, fried ham, slices of beef that still steamed their fragrance into the air. Fresh-baked bread, marmalades, jams, even a dish of stewed dried fruit. A pot of tea sat in its brace above the burner, keeping warm.

The only other person in the room was his father, in his usual place at the far end of the big table. "Get yourself some breakfast,

Damon, before we are interrupted." Edward nodded at the spread. "If we plan it well enough, we might be able to avoid our guests for a whole day, and then hopefully this will be the last time for a while that we'll have to put up with them."

Damon smiled. His thoughts exactly. "Bold statement, Father. And how are we going to pull this amazing feat off?"

"The men wished to go out shooting again. They will be gone most of the day. After that, I intend to see that they leave."

"I wish you every success." *Shooting.* Damon remembered Verbena's outrage that the villagers who had lived here for generations, had hunted in those very woods, were now banned. Of course they heard the guns. What must they think as guests hunted for sport while those who lived here could not hunt for food?

The land still belonged to his father to do with what he wished, but when his father was gone, fences or no fences, he would let the villagers hunt again.

He stopped at the bacon, and looked over his shoulder. "You will keep your word about the settlement with Edeline." It was not a question.

His father scowled, his eyebrows nearly meeting. "This again? If I am going to keep you from dragging our name through the dirt by supporting that woman yourself, I shall have to, won't I?" Edward lifted his cup of tea to his mouth. Damon could smell the hot brew from where he stood. "I gave my word. That should be good enough for you."

He walked over to his father's right, a footman pulled out a chair, and he sat down. The man poured him a cup of steaming tea. Damon nodded his thanks. "We won't need you further. Thank you." The footman nodded back and both of them exited.

Edward waited until the door had closed. He set down his cup with a clink. "Your concern for them troubles me. You worry that I will not keep my word. I worry that you will not keep your own. You say you are not interested in your sister-in-law, but I see no reason to believe you."

Damon cut his father off. "I barely know the woman. Regardless, my interest lies elsewhere. I am only interested in justice for Edeline. That is all." That was not exactly a lie, Damon decided.

"I am relieved it hear that." His father's face relaxed. "I suppose you will not give me this fortunate woman's name?"

"It is much too early to speak of it yet."

A smile pulled his father's mouth upward. "Is this mysterious woman someone I know?"

Damon looked his father straight in the eye. "I think not."

Edward gave a sharp nod. "I understand. Well, do let me know as soon as it is settled, will you? And as for your sister-in-law, I know you are not happy with the sum I decided upon, but I will not beggar us to keep that woman in funds."

"*Beggar?* Two hundred fifty pounds a year?"

"Damon," his father interrupted, which was probably just as well. "I know that family and you do not. I thought we settled this matter yesterday. I tell you they are all greedy, grasping, money-grubbers, and the father is no more than a drunken sot."

Damon stopped cutting at his beef. "They are land-owners, just as we are."

"They won't be land-owners long." His father puffed himself up as if taking credit.

And maybe he was. Damon went cold. He set the utensils down. "What have you done, Father?"

Edward looked honestly surprised. "Me? Nothing. I have done nothing. I don't need to. Parliament is doing it all for me. I am not even in Parliament. You can hardly place the blame for their downfall on me. But neither will I mourn if they lose their land and have to move away. I will be more than glad to see the back of them."

Damon could not move for a moment. His breath seemed to stop. Verbena, Julius, Matthew, the girls? Losing their land? He knew things were difficult at the Barnes' but he did not think it this serious. Where would they go, what would they do? He had seen too much of starving to wish it on anyone, much less this family of whom he had become so fond.

His appetite deserted him. "I don't think I'm as hungry as I thought. If you will excuse me?" He rose and gave a stiff bow.

"I find the same thing myself. I have not felt like eating since your brother died. Go out, get some fresh air." Edward's mouth, so recently smiling, turned down. "If you can find any unpolluted by guests."

Damon had not reached the door before his father called out one last command. "Be sure you join the rest of us in the office in an hour. We have plans to make as a family. Your mother needs all of our support."

It had been a near thing. One of the tittering, twittering guests, a young woman just out of the schoolroom and anxious to make a success of her first season, followed him to the room where the private family meeting was held. "I'm so glad I found you. I would be happy to help you through the garden. It is beautiful this time of day."

She would escort *him*! As if he was so crippled he needed help to walk around his own family's garden! Damon refused to think that a few short months ago, he would have needed that very help. He had nearly lost his patience, and only managed to turn her away by saying, rather firmly, "Thank you, but no." He then slipped inside and shut the door.

From where he stood by the bookshelf, Damon looked around his father's study. The entire family had indeed shown up here, out of earshot of any curious guests. Entire *remaining* family, he corrected himself. Andrew's absence was a gaping hole, all the more so when they gathered like this.

Silhouetted against the glare of the window, Edward stood behind the desk, next to Imogene, who sat in the big leather-covered chair that normally belonged to the family head. It matched the desk in size, big furniture designed to intimidate any poor soul called to account. Damon knew. As a child he had been dragged into this room for punishment more times than he cared to remember.

Edward rested a hand on his wife's shoulder. "I think it best for all of us to leave this place. We will return to London tomorrow morning. There are . . ."

His mother interrupted. "We have been here long enough. Of course, we will miss the rest of this Season because we are in mourning, but that is no reason not to be seen about London." Imogene turned to the girls. "You two will be able to reenter Society by the time the next Season starts in the spring, so we want to make the most of our time the next few months. We will remain through the winter. Our choices of where we can properly be seen will be limited, but one never knows who one might run into in something as innocuous as a trip to church."

Edward patted his wife's shoulder. "Now, Imogene, we have more important things to think about than husband-hunting."

She swiveled the big chair and glared up at him. "Nothing is more important for your daughters than that!" She rose and walked around the desk. "As your father said, we will be leaving early, so I suggest you pack only what you need for the trip. We will of course have to get a new wardrobe for our mourning when we get into London."

She got to the door before Catherine and Margaret even got out of their chairs. "Girls? Come along! There is no time to waste." And she ushered the girls out.

Damon turned to his father. "We still have guests. What do you plan to do with them? Push them out onto the lawn?"

Edward glared at him. "It is time for them to go. I can't be the only one who is tired of them. I intend to see everyone is informed by this evening that we will be leaving."

"What about the servants?"

"Most will come with us. I plan to close Thernwood up, except for the barest of staff. I would rather not come back for a while. It will do us all good to spend a winter there, instead of surrounded by painful memories."

Damon said nothing. He had promised to bring back some treasured pieces for Edeline. She had given him a list of gifts she had received from Andrew that she wanted back, but there were other items as well. He had seen in it the war where fancy gifts were few, widows clinging to a glove, a hat, a belt, anything they could save that would bring comfort and hold memories.

It seemed Edeline was no different.

Perhaps in his efforts for her sister, Verbena would see that he could ensure she would not receive the same treatment as Edeline had at the hands of his family.

***

IT WAS time to put the final part of his plan to help the Barnes into effect. Damon dismounted, and walked through the small collection of stores his village boasted, from the carpenter to the blacksmith to the apothecary who vied for business with the doctor, to the small storekeeper who sold oddities like covered oil lamps, dishes and woven fabrics from local weavers and as far away as London. The man even from time to time quietly sold wine from France, though Damon had never asked how it got this far inland, or who wooed it away from the smugglers.

At each shop Damon requested that if the Barnes came to purchase anything, the bills be sent to him. To protect everyone's reputation, he made certain they knew it was for Edeline's sake, that his family was taking care of both her and her family while she recovered.

Not too many years ago, he would not have been overly concerned about gossip. This new concern for the proprieties sat easily on him, and he liked the feeling. He did not know if Verbena ever came to the village to shop, but if she did, he would smooth this part of her life for her, even if it had to be done on the premise that it was because of her sister.

It would go a long way to redeeming his family in her eyes.

After the last store, Damon remounted his horse and found

himself facing the dusty road that could take him to Verbena's house. He drew his horse up and stopped, looking down the break in the heavy trees.

He did not know how long it would take to get the business in London completed.

He could only hope he would not be gone long.

13

DARKNESS WAS FALLING. Verbena stirred the soup, grateful for the heat of the fireplace. Despite their efforts to keep the inside warm, winter had been particularly nasty and the boys had to go out every few days to scavenge for wood. Storm followed storm, and the wind pushed the snow into fantasy shapes all around the house and the trees.

Another gust rattled the windows, and a tendril of cold seeped across the floor, to tease her ankles under the skirt.

Annabelle and Lizabeth sat behind her at the table, working on their studies, and today it was spelling. "Annabelle, the next word is America."

"America, a-m-e-r – "

"You forgot something. Do you know what it is?"

"I do, I do!" Lizabeth piped up. But to her credit, and after a number of scoldings at her taunting of her younger sister, she said nothing more.

"I can do it!" A moment of silence followed. "Oh! I remember. Capital A, m-e-r-i…" Another pause. "C? No, k. No, c? a?"

Verbena had to turn around to smile at her sister. "Very good!"

She did not know how much of the improved behavior was Lizabeth maturing, how much was her own efforts to play Mother to the girls, and how much was having regular hearty meals and a – mostly – warm house. Whatever it was, she was grateful. Mingled in with the gratitude was a painful twinge of humiliation. How she hated being a burden! Were it not for the children, she did not think she would have been able to accept such constant charity from Edeline.

Not just Edeline, either. Damon had worked something out with the storekeepers so they did not have to pay for anything. The food they ate, the soaps they bought, even fabric for a few, a cautiously few, new pieces of clothes for each of them, all had been covered. Matthew got his own new pantaloons, and Julius bought two books on science, which he was still happily devouring. "Young Thern said it were all paid. For yer sister," one of the storekeepers had said the first time it happened, when she was ready to pay for her purchases and pulled out the pound notes Edeline sent. "E said it were 'er allowance, like."

Then he had leaned close, bad breath and all, and added, "Personally, I thinks old Thern ain't in on it. If it twere me, I would not tell the old man nuthin neither."

If the villagers were surprised at the sudden communications going back and forth between Verbena and her aunt, no one said anything. And if anyone surmised that Edeline had gone there, no one said anything about that either.

Thernwood was silent, as if the Thern family had never been there at all. No, not the family. Damon. He had not been back. The boxes of Edeline's treasures had arrived, but not him. Inside the box had been a polite note apologizing for having to send them by messenger, but that family affairs had not allowed him to deliver in person. He hoped all was well with them, and concluded with a 'most sincerely.'

She tried to remember, but she did not think he had actually said *when* he would come back. Would it be for a summer house party, with an added visit to a distant relative?

Each time that thought cropped up, a strange pain bloomed in the middle of her chest, right where her heart was.

A totally inappropriate response, she told herself. There had been nothing between them. One walk and several visits, even repairs to the house, did not a courtship make.

Yet, Verbena missed him. No doubt he was squiring some young heiress about London. He had done what he could for his sister-in-law and her family, and now it was time to concern himself with his own responsibilities.

"Bena? Bena?" Lizabeth's voice sounded worried. How long had she been lost in her thoughts? "What is the next word, Bena?"

Before she could answer, before she could remember which word she had even chosen, a sharp rap shook the front door.

"Who can that be?" Maybe it was a letter from Edeline. She wiped her hands on her ever-present apron and went to the door.

She did not recognize the old man standing there in the icy twilight.

"Miss Barnes?" Her name came out on a cloud of frosty white air. When she nodded hesitantly, he held out a large envelope. Verbena immediately recognized Aunt Mabel's handwriting.

Aunt Mabel had never delivered a letter by messenger before.

"Please, come in out of the cold." Verbena swung the door wide, and stepped back.

"Most kind, miss, most kind of you." The man stepped into the vestibule, taking the time to close the door behind him and seal the biting cold out.

The letter was bulky. Something inside slid around when she turned it over to find the opening. She ripped her aunt's seal off, and unfolded the paper. Money fell onto the floor in a solid thump, tied with string to hold all the notes together. The man bent over and retrieved the stack while she stared in astonishment at such a large sum. She'd never seen so many pound notes in her life. It was as thick as a slice of bread. She shook herself and scanned the large, wavy letters that sprawled across the page.

"Verbena, I hope this reaches you in time. Your sister nears the end of her confinement, but all is not well with the pregnancy. I am most concerned."

The words became hard to read. Verbena realized the letter was shaking in her hands. Her breath shuddered as she fought the cry of fear building inside. She forced herself to continue.

"I am including funds for you to hire someone to watch the children and for your trip. Please come with all haste. Aunt Mabel"

Verbena looked up at the man, who handed the solid package of money over. It was heavy.

The cold had turned his face red, but areas showed spots of white. Her own feet could still feel the chill he had brought in with him. Verbena suddenly realized the white of his hair under his hat was not snow – he was old. His hair was thick, but totally grey, and his hands, when he took the gloves off, were wrinkled, and liberally covered with age spots.

"Come into the kitchen. It is warmer there, and I will get you a cup of tea. Please, give me your coat."

The man took off his greatcoat, stiff with cold and raining snow onto the floor. He was dressed in some dark green livery with gold braids on the shoulders and cuffs, but the braid was fraying, threads had come loose, and the green of his jacket was shiny with wear. He scraped his boots off and followed her. Annabelle and Lizabeth still sat at the table.

"What is that?" Annabelle asked, staring at the stack in Verbena's hand.

"Is that *money?*" This time it was Lizabeth who had the wide eyes. "Why did he give you money?"

Verbena looked down at the bundle of notes she held, and back up at the old coachman's uniform. What had they done when they sent Edeline off to Aunt Mabel's? What kind of burden had they placed on their mother's sister?

"I'm supposed to bring you right away, miss." The coachman

turned his hat around in his spotted hands. "It will take us a good three days to get back, specially in this weather, and yer aunt is a bit worried, she is. I planned on us leaving right now."

As if in warning, another gust of wind whistled around the corner of the house, shaking the windows. In those few minutes the light had faded to a faint grey. How long could they possibly travel tonight? "We are waiting for my brothers to come back. I won't leave until I know they are home safe. A woman in the village has helped us from time to time. I will ask her again."

Before he could protest again, she added, "There is a small inn in the village, next to the tavern. The food is good, and I hear it is clean. Why don't you spend the night there? By the time arrangements have been made, the day will be gone. If we leave early tomorrow, the storm might be over. We will have all day to make up the delay."

She poured a cup of tea into her father's large mug and set it in front of the empty chair. "Please sit. You need something warm inside you before you go out again."

The coachman said nothing for a moment, then smiled. The smile softened his old face. "Well, I don't mind tellin you I did not look forward to headin back out in this weather." He sat down with the stiffness of age and breathed in the fragrance, then took a careful sip. "Thank you. This will hit the spot."

Annabelle looked at her with large, suddenly aware eyes. "Where are you going? Can I go, too? You are not leaving me behind, are you?" Her gaze went from Verbena to the man.

Lizabeth chimed in, "With him? Who is he? Why does he want you to go?" Her hazel eyes narrowed in suspicion.

"We don't know him." Annabelle seemed to have decided the issue for them. "You can't go with him. He is a *man*. You can *not* go with a man, not unless it is Damon." She folded her arms and glared at the coachman as if it was all his fault and this proclamation from her could settle the matter.

Damon again. Verbena never knew when the girls would mention his name. Despite the stab of pain every time he came up, it was comforting to know she was not the only one thinking of him and missing him and waiting for him . . .

She gave herself a mental shake. "This man is from Aunt Mabel."

"I don't know any Aunt Mabel, and I don't know him. And you don't neither." Annabelle's little chin came out pugnaciously and she switched her glare to Verbena.

The kitchen door burst open, bringing in more cold and the boys, thank goodness. Their arms were full of branches. They stopped short on seeing the stranger sitting at the table. Matthew remembered to shove the door closed.

Julius asked first. "Who are you, and what are you doing here?"

"Boys, I have to leave tomorrow, the earlier the better. I have to go to Aunt Mabel's." Verbena motioned at Aunt Mabel's man.

"Aunt Mabel?" Julius's brow furrowed. "But that is where Edeline went, isn't it? She already has Edeline there, why does she need you as well?"

The girls did not know the full extent of the situation, and she did not want them to. Verbena turned to the man. "I need to speak with my brothers privately. Please. Rest. Warm yourself. Have as much tea as you wish. The kettle is full." She headed toward the parlor, and the boys followed her, tracking snow across the floor. The parlor doors pulled shut smoothly. Damon's gift. She blurted out the news. "Edeline is having a baby, and Aunt Mabel wrote that something is wrong."

"With Edeline?" Julius's eyebrows came down in a worried frown. "She is having a baby? How long have you known? The whole time?"

"Yes." Old guilt rose again. "The whole time."

"Oh, Verbena." His worried eyes matched her own, she was certain. "You should not have let her go. She should be with the Therns. She would be in better hands there. They can afford doctors, and besides, that will be the heir. If it is a boy."

"Julius, there is so much she never told you. Things about which she did not want to burden you." Verbena looked into her brother's face and suddenly realized how close to being a man he was. "Things were not – easy for her there."

"Because we are poor?"

"Partly." She hesitated. "Mostly. Anyway, it was her decision."

"Verbena, the Therns are in *London*. There must be hordes of midwives there. And doctors, too. And they have the money to get her care." He braced fisted hands on his thin hips.

"Well, she did not want to go to them. She had her reasons. I did try to talk her out of it. But it was her decision." Verbena swiped a hair out of her eyes. "Aunt Mabel lives in Bath. There are plenty of healers there. No doubt she could receive as good care there as in London. I don't know what the problem is. I have to go to her, so I will be leaving first thing tomorrow morning. Aunt Mabel left us enough money for my trip, and for Mrs. Downs to come again."

Matthew rolled his eyes at his brother, but kept his mouth shut.

She looked from one to the other. "You two must help out with the girls. I don't want you to neglect your studies, though."

Julius gave a shrug. "Well, if you are determined to go, I will see if Mrs. Downs will come and cook. Don't worry about the girls. I promise to take over teaching their lessons." He nodded toward the kitchen. "How much do you want the girls to know?"

Verbena took a breath, startled by how heavy her chest felt. For the first time, she realized just how very alarmed she was. She might have shoved it aside by concentrating on details, but her body had kept worrying. "I don't want them afraid. It might be different if they had not come to know her while she stayed, but they were beginning to grow attached to her."

Julius nodded. "They are already alarmed. They need to know *something*. Say Edeline is ill and needs your help. Even bad news is better than not knowing." Again, she saw the first signs of adulthood, even young wisdom.

"Thank you, Julius." She gave him a spontaneous hug. "You, too, Matthew." Verbena stepped over and pulled him in for a hug as well. "I am so proud of you two. How would I have managed this winter without all your help?"

Matthew shuffled his feet. "You would have thought of something. You always do. Besides, Damon's money helped."

Verbena reached up to ruffle his hair. "It did, indeed, but you helped us not be a bigger burden than we had to be." She waved toward the doors, and the kitchen beyond. "Will one of you go with him to the village and hire Mrs. Downs again? If she is willing? There is plenty of money to pay her wages."

ON THE SURFACE, it was a happy meal that evening. Mrs. Downs promised to be over by midday the next day. Despite the few new gowns Verbena had been able to make with Edeline's money, she had so little to pack that it did not take her long to get everything ready. Her soup, the quickest way to prepare a small meat meal, filled the air with richness. Carrots had been available, saved through the winter by being packed in sand at the general store. Verbena was comforted to know that, with Aunt Mabel's money, the children would be set for weeks. Not that she would be gone that long.

There was enough flour for bread, and the oat bin was full. They had a dozen duck eggs, a string of sausages, a leg of lamb, dried apples and cherries for tarts and pies, and herbs to flavor the food. Julius even had bought walnuts to put in cakes.

Every now and then the laughter lagged and Verbena knew they – the three eldest – had Edeline on their minds. But for the sake of the two younger, they pretended to be carefree.

After everyone was in bed and the girls had been kissed and hugged extra-long in case they did not wake in time for the morning's farewell, Verbena lay in her own bed and tried not to think about the journey and what waited on the end of it.

How bad was Edeline? Was Aunt Mabel being overly pessimistic?

What frightened her most was that her aunt was right and all was truly not well and she would get there too late. Maybe she should have packed her bags and rushed off immediately.

And blunder through the storm? With an old coachman who had not had any time to get warm? Or be fed? Or have any sleep at all to keep him awake during the terrible journey?

It would not do anyone any good at all to drive off the road in the swirling white and die of exposure. It had happened, and more than once. Carriages and stages had been found in drifts nearly to the roof, with the passengers frozen to death inside.

No, she had made the right decision. She would just have to pray that things were not as bad as Aunt Mabel feared.

But in spite of her reassurances, sleep was slow in coming.

MORNING DAWNED BRIGHT AND CLEAR. The world was white and beautiful, but the air hurt the lungs to breathe. The children all were up, handing her last-minute items, the remnants of last night's soup, carefully packed in a crock, one of Father's flasks rinsed and filled with water, his greatcoat wrapped over her old pelisse for warmth. The coachman, Cranley, said the carriage had a heavy blanket.

Verbena decided he needed it far more than she would, and packed another pair of socks.

The minutes passed by with increasing speed while she peppered them with additional instructions. Food, schooling, "and don't forget to help Mrs. Downs wash the clothes, be good, I know you will be," portioning the money so there was enough for her to stop at inns for meals on the way and at least two nights lodging, a promise to write, and at last hugs all around. She had a few seconds of disguised panic when she climbed into Aunt Mabel's large carriage with the wool padding showing through the fabric of the seats, the once-grand glass windows cracked, and the poor old man in the bitter cold on the driver's seat.

The carriage lurched as the horses braced themselves against the thick snow and tugged. Another jerk, the carriage groaned and slid, and then the wheels began to turn, the snowdrifts whooshed and swished against the underside, and the house eased away. The long ride down the drive, trees weighed with the heavy white that sparkled like a world of diamonds, and the small figures of the children standing in the cold at the front door waving grew smaller and smaller.

She was alone in the carriage with her thoughts, and they were not pleasant company. Was Julius right? Would Edeline have done better in London?

No. If Edeline had gone – or been dragged – to London, she would have been miserable. Worse than miserable. Edeline had been truly afraid.

All is not well with the pregnancy. I am most concerned.

She was most concerned now, too.

14

DAMON STOOD BY THE COUNTER IN THE BOOKSTORE AND WAITED for the attendant to return with Margaret's book. What had been delicate white flakes for the past day was now coming down large and heavily, pushed by the wind. He was surprised that in this weather the store was as busy as it was, but those who had stayed in London for the winter needed something to distract themselves. If they could just beat the worst of the snow to come, everyone could nestle in front of a fire and read.

He wondered if his father had been right keeping his family in the city over the winter instead of joining the migration back to the country like most of the *ton*. Perhaps the sickness that had plagued the women would have found country dwellers as well, and they would not have been safe wherever they stayed. A nasty cough that was slow to pass had started first with Catherine. It moved down into her chest, and for days they had wondered if they might lose her so soon after Andrew. The memory of seeing his younger sister, the one so like him in looks, her own dark hair matted and dull, her face flushed and dry with fever, still made him shudder.

Leaving London then had been unthinkable. The doctor had

done all he could but told them he had other patients just as ill, and left them to mop her brow and pray alone.

Catherine's fever had finally broken, just in time for the sickness to move onto his mother. Once again, he had given up all thought of travelling north. They had just believed their prayers for her had been answered when Margaret began coughing. It had been a desperate time. Imogene was still hot. Her cough brought up ugly green mucous. Margaret's fever seemed to rise with no end in sight.

Damon would stand outside the door of one or the other and, between his own prayers, wonder if this desperate sickness reached beyond London. Reached as far as Thernbury, and that little house on the edge of the village. One letter to his sister-in-law and a box might be overlooked. A second letter would cause the very talk he most wanted to avoid. Not to mention linking him to Edeline.

He often thought of traveling back to Thernwood, but leaving now, with this frightening sickness raging through his own family, was impossible. He had to content himself with letters to the housekeeper, and the desperate wait for a reply. Word came back that no one there was ill, but nothing had been said about the villagers.

Visits to the apothecary became an almost daily event. Packets of herbs were stirred into water they had to fight to get the two women to swallow.

Only he and his father seemed to have escaped its ravages. Even the servants spent days dragging through their chores and hacking. Thankfully there had not been a new case in the house for a week or more now, his mother was eating again, and Margaret finally felt well enough to become demanding. Hence this trip in the snow and cold.

He had kept his word – of sorts. He had not gone back in person, but rather sent Edeline that trunk of trinkets and keepsakes from her house. He hoped he picked correctly. One coat or hat looked much like another. He had chosen other things as well:

vases, jewelry boxes with necklaces and bracelets, a couple books with Andrew's signature in them, and other odds and ends.

The thing that kept his hopes high and the waiting both easier and harder, was that the grateful reply had come not from Edeline, but from Verbena. And it had been both formal and warmly informal, starting with the salutation, "Dear Mr. Thern," and ending with "warmest regards."

That same letter rested safely locked beneath his accounts book in his desk drawer in his study. The bills from the village stores took on a new, more intimate tone, as if her purchases of fabric, mutton and dried fruit were in lieu of another letter.

Damon leaned back against the counter and scanned the store. An elderly woman in rich fur with a hat nearly as tall as she was strolled along the shelves. Her companion, clearly her maid, holding a basket and the woman's gloves, trailed by her side. Several young bucks browsed by the section on military history and bragged about what they planned to do to Napoleon when they were able to join the army.

Damon hoped Napoleon was long dead before they could join. There were horrors in war that did not belong anywhere, especially not in a peaceful bookstore in the heart of London's fashionable district.

A young woman browsing the shelves against the far wall must have finally warmed up. He smiled as she impatiently brushed the hood of her cape back off her head. Beneath the bonnet the hood had hidden, her hair peeked out and caught his eye, as yellow as summer sunshine, with a hint of curl.

He knew that hair, that wash of golden curls. How had she gotten here and what was she doing in London? He took a step forward, only to be blocked by a large woman and an equally large basket.

The young woman turned. It was not Verbena after all.

Of course it would not be. She was stuck in that tiny village, taking care of her brothers and sisters.

But when the bookstore's door opened and another patron

scurried in, bringing a wash of cold air, Damon could not stop his mind from traveling back to that small, worn house where the Barnes would likely be facing the same storm that swirled outside.

Was it as cold in Thernbury as it was here in London? At least he knew Verbena – and Edeline and the children, of course – were being cared for. It made the months easier to bear.

"My lord? My lord, I have the book for you." The words penetrated his thoughts, sounding like they had been repeated several times.

He turned around to the shopkeeper and had to blink to bring himself back from Thernwood and a head of curly blond hair and green eyes, colors of spring and warmth. He plunked down the coin, took the wrapped book and left, taking one last glance at the young woman against the wall in spite of his every effort not to look.

Just as he reached the carriage door and grasped the latch, his young tiger hanging onto the strap behind the carriage, too cold to move, the raw reddened face sending a new lash of guilt through Damon, a rich feminine voice called his name.

"Sir Damon! Sir Damon! What an unexpected surprise this is!"

Unexpected for himself, Damon thought, but he highly doubted it was as much a surprise for her. Banging his head against the carriage door in frustration would attract attention he did not want. After months of dodging the woman from his gazebo, even avoiding balls and operas where he knew she would be after he learned her name, she had finally trapped him. Madelaine Osgood, the wife of a school friend of Andrew's.

He did not know Osgood, he and his brother had been just far enough apart to have belonged to different sets at Cambridge, but it seemed that only made him prime bait.

Taking a moment to remove all expression from his face, Damon turned slowly, and bowed. "Mrs. Osgood. What brings you out in such inclement weather?"

"I was on my way home," she smiled at him from under a small-brimmed hat liberally dusted with snow. He wondered if she had been standing there waiting for him to come out so she could waylay him without an audience. "How very fortunate to run into you. Might I request a ride the rest of the way?"

His jaw clenched. Where was her own carriage?

He glanced up at the coachman, and back at the young boy getting colder by the minute, and made his decision. "I was going to allow my tiger to ride inside before he got sick." He beckoned to the boy and opened the door. One quick look at Damon and the youngster wasted no time jumping down off the back and scrambling in.

Mrs. Osgood's nose wrinkled, and her lovely brows came down in a scowl. "You would have me ride inside with your servant?" She tossed her head, and flakes drifted off, sliding down her curls.

"Then let me hail you a hansom cab." Damon stepped in front of the carriage door, blocking her entry.

Mrs. Osgood shrugged, her black eyebrows arched as her dark eyes taunted him. "I merely wanted to ask how it felt to be an uncle. Your parents must be delighted at the new addition."

His hand clenched on the carriage door. "You are mistaken, madam. I have neither niece nor nephew and I assure you both of my sisters are above reproach. I would be careful about spreading such a slanderous story."

She chuckled, low and throaty. "I was not talking of them, Damon." His name rolled easily off her tongue even though he had not given her leave for such familiarity. "You have another woman in your family, and I assure you, she *is* in the family way."

Damon stared at her.

She clapped a gloved hand over her mouth in overdone disbelief. "Don't tell me you did not know? Surely you must have guessed!" She smiled a mocking smile. "Well! This is rich! If your family had not been so shocked by Andrew's death, they would have seen. The symptoms were unmistakable. My room was near hers, and I heard her be sick every morning. How very odd, though," she tapped her chin with a finger, "I have not seen your brother's widow for some time. Is the pregnancy going hard on her?"

The cold burned his lung as he gasped air in. "Edeline? Are you speaking of Edeline? She is not – " but he could not finish the sentence.

Edeline, so pale and white, weeping all over Thernwood, and leaving endless plates of food untouched. The mysterious message that needed such secrecy. Verbena and the absolute disgust in which she held his family. No wonder, turning out a pregnant woman!

He whirled to the coachman. "My house, quickly, man!" and leapt inside with such lack of caution the pain at his sudden movement did not catch him until he was already seated. He slammed the door behind himself, leaving Mrs. Osgood smirking on the sidewalk.

DESPITE THE FEBRUARY sun shining through the carriage windows and glinting off the mounds of snow, threatening to blind everyone nearby, it gave no heat. The cold cut through Damon, making his wounded leg throb and pained sweat break out all over his body. It immediately chilled in the bitter temperature of the carriage, making the pain grow worse. After the past three days of this, he firmly expected to fall flat on his face when he tried to get out. That would be a lovely way to present himself to Verbena and her family, especially when he wanted to stand there, in high dudgeon, and demand answers from Edeline. It was hard to demand when one was lying flat on one's face in a pile of snow.

At least it was not mud.

If Mrs. Osgood was right, depending on how far along Edeline had been at the funeral, she might well have a babe in arms by this time.

Why did she do this? Relations with his family had not been good, granted, but to deprive a child of his rightful inheritance?

The carriage turned into the entrance to the rundown estate of the Barnes'. The chimney sent hearty smoke into the air, its dark grey color peeking above the bricks before being caught by the wind. He caught a whiff of the woodsy smell, and just the thought of it made him feel warmer.

Damon rapped on the carriage roof, and the trapdoor opened. The coachman's chapped red face peeked through. "Yes, my lord?"

"Get us out of the wind. Pull around to the side of the house. I'm not so conscious of my dignity that I insist on the front door. I just want out of the cold."

The red face grinned. "I agree. Will do, sir."

The carriage turned neatly around the corner, and Damon immediately felt the difference in the wind whistling past the cracks in the door. The carriage swayed as the man climbed down and opened the door. If Damon thought he had been freezing before, this was a whole new level of cold. The porch steps were marked with tracks of all sizes, from larger boots to the smaller ones that were obviously from the girls. He saw signs that someone had tried to shovel, but the snow had fought back.

Damon dragged his aching body out – to promptly slip on some hidden ice and fall spread-eagled on the porch floor, staring up at the porch roof and icicles that hung poised like bullets stopped in flight.

Damon glared at the icicles. Forewarned was clearly not always forearmed.

The door opened. "Damon!" Julius appeared above him, looking down with utter relief. "Thank goodness you are here!"

Damon spit snow out. "Get me up, will you?" Julius's face was followed by all the others, and one more he did not expect to see, Mrs. Downs. Hands appeared for him to grab. He was hauled to his feet with surprising dispatch and busily dusted off.

"Thank you." He looked around at the clustered group staring back at him. Tasty aromas drifted through the open door, fresh-cooked bread, a roast just reaching the point of doneness, and carrots sending their summer reminder into the air.

What was Mrs. Downs doing here?

"Come in, hurry, you must be cold," Julius said with such an adult manner that Damon wanted to smile. Maybe once his face warmed up, it would break through. The children still blocked his path, seemingly immune to the cold that bit through his greatcoat.

He looked at the face that surprised him most. "I did not expect to see you here, Madam."

"Well, as to that – "

Mrs. Downs was drowned out by four other voices. "Some aunt sent it – " "Edeline is sick – " "Verbena had to leave fast – " "We did not even know Edeline was with child."

That last sentence grabbed his attention. One question answered in the din. Mrs. Osgood had been right.

The four young faces held varying stages of worry and excitement. He would unravel the whole story from the warmth of the house. "Might we all go inside? And once my driver takes care of the horses, may he come into the kitchen to warm?"

"Of course!" "Come. Come!" "We missed you!" He was dragged in amid a second chorus and divested of his coat and hat. Seated, a heavy cup of hot tea in one hand and a plate of slices of buttered bread and meat close to the other hand, Damon felt pummeled with words from all four, no five, voices, making a disjointed picture in his mind of letters and cold and money and Verbena whisked away in a great carriage.

He raised a hand to quell the hubbub. "Now, one at a time. What is going on here? When did Edeline leave, why is Verbena not here and who took her away?" He had to take a breath to calm himself.

"Hush up, everyone! Let me tell it!" Julius shouted them down and answered. "A letter came over two weeks ago from our mother's sister. Edeline went to live with her after you left. She was in the family way, but no one knew. I did not know, either." A touch of injured dignity slipped through in that last sentence. "Aunt Mabel sent money for us to hire Mrs. Downs again so Verbena could go there because something is wrong."

Damon's breath caught. Something was wrong? How bad was it? That was Andrew's child! What was Verbena expected to do?

Julius was still speaking. "I don't know what is happening now." He looked pointedly over at the girls.

Damon beckoned the girls over, and they pressed close, as if he was their savior. "I need you two to stay here in the kitchen with Mrs. Downs and help her take care of my driver, when he comes in. Julius, is there somewhere we can talk in private?"

Lizabeth did not move. She glared at him. "Again? Every time you come, you always send us out. We never get to hear anything."

He fought the smile. "I am very sorry, but I have to do it again."

Matthew said, "I will stay with the girls." His eyes were ringed with red. Damon suspected the boy had been crying in private.

Julius led the way out of the kitchen. "The only room is the parlor." He started talking before they had passed the dining room. "My sisters were close before Edeline married, and when she came back this summer they were thick as thieves again. Edeline stayed a week or so after you left, and then said she had to go, and went away."

He pulled open the parlor doors. Damon noticed with a passing flash of pleasure that they were still working.

Julius waved into the room. "Sit wherever looks most comfortable. Anyway, the girls cried when Edeline left, but Verbena said she needed a place alone to mourn, so I never questioned it." He dropped down into one of the straight-backed chairs, and leaned forward, arms propped on his knees.

Damon chose the settee. "Did you know she had gone to live with the aunt?

Julius nodded. "Oh, yes. They told us that. Just not the other. When I found out about the baby, I said Edeline should have gone to London, where there are lots of midwives, but Verbena said she did not want to go. She fairly told me to mind my own business."

Damon tapped his finger against arm of the settee. "And you don't know where this aunt lives?"

Julius shook his head miserably. "Bath, but I don't know more than that."

"Big town." Damon thought for a moment. "Where is the letter from this aunt? Do you still have it? Or did Verbena take it with her?"

"I don't know. If she left it, it would be somewhere in her room, most likely."

"Let us find it." Damon pulled himself to his feet.

Julius led the way, retracing their steps. A spate of laughter met them as they entered the kitchen, a good sign that the grownups were working hard to keep the mood up.

Julius opened a door tucked away in the corner. Despite the cooking Mrs. Downs had been doing, inside Verbena's room it was bitterly cold. Damon frowned down at the thin mattress, the broken bits of straw that had fallen out of the casing onto the otherwise spotless floor, the worn blankets. Verbena slept on that? She should be on a featherbed, with down quilts, like his . . .

He forced his attention to the room. There was a notch in the wall, perhaps once a closet, with hooks for gowns and two small shelves above, holding a couple of bonnets, long out of fashion, a comb, two worn books – Shakespeare, he was not surprised to note – and other miscellany.

"Damon?" Julius's voice was low, and he looked anxiously over his shoulder as if afraid of being overheard. "Verbena has been gone too long. She wrote to say she had arrived, to tell us about Bath, but she never mentioned when she would be back. Two weeks, Damon! She would never be gone this long if everything was all right."

Damon was afraid of the same thing, but he clapped a reassuring hand on Julius's shoulder. "I intend to find out what is going on."

They began moving items, the hats, the books, even checking under the covers on the bed. Damon shoved aside the uncomfortable feeling of violation as he laid the covers, such as they were, back into place. She would not be sleeping in this excuse for a bed again. If he had to defy his entire family, he would find a way to wed her.

Why had Edeline abandoned her child's inheritance? Nothing could have been that bad. Well, now she had someone to protect her.

The whole family had someone to protect them.

At last, checking any last places they might be hidden, on the back of a shelf Damon picked up an old corset he doubted Verbena had ever worn or ever needed to. A small collection of letters and a fine white handkerchief fell out onto the floor. He plucked out the letters but folded the handkerchief and replaced it.

How easily the packet might have been overlooked. Inside a corset, of all things!

The letter on top was done in an unfamiliar feminine hand. And it had an address. From Bath. Damon slipped it into his coat pocket. "Thank you, Julius." He squeezed the boy's shoulder, realizing as he did so that in the time he had been away Julius had grown from a boy into a young man. "I promise I will find out what is happening, and bring your sisters back."

He hurried into the kitchen to pick up his greatcoat. His driver took one look at him, rose and slipped out the door.

"Take care of the children," Damon told Mrs. Downs. He pulled out some paper notes. "Use this, get whatever you need."

And he headed out into the bitter wind.

15

To say their Aunt Mabel lived 'in' Bath was a bit of a stretch, Damon thought as the carriage turned into a drive. The post they had passed, tall, wooden and layered with snow-crowned boards announcing names and accented by arrows, gave the house he was looking for, and the arrow had pointed this direction.

Three more days of struggling with snow covered roads and rutted puddles when the snow melted. And wind. Always the wind. It had followed him all the way from the north country, and now Bath was having one of its rare winter storms. The wind battered the flakes that tried to settle on the ground, and drove them through the carriage door seams. A layer of white edged the floor by each opening.

It had been a hard journey. Worry dogged him every mile, reinforced by frequent re-readings of the aunt's letter. Guilt battered him along with the worry. His father had tossed Edeline out. No matter how one tried to pretty it up, that was what it amounted to. Tossing her out. They bore the responsibility for anything that happened to either Edeline or the child. Had she stayed, she would have been in London, with access to the best of doctors.

Granted, Bath was a veritable healing center. Perhaps the care she had received here might be the equal of anything she would get in London.

Although he did not put much faith in the supposedly miraculous powers of the hot springs.

The house finally could be seen in bits and pieces, screened by trees, some bare for the winter, others evergreen. Through the swirling snow and the needles and branches, Damon saw mourning black hanging on the door.

Damon held the carriage window's curtain aside and stared at the big black wreath. It grew larger and more ominous the closer they came.

Death had visited here. A weight spread in his chest.

The vehicle rocked to a stop. His driver opened the door and flipped the step down. Damon climbed out, straightened his shoulders, took a deep breath of the cold air that chilled his lungs as the wreath had chilled his heart, and walked to the door.

For whom had they hung that black wreath? The aunt? Edeline? The child?

The heavy knocker's clang echoed in the clearing, a rude noise in the light of the black crepe he could now see draped across the inside of the nearest window as well. But the rumbling sound had the desired effect – the door eased open and a young woman in a maid's cap poked her head out. "May I help you?" She made no other move, just stood there with only her head showing, her eyes wide and uneasy.

"I am Damon Thern. Mrs. Thern is my sister-in-law," he said. Her eyes only narrowed, unease becoming distrust, and to his amazement, in one swift move she swung the door shut.

Or started to. He caught it with his hand, and pushed it open, slipping past the door's edge the moment there was enough room. "For whom is the mourning wreath on the door?" His voice was too loud in the still house.

"Wait here," she snapped, no welcome in her words or her manner, then scurried across the poor excuse for a foyer, in actuality little more than just a space in the hall, and up the dark stairway that ran sideways directly in front of him, her hand barely skimming the handrail. The steps were built tight to the wall, and at their foot an open doorway indicated more house beyond. At the top of the stairs there was a railed opening as wide as the staircase that climbed toward it.

Clearly, everyone was upstairs. Damon wanted to follow her, the house was again quiet and he could plainly hear the sound of shoe heels clicking not far away. If this place had a drawbridge, it would have been pulled up tight. He waited, hearing footfalls back and forth in the floor above him, and voices like a faint hum running along the walls.

His greatcoat had done its job and he finally felt warm. Or warm enough. Damon would hardly call this house heated. He glanced around for a place to hang the heavy coat, since the maid had not offered to take it. Although clean, the house had a musty odor, as if no one had done any real scrubbing, no polishing to scent the air. Of course, in light of that awful black, they had had other things on their minds.

A dark door was shut tight to his right, and a matching door closed equally tight on his left. There was no place to sit, no bench even for removing boots. He had done too much sitting anyway in the last week, but his leg did not want to take his weight.

It was a small suffering in view of what had happened in this house. Damon straightened his shoulders and continued to stand.

It probably was not as long as it seemed before he heard a light step walk toward the stairs. He looked up.

Verbena stood there, looking paler than ever in the black dress, her fair hair shocking against all that darkness. Her green eyes seemed too big for her delicate face, and shadows stained the skin underneath. She walked down as if each step pained her, slow and careful, her gaze fixed on him. Halfway down, she wobbled. Damon snapped out of his own stillness, and strode across the foyer to the bottom of the steps, ready to catch her.

"How did you find out where we were?" She shook her head, her hands clenched and unclenched, quick movements, as if they did not know what to do with themselves. And then her eyes filled with tears, she started to tremble, and to his utter shock, hurtled down those last steps, threw herself against him and began sobbing. "Where have you been all this time? Where were you when we needed you?"

After the first moment of disbelief, his arms wrapped around her to hold her close, frightened by the shudders that shook her slim body.

She was so slight, he was afraid he would break her. He forced himself to gently ease her back. He could not make himself let go of her arms, just moved her out far enough to see her face, her sad, pale, tear-stained face.

In a quiet voice, he asked, "Who was it?"

Fresh tears filled her eyes. "Edeline." Her voice broke. "Aunt Mabel said things were not going well at the end." She hiccupped. "That is why she sent for me." Those waiting tears slid down her face, her eyes were stained red from crying. "Little good I was."

What did he say to that? *I am certain your sister was glad to have you in her final minutes?* When Edeline knew she was leaving her child behind? Or had the baby died, too? "Oh, Verbena. I am so sorry, my dear. So terribly sorry. And the child?"

A cold change came over her face. Verbena wrenched away, her tears dried up, just the silver tracks remaining. She glared at him. "That is all you care about, truly? The baby?"

The baby. He did not know if that was an answer. "No, it is not all I care about." He looked back at the nearest closed door, took her hand, so small and cold and trembling, and pulled her behind him. *Ask her about Andrew's child.* "We are not discussing this where anyone can overhear."

The room he entered proved to be a small study, with a solid desk, several old chairs whose upholstery had gone shiny with use, and inadequate bookshelves that came barely to his chest, jumbled with books that were at least part of that hint of mildew on the air. He pulled the door nearly shut behind them, just enough for privacy but not so much as to cause talk. He did not care about the talk, except for her sake. It would only serve his purpose.

In the dim room, the heavy blackness of Verbena's gown drained what color remained from her white skin, barring the high spots of anger across her cheekbones. "I have heard a lot more these past weeks about what my sister went through with your family, and it was not pretty. Throwing her out in front of a whole house of London society was the least of it. As if there was a soul in the house that did not know your family was washing their hands of her!"

He had seen this often, grief turned into anger that hit out at anyone near. If she needed to lance it on his head, it was small atonement. "There is no way to apologize for how she was treated. She must have known, though, that the child would have received Andrew's estate." Whatever his father would not give to Andrew, he would certainly save for his child. And, of course, the boy would get everything in the end. Yet, knowing that, Edeline had fled to this cold house with musty books? "Why did she not tell us she was with child? If she had, she would hardly have been pushed out of my father house."

Verbena backed up, staring at him with her big green eyes. She took a breath, and he saw her visibly retract, her words unsaid.

He asked, his words quiet, "How is the baby?"

Her hands came down and clenched in small fists in her gown. "You can't have him! I won't let you! She made me promise to raise him. I gave her my word, and I will keep it! You Therns think money can get you everything – well, not this time. I am his mother now, she left him to me! She even wrote it down in her will!"

Andrew's child was a boy, and, yes, alive. Damon's chest swelled with relief, but he immediately tamped it down. There was no room for happiness here, not in this house, not before Verbena and her grief.

He had just been handed the very tool he needed, a way for them both to get exactly what they wanted. If he went through with this, he would be dragging Verbena into the very battle her sister fought. Only this time, she would have someone to take her side. And, Damon thought, unlike Edeline, Verbena would be able to hold her own.

Any halfway decent solicitor could overturn Edeline's paltry will, but he let that slide. "Verbena, please calm yourself," he said, keeping his voice soothing. "I only asked after the child. My nephew. I appreciate your devotion to your sister. I always admired your loyalty to your family, and now to this little one. I know you would like nothing better than to see the last of all of us Therns, but I am part of the father's family, and no one will question whether we can care for our own."

She straightened her spine, and looked for all the world like a little black wren taking on a hawk. "Are you saying you will take him away from us?" Her eyes were angry pools of green. The vulnerable red rims around them rather spoiled the image of indomitable strength she wanted to project. "I won't let you do that. I have just as much right to the child as you do, more even because of my sacred oath, and Edeline's written wishes."

He hated the fear that leapt into her eyes. Keeping his voice low and gentle, he went on, "I know you love him already. I would never deny you that. But despite what you think, despite what you have been told, and despite the admittedly unsavory behavior of my family, we are not monsters. There is another side to the story besides Edeline's. I grew up in that house you despise so much. My mother loved Andrew, she will love his child."

He had this chance, like a gift from heaven, and he was not going to waste it. He would take the child, he had no choice. It could not be left in a house with a drunken, violent grandfather and not enough food unless provided by others. He wanted Andrew's son safe and healthy. But he wanted the baby's new mother as well.

It was time to make her see logic. "Before you rush off with the baby in a fit of righteous zeal, you must plan. How do you propose to care for it? How will you take care of your other brothers and sisters with a tiny baby?" There had been infants in his company in Europe, both from wives and hangers-on, so he knew a few things about babies. "They don't sleep. Will you trust yourself to cook over an open fire with no sleep all night? The thought of you standing next to a fire when you are that tired frightens *me*. Will the baby live with you, or will you have to leave it with a wet nurse? Can you even afford a wet nurse? How can you be certain whoever you find is taking good care if it when you are not there to oversee what is happening?"

She bit her lip, then retorted, "My aunt has given us money. We can pay well enough to ensure he gets care."

Damon resisted the urge to look at the worn furnishings around them. "I see. *'He gets care.'*" He repeated her words to her. "But what kind of care? If you hire a wet nurse, where will she live? Your house is not big enough for anyone else to live with you. I am not even certain you have room for one tiny baby. He *will* have to stay with the wet nurse, at least for the first few months. How often will you see him? Is that the kind of care Edeline would have wanted? To leave your nephew – her son – with a stranger? And how long do you want him nursed before he is weaned and you can take him home?"

"As long as is best for him! You would have the same problem, hiring a wet nurse."

The fear was building in her eyes, but she held her ground. He felt a thrill of pride in her. How valiant she was! "Certainly I would, but it will hardly be a problem for me. There are widows aplenty with babies glad to live in their own apartment in my house, where I can watch over his care. I have plenty of room and more than enough money, and I will not think of the cost as a burden. Assuming you had a place for her, where can you find a woman you can pay enough to live in your house?"

She was wavering, he could see it in the sheen of tears in her eyes, and the slump in her shoulders. It was one thing for her to grab the baby and whisk him away in a burst of fury, it was quite another to work out all the myriad details.

He wished he could reach out and catch her hands, hold her in the security of his own. "Verbena, I am not trying to hurt you, but you must see how difficult this task is. How long do you think your aunt can afford to support you? Edeline was not her daughter, he is not a grandchild, but rather a distant relative. What if she decides the cost is a drain?"

"She won't." The anguish in her eyes stopped him from adding more arguments to his case.

It was time. He stepped closer, and made his voice soft and alluring. So much depended on the right words, the tone of his voice. "There is another solution, one that would protect both our familial rights, and not threaten your sister's will."

Ah, there it was, that flare of hope, quickly squelched but unmistakable. "And what might this miraculous solution be?"

He caught her hands at last, small, strong things, so capable of handling whatever life had thrown at her. They were nearly as cold as his had been in the carriage when he saw that black bow hanging on the door. He lifted them to his mouth one at a time, and pressed his lips to them. "Marry me."

Her big green eyes went so wide they threatened to fall out. Her mouth dropped open and a little squeak came out. "Marry you?"

"Yes. Marry me." He took a chance and reached out to smooth a loose strand of hair behind her ear. "That will guarantee your rights. I can afford to hire a wet nurse, and bring her to my house – *our* house, under your watchful eye. No one would dare take a child away from my wife."

16

VERBENA'S EARS BUZZED, AND SHE FEARED FOR A BRIEF MOMENT SHE was going to faint. He had said the words twice and they still did not make sense. Marry him?

Marry Damon? Become his wife? Walk right into the Thern family, like a lamb to the slaughter?

Keep Roderick?

Kind as Damon had been to the children – and herself – she could not get past the stories Edeline had told these past days. Verbena forced herself to breathe around heavy pain of the empty space where her sister had been.

She pulled her hands free. Small warm spots remained where his lips had been. "I won't marry into your family. I can't." Her chest hurt. "I gave my *word* to Edeline, I would keep him safe from you – your family." She had not meant to lump him in with his family, but neither could she separate him. "I know what they did. They never accepted my sister. She was never good enough. Which means I will never be good enough. Julius and Matthew and the girls will *never be good enough.*" Verbena forced herself to take a quick breath. "I appreciate the offer, but I will follow her instructions. Her whole purpose was to keep her child safe."

"Safe?" He closed in on her, moving forward slowly like a prowling cat. Despite herself, she kept retreating until her back was against the nearest shelf. He braced his hands on either side of her head. His swarthy face was so close she could see the fine lines pain had etched around his dark eyes. A swath of black hair fell across his forehead and she had to clench her hands in her skirt to keep from reaching up to push it back.

Verbena stood straight, even though she knew how easily this latest burden could be the one to break her. How badly she wanted to trust him. She was tired, so tired, and afraid of the very things he had just put into words, worries she had had for months but had shoved away.

"Safe?" He repeated the word. "Verbena! Sometimes I don't understand you. Edeline was living with a relative who it seems barely knows her, in a house your aunt does not even keep warm enough for a baby. And now you are going to take this baby back to your home? I wish there was a way to say this without giving offense, but you were living one step away from the poorhouse, with a drunk for a father. What will your father do when the baby cries at night? Do you think I did not see the girls trying to stay out of his way? And you would bring my nephew to that?"

Verbena flinched. He was right. Father would not want another mouth to feed, however tiny. And with such connections available?

"You don't trust my family." He straightened, and she took a breath. Her teeth began to chatter. She did not know if it was from the cold in the room – he was right about that – or the fear that dogged her. The decision he held out, one that might so easily solve most of her problems, buffeted her with conflicting loyalties, promises given, threats and betrayals.

Damon had not broken his thought. "I understand that, I even can sympathize. This distrust goes both ways. I must be blunt and say I don't trust your father. When he comes back from the sea, what then? The thought of him in a house with a tiny baby is enough to deprive me of sleep. Let us not forget that you already have too many siblings to care for. One of us must make the first step to reconciliation. You have done well, but this is too much for you, and it is unfair for Andrew's child."

"You see?" His words gave her the anger she needed to stand up to him. "You did it again. Andrew's child. Nothing about my sister."

"It was a slip of the tongue, nothing more," he said, sounding almost as tired as she was.

Verbena sighed and rubbed at the ache behind her forehead. "The leap of faith you are asking of me is too much. I cannot over- look that I gave her my solemn oath. You say this decision would allow me to keep my word to her but how can I know I will be able to raise him as Edeline would have wanted? She told me about the very world you live in, how people walk past starving children and only care that they are in the way."

Damon pressed a finger over her mouth, a gentle and implacable touch, and she stopped speaking instantly, shocked by his sudden contact and the warmth in the soft pressure of his fingers. "You can find people without conscience everywhere. I could tell you tales of the worst of humanity that happened among the poorest of people. I saw dying men be robbed of their boots, rings cut off fingers of men who were too injured to stop the thieves."

She blinked at the passion in his voice, the pain she heard there. Had he had his boots pulled off when he was too wounded to stop them? The pain of grief in her chest made room for a whole new ache as she looked up at his burning eyes and saw the shadows of nightmares there. His finger still held her words inside, only she could not have spoken anyway.

He towered over her and she reminded herself that he was alive and healed, if not whole. "We can argue class all day long," he said, his voice soft now, his eyes hiding his secrets again. "It won't change the situation. We both have a child to care for. You can give him love, I don't doubt that at all, but that is not the point. The point is, how will you feed him? Keep him safe? Keep him warm? Clothe him? I can give him food so he will never want, surround him with guards if necessary, and provide him with the best schooling."

He lifted his finger, and her lips felt the loss of its warmth just as her hands had moments ago. She sensed his mind churning.

"And I can give him you, if you marry me." Damon's eyes were suddenly determined, his jaw set. "What about Julius and Matthew and Lizabeth and Annabelle?"

The children's names slipped off his tongue so easily, almost as if he had been thinking about them these past months.

He did not pause, just went on, his words an inexorable litany of her own worries. "Do you think I don't know the boys wish to learn? What can they get in a small school? Is there even a school there most of the time? Where will they learn the sciences? I can get them tutors, teach them as many languages as their brains can hold and whatever else they wish to know. Will your sisters learn Italian, or even French? Learn to paint? To play an instrument, or any of the other accomplishments that will attract a husband?"

He was using her siblings deliberately, she knew it, and it was working, forcing her to face the empty future they all were condemned to live. There was no choice, had not been since he learned of her sister's pregnancy. All these months she had battled to hide Edeline and the baby, knowing she was fighting a battle only a miracle would let her win.

She made one more attempt to refute him, the final and insurmountable problem that assent would leave her to fight. "Will you protect me from your family and the scorn Edeline endured?"

Damon's expression went blank. Verbena watched him draw inside himself, and felt him gather his resolve. She braced herself, and wished she had never made that vow to Edeline.

He exhaled sharply, the sound hissing in the quiet room. "We will not fight over a dead woman's words. We can't raise the baby in a world of bitter words and resentment. Your sister is dead. I understand your hurt. My brother is dead as well. You are not your sister – I am not my brother."

In that deep, methodical voice, Damon continued, "That battle is over. It is done." His eyes narrowed. "We will not fight your sister's war. Whatever her grievances, they were hers alone, and they died with her. It was unfair of her to burden you with them."

Verbena felt her spine stiffen. She opened her mouth to rush to Edeline's defense, but he raised a cautionary hand. "I will leave your father out of our marriage, and you will leave my family out. Our marriage will be between the two of us. Do you understand?"

"I don't take orders well," she snapped.

He smiled, and the amusement reached his eyes. "I have figured that out already. I will not be an unreasonable husband."

She thought back to the summer, all the kindnesses Damon had showered her and the children with. What had she given in return? Just Edeline's angry words. Just Edeline's accusations.

Maybe Damon was right, maybe Edeline had burdened her unfairly. Goodness only knew, holding Edeline's secret all these months had nearly broken her. How many times had she wanted to have someone, no, not someone, wanted *Damon* there to help her? When she was injured, despite his own grief he had found time to visit, and when he could not he had hired people who could.

But that did not change Edeline's situation. Verbena did not doubt her sister's story. There had been too much pain in Edeline's eyes. Whatever she had suffered had been real, and had come from Damon's family. The line between the classes was harsh and vigorously enforced, she knew that. If Damon, or his family, wanted to take Roderick, there was nothing she could do to stop them.

Verbena shivered.

His hands came down on her shoulders, and she could not make herself step away. "I think part of your sister's problem was that my brother lived in his own world. I do not. He probably was unaware of Edeline's unhappiness. I will make certain you are accepted." He sounded so confident.

He looked it, standing there with his dark head held high, so tall, so completely assured of his ability, as if his wounded leg mattered not a whit. "You need not fear sharing a home with my family. I have my own house, my own servants, my own income. I depend on my family for nothing, they have no monetary hold on me. And while you will have to take my word on all of this, you will also have to take my word that my family will love this child."

He always had been something far beyond any male in the village, with his height that stood above most of the other men, his piercing dark eyes that compelled attention and made her shiver. She knew now that those eyes could dance with humor or ache with sadness.

And he wanted her to marry him. Verbena's heart fluttered in her chest, but she did not dare put her hand over it to steady it. She had to remember it was not safe to love a Thern. Edeline had, and look where it had gotten her, hated and scorned and driven out, and now dead.

But Damon was right, she was not her sister. While Edeline had suffered in silence, she herself would fight back. Verbena knew she had to make this decision with her head, and then keep her wits about her.

It was hardly the way she had dreamed of marriage. Her heart longed for those youthful dreams. Her head said her brothers and sisters would be secure. They would be warm, well-fed, well-dressed. Julius would have schooling, Matthew – well, Matthew would be able to find his way. They would have servants and she could finally rest.

Oddly, she knew she could trust him in that. If Damon said the children would have schooling, they would have schooling. The girls would have a governess, and learn to paint. How they would love that!

And Damon would have Roderick. But she would have him, too. *Our marriage will be between the two of us. I will make certain you are accepted.*

Verbena fought back the panic that rushed at her. Her mouth dried. She ran her tongue across her lips, but it did no good. *No one would dare take a child away from my wife.*

His eyes gleamed as they focused on her mouth, then he met her gaze. "Well?"

She had one more question, hard to ask. "What kind of marriage would you expect?"

"What kind of marria – Oh. I see." His eyes actually twinkled. "Do you mean, will we share a bed?"

Heat rushed up into her cheeks. She must be as red as an apple. "Yes."

The twinkle faded from his eyes. He picked up her hands again, and pressed them between his own. "Verbena, I would never marry a woman in name only, however good the reason. I have always wanted a marriage with a woman I could respect. I certainly . . . respect you, and I hope you hold me in at least some esteem. So yes. This will be a real marriage, and I look forward to having more children of our own."

Oh, Edeline, I promised, but what else can I do? Her heart raced as if she had been running hard, and maybe she had been. Running from hunger, from cold, from a house that threatened to fall down on her head. From the crushing weight of poverty and the constant threat that her father would some horrible day lose everything because of his weakness for drink, and they would have nothing left, truly nothing at all.

"Very well." Her chest was tight, the words sounded weak. Verbena cleared her throat and said, "I will have to marry you."

I will have to marry you. As acceptances went, that must surely rank as one of the least enthusiastic, Damon thought as he rode down the street in Bath. He wished he could give Verbena a few weeks to get used to the idea, and to rekindle the friendship they had begun last summer. Not having met the aunt, who it turned out had been meeting with the local vicar planning the funeral when he was busy proposing, he had no idea what her reaction would be. Many the widow who, having got her freedom, chose never to remarry.

There was another reason to get the wedding done quickly. His own family, particularly his father. Verbena was not far wrong about the enmity. He remembered his father's biting words, and there were plenty to choose from. *They are all greedy, grasping, moneygrubbers, and the father is no more than a drunken sot. I did not approve of Andrew's choice of a wife. I never will consider her to have been his equal. If only she had contracted the fever and died instead of Andrew.*

No, best to present it as a *fait accompli.*

Thank goodness there were other things to keep his mind occupied. Right now, he had several items to purchase. She simply could not wear her mourning dress at the wedding, it just was not done, but he knew without asking that she had nothing worthy with which to replace it.

It was a good thing her aunt lived in Bath. Anything he wanted could be found here just as easily as in London. And thinking of London brought him to the furor this marriage would cause among all who knew him.

He could already imagine how hard his friends would laugh. He could hear them now. *You have how many children! You, Damon, a family man? Did you injure your leg in the war or your head?*

Perhaps it was time to find a new group of friends.

Shops slipped past, a tailor, a stationery shop – that one he intended to avoid at all costs, he had no intention of informing anyone by mail – an upholsterer, a cobbler, another thing to add to the list of things she needed. And at last, a modiste. Complete with premade gowns in the window.

He turned his horse and dismounted, scanning the gowns set out in the window display with a careful eye, one navy, the other green. The green one on the right was definitely too large, not to mention it was too bright and there was too much shine. If he knew Verbena – and he thought he did – she would stick to convention as much as possible, which meant dark and subdued. Respectful.

So the navy one it was. He gave it a more detailed perusal, and something else caught his eye, an attached cape that draped from the shoulders all the way to the floor, over the gown's full back gathers. He could not wait to see her in it.

He walked up to the door, but just before he pulled it open, he spotted a silvery fur cloak that looked so thick he thought Verbena might get lost in it, draped over a chair on the far side of the window display. Perhaps there was enough fur left over to make a muff.

While he was thinking about it, Damon added gloves to the list of wedding presents.

At least she would be warm for the return trip. If he was very lucky, and very crafty, he might be able to convince her to share the carriage blanket with him in his far less adequate coat. Of course, if she was warm enough, she might push the entire blanket over to him and sit there in her bundled splendor.

He looked at the cloak again.

Damon smiled and pulled open the door.

AUNT MABEL BUSTLED into the room. Her grey curls bobbed under her cap. Her gown was rich velvet, done in a purple so dark at first glance Verbena thought it was black. Only when she moved did the true color show, and she was moving a lot, fluttering around as if about to take wing.

"Come, come, my dear. Your groom will be here soon. You certainly don't want to be late for your own wedding." Aunt Mabel picked up the hat the modiste had whipped up, a confection of navy blue velvet and net and the most cunning pleated crown and small brim. A subtle, bow decorated the back of the bonnet, complete with two long tails that could drape down her back or be pulled to the front as she chose. He made sure she knew that it was designed specifically to go with the gown at his request.

She adored it instantly. The man knew women's fashion. She did not know what to make of that bit of knowledge.

Accepting clothing from him had given her a moment of embarrassment. The step she was about to take had been brought home by those carefully wrapped packages. Two dresses, one black in honor of her mourning, the other a blue as dark as the purple hue in Aunt Mabel's, and of velvet as well.

Both gowns fit perfectly, another bit of unnerving intelligence.

"You look beautiful." Aunt Mabel stopped her fluttering when the maid finished tying the last bow on the back and turned Verbena around.

"You can look now," she said, and stepped away. Verbena turned around to the mirror, something the maid had forbidden until she was done.

She went as still as her aunt had. The blue gown was beautiful, starkly simple with its high waist and low neck unembellished by any unnecessary ruffles or gathers. That had been saved for the long sleeves that rose at her shoulders to narrow near the elbow, and the gown's back. Verbena felt the weight of the fabric draping off her, and saw the wide ruffled bottom peeking out the skirt's side.

For the first time since she had given her agreement, she felt like a bride.

In the mirror's reflection, she saw her aunt fish a lace handkerchief out of her own sleeve. "I wish your mother could have lived to see you like this."

Verbena felt her mother's loss as well, someone to hold her hand and hug her and promise it would be fine. She took a deep breath, hoping it would slow her heartbeat, which until that first look in the mirror had been only mildly fast.

Now her heart beat in her ears like a racing horse.

The heavy knocker sounded through the house, a deep knell, startling all three of them.

Aunt Mabel began fluttering again. "Oh! He is here, he is here. Oh my! He has come!' Relief drenched her voice, as if until he actually arrived, there might be some doubt he would go through with it.

"Quick, put on your bonnet. Mary, where is the cloak? And the muff? Oh, my goodness," she stopped to clap her hands over her flushed cheeks. "Oh, my goodness, how exciting this is! How fortunate that you had been here just long enough to make this simple. The bishop was very agreeable to give the license. If your young man had had to go all the way back to London for a special license, just think how much more time it would have taken."

That did not sound like such a problem to Verbena at the moment. She would not mind at all another few day's respite.

Aunt Mabel turned to look at Verbena. "What are you waiting for, my dear? Come, come, get your cloak on! And your bonnet, but don't muss your hair. You look absolutely beautiful. Pinch your cheeks, dear, so you don't look quite so pale. Why, I remember the day I was wed. My own dear mother – your grandmother, you know – made my brother walk beside me all the way to the vicar's just to make sure I was not going to fall down, I was that pale."

Verbena looked back to the mirror. Aunt Mabel was right. The color had leached from her face, leaving her looking like she was indeed about to faint.

She was marrying Damon Thern. Today. Now.

Where is your courage, she asked the white-faced reflection staring back at her. *Think of the children. Think of Roderick.*

Mary came up from behind and slipped the rich fur cloak over her shoulders. The warmth was welcome. "Here you go, miss. Don't forget your muff."

Verbena took one last look at the face in the mirror, and turned her back on it. She needed all the strength she could muster, and that wide-eyed, shocked reflection did not help.

Not at all.

Damon tapped his hat against his leg as he waited. Servants scurried back and forth across the open space at the top of the stairs. Now and again, one would smile down at him with an air of suppressed excitement as they hurried past.

She was not going to back out, was she? It must be a sign of his own nerves that he even wondered. Verbena was not that type. If she had decided she could not go through with it, she would have told him to his face last night when he came to work out the final arrangements. Ten o'clock in the morning at the church. The vicar promised to be waiting.

Damon patted his vest pocket to ensure the license was still there. It was, of course, as it had been the other five or six times he had checked. The delay that had so worried Julius plus the time it took for him to get to Bath worked to his own advantage. It put Verbena easily over the fifteen day residence limit to qualify for a common marriage license and spared him a jaunt back to London for a special one.

Testing her resolve that long would have been a very bad idea.

Measured steps and the rustle of heavy skirts pulled his attention back up. The aunt came first in a purple gown so rich it surprised him, her face beaming.

"You are here! How glad I am to see you. What a happy, happy day this is." She did not come down the stairs, just stood there smiling between him and something beyond the wall, just out of view.

Irresistible compulsion drew his own gaze after the aunt's. She had the advantage of knowing what was coming. Verbena seemed to float past the wall's barrier, and his breath caught. She was a vision, her beauty set free. The gown had been an inspired choice, accenting her slenderness, making her look taller than she was.

Someone had put her hair up in curls that cascaded down the back of her head beneath the blue bonnet. Smaller curls brushed her cheeks, accenting her dainty features, her delicate nose, her high cheekbones, her wide eyes.

Her face was whiter even than it had been the first day he arrived, when Edeline's death had shocked all color from her skin. She looked down at him. For the first time, he saw real panic in her eyes.

In two great steps, Damon reached the bottom of the stairs, ready to catch her if she collapsed on the way down. It would not be the first time he had rescued her on these very stairs.

But this time she made it on her own. Her eyes got larger with every step until they seemed to fill her whole face, her steps slowed, but the aunt kept hard on her heels. To ensure Verbena would not break and run back up?

He did not want to chance it, so held out his hand. And hoped she would take it. Once he had her hand in his, he had no intention of letting it go.

Letting *her* go.

17

Damon wore a black coat and blue trousers, white shirt and cravat. He was always handsome, but today looked so magnificent she could hardly believe she had had the courage to turn his first proposal down. And with such fervor!

He would never be washed out wearing dark clothes, not with his warm skin and black eyes. He had even made an effort to tame his curly hair, brushing the thick waves back from his forehead. He was so tall! She had walked beside him previously, had sat beside him, and never before had his height intimidated her.

But those other times, she had not been tying herself to him for life. Verbena tried not to shiver during the brief and sadly impersonal ceremony.

Impersonal except for Damon's hand gripping hers so tightly she could not move her fingers in his grasp, so tightly she almost thought he truly wanted this and was afraid she would run away if he let go.

Aunt Mabel stood behind them, her relief a visible and uninvited guest. 'A good match,' she had crowed almost like a chant ever since Damon had told her their news. At least one of them was happy.

What was he thinking? Words came at them, love, obedience, fidelity, children. Twice she saw Damon give a quick nod, but she could not tell to what.

When he said his vows, his eyes fixed on hers with almost frightening intensity. "I, Damon, take thee, Verbena, to my wedded wife, to have and to hold, for better for worse, for richer for poorer, in sickness and in health, to love and to cherish, 'til death us do part, according to God's holy ordinance; and thereto I plight my troth."

Then it was her turn. She tried to clear her throat but something seemed stuck there. "I, Verbena, take thee, Damon, to my wedded husband, to have and to hold, for better for worse." Her throat closed.

The vicar gave her a stern glance. "For richer for poorer," he prompted.

She had to take a deep breath before she could begin again. "For richer for poorer, in sickness and in health, to love, cherish, and to obey." Once again her throat went tight. *Obey.* What a frightening thought. Her life would never be her own.

"Til death..." The vicar seemed to be losing his patience.

Then the strangest thing happened. Damon lifted her hand to his mouth and placed the smallest of kisses there, his eyes holding her as warm as an embrace. The vicar cleared his throat in sharp reproof.

Damon's eyes twinkled, his mouth crooked upward in a mischievous smile and the tightness that had been near to choking her released. The words came out strong at last, "'til death us do part, according to God's holy ordinance; and thereto I plight my troth."

"You may kiss your wife."

Verbena gave a start. Neither moved for a moment. Damon breathed first, a strange sigh. He touched her face with the hand that had not been holding hers. His face drew nearer and nearer, and finally his eyes closed. Unless that was her own? She felt his breath first, faint as a whisper, before something even softer brushed her mouth. She did not know what to do in return. Did she pucker her mouth as she had as a young girl, pretending by kissing her own hand?

And then his lips melded with hers. So this is a kiss, she thought, before thought fled, his lips pressing warm and soft against hers for a powerful instant. He was shaking the merest bit, like a wire stretched too tightly.

He pulled away, and rested his head against her forehead for a moment. In a whisper for her ears only, he said, "That will have to do for now."

Then he straightened and shook the vicar's hand. "Thank you, good sir. I am most grateful."

In all that time, she realized, he had never let go of her hand.

DAMON FOUGHT the impatient urges to drum his fingers on his leg, shift restlessly, whistle, and whatever else would release the tension that kept building every time he looked across the carriage and saw his wife.

His wife. She was finally his, with all her blond hair and green eyes, her soft skin and sharp tongue and the prickles that made him want to tease her.

It had been a long day. After the wedding, they had all ridden back the way they came, up the hill to Aunt Mabel's house and the feast the servants had been working on during their absence, back to the packed trunks that held her gowns and clothes for Roderick.

Damon decided not to stay the night. They had been away from the other children too long.

He still had to tell his parents about the baby.

She insisted on changing out of the blue gown before they climbed into the carriage. "It is far too fine to wear riding in a carriage for hours. I could not bear it if anything happened to it."

It was a wrench to see Verbena back in the shabby, old dyed black gown. She would, of course, insist on the full six months of mourning for her sister, but after that he would deck her in the finest fabrics he could find. Perhaps a bit of feminine finery would help in his final goal. He had almost accomplished everything he had set out to do. Verbena as his wife, and the true heir back into the Thern fold.

Just like her mourning period, the real work was still ahead. He could tie her to him with legal vows, but that would not make her love him. Without that, their house would be as cold as the weather outside.

Damon looked out through the fogged glass window at the expanse of white that crowded close to the rutted road. They would have to find an inn suitable for a night's stay soon. For safety if nothing else, he would book them together in a single room. He sincerely hoped Verbena would not have a fit of the vapours when she found out.

A smile tugged at his lips. Verbena, have the vapours? Hardly.

A faint squeak from across the carriage pulled his attention back inside. The smile faded as Damon stared at the basket with the soft blankets he had managed to purchase before they left. He knew that under the bulk of coverings, Verbena was holding Roderick safe against her side. After raising her siblings single-handedly, it might take a while to convince her that men could be useful with babies, too.

He heard another whimper, the warning of coming wakefulness and wails. He had not held his nephew for more than a few minutes at each stop while Verbena was putting on her new fur cloak. She may have removed the blue dress, but she did wear the other gift.

He had set himself quite a task with his wife. He smothered a sigh, and looked out his own window.

Verbena shifted in her seat for the second time in that many minutes. Damon knew how she felt. His own bottom had been trapped in a carriage far too much this past week. "Yes, my dear?"

She smiled. A little one, but a smile nonetheless. "I think we need to find a suitable inn for the night. Roderick is getting hungry again and he needs to sleep in something that does not jounce."

Verbena turned to the small window. It was frosted around the edges and at the whim of some childish urge, she leaned over and blew on the glass. Her breath froze and blocked her view.

A soft chuckle from across the carriage seemed to tickle against the skin of her face. When she glanced over, Damon's gaze met hers, and sure enough, his eyes held a twinkle even though he had wiped away any smile.

How strange to be alone with him.

The carriage driver gave a call and Damon stood against the jolting over the frozen road and lifted the door in the roof. The carriage hit a hole and lurched hard. Damon grabbed the frame.

"A biggish town ahead, sir," the driver called back, his voice coming through the roof opening. Verbena scrubbed the frost off her window. Sure enough, a valley spread below them, filled with snowy roofs and chimneys billowing smoke.

"Find the best inn," Damon said clearly, and then sat down, wincing and rubbing his left leg.

She wanted to ask about the pain, but did not know if it would embarrass him. Verbena clenched her hands and tucked them back under the carriage robe. If they had courted and fallen in love, shared hopes and dreams, spent hours planning their future, she would know these things.

But they had not, and her stomach tensed. How long would it take before she knew what he expected, and just where her place was in this muddle?

"A town ahead," he said unnecessarily.

"Yes, I heard."

Conversation died again. The town closed around them with surprising speed. A prosperous town, she could tell, with window boxes under the windows, empty now but promising colors for the spring.

Verbena peeked out the small clear patch in the frost-rimmed window. "I have never seen a town this size with such wealth." She bit her lip. Maybe that was not the right thing to say. After all, she had already let him know what she thought of the Thern's attention.

"I know this place," he said with faint surprise, as if he had lost track of their route. "It belongs to a friend of mine. The family has found many ways to help support the shops here." Damon shifted on the seat, looked out the window and then looked back, clearly weighing his next words. She might not know him well, but she could tell that much. Verbena braced herself.

"Under normal circumstances there would be nothing amiss about stopping at my friend's house and asking lodging for the night, but I think it best that we stop at the inn, instead."

She waited.

A faint red seemed to creep up his cheeks. Of course, it might have been the way the lowering sun crept through the window. "I was not always the upstanding citizen you see today. When I was younger, I got in with some friends that – well, I have been thinking lately that it is time for me to cultivate a new group of associates."

Verbena forced herself not to smile. Apparently he was not aware that she might have heard of his less savory exploits. Damon the Demon, indeed! "I have no objection to an inn. It might well be the best place to find a nursing mother. Or at least find some milk. Roderick can't wait much longer."

EVERYTHING WAS SO simple when one had wealth, Verbena marveled anew. Damon's orders were fulfilled as quickly as he spoke them. Two bowls of boiled mutton stew and potatoes sat on the small table, along with a steaming pot of tea. Across the room, a plump woman was breastfeeding Roderick, and the poor babe nursed as if it were his last meal.

Damon had taken a room with a small fireplace. With impeccable tact, he had left her alone with the wet nurse, giving the woman privacy. The fireplace did not keep the room very warm, it really was small but the room was big enough for the largest featherbed she had ever seen, two chairs, and even a small table. Regardless, the meager relief of that much heat made her shudder.

To think that an inn would have a finer room and better furniture than her own house. Verbena looked down at her worn, dyed gown, and abruptly hated it with fervor. She groaned before she realized she had made a sound.

"Somethin wrong, ma'am?" The wet nurse looked over with open curiosity. She was a jolly woman, with brown hair up in a sloppy bun, a round face, and matching body that spoke of several other children at home. "Ye needn't feel bad that ye cain't nurse yer own babe. Many's the woman what could not."

Verbena managed a smile. "He is actually my older sister's child. She died in childbirth."

"I's truly sorry to 'ear that, ma'am." A moment of awkward silence fell as they both absorbed those stark words. Tucking her breast back under her bodice, the woman raised Roderick to her shoulder and began patting his back. "It's good o' yer man to take 'im in."

"Yes, it is indeed." Disregarding all the other complications, it was good of Damon.

If she was truly honest with herself, Roderick was not the only reason she had accepted him. He was just the reason she could safely admit to. It would hardly do to say she found Damon physically beautiful, with his piercing dark eyes, that thick black hair that curled over his forehead, his tall body, strong broad shoulders, and the warm deep voice that sent tingles through her. All he had to do was say something, and she was half in his power. A smile from him threatened to melt her completely.

Not that she would admit to it, of course. A woman had to have some pride. And right now, alone in the room with a stranger while he was off doing she knew not what, pride was all that held her together.

"Doubt ye'll ever 'ave to worry 'bout feedin the little tyke. That man looks like e can afford 'bout anythin." Roderick interrupted with a surprisingly loud burp. The wet nurse laughed and looked at the baby with motherly amusement. "E'll be ready for more, I'm thinkin." She put Roderick to the other breast, and was rewarded by having him take hold again. "Are there more at 'ome waitin to welcome this un?"

"No. We're just married." She did not dare say they had been married just that day.

"Oh." The woman was silent for a few minutes, as if weighing this odd arrangement. "Well, it be good yer man is willin to take the little tyke regardless, and that the weddin ain't been put off even with you in mourning an all, and 'ow nice the first babe be a boy. Me man an I got three boys, but me sister's only 'ad girls. Er man ud be glad fer a boy, no matter where it come from."

Verbena only nodded. "Can you come again in the morning?"

"'Course I can. Me own little un is up bright an early so I'll jest head on 'ere once 'e's done."

The woman finished, tucked Roderick into his basket, picked up the coins Damon had left for her, thanked Verbena profusely, and left.

A faint crust lined the edge of the stew, warning of cooling. Verbena paced the room, trying not to look at the bed, a very large bed compared to her old one, clearly designed for two, and caught herself picking at a stray bit of thread coming loose from the sleeve cuff. The sunset turned the room pale wintery gold, and her stomach began to rumble.

Damon still had not returned. He said he had friends here. Whatever he was doing, she had given him enough time to come back and join her for their meal. If he was anywhere near the inn, he should have seen the wet nurse leave and known he could come back up.

Verbena sat down at the table set for two and began to eat.

<hr>

THE BED WAS VERY small after all, when two people shared it. Verbena wished for sleep so she could stop thinking and wondering, wished for her heart to slow its hectic beat.

Damon's courteous explanation rang in her head. "I have decided that an inn is hardly the place for our first night. I want it to happen in my own house, with no interruptions to disturb us."

As if timed, a ribald shout drifted up from the dining room, words that made her blush. They both had winced at the same time.

"Do you see what I mean?"

She had nodded, and wondered even then, as she did now, if the waiting was worse than the smells and sounds.

Her husband had had no trouble falling to sleep. His deep, regular breathing whispered through the room during the fleeting moments of quiet.

The ceiling had a small crack running along one corner, barely visible in the light reflected from the busy crowd below. She had not noticed it before, but before there had always been something else to look at.

Maybe Roderick would wake and give her something to do while she waited for sleep to come.

They had two more days on the road. She was going to be very tired if sleep fled each of those nights.

She never thought she would be anxious to get to Thernwood.

18

———————

The Barnes' house loomed before them in the brittle twilight. Only the sunset gave any glow to the curtained windows.

"They are still up," Verbena said unnecessarily. Her teeth wanted to chatter, and not from the cold.

"They will be delighted to see you. And Roderick will no doubt be a comfort to them."

It should not seem strange that they were thinking the same thing. Roderick was, after all, the reason for this whole situation.

Damon's eyes were dark pools in the dimness of the carriage. "I think you do yourself a disservice. Undoubtedly you have eased them into other bad news over the years, and they have survived the telling." He leaned forward and grasped her hands. How his could be so warm when he was in this cold carriage, too, she did not know. Her fingers curled around his. She told herself it was just to grab what little heat they could.

The carriage slowed to a stop at the front door, the traces jingling like the clarion call of a thousand bells. Verbena looked down at Roderick in his basket, his little face so vulnerable and peaceful. Just the fact that his future now could be as peaceful as his sleeping face was all due to the man across the carriage from her, calmly preparing to climb out and confront her family with their startling news.

He was right. The children certainly would be delighted with this part of their news.

Damon climbed stiffly down the steps the coachman had flipped into place, and turned to hold out a hand. Verbena stared at him, her thoughts pulling at her. He gave her a quizzical look in response but held her gaze. His second hand joined the first as he lifted her out of the carriage and held her still in front of him, his grip firm on her waist.

Verbena tore her gaze away from Damon's as she turned and picked up the basket in which the baby was nestled in so comfortably. Another bit of credit for Damon, he had chosen well when he purchased it. Woven reed, it was so light and so well made carrying it was nearly like carrying nothing. Roderick whimpered inside his mound of blankets, but did not wake.

Damon rapped sharply against the doorpost, the sound echoing faintly. Standing before that familiar door, Verbena suddenly wondered why she was waiting outside in the cold. This was her house. Bracing the basket on one hip, she stepped around Damon and reached for the latch, but Damon caught her hand.

"No."

She looked up at him, confused. "But it is cold out here. There is no reason to keep Roderick outside, when it is – mmph." Damon touched a finger to her lips, and her words stopped, from more than just the sudden contact.

"No." The word was hard. Damon lifted his finger. "No, it is not, not any more. This house now belongs to your brother Julius while your father is away, and you will wait to be invited in."

The door opened just then, sparing her from any more thinking. Julius stood there in the small entryway. When she saw the girls jumping and squealing in the background, running for the door behind Julius, relief and love bubbled up. With a careful one-armed grasp on Roderick's basket, she caught each close, to hug and kiss and make up for the last long three weeks.

Annabelle pointed at the basket. "What is that?"

Before she could answer, Julius asked, "Where is Edeline? Why is she not here?"

"We have bad news, I fear," Damon said quietly. His somber voice told the boys all they needed to know. After a horrified look at Verbena, pleading for denial, Matthew dashed up the stairs, hiding rather than be seen crying. Julius was old enough to know how to hide his pain until out of public view. He stiffened, even his face going still until he could speak without his voice breaking.

Verbena mourned anew, and held the basket a little tighter. Details of the feminine mysteries of giving birth and the dangers with it were not for men or little girls, so all they said was, "Edeline died in childbirth." It was not an unusual tale.

As they passed the dining room, Mrs. Downs stepped away from where she had been bustling at the far end of the table, stacking and scraping. Her face was sober. "I weren't eavesdroppin, but I 'eard the news. I am so sorry. I worried 'bout 'er. She seemed to 'ave lost 'er will, you know?" She paused, picking up a plate as if she needed something to do. "Am I right in thinkin some congratulations be in order, the two of you comin together an all?"

"Yes. Thank you." There was no time for any more conversation, for which Verbena was grateful. Damon's hand in the small of her back moved her away. She was not ready to discuss this odd marriage she found herself in. Clamping her hands even tighter on the reed basket with its precious contents, Verbena made herself step into the parlor.

Acting very much the man of the house, Julius took their coats and draped them over the chair by the settee. "Are you hungry?" He stood with his hands behind his back. Verbena watched his arms flex and shift, and knew he was wringing his hands out of sight.

His lips trembled at the effort to maintain control. She looked away, and busied herself unwrapping Roderick, the basket balanced on the settee. His little eyes stayed tightly shut, but his mouth started sucking. In a few minutes, he needed to be fed yet again, but they had a little time to enjoy his curled-tight babyness. She picked him out, careful not to wake him before time.

Damon shifted the basket onto the floor and waved her to the settee. He did not join her but remained standing, his hands braced on the back of a chair. His knuckles were white as he gripped the wood.

For the first time in her life, Verbena found herself feeling awkward sitting in this so-familiar room. She tried to orient herself with the mundane.

Books lay scattered about. Hopefully that meant the children had managed to go to the village school per her instructions before she left. What looked like a pair of breeches liberally dusted with straw was draped over the back of a chair, probably from the last visit to the sheds for the eggs. That had probably been done recently, since she could not imagine Mrs. Downs with all her energy leaving dirty clothes sitting about very long.

"Is Edeline really dead? Just like Mother?" Annabelle crowded by Verbena's knee. Were it not for Roderick, Verbena thought her little sister would have climbed onto her lap for comfort. How she had missed them all!

Drawing her youngest sister as close as she could with Roderick in her other arm, Verbena murmured, "She left us the baby to remember her, dear. It is right to feel sad, but we want her baby to be happy, so we will all learn to laugh again." Tears crowded her throat, but she swallowed them back.

Roderick was wonderful distraction.

Julius cleared his throat and surprised her by saying, after that awful pause when everyone pretended he was not fighting his own tears, "I don't think she wanted to live without Andrew, anyway."

Matthew came back down, his face marred with red patches, his shoulders unnaturally stiff. He said nothing.

Damon did not attempt to draw him into the conversation, just let him blend into the group with his dignity intact. "We do have some good news."

"I think I can guess." Julius managed a smile.

"You are probably right." The two exchanged a manly look, then Damon looked around to the other children. "Verbena and I are wed. We would have liked all of you there, but there was not time."

"Yes!" Annabelle shrieked, and with the resiliency of childhood began jumping up and down. "I knew you would!"

Matthew perked up. "Really?"

"Do we get to keep the baby?" Trust Lizabeth to put her finger on the very reason for the marriage.

Damon smiled at her. "Yes, Lizabeth, we get to keep the baby. No one will ever take him away from us."

"Good!" The single word had so much conviction in it that Verbena had to bite her lip not to smile. "I like babies."

She looked around the room at the four children. Where did Damon mean to put them? He had made such promises when he pushed her into the marriage, schooling for the boys, good marriages for the girls, but he had never mentioned exactly where the children would live. Or had he? So much of that day was a blur. So many questions she should have asked then but was so sad and overwhelmed that she did not. Would he hire tutors to come here to this little house? Would he pay governesses to live nearby for the girls?

Our marriage will be between the two of us. Those words she remembered clearly. Damon could clothe the children and find tutors and still leave them here, in this tiny village.

Julius was almost grown. He belonged in school, not trapped raising the other children, picking up after the others, sweeping the floors or helping wash clothes. If he got too far behind in his studies, burdened with the weight of new responsibilities, Verbena did not know where he would end up.

Matthew with his constant restless energy, Lizabeth and Annabelle with their bickering. They all needed her. If Damon removed her to London and told her to leave them behind . . . the thought was terrifying.

Who knew when their father would be back? She thought of

what he would say or do if he came and found a tutor or governess in residence, and shuddered.

Damon turned to Julius, and said, "I think it best this house be closed. Do you think you can help the other children pack whatever they want to keep? I know this will come as a shock, but I am going to bring all of you with me to London."

Relief rushed through her. Her arms shook as they held Roderick, her lungs exhaled an audible breath as she looked around at her brothers and sisters. Four pairs of eyes were not looking at her at all, they were staring at her husband.

Lizabeth, not surprisingly, was the first one to find her voice. "London? Why do we want to go there?"

Damon smiled down at her. "That is where I live. Now that your sister and I are married, we will be living in the same house, and I want you to live with us. It is a nice house, and there are lots of things to do in London. There are museums and parks. You girls will have a governess, and she will teach you painting and languages and all manner of things."

He turned to the boys. "I need to assess your schooling, both you and Matthew. I have plans for the both of you, but first things first. Start sorting what things you do not want to leave behind before you go to bed. You can spend tonight here. I will leave Mrs. Downs to help the girls. She can stay for the night. Tomorrow the servants will come over and help you take whatever you have set aside to Thernwood, so it can be packed up with the rest of what we need to carry. I plan to stay a day or two there while we let poor Roderick recover before he gets loaded for another journey."

Roderick was not the only one who needed to recover from the trip, Verbena thought, and watched Damon with narrowed eyes. How like a man not to want to show weakness. If not for those white knuckles, she might not have noticed herself.

She would pay more attention from now on.

"Pack and get the house ready to close up." Damon shared his smile equally with all the eyes staring at him. "In a few days we will be off for London."

19

"THIS IS YOUR ROOM. THAT DOOR,"' DAMON POINTED TO A DARK wooden door in the middle of the wall that also held the fireplace, "leads to my room. I will let you get ready, and then I will come visit you." He gave a bow, slipped out and shut the door behind himself.

Verbena stood unmoving in the massive bedroom. The fireplace warmed her back, and candles stood on the two small night tables, one on either side of the bed. She could never have imagined being in a bedroom big enough for two chairs, three tables, an armoire and a bed the size of her kitchen. It was not just the size that was imposing. The wood it was made of caught the eye as well, a heavy dark wood, four poles so big around she could not circle them with her two hands, going up to form an open rectangle. At one time it might have been draped with a canopy, but the frame overhead was empty, which struck her as rather strange.

She could not take her eyes off that connecting door. His bedroom was just on the other side.

The tapes of her cloak were stuck in a hopeless knot. Verbena fumbled with it, picking at the ribbon, fighting to get the knot to unravel. Each tug made it worse. *Relax*, she ordered herself, and took a deep breath somehow, past the constriction of her lungs.

A knock at the hallway door startled her just as the cloak came free.

Two burly male servants stood outside, identically dressed in the family uniforms she had spotted often from a distance, carrying a large round basin, bigger than any tub she had ever seen. "Sir Damon said to bring your bath," one of them said, and they shuffled past her and into the room, setting the basin before the fireplace. A young maid followed them, carrying towels, a basket of small bottles that no doubt held perfumed oils, a small cloth that draped over the basket's edge, and a pale pink silk robe over her arm that shimmered in the light.

"Mr. Damon said this was for you, with his compliments." The young woman laid her burdens on one of the tables, turned the covers down across the whole width of the bed, and curtseyed.

A curtsey? For *her*?

"I can help you get those clothes, ma'am." The maid curtseyed again.

"Oh!" Verbena looked again at the young woman. She was not just a maid, she was a *lady's* maid.

The idea of anyone else being here as she got ready for her actual wedding night was appalling. "Perhaps not tonight, thank you." The girl's face fell. "What is your name?"

The maid's face brightened. "Mary, ma'am."

"Well, Mary, I'm certain I will be grateful for your help in the days ahead." Just not tonight, Verbena thought. Tonight her blushes were just for herself, not for the staff.

When the footmen left the tub full and steaming before the fireplace, Verbena hesitated, listening for any sounds from next door. She wanted that bath. It had been, oh goodness, how many days since she had been really clean? Her wedding day, maybe.

The basket held a small dish with soap. She flung off her gown, and peeled off her corset and stockings, grabbed the soap, towels and that pink robe, setting them close, then slipped into the water. Oh, it felt good! Warm but not too warm, and the soap a soft cake, perfumed even, so unlike the harsh lye and ash-base stuff she had always used.

Verbena lathered her hair first, rinsing it off in the tub, and smiled at the glistening suds that floated around her. She used the small washing cloth to smooth the bubbles over her skin, then slid down and leaned against the rim, letting the heat relax her muscles. A pail of water had been left for rinsing, and it must have been near boiling because it was still pleasantly warm when she stuck a finger in it to check.

She wanted to luxuriate in the water longer but sounds suddenly slipped through from Damon's room. Verbena froze, listening to two male voices and the tone of dismissal before the outer hallway door opened and shut. She stood quickly and poured the rinse water over her.

His valet was leaving. Damon would be here in seconds! Skidding on the floor, she grabbed frantically for towels and the pink robe.

No sooner had she wrapped the robe around herself and tied the belt, her hair wet down her back, when the door opened. Damon stood fully illuminated in candle and firelight, his features limned by the flickering flames. He crossed his arms and leaned on the jamb. He was a beautiful man, with his black hair and eyes as dark as the most moonless night. The long dressing robe covered his body, only his hands and forearms showing.

"You knew I was coming – that this was coming," he said softly, his deep mellow voice the first touch.

"Yes," she said just as softly, for really what else could she say? "Where is Roderick?" Anything, she thought, to change the subject, to delay what was coming.

"He is with the maids. They are nearly fighting over who will watch him." A smile tugged at his mouth. "Come, come, my dear.

You will not get rid of me that easily." Then he sobered. "How much do you know about what happens between a man and a woman?"

"Nothing," she answered. Maybe if he knew how very ignorant she was, he would go slowly and let her get used to this awkward intimacy. It was bad enough having a man walk into her room, even after the past two nights. But those hardly counted, since they had been dressed for both of them.

She knew he wore nothing under that dark brocade.

Oh, she was not ready for this! She wished she could turn the clock ahead until tomorrow when this was done and she knew all there was. But the only way out was through.

He crossed the room toward her. She wanted to stand still, to face him bravely, but she backed up despite her own wishes until her legs hit the edge of a chair close to the fireplace and she tottered.

Damon caught her hands before she went down, only he did not let go once she was steady. Or was she steady? Maybe she would never be steady again.

"Your hair is wet," he said, and smiled. "Give me the towel and I will dry it for you." He looked beyond her. "There must be a comb in that basket."

She did not know, she had looked for just the soap, but Damon was right. He shuffled through the bottles and came up with a silver comb.

A silver comb. It would have bought them food for a whole week, maybe longer, and she was going to pull that through her hair!

Only she did not use it. Damon did. He wrapped the towel around her hair and squeezed it section by section until she felt the cold wetness leave.

No one had combed her hair since her mother died. The gentle scratching of the teeth against her scalp sent tingles down her arms. He worked through the snarls with care, and she shoved aside the question of how he had learned to comb a woman's hair so gently. He was preparing her for what was to come, and she knew it.

This will be a real marriage, and I look forward to having more children of our own. Children. Her breath came faster as memories returned, Edeline, screaming as she fought to push out the baby. And herself, watching her sister's life drain away as she stood helpless, cradling the tiny newborn.

Damon must have noticed the change. He turned her around. "What is the matter? What has happened?" His hands moved from her shoulders to her arms, holding her still as he scanned her face.

"I'm afraid. I'm afraid of dying," she gasped out.

His fingers tightened. "Dying? There is nothing – Oh. I see." His face softened. Pulling her gently against himself, Damon wrapped his arms around her. His voice crooned in her ear, "Oh, my dearest, I can only imagine what you went though." His hands stroked up and down her back. "I did mention children. I cannot promise that I will not make you pregnant tonight, but I can promise that you will receive the best of medical care."

Then he smiled ruefully. "This is hardly the discussion for our wedding night. Before we get to pregnancy and birth, we need to consummate our union, and consummation is," he gave her a roguish smile, "wonderful. So, if we can go back to where we were?" He did not give her a chance to answer, just leaned down and claimed her mouth.

"Augh!" The sudden bellow startled Verbena out of sleep. She sat bolt upright, her heart pounding, wondering what pulled her awake. Cold air bit at her skin. Her eyes would not open but, when she wrapped her arms around herself, she realized she was naked.

The night came back in a rush, and heat, the only heat in the entire room apparently, flooded her cheeks. She flopped back down and tugged the covers over herself. Maybe sleep would claim her again, and she could dream about the night's wonders.

Her lips curved upward. Who could have known the sweetness in the marital bed? In spite of the other travails in this marriage, the smile did not go away.

"Gaw!"

Her eyes flew open.

Damon rolled to his side, groaning with pain. Verbena recognized the sound of agony, and popped back upright. She watched in dismay as he lay taut, his hands tight fists holding the sheets like a lifeline, his jaw clenched so tightly she feared his teeth would crack.

"Damon! What is the matter? What happened?" She reached out but, afraid to cause more pain, her hand hung suspended just above his shoulder. "Damon?"

"Don't look," he begged past those clenched teeth, and turned his own head away as if humiliated.

"Don't be silly." Verbena looked around for her robe. He remained turned away, still wrapped up in his pain. Her legs wobbled when she slid out of bed, another surprise. When she got the robe tied, she looked back at him.

And caught her gasp.

The covers around him had slipped away with his tortured thrashings. The leg was the worst, his poor, damaged leg, a deep gouge of torn muscle where a bullet must have traveled, several small holes where others had gone straight in, and a small puckered hole just above his hip, matching another ugly ring several inches away. She did not need to have been in battle to know what those two circles were, an in-and-out path from yet another bullet.

Amazing that he could even walk. As he lay, fighting pain, his head still turned away, his eyes pressed tightly shut as if he could ease the pain if he could not see the wound, he held the leg stiff, the muscles pulling so tight she could see each one, thick uneven ropes, bumps of spasms standing out under the reddened skin.

Someone had shot Damon when he was already wounded, she knew it with a rage that shook her own body. Had he rolled away to keep the bullet from hitting his heart? Is that why it had almost miraculously hit in such an innocuous part of his side?

He would not want pity. He needed relief, and thanks to the bottles of lotions, and the time she had spent learning to ease her dying mother's pain, *that* Verbena knew she could provide. There would be time later to weep for the hurt he had endured.

Compassion washed through her. Her poor, brave, wounded husband. She had wanted to learn more about him. It appeared she would get her wish and then some.

They needed warmth. She replenished the fire and pulled the screen into place, then turned toward the basket still on the table by the fireplace. Good. The lotions would be warm.

She lifted out the colorless one, and pulled out the stopper, to be knocked back by a wash of thick scent of flowers and femininity. Stoppering it as fast as she could, Verbena waved the fumes away from her nose and pulled out another, and another, each more flowery than the previous. The last one, a small pot, finally was what she needed, a smooth, thick white paste, and thankfully little smell.

Verbena carried it to the bed and, gathering her courage, climbed up to kneel by his side. She scooped out a small palmful, rubbed her hands together to soften it and leaned over him. He jolted at her touch.

"Shhh," she whispered. "Just relax." She slid her hands down over his knotted leg. He exhaled, and a shudder rippled along his skin.

Verbena froze. Was that good, or bad? His jaw was not quite so tight, she thought, and it gave her heart. White paste melted into his skin as she worked down his thigh, calf, ankle, leaving them shiny.

Shiny and smoother, the knots gradually released under the steady pressure of her rubbing. The clock ticked, and a log snapped apart in the fireplace. How long had she been at this? Her hands were aching. Funny, she had not felt it until now.

Quiet, slow breaths told her Damon had fallen asleep. At last.

Verbena rubbed away the remnants of her handful on her own skin, and grabbed the blankets from the bottom of the bed, pulling them over him to keep him warm.

She climbed in with her robe pulled tightly around her, and huddled under the covers until the heat from his body warmed her.

This is nice, she thought on a yawn, and closed her eyes.

20

DAMON STRETCHED, AND OPENED HIS EYES TO SEE A TOTALLY unfamiliar ceiling. It had been a while since he had not recognized the room he woke in. He went still when he realized he had stretched without pain. He enjoyed the loose, relaxed feeling, and tried stretching again, to have his fingers brush against something soft, wrapped in silk.

Verbena.

He had shared her bed last night without a thought of moving to his own room. At the memory of what had happened here, Damon smiled. He was well and truly married. Whatever happened outside the bedroom, at least inside her bed he was quite content.

Rolling to his side, he propped his head on one hand and watched her sleep. A slender mound running down the bed, she lay facing him. Her lips were soft and still puffy from the kisses of last night, her cheeks glowed pink in the soft light. Strands of hair slipped down along her jaw and across her neck, tickling her even in her sleep. One slender hand came out from under the covers and brushed at the annoying itch. Soon it would wake her, and he was not ready for that. He was not done looking. Damon caught the tendrils and slid them behind her ear, careful not to touch, tempting as it was.

His finger hovered over her skin, tracing in the air the shape of her jaw, showing determination in such a tiny woman. Her cheeks a beautiful color, the palest ivory with the softest hint of pink, but too thin. Rest and good food would take care of that. Moving on, his finger went, close but not touching, to her nose, so pert and so refined, and her lashes, dark on a woman so fair. Lastly her brows, just darker than her hair, lighter than her lashes, and so expressive, a perfect frame for the summer-green eyes and, he had learned, softer than he could have imagined.

A shiver told him it was time to get up. Damon got out of bed, careful not to wake Verbena. The air outside the covers was sharp with cold. Shivering in his robe, Damon stirred through the blackened chunks in the grate, each sound seeming as loud as thunder. Surely Verbena would hear and wake, but the bed was still, her shape unmoving.

A thread of orange peeked through the black. Damon fed it kindling from the basket until the coals went red, and a tiny finger of flame stretched up into the icy air of the fireplace. He held his hands out to catch the first tendrils of warmth. A sound from the bed made him turn.

Verbena yawned, gave a mighty and unladylike stretch under the covers, then froze in that silly position like a deer who senses trouble. She looked up, staring at him with huge startled eyes.

They gazed at each other for a long, heavy moment. Red rushed up her face.

Damon enjoyed the sight and let it go unremarked. "Good morning, wife." He leaned against the mantle and just looked at her, enjoying the rumpled sunlight strands and her bleary green eyes. "If I woke you, I apologize, but we must collect your brothers and sisters today."

She rubbed her eyes as if trying to brush away the sleep. "What time is it?"

Damon looked for a clock. "Nearly eight."

"Nearly eight!" Her mouth gaped. "I have never slept this late!"

"We have an excuse, don't you agree?" He grinned at her.

The color that had begun to fade came back. She shifted the subject. "Is your leg better today?"

Damon bowed to her. "Yes, it is much better, and I thank you. I see I married, not just a beautiful woman but a woman of many skills. I believe I have chosen well." He walked over and sat down on the edge of the bed, suddenly sober. Perhaps he should have done this with more ceremony. "I want people to know at a glance that we are wed."

Leaning over, he pulled open a drawer under the rim of the table next to the bed and lifted out a small black velvet pouch tied with satin strings. It looked feminine and out of place in his large hand. "I meant to give this to you last night, but other things drove it from my mind."

He untied the string and pulled the sack wide.

VERBENA CAUGHT a glint of shiny yellow, and held her breath, not wanting to breathe for fear the moment would vanish like a bubble, she would wake and find this just a dream.

His large fingers pulled the shiny circle out and her eyes filled with tears, staring at what he held. He set the pouch aside. Almost lost in his hand sat a solid gold band, wide but not ostentatious.

When he looked up at her, his face was both determined and vulnerable. "I know I did not ask you what kind you would like, I don't even know what your tastes are yet, but this reminded me of you, both strong and delicate. It was from my grandmother's jewelry, held for when I wed." He reached for her left hand. It shook, she could not make it stop. "It is yours."

He lifted her hand to his lips and pressed a kiss on the finger where the band would go. "Now the world will know how much I value you," he whispered as he looked up at her through the ebony curls that always tumbled over his forehead.

It was cold as it slid over her knuckles, but it fit perfectly, and began to warm with her body's heat. How had he known her finger size?

She felt his eyes like a touch, but could not take her gaze from that golden band. Everywhere she went now, people would look at her and know that she was wed. No one would be able to call her a dirty name.

A silver drop fell on her hand, shimmering like a jewel there. Value. He valued her. He was suddenly playing father to nearly-grown young men and being followed around by two little girls whose very name was an affront to his own family, taken on his brother's child, and he *valued* her.

She scrambled to her knees on the bed, and reached for his face, holding it in her hands – her *strong and delicate* hands – and looked at him, into his dark eyes that were like pools of midnight, pulling her inside to drown and be safe. His lips began to curve, and she leaned close until she could taste them, pressing her mouth against his, trying to thank him in the only way she had to give.

He did not move for a frightening moment and she felt a flash of fear and embarrassment, then suddenly his arms came around her, holding her tight.

THE CHIMING of the clock reminded him of all the work still ahead. "I am going to dress. There is a lot to do before we leave for London, starting with collecting your brothers and sisters this morning. I want plenty of milk for Roderick to carry him through today and most of tomorrow, carriage robes for all the children, and food for us. Do you have carriage blankets over at the house to bring for them?"

Verbena shook her head, and frowned, but it did not stay long. "You know we don't." Her gaze slid back to the ring.

Going through his grandmother's jewelry had been a stroke of genius, he thought smugly. "I'm going to have the staff check through the attic for clothes from my brother and myself for the boys. I think we might find something up there that would fit for the girls as well. There must be trunks filled with my sisters' outgrown dresses."

That was the wrong thing to say. Her dreamy expression vanished. "You can't think of giving away clothes from your family without asking permission! You are going to cause us trouble!"

Damon scowled at his wife. "In the first place, any clothes for your brothers would be mine and my brother's. He is dead, and I certainly have the right to give my clothes to whomever I wish. As far as my sisters, why would they mind? They are both out of the schoolroom and far too stylish now to care about the children's clothing they wore ten years ago."

He heard the sharp edge in his voice. With a calming breath, he continued more quietly, "I doubt Margaret and Catherine will even recognize them. We just need clothes that fit until we can get to the tailor's and modiste's and get everyone fully garbed. Once their own clothes come, if you wish you can box these back up and ship them back here."

He took her hands, running a thumb over the ring he had just placed there. "It is both my pleasure and privilege to take care of your brothers and sisters. This is not a burden for me. I like them, all of them, and I have plenty to share. Please let me do it."

Verbena watched his thumb move over the ring she already loved. *Pleasure and privilege.* No one before Daman had been the least bit interested in her because of the children. She had never received so much as an invitation to go for a walk. The very least she could do was give in gratefully. And hope she was wrong about the antipathy between their families. "Very well. I am certain the children will think they are in heaven."

Roderick had been left at Thernwood with a couple of delighted maids who would much rather cuddle a baby than mop floors. It was a wrench to leave him with anyone belonging to the Therns, but Verbena suspected there would be bigger battles ahead. Besides, they would be back soon.

The children were happily eating when she and Damon arrived at what had been her house. The breakfast spread across the scuffed table was nearly identical to the one she had eaten, or at least tried to eat, in the small, elegant breakfast room at Thernwood: eggs, bacon and ham, muffins and sweet rolls with currant preserves.

Their meals would likely be this fine from now on. Verbena found that hard to imagine, endless food that someone else had cooked, dishes that someone else would have to clean up.

Verbena watched a maid – a real maid in her house, fancy that! – scurry around the table, refilling familiar worn, chipped mugs with milk, serving eggs from gilt-edged plates with silver serving spoons that had clearly been carried over from Thernwood

She looked at the old dishes her siblings were eating from. They were like those little cracked dishes, poor and worn and faded. Soon they would be surrounded by well-dressed, fancy people as elegant as the furnishings that surrounded them.

The children had no idea what was ahead of them. They had never even been in Thernwood, seldom even seen it from outside. It was shielded by trees and they were held away by the fences.

Frankly, even after a night at Thernwood, footmen carrying in her bath, a maid offering to help her undress, not even she knew exactly what lay ahead.

It had to be better than what they were leaving behind. By the end of the day, they would have decent clothes. She looked around the room, and remembered how hard she had worked in the kitchen cooking whatever they could afford, how often she had scrubbed the floors on her knees. She had sat in the parlor and patched pants, cut and stitched old gowns into dresses for the girls.

And done without.

She felt the first stirrings of excitement. Those days were over. Thank God.

And thank Damon. But that did not mean she was not nervous. Scared was a better word. Edeline's tales were stuck in her brain like a bell bouncing from the hills. They might fade for a while, but like an echo they kept coming back.

As she looked at him, Damon directed his attention to the children sitting around the table. "How is the packing coming?"

Lizabeth propped her hands on her hips. "I don't want to go to London. Why do we have to leave?"

"Me, neither," Annabelle piped in, with a rare agreement.

"I already explained that to you yesterday. I live there." He smiled down at them, his gaze going from one to the other, but Verbena could tell he had not expected this outright rebellion.

London was much larger than this small village. It had to be much easier to avoid the Therns there. "Girls, you will have a wonderful time in London."

"I want to go." Every head turned to stare at Julius. "Well, I do. I never thought I would be able to see it, and now that I can, I'm glad."

"Damon is kindly sending more servants over to help you carry whatever you wish to bring to London, so go get whatever you chose last night." Fixing the children with a narrow-eyed stare, Verbena added, "Now."

The girls looked between her and Damon, and slid away from the table. Julius and Matthew followed.

As they dragged themselves away, the maid came back to the table from the counter where she had been trying to be invisible and began collecting the mugs. Verbena took a knife and scraped the breakfast leavings off the nearest bowl. "I will get the dishes ready for you, we can get it done in twice the time," she said to the maid.

Damon firmly took the bowl from her hand and returned it to the table. "Come with me." He marched her into the parlor and pulled the doors shut, then faced her, his folded arms straining the seams of his coat. "Verbena." He shook his head. "You don't have to do that work anymore.

That work. She could not read his voice, did not know him well enough to tell if there was a hidden meaning in the words. Was he ashamed of her? "I have worked in this house my whole life. It feels strange to sit around and do nothing." Verbena rubbed her forehead against the sudden twinge of headache.

Damon crossed to her. His hands came down warm and heavy on her shoulders, his fingers soothing the tense muscles there. "I know. But I am trying to make your life easier. Everything you used to do, I have servants to do for you now. You don't need to divide your attention like you used to, raising the children, cooking, cleaning, washing and mending. All you have to do now is raise Roderick."

Verbena thought she saw a bit of emptiness in the world ahead of her. She did not mind *less* work, in fact relished the possibility. But if she did not do something useful, would she lose herself? "I don't think I know how to be indolent." Her jumbled emotions fought for words. "Damon, I've done this very work ever since I was old enough to reach the tabletop. It is good, honest work, and I will not ever apologize for doing it."

He drew back. "I never said anything to make you feel you had to apologize."

Verbena grabbed his hands, and clutched them tight, holding him so he would not move any further away. She would not think about how easy it was now to touch him, even for something so innocuous. "No, you never have. I just want you to be aware that this is not easy for me. I realize I will make foolish mistakes. Before you carry us off to London, you need to know how patient you must be."

Somehow their hands shifted, and he was now holding onto her. He squeezed her hands. "Now you are being a snob in reverse. You are far more refined than you realize, my dear. Trust me when I say, you will fit in."

Without warning, he gave her a quick kiss. Resting his forehead against hers when their lips separated, his breath tickling her mouth, he murmured, "If I had been ashamed of you, why would I have asked you to marry me?"

"For Roderick," she answered without thinking, wishing she could take the words back as soon as they left her mouth. They were unworthy of her, unworthy of him.

He had already let go. "Yes. Roderick. Of course. By all means, let us not forget Roderick." He sighed and moved back another step, out of arm's reach, running a hand through his hair, tousling the night-dark waves.

Feet clomped above them.

Damon ushered her out of the parlor in a rush and pulled the double doors shut. It was too late to apologize.

They were standing in false calm when the children came down with their scant prized possessions wrapped in lumpy scarves.

Verbena looked at those pitiful bundles and was fiercely glad to leave.

* * *

VERBENA LOOKED at the room before her. Damon's hand rested lightly on her shoulder. Like a true wedded couple, she thought. No one watching could possibly guess how awkward they were together.

"I thought the boys could stay here tonight," Damon said in a matter of fact tone, not even looking at her. She could hardly blame him. "This was Andrew's room," he continued. "Mine is next door. The girls' rooms are across the hall."

It looked masculine. And large. The decoration was plain, the bed and matching armoire were unadorned and cut out of some dark wood. Just to add to the somberness, the walls had been painted deep green.

"Verbena, Damon says we are staying here until it is time to go to London. Can you believe the size of the bed?" Matthew pulled open the armoire doors without even asking permission.

Verbena gasped. "Matthew! Don't open things without asking permission first. We are guests here!"

Damon's hand tightened. "I don't mind, Matthew," he said, his voice calm as a summer lake. "What do you think about going to London in style?"

The footmen walked in just then, a mound of breeches and shirts, waistcoats and coats in their arms. Matthew's eyes went huge.

"I want you and Julius to pick out enough for the trip to London and at least another two weeks after that." Damon turned her around toward the door. "There will likely be clothes for the girls in the room next door, Verbena. I will help your brothers go through their clothes if you would be so good as to check what was found for the girls."

"Yes, Verbena," Matthew agreed, hardly able to drag his attention from the wealth of clothes waiting on the bed. "We can't get dressed with you watching us."

Damon stepped out into the hallway with her, pulled the door mostly closed, and took her arms. "I want you to remember, Verbena, I knew what I was doing when I asked you to marry me. Everything will be fine." He drew her closer, and closer, until the tips of her shoes brushed against his boots. She stared up at him. They were in the hallway! Anyone could see!

He ran a finger down her nose, stepped back, and turned her toward the room across the hall. "Go help your sisters."

Verbena pulled the opposite door open and stopped short. It was pink. Pink walls, pink curtains, pink coverlets. Even the wooden bedframe had a distinct pink wash. The room was a veritable pink frame for the display of garish wealth that confronted her. The girls' beds were laden far heavier than the boys'. Her little sisters were pulling gowns off the pile as fast as they could grab.

"Look, Verbena!" Two excited voices spoke in unison.

Annabelle held out a gown. "I want this one. Damon says we can have anything that fits. Can I have this one? Can I, please?"

Beribboned gowns in every color imaginable and petticoats with ruffles, bonnets and miniature pelisses mounded both beds. Verbena was horrified that any girls could own so many gowns when she and her sisters had barely managed two or three apiece.

This was not about her, she thought, not about her struggles with the past. This was about now, and now the girls' faces were glowing. Verbena felt a smile start down in the middle of her chest as she watched them dig through the mass of colors and fabrics.

Annabelle already had her own worn dress off, all the morning's careful combing of her hair totally ruined in her eagerness, but that first coveted gown did not fit. Nor did the second or third, but the fourth was perfect. Lizabeth was not far behind her sister, making two increasing piles of clothing, those that fit and those that did not.

It was not long before bubbles of laughter started. Verbena felt herself joining in helplessly. Gowns too large had to be put on and paraded, even if the sleeves slid off shoulders and sashes could go around twice. Gowns too small became headdresses or oddly shaped shawls. She could only make sure that nothing was damaged, but as long as the girls were careful, she let them have their play.

There had not been enough of that in their lives, Verbena thought as she folded another discarded gown. She could not stop herself from sliding a finger along the shiny ribbons, and caressing the delicate lace.

A knock came at the door. "Come in," she called.

She was not surprised to see Damon.

"Damon! Damon!" Annabelle bounced up to him and twirled, her brown hair flying. "See my new gown? It is so pretty! I have never had anything so pretty in my whole life."

Lizabeth would not be outdone. She scampered over, and shook out her own skirt. "I took two pink ones and a yellow one, and two green ones, and this blue one. And we are not even done," she said, and pointed back to the bed. "See that pile? It is all mine." Verbena was struck by Lizabeth's unerring sense of what would look good with her blonde hair.

Damon smiled down at both of them. "I'm glad you found things that fit. You won't need many for now, just enough for the trip and a few days until you get the rest of your clothes made. I'm going to have a whole wardrobe sewn for both of you when we get to the city."

Annabelle and Lizabeth exchanged glances with silent "oh's" of acquisitive delight. Verbena watched them, and the look on their faces gave her concern. She was not going to let them become greedy, and surrounded by this sudden luxury, her task was going to be a big one.

Damon turned to her, pulling her away from her heavy thoughts. "I will send a maid up and we can give them the ones to wash for the journey. We will leave tomorrow or the next day, depending on how fast we can get everything ready." He turned both girls around and eased them toward the bed again. "It is going to be cold on the journey, so make certain you have nice warm pelisses."

With the girls' attention again distracted by the mound of clothes, Damon reached for Verbena's hand. "Come with me, wife. The maid will help the girls find whatever else they will need."

He hustled her out of the room and into the dim hall, tugging her along behind him as they passed door after door. Verbena looked at the back of Damon's head, that rich curling hair. Now she knew how it felt against her fingers, how silky it was. Who would imagine a man's hair could be so soft? She knew, too, the taste of his lips. Knew and craved them. Every moment, he burrowed further into her life.

He stopped in front of a door, heavy wood like all the others in the hallway. "On the other side of this door is an armoire filled with gowns." He pressed her hands together like a prayer. "Yes, they are from my sisters, but this is the closet where all their discards go. They may not be in the latest styles, but any of them is better than what you own. The two decent gowns I bought for you are not enough to carry you until the London modiste can finish a new wardrobe. Forgive me for being so blunt, but we both know it is true." One eyebrow cocked, and his eyes challenged her.

She swallowed, remembering the feel of the ribbons between her fingers.

His hand closed over the handle. "I know how much you hurt. I share that. We both have suffered the same loss. Before you feel you must reject this gift out of hand, no one will expect you to wear black indefinitely, so think of the colors you like best, and don't be afraid to pick your favorites." He pushed the door open.

Verbena stepped inside. A white-canopied bed with matching curtains draped down each of the heavy carved posts and drawn away on the sides, a massive armoire twice the width of the one in her room, a lovely table with a mirror above and a stool whose pristine skirting matched the curtain around the bed.

Damon strode over to the armoire and opened it. A rainbow of colors, pinks and blues and greens and golds, ruffles and petticoats, silk and satin puffed out at him as if they had been chained behind the door. Verbena wondered how they ever got the doors shut, and if Damon would be able to close them once she was done.

She faced him, trying to ignore the profusion of glorious colors and fabrics at the edge of her vision. She had never owned such beauty. She had never expected it to be this hard to do the right thing. There was a limit to how much of herself she would give up. "I must do something for mourning. She was my sister, and I loved her."

He just looked at her for a moment, then nodded once. "I wore an armband for Andrew for months. However, we have to get to London. I will order you mourning clothes once there. This is just for now."

Damon shoved at the ruffles, swatting bits aside as he dug through the colors. He pushed another swath of fluff aside, looking bewildered as he gazed at the feminine frippery before him. "To think, this is only part of their wardrobe," he muttered. "Good lord."

He turned back to her. "Pick out something you like. I know there must be respectable colors in there." His eyes finally twinkled. "I know my way around corsets and ribbons. I will be happy to help you dress."

She straightened her shoulders, and walked toward the armoire. "I will pick out a few on my own," she said, and waved him away. "There is no need for you to watch."

"I have no intention of just watching," he said with a wicked grin as he moved over toward the curtains, to pull them apart and let the faint winter daylight come through the thin lace curtain hiding behind the heavy ones. "You select what you want to try on, and I will play maid." He left the window and walked over to the bed to flop down onto it, staring up at her with those keen black eyes. "Come, my dear. No one will interrupt."

"Damon!" Verbena felt the heat rush up her face.

"Verbena," he mimicked. "We are fighting against time. We are married. I have seen all there is of you, there are no more secrets." Sitting up, he made to rise. "Pick out a dress, Verbena, or I will pick one for you."

She turned back to the armoire. It took a moment, but finally the jumble of colors, of blues and primroses and jonquils and puces and emeralds, began to separate into individual gowns with their own styles, some with collars around the back of the gown plunging into low-cut bodices, some with longer, close-fitting sleeves, others with soft, ruffled styles that just covered the shoulders, some with embroidery all over the dress, others with hems of any manner of design from ruffles to braiding. Muslin, silk, lawn, cotton, and a few she would have sworn were wool, but not like any wool she had ever felt, soft and fine as a breath of air.

She took a breath, and reached into the pile.

THE HOUSE WAS FILLED with happy conversation and laughter as they all sat down for supper. If breakfast had been elegant, supper was beyond lavish. Verbena stared in amazement at all the food that had been cooked just for them. Fish, chicken, mutton, Yorkshire pudding, not even mentioning the sauces and a fruity cordial for the older ones, served in etched stemware glasses that caught the candlelight. She watched the children anxiously, wishing she dared whisk most of the dishes away, afraid they would get stomach upset from all the rich foods.

"What is London like?" Lizabeth asked between bites.

"Big.' Damon smiled at her. "It is people and buildings as far as you can see. Parts of the city are beautiful, with parks and trees and flowers growing in boxes under the windows. There are stores selling everything you can imagine." He turned to Julius. "Bookstores fairly litter the streets. You will never run out of things of read."

Then he sobered and looked around the table. "I want you all to listen to me. You are used to being able to roam outdoors. That is not possible in London. There are pickpockets and footpads roaming the crowds to fleece you of whatever you carry, so when I say you must never go out unaccompanied, I mean it."

The children stopped eating and gazed at him. Even the boys were sober.

Annabelle had a puzzled frown on her face. "What do the feet wear?"

Damon blinked at her, then glanced over at Verbena for translation. It even took her a moment to decipher. "Footpads, darling. I don't know why they are called that, but they are dangerous men who live by stealing from other people."

"Did their mothers never teach them better?" Annabelle asked innocently, looking between Damon and Verbena with her big blue eyes.

Damon bit the inside of his cheek, Verbena felt a giggle threaten, but swallowed it down. "Likely not." She did not dare meet Damon's eyes for fear they both would lose control.

A couple deep breaths later, once again somber, Damon continued. "We have a long journey ahead of us. It will take us at least three days to reach London, and along the way we will be stopping at inns. Everything I said about London applies to them. No one goes around the inn unaccompanied by myself or one of the outriders. I will do my best to get us rooms together, but that might not be possible, depending on how full the inn is. Each and every one of you will do exactly as I say. If I tell you to stay in your room, you will do that. And when I say we have to leave immediately, anything that is not back in the bags is left behind. Is that clear?"

"I don't know why we are even going, if it is that bad," Matthew muttered from where he sat across from Verbena.

Damon must have heard, because he fixed Matthew with a fierce glare. "My home in London is in one of the best areas, so when we get there, we will be as safe as I can make it, but only a fool ignores danger signs. I trust none of you children are fools." He looked around the table. "I want you with me. I have plans for your futures, good ones that will guarantee security for the rest of your lives, but that can't happen here. Some day when you are older I want you to look back on this move as a happy one."

He put his spoon down. "Tomorrow morning, the trunks will be packed. My goal is to begin our trip by midday, no later. Can we do that?"

Five faces looked at him, serious under the current of excitement, and nodded.

21

———————

The carriage creaked and groaned as it lumbered up the hill. Inside the box, Verbena looked around at the tightly packed group and tried to calm her nervous stomach. Damon had promised when they awoke this morning that they would reach London today. Word had been sent to his London home the first day of their journey, so rooms should be ready.

Servants. Her own servants. Every time she thought of that, her heart fluttered with incipient panic.

In a way, she was glad the trip was almost over. Despite the luxury of riding in a carriage, the trip had not been comfortable. The three males sat on one seat while she, the girls, and Roderick in his tidy little basket had the opposite seat, as they had for the past four days. Each morning they all took their respective places in the carriage. Carriage seats, Verbena discovered watching the men opposite, were not meant to sit three adults comfortably, and the boys really were adult-size. Elbows and shoulders had become annoying.

At least they had managed to stay relatively warm, far warmer than she expected. Damon had provided them with the thickest of bearskin carriage blankets. While they all might have been warm under the blankets, the air around them was crisp. The windows were fogged from all their breathing. Stops for nature's calls had become welcome breaks if only to be able to bend arms. She had seen Damon and the boys stretching and flapping to get the kinks out before they climbed back in.

The inns had been better than she expected. Granted, few places were prepared for a baronet's son to arrive with four children, a wife and a baby, so one or two nights they had slept in tight quarters, but the beds were clean, the sheets smelled fresh, and no one left itching.

All in all, a successful journey.

They crested a hill and the carriage air was sucked away in a collective gasp as chimneys rose above the horizon, row after row of shadowy square spokes spewing black into the darkening sky. Buildings spread as far as they could see. A grey haze hung over the air.

Misgivings rose again, giving Verbena a moment of panic. They were driving into gloom. How could anyone see the sun in this place?

"Is that London?" Julius asked in a hushed voice.

"Yes. You will love it." Damon smiled at him first, then the rest of them, rubbing his hands as if in glee. "I intend to get you tickets to Astley's Amphitheatre with more horses and dogs than you ever saw before. After that, I thought we would go to the opera."

They were here and there was no turning back. Verbena looked at Damon and wanted some of his enthusiasm.

He grinned at the girls across the carriage. "You have not heard music or singing until you have been to the opera." He turned his attention to the boys at his side. "It can't be described, it has to be experienced. I know this is a change for you, but once you start school, you will make new friends. Eton in particular is designed to accept those without privilege, so you don't need to worry about fitting in, and you won't be far away."

The children nodded and went back to staring out the frosty glass.

"We are coming in on the West End," Damon said, and leaned back in satisfaction. "It is by far the nicest part of London."

By 'nicest,' Verbena thought as she watched him, read 'wealthy,' and sure enough, town houses soon appeared, some set far back on snow-covered swaths of grass.

And, much to her relief, there were trees. Not the forests around Thernwood, for which her heart suddenly ached with a sharp sense of loss, but at least something green did grow here. If plants could survive, maybe the children could manage, as well.

Verbena sat up straighter. Ever since Damon had announced the trip to London, the city itself had felt like another load for her to bear. Looking around the carriage at her family, Verbena tried to find a bit more courage. She had taken over the children when Mother died, and she had been much younger then. She had traveled off to take care of Edeline, and survived her death as well.

Damon looked across the carriage at her. His dark gaze sharpened, and Verbena could not look away. She did not like the frightening sense of surrender, but she could no more break the connection than she could make herself invisible. She lifted her chin, trying for a semblance of her old confidence, and smiled.

Damon's eyes softened, and he gave a quick nod. "That's the way, my girl," he murmured so softly that she knew none of the children heard.

For the first time since nearing London, Matthew perked up. He pressed his face against the glass window and gaped. "Lookit how fast they go!" He flinched as a small two-wheeled vehicle whipped past so close Verbena was surprised the two vehicles did not get tangled together and overturn.

When the sporty little gig had rattled out of sight, Matthew sat back, staring dreamily ahead, no doubt planning his own race down the street.

The further in they went, the thicker the city became, streets crossing each other like tangled yarn. They turned down one of those streets, getting a closer look at those houses, stretching tall, three and four stories high, curtained windows on every floor.

Wherever there were not houses, there were tall stone walls that held the sidewalks at bay and kept eager eyes from peeking in.

At the end of one street, a four-story house edged with a stone fence dominated the corner, the house set back far enough for a span of snow-clumped grass and a tall, sweeping tree. A walk led up some stairs to the door, with elegant scrolled wrought iron railings stark against the white background.

The carriage slowed, the driver called, "Whoa," and it gave a settle, adding a final punctuation to the journey. Leather reins slapped as the horses shook their heads, a sound with which she was now quite familiar.

"Take a look, everybody. Your new home. *Our* new home." Damon's good spirits added sunshine to the carriage.

Verbena took a bracing breath and made herself look objectively at their new home, or what was visible in the last rays of twilight. Three stories? Or was that four? Steps led up to the door, which might take off some height inside. This was the kind of house, she decided, that should be seen in the bright of day. Designs appeared to embellish the brick front, but they were hard to see in the fading light. She would have to go outside tomorrow at noon and get a better look. What it must be like in the summer, when the trees were green!

She remembered their house, and the leaning porch, and faded paint, the roof that was just waiting to spring a leak. No leaks here, she was certain. Undoubtedly the rooms were twice the size of their old ones, or more, and the children would never have to share beds unless they wanted to. Wallpaper would not dare peel, and the chimney was strong and solid.

She looked again at her new home. At the moment, the windows were dim, as if the only light was coming from the back. Where the servants were? Of course he had servants. No one who lived in a house this big took care of it alone.

"Everybody out," Damon said, and the girls clambered around the others' legs in their eager rush. Lizabeth wrested the handle without waiting for help and jumped down as if she never even noticed the dismounting steps should be there at all, typical of her. One of these days the coachman would get there first and she would trip over steps she did not expect. Verbena smiled at her thought and heard the brake groan into place.

At the carriage door, Annabelle looked back. Peeking shyly up at Damon, she asked, "Is this really where we are going to live? Really?"

Damon smiled across the carriage at her. "Yes."

"Come on, Annabelle," Lizabeth called from outside. "I want to see it."

One of the outriders appeared around the corner of the carriage just as the boys grabbed the strap and swung themselves out. Matthew poked his brother and pointed up past the stairway to the house. "Lookit that, Julius," he crowed with clear pride, as though staking ownership already. "I bet we get our own rooms!"

The carriage was finally empty of children except for Roderick, as he lay in his basket staring up at the ceiling with bleary eyes. Damon slid over and pulled the door shut, sealing them in and the sounds of the children out, cocooning them. He leaned over to catch her hands between his own. "What is wrong? I see it in your face. Talk to me. How can I help if I don't know the problem?"

The sudden privacy felt odd. The children had been a wonderful buffer between them for four days. She took a deep breath. He had asked. He needed to know. "I knew London would be different from what we were used to, but this is beyond anything I imagined." She shook her head, but a smile started. "Did you see Matthew? He already wants to race carriages down the street."

Damon grinned at her. "I will teach him how to do it safely."

"Oh, you!" She shook her head. "I don't want him racing down the streets at all."

He eased across the carriage to her side, and put his arm around her. "You are not doing this alone. The children seem to trust me. I can use that to guide them through the changes they will be facing. There is so much here to entertain them, so much to see and do. I want them to be happy here."

His dark eyes looked at her as though they could see right through her. "I think they are pleased we wed, but I agree this move has been a big change for them. Because it was my idea, if they run into any difficulties, they might hesitate to come to me." He nudged her with his knee in a playful gesture. Against her will, the gesture charmed her. She wanted to have his same light-heartedness.

He picked up one of her hands and kissed it lightly before setting it back down. "We are a team, now, you and I. If they tell you anything I should know, will you tell me, so I can fix it?"

Words caught in her throat, tangled there by the wish for him to kiss her mouth as well. They had not been intimate since the journey began, and she was surprised that she missed it. His eyes warmed as if he had the same thought, and he leaned closer, his mouth coming so close his breath tickled her face.

"Promise me you will come to me if there are any problems?" His lips claimed her, sealing any answer in her mouth, his scent carrying faint traces of the soap he used to shave. He shifted and she felt his muscles cord and ripple despite coats and layers of clothing.

"What is the matter in here?" Lizabeth's face poked in through the doorway, popping the mood with the dash of cold air pouring through the opened door. "Are you coming out? I can't wait to get inside, and besides, we are all *freezing.*"

Damon pulled back abruptly. "We are coming," he said but he did not take his gaze from Verbena.

"Oh, good. Can we go in without you?" Lizabeth bounced on her toes, whether from excitement or cold, Verbena did not know.

Damon finally turned toward impatient Lizabeth, breaking the hold of his gaze. "Certainly. In fact, I would be surprised if my butler is not already waiting for you to walk up. Go on ahead." He slid across the seat toward the door. The steps had been put into place, Verbena had not even noticed anyone do it.

Damon got out and reached back into the box. "I will take the basket so you can get out. Hand Roderick over, please, my dear."

He did that so often, slipping endearments into his sentences, endearments that tugged at her heart and pleaded for belief. But it was too early to give her heart yet. Much too early.

She handed out Roderick, to discover a young maid wrapped in a shawl behind her husband with arms already outstretched. Damon passed the basket over, then held out a hand again, but her gaze would not leave the maid, hurrying with the precious burden toward the big doorway where light drifted out.

Her husband caught her just as she reached the steps, one large hand closing around her arm, stopping her in mid-stride. Verbena slipped on the frosty walk. His firm grip was all that kept her upright.

The maid and Roderick were inside. Without her. Verbena whirled around to him. "Why did you do that? Where is she taking my baby?"

Damon did not release her. "He is fine. You keep forgetting that he is as much my nephew as yours. And I stopped you because you are not going in without me."

He sounded angry. He looked angry as he leaned down to her, his face close enough for her to see his expression in the dimness. "You are my wife now. We are going to present a united front just as we did at your old house, both to the children and the servants. We are not having you dash inside and leave me standing out here as though I were nothing more than a coachman. No one will ever be allowed to say that you were more eager to be with your nephew than your husband."

He wrapped her hand around his arm and held it there with his other hand, his grip unyielding. "Now. We will proceed in and I will present you to our staff."

Our staff. She, Verbena Barnes, lately of the run-down house on the edge of Thernwood, was indeed going to have servants.

Verbena forced herself to take a deep breath. Her hand clamped down on Damon's arm, needing something strong to hold on to.

Our staff, both his and hers. This was not Damon's parents' house. And the other children were already inside. No one could take the baby away.

The door opened and they stepped into the light of candles whose sweet scent proclaimed them to be of beeswax. A line of servants traced the wall of the foyer, all of them staring at her with ill-concealed curiosity. After the first startled look when uniforms blended and the faces seemed to stretch down the hallway, Verbena realized it was really a small staff.

Thank goodness.

And at the far end, the young maid stood, still holding the basket with Roderick.

Damon pulled off his gloves and handed them to what had to be the butler. He turned to her, untied the bow of her bonnet and lifted it off her head. "Your cloak as well, my dear?" That, too, was handed over, along with Damon's greatcoat, to be passed down to the next servant in line.

Moving behind her, standing like a guard at her back, Damon's hands came down on her shoulders. "As you all have no doubt figured out, this is my wife, Mrs. Thern. Verbena, this is our staff. First of all, my butler and all around right-hand-man, Samuels."

Each step into this new life brought changes that, however welcome, did not sit easily. Verbena took a bracing breath, stepped forward, and stopped in front of the butler. He stood rigidly before her. "I'm glad to meet you, Samuels. We are all new to London, and any help you can give us will be appreciated."

He bowed to her, no smile yet, but Verbena thought she sensed pleasure. "I am happy to help you in any way possible."

She looked back at Damon, and there was no mistaking the satisfaction on his face. After that it was easier to go down the line, trying to memorize names. There was a Tom, a Reggie, a Bob, all footmen, tall and broad-shouldered, easily capable of carrying up loads of firewood and bathtubs. Damon had outfitted them in uniforms that resembled those at Thernwood, subdued in digni-fied navy blue with stripes of grey. Next came Mrs. Thompson, the housekeeper, and two maids, Nan and Tessa, whose rough red hands announced they worked in the kitchen. They were young, maybe Julius's age.

At last, at the end of the line, almost blended within the clump of her brothers and sisters, the little maid with Roderick. Now that she got a good look at the girl, Verbena was startled at how very young she was, halfway between Lizabeth and Matthew. How sad the world was, that a child had to go to work alone and away from her family. And such a pretty child, delicate features, long hair a blonde so light it looked white, and big eyes so blue they put the sky to shame.

All Verbena's protective instincts rose up. "And your name?"

"Alice, miss – er, ma'am." A soft blush rose up her cheeks.

"You can put the basket down, Alice. Roderick will be fine."

"Oh, no, ma'am," the girl protested. "I don't mind holding 'im." Despite her brave words, she was beginning to bow backwards to offset the weight of Roderick, the basket, and the mound of coverings tucked around him.

Damon said in a gentle voice, "It is fine, Alice. You can put him down. He has been in a carriage so long I'm certain solid ground would feel good to him."

"Yes, sir." Alice quickly set the basket down and bobbed a curtsy, relief washing over her face.

Damon beckoned to the children. Gesturing to one child after another, he gave their names, then nodded at the butler, who dismissed the staff. As the foyer emptied, Damon beckoned Mrs. Thompson over, and whispered something in her ear that brought a bright smile.

"Yes, sir," she beamed up at him. "You know you can count on me."

Damon gave her a hug, just like he might have done with his mother if his mother was the kind of woman who welcomed such an affection. Mrs. Thompson giggled, actually giggled, and scurried out of the room like a woman on a mission.

He watched her go with a chuckle, then rubbed his hands

together, and looked around the group still clustered in the foyer. "All right. Let us all get out of the hallway and into the sitting room." He waved the children ahead of him into a room off to the right. As he held out his hand for Verbena, he kept talking. "Mrs. Thompson will bring us some refreshments. She is a magnificent cook. I know I can't be the only one who is hungry."

Well, now she knew something about handling the housekeeper, Verbena thought as she followed the children through the door. If she wanted to stay on Mrs. Thompson's good side, she had to make Damon happy.

Verbena looked around at the room. It had the stamp of a bachelor's domain. A large fireplace faced her from the far side, brick stained above from years of fires. A heavy darkish wood mantle ran along its length and more heavy wood went up to the ceiling on either side. The same wood was in the floor in wide planks. The floor was scuffed, the finish nearly worn through.

While it was wonderful to be in a house that did not threaten to fall down on her head, this well-used room held out a welcome better than the finest decorations.

Except for one thing. Everything was distinctly . . . dreary. Chairs, all large and heavy, with dark wood and equally gloomy upholstery, sat scattered around the middle of the room. More chairs of simple bare wood lined the side wall facing the windows.

Not that anyone could enjoy the view. All the windows were covered with dark draperies. The walls were a dark green half-way up, with cream above the chair rail, the softer paint the lone brightness in the room's decor. Only a few candles were lit, making the room even more oppressive. Was the entire house this dark?

Something must have shown on her face, because a deep male chuckle vibrated the air nearby.

"Don't blame it all on me," Damon said. "I bought it as it was. The colors suited me at the time." Hands on his hips, he looked around the room. "Do what you like to it, just don't paint it pink, and don't put up flowered wallpaper."

Do what you like to it? A bubble of excitement, of optimism lifted through Verbena's heart. *Do what you like to it.* She looked around the room again, ideas and dreams popping up like colored sketches.

Damon walked across the room, going past her without stopping, his limp more pronounced than she had noticed in a while, and leaned against the mantle. Julius and Matthew strode past her over to Damon. The boys, too, leaned against the fireplace on opposite sides, trying hard to look as masculine.

"Roderick will have to sleep in our room," Damon said when she reached his side. "Until we can set up a nursery and hire a wet nurse to stay with him, we need to keep him close." Verbena thought she saw white lines around his mouth. He would need her ointments tonight. She felt a tug of pride at his stoicism. He was the best example her brothers could have of facing adversity with courage.

"Well, bless my soul, and if you are not the prettiest little girls I have ever seen." Mrs. Thompson's warm voice crooned behind Verbena.

The housekeeper and two maids came in, carrying trays laden with food. The large trays were set on side tables. Elegant cups were filled with tea, and plates were loaded, chicken and thin slices of ham, flakes of smoked fish and finely-sliced, fried potatoes, with small frosted sugar cakes for dessert.

"Julius? Matthew? Come get something to eat."

Verbena nodded to the kitchen servants. "Thank you very much. We will carry everything down when we are done. Damon can show us the way to the kitchen."

Mrs. Thompson raised horrified eyebrows. "Oh, no, Mrs. Thern. You can't be carrying your own dishes about the house. You just ring, and we will come get them."

At least she had made the offer to help, Verbena thought, and Mrs. Thompson liked the girls. That was a point in their favor.

Maybe they could fit into Damon's household.

That only left his entire strata of society.

And his family.

22

DAMON STOOD IN THE HALLWAY OUTSIDE THE DINING ROOM, dressed for the first formal family breakfast, and watched the children practice being seated at the table. The scents of breakfast teased his nose, eggs and bacon, fresh-baked bread and muffins. Morning light shone on the polished table, reaching to the plates and bowls, the tableware and china cups.

He grinned as he stood silently watching the tableau before him.

His footmen, much to his delight, had clearly discerned the children were totally out of their element. Instead of upturned noses or rolled eyes, the men went through the routine again and again of guiding the boys into pulling out the chairs, helping the girls into them, and pushing them in.

"No, Mister Julius, push it in slowly, and don't make the lady fall into the chair."

"But how do I know when she's going start sitting down?" Julius was definitely frustrated.

"It's an art, Mister Julius, it is indeed an art." The footman motioned him toward the chair. "Come now, Miss Annabelle, it is your turn. We will work on the smoothness. It should look like one movement."

Annabelle giggled and bowed to the footman instead of a curtsey. She had obviously been paying attention to the boys' instructions, with not so much concentration on her own role. Damon waited for the footman to laugh. Even though he was clearly biting the inside of his cheek, the man did not release so much as a snicker, just bowed politely at Annabelle as if he had received the most graceful curtsey.

The other footmen looked away for a moment while they got their faces in order. Trying to hide his smile, one of them found himself looking directly at Damon. After a shocked second, he suddenly snapped to attention. "Sir Damon! Excuse me, sir, I did not see you there. We did not – we were just – May I help you?"

Damon shook his head. "No. I did not mean to interrupt. Things look fine in here. I will go get my wife. Carry on." Whatever possessed him he did not know, but he winked at the footman by Annabelle before he left.

Now all he had to do was find his wife. After their slow, leisurely morning of loving once Roderick had been turned over to Alice, it was no wonder the children had beaten them down to the dining room. He thought again about the scene he had interrupted, and a chuckle slipped free.

Verbena had thought they would not fit in! If they charmed London as easily as they had charmed his household, their success was assured.

He climbed the stairs to the floor above their bedrooms, and started down the hallway. He heard Roderick crying before he reached halfway and picked up his pace.

Two strained female faces turned to him, eyes alarmed.

"Oh, thank goodness you are here!" Verbena was doing the jiggling move that mothers did, jouncing Roderick gently and swaying from side to side, but it did not seem to help. Her hair looked as if no one had styled it yet that morning, sun-yellow strands poking out at odd angles from the ribbon that was coming untied. Roderick's tiny head drooped over her shoulder, and his tiny legs were pulled up into a tight curl. His little fists flailed around her ears. Behind her, Alice looked ready to cry herself. Her eyes were ringed with dark circles, and her young skin had an ashen hue. "Here, you take him. I have tried everything I know."

Verbena startled him by settling Roderick in his arms, the first time she had relinquished him willingly. Damon stared down at a tiny gaping mouth, shocked at the volume coming out of it. He had heard his nephew cry before, but nothing like this. No point in making the rest of the household suffer. He eased the door shut with his foot.

Over the din, Verbena went on, "We can't find the last jug of goat's milk. I was so sure there was another jug, but we can't find it. He is so hungry again he won't stop crying. Have we found a wet nurse yet?"

He stared down at the squalling bundle. In addition to the sound that was making his own ears ring, he felt a distinct wetness against his hand. "I sent out one of the maids to bring someone she knew back in the carriage. Apparently there is a widow nearby who was about to wean her own child."

Not knowing what else to do, he rested a knuckle against Roderick's mouth. He had seen one of the mothers in the army followers do that. Her child was older and teething at the time, but the ploy had worked wonders.

Roderick tasted his knuckle with soft brushes of his tongue, like butterfly kisses, then tried to suck it inside. It was too big, but the challenge distracted him into silence.

The room went so quiet the lack of sound almost hurt. He beamed at Verbena, who rewarded him with a lift of skeptical eyebrows. "He is diverted now, but mark my words, it won't last long."

He gave her a superior smile. "I'm grateful for whatever quiet I get."

Sure enough, the words were no sooner out of his mouth when Roderick pulled his head away and stuck out his tongue. Damon tensed, and saw the same wince on both Verbena and Alice. A rich, moist burp rolled out of the rosebud mouth, so impressive it startled Roderick into wide-eyed silence.

"Oh!" Verbena whispered and she and Alice exchanged hopeful glances and held their breaths. Damon sensed something changing in the little bundle he held, a softening, a tiny baby breath, and went still, afraid to move for fear he would break the spell.

Roderick yawned, the little mouth opening wide to show toothless gums, and his eyes did a slow blink that hung suspended, then the blue-veined eyelids fluttered and closed.

A sharp knock came on the door. Roderick's eyes popped open, his mouth opened, and the screaming began again. Damon's ears were ringing. Verbena scurried over and jerked the door open as if rescue was on the other side. "Yes?"

"There is someone here to see Sir Damon."

It had better be the wet nurse.

Damon raised his voice to be heard over the baby's screaming. "I will meet them in my study, if you could bring them there." He plopped Roderick back into Verbena's arms, and escaped.

This wet nurse had better work out. There was a limit to how much of a baby's screaming any sane person could handle.

Verbena watched him leave. Irritation surged. Typical man, to leave them here with a screaming baby.

Unless . . . he had said something about a wet nurse. Verbena stared at the door. He would not interview the wet nurse without her, would he?

"Do you think you can take care of him for a few minutes? I won't be long." Verbena set Roderick back into his elegant little bed. "You can try the finger trick again if you need to." Never mind that they had tried it several times before Damon and his intriguing masculine finger bought them a few seconds of peace.

Just as she reached the main floor, all out of breath, she heard the study door shut, a solid sound. A curl, still moving after she had stopped, flopped down over her eye, and the rest of her hair, as if playing a follow-the-leader game, tumbled down around her ears.

Until that moment, she had forgotten what she looked like, her hair tumbled and tangled, her gown limp and wrinkled, and smelling distinctly of baby. Well, any woman who was fit to be around her baby had better be aware of the pitfalls.

Taking a deep breath, Verbena pushed the hair away from her face, tucked what curls she could behind her ears, and strode toward the study door.

A few steps away, a sudden doubt popped up. What if it was not the wet nurse after all? Damon would not be happy.

And, considering how she looked just then, she would be totally embarrassed.

The study door looked very forbidding up close, all dark wood and carved panels. Before she could change her mind she took a deep breath, gave one sharp knock and wrenched the handle.

The room was much bigger than she expected. Damon was sitting behind his big desk, his eyebrows raised in mock surprise. Between herself and her husband's desk, in one of the big chairs like an unwilling arbiter in a war, sat a woman not much older than herself, her face mild but care-worn, her fashionable clothes announcing she had only recently fallen upon hard times. Her dark hair had streaks of grey, but her young face, tired and sad though it was, belied the grey hair. A child, looking to be about a year old, clung to her like a limpet.

The sight of that baby stopped Verbena in her tracks. Of course the wet nurse would have to have a child, but Verbena had not expected to find it here, in Damon's study.

With a resigned sigh that Verbena knew was for her, Damon rose and gestured in her direction. "This is my wife. My darling," his voice held a touch of dryness, "this is Mrs. Smythe, and I believe she is the answer to your prayers. She is the woman I was told of, newly widowed with a son not yet a year old."

He motioned Verbena to the other chair, brown leather with some kind of padding and carved wood legs and arms. She shoved herself as far back on the seat as she could, only to find that her feet did not reach the floor. Probably no woman had ever spent any time in this room. She noticed the other chair was just as big, but Mrs. Smythe was taller than herself. "I am *so* glad to meet you. Would you like some tea?"

"It has already been sent for, my dear." Damon turned his attention back to the woman. "To answer your earlier question, the baby was born just under a fortnight ago."

Verbena gave a start. A fortnight already? Roderick had been a day old when Damon arrived. Nearly two days to arrange the wedding, three days from Verbena's Aunt Mabel's house to Thernwood, a couple days there to pack up, then the four days' journey to London – yes, this was indeed the twelfth day since Roderick was born and Edeline was buried. Her finger rubbed the heavy ring she wore.

"Do you have an objection to living in? If you have several children, I am not certain we will have room for all of them. We really require someone who can remain in the house."

"I have just this one child," Mrs. Smythe said. "My husband died little more than a month ago. He had been ill for a while, the doctor needs paying, and creditors are hounding me. Yesterday I was told there is no saving my house." The words came out in tight breathlessness, and she pulled her son closer. "Forgive me, I don't mean to put my burdens on you."

Verbena knew that fear. It seemed one did not have to be threatened by the Enclosure Acts to live on the edge of desperation.

She could not take her eyes off the child, sitting so close. Mrs. Smythe held the baby on her lap with interlocked hands. The round, cherubic face looked up at Verbena, and he stuck a fist in his mouth, drooling around it while he gnawed on a finger.

Teething, no doubt.

When she smiled at him, the baby ducked his head, squirmed

around and scrambled to his feet despite the restraining hands. The instant he got upright, he dug his little head into his mother's neck. Drool dripped onto the bodice. Mrs. Smythe did not seem to care.

Was this not the very kind of woman she wanted?

She dragged her attention back to Damon's interview. He raised his eyebrows. "Do you have anything else to ask?"

Verbena's eyes widened. She had been so distracted by the baby that she had not even paid attention after the first few answers. It was very aggravating. But had she not already seen all she wanted?

Everything pointed to Mrs. Smythe as the perfect choice for Roderick. She was soft-spoken and intelligent, her face was kind, and she met Verbena's gaze without hesitation when she smiled. Most of all, the baby was obviously happy and secure. Regardless of the fears Mrs. Smythe faced, she had hidden them from her child.

"Very well, then," Damon said, "we will consider the bargain struck. I will send some footmen and the carriage over to your house after Roderick has been fed – that really comes first."

"I understand," Mrs. Smythe said, everything about her, her voice, her posture, the lift of her head, proclaiming her relief. "If you will show me where the baby is, I will see if he will take to me."

THE ROOM SELECTED as double duty both for Roderick and the wet nurse, the better part of an entire floor, had only a cradle, a rocking chair, and two straight-backed chairs, so there was plenty of space for Mrs. Smythe to make a small home for herself and her son.

"We have not got the nursery set up yet," Damon said as she stood awkwardly in the opening and looked at the nearly empty, echoing room. "I wanted to make a place for you and your son, since you will be with us for some time. You will have some of your own furniture here."

"That is more than kind of you, sir. I cannot thank you enough." Her gaze went down to Roderick, nestled in Alice's arms, hiccupping from so much crying. "If I may?" Her son began squirming, fighting to get down and run in this new playroom with plenty of bare space. Mrs. Smythe set him down and straightened with her arms extended.

Just that quickly, Roderick was turned over. Mrs. Smythe walked over to the rocking chair and sat, holding Edeline's son. Roderick immediately began nuzzling the woman's breasts.

Damon turned away, and took her arm, pulling her toward the door. "Give the woman privacy, my dear," he whispered in her ear, and pulled the door shut in her face once they were in the hall. "He will be fine with her."

"I know." Tears pushed at her eyes. Edeline, had she lived, would have fed him, *wanted* to feed him. During their stages of the journey, the hunt for milk, village after village, had distracted her from the loss of her sister. Now, godsend though she was, kind as she appeared to be, Mrs. Smythe had brought back the void.

She should not be so selfish about her sorrow. Each of them grieved.

Damon's hands gripped her shoulders. "I wish you would trust me. I know you came down because you did not think I could find the right woman for him, but I love that child. I love your brothers and sisters. I love – " he caught himself, and in a calmer voice went on, "I love being part of your family. I know I am new to it, and compared to you must look like the rankest amateur. You have done all the mothering for so many years that it comes naturally to you. You never really had to share any of your brothers and sisters. If you will forgive my plain speaking, your father never wanted any part of them."

It was never easy hearing the truth about one's family from an outsider, Verbena thought. "You are right," she said slowly, the reluctant admittance wanting to stick in her throat. "I never really did have to share any of the children." She looked back at the door. "I should be glad we have found someone to help care for him." It was time to be practical, no matter how difficult it was. "I think she will be a good choice."

He lifted her chin up. "You *can* trust me, you know."

"I know." Verbena brushed at her cheek with the back of her hand. "I was just thinking – how very much Edeline wanted . . ."

Damon found the tears she had missed, and caught them. His fingers were always so gentle, she marveled. He tipped up her chin. She felt the coolness of the remnants of her tears in the soft touch. When she met his gaze, he said, "He *will* be fine with her." He tucked her arm in the crook of his elbow and held it there.

Even after his finger moved away, Verbena still looked in his dark eyes. They had softened, like a rich dark chocolate drink. And like the drink, their depths hid something swirling inside, something warm and tempting. His words whispered through her again. *You can trust me, you know.*

It really was about trust. Trust in Damon, trust that she would not lose herself now that her main reason for being here had been turned over to another.

Someone had to feed Roderick.

He moved her away from the door. "I forgot to tell you that breakfast was served," he said as they walked. He sounded so conversational. How did men change subjects so easily? He gave a half chuckle. "It must be cold by now."

"I can eat cold food." She managed a smile, thinking of some of the meals the children had eaten when she was first learning to cook alone, without her mother's advice.

"Mrs. Thompson will undoubtedly remove the cold food and replace with fresh when she sees us coming."

"Such waste." When she was confident with the role of mistress of the house, and hopefully it would not take too long, she would have to put a stop to it.

"Don't feel too badly." Damon patted her hand where it rested on his arm. "The servants will eat what is edible, and the rest they will feed to the dogs. Everyone gets something."

A footman scurried over to open a door for them. It was the

dining room, and the children were all there. Damon seated her, and unless she was very much mistaken, exchanged a wink with Julius.

Verbena looked around. The walls in this room as well had dark wood wainscoting from the chair rail down, but the upper part was just a pale green paint, and only a clock and a mirror decorated two of them. A chandelier utterly devoid of crystals hung from the ceiling.

She did indeed have her work cut out, making this a welcoming family house. The bare chandelier drew her attention again.

This might be fun.

A long server by one of the undecorated walls held the last of the eggs and bacon and a plate with a few pieces of cold toast. On the table were crystal jars holding the remnants of the jams, and empty tiny cups that held only the scent of hot chocolate. The children were still there, talking over each other, comparing food and each other in the most candid terms.

"Verbena," Annabelle said happily, "we had chocolate! To drink! Did you know they cook their eggs one at a time? And there was no water in them, either."

"And they gave us bacon, too," Matthew could not resist. "Eggs *and* bacon."

Verbena wrinkled her nose at him. "If you want to eat like this when you are grown, you will have to study hard."

Matthew wrinkled his nose back at her. "I wish I would hold the books to my head and have all the words slide off the page into my brain."

"They would probably slide right through and out the other side." Lizabeth sniped, ignoring Verbena's sharp look.

"I don't notice you studying that hard," Matthew sniped back.

Verbena rapped out, "Children! Damon is going to think you have no manners whatsoever."

They subsided, with quick glances his way. Annabelle tilted her head back to get the last drops of chocolate out of the tiny cup.

Julius did not even seem to hear the commotion around him. He had a few scrapings of eggs left on his plate, and was busily chewing a piece of toast. Verbena had seen him stop outside the library door yesterday to stare open-mouthed at the abundance inside. From long experience they all had known he considered the time eating as time he could better spend inside a book. It would not take long before he excused himself and slipped away to do that very thing.

Samuels came in with the mail on a silver tray. All her brothers and sisters watched the little ceremony with respectful quiet. At least it put a damper on the conversational din.

Annabelle broke the silence first. "You eat paper?"

Verbena smothered a smile. She was used to Annabelle's flights of imagination. Damon looked at the tray, and he laughed, a rich and delighted sound. "No. I'm sorry to disappoint you, but that is just how I get my mail."

"We get ours from the postmaster's house. We don't get mail very often."

He smiled at Annabelle. "Unfortunately, I get all too much mail." He set the tray of mail aside. "This is not the time to deal with it, however. Today you will learn your way around the house, and I will begin the search for a tutor and a governess."

"What is a govn'ness?" Annabelle asked. "Is she the one who will teach us to paint?"

"Yes, she is." Damon smiled at her.

"You said she would teach us languages." Lizabeth made it sound like an accusation.

His eyebrow went up. "Yes, she will."

"Will she teach us French? I was told great ladies only speak French."

"Great ladies certainly speak French, but they speak other languages, as well. Like German and Italian."

"We learned how to sit down already," Annabelle interjected. "And how to bow."

"That is a very good start." Damon seemed to be hiding a smile.

He looked across the table at Verbena, and met her gaze with a moment of instant and silent accord. "As soon as you learn your way around the house, Julius, you may go to the library. It would be good for you to become familiar with what is there. You never know what might help you in your studies."

He knew what each child was thinking. It was a marvelous thing to have him understand her brothers and sisters so well, and she smiled back at him, a happy glow filling the ache in her middle.

"Thank you," she mouthed, and across the table his smile broadened.

AFTER BREAKFAST WAS DONE, and the children had been sent off for a tour of the house, Damon gave Verbena a long look across the span of the table. "I need to discuss something with you. I prefer to do it where we cannot be overheard. My study is, as you already know, private." He came around, tucked her arm around his and led her out.

She had not paid much attention to the room this morning, just that his study was all dark colors and very male, with a big desk and oversized brown chairs. This time she did not try to slide back.

Damon stood in profile to her, looking out the window, an ominous air hanging about him.

She glanced quickly around the rest of the room. Tall bookshelves, but no one had finished filling them, and the few books had fallen on their sides in the big empty spaces in each shelf. The walls were painted a deep red, and were stark and undecorated. No paintings, no trophies of war, no swords, no emblems, no medals.

Just dark red paint, a big desk, and three big chairs.

Damon seated himself behind the desk, and leaned back, watching her with half-closed eyes. The curtains had already been opened, and the sunlight through the window behind him cast his face into shadow. She could not help but notice that he fit his chair very nicely. Or that with the sun at his back, she could not see the expression on his face.

"I'm going to tell my parents about Roderick today."

Verbena studied him. Of course he would tell them. Roderick was their grandchild, and she had known this was coming from the time she agreed to marry him. "You have not even written a letter?" Dread mixed with relief. They did not know yet.

Damon picked up the quill laying loose on the desk and turned it around in his hands absently, but he did not take his gaze off her. "When I heard the rumor that Edeline was with child, I left as soon as I could pack." His eyes narrowed. "My source was not – trustworthy. I did not want to raise my family's hopes if I was on a fool's errand. Therefore, I chose to say nothing until I was certain. It is the kind of news one must give in person."

He paused. There was an ominous feel to the quiet. "It is possible," he said slowly, "that my source might already be spreading it. The news might have reached them by now."

"I will get ready," she said, and started to rise.

"No." The word was said without inflection, but it cracked on the air. "I would prefer to do this alone."

"Why?" Verbena sank back down onto the chair's edge.

"I think it best that you not be there." Damon said nothing more, just looked at her with those eyes that could hide his thoughts so easily.

A sudden thought, a burst of intuition, hit her. "You have not yet told them we are wed."

"No." The word was stark and unadorned, just *no*.

Pain stabbed her, but she forced it back. This was not the time for hurt feelings. The air was thick with a different tension, one she did not understand.

Damon stood and went to the window, looking out at the cold street. Verbena stayed on the edge of the chair and waited for him to say something, anything to explain himself.

He had not told his family that he had married her. No, not *her*, but a Barnes.

He had gone through his family's closets to clothe them, but a moment of that day came back. She had said she hoped this did not cause problems with the family. Instead of saying, *of course it won't*, he had returned, *I knew what I was doing when I asked you to marry me.* A chill slid down her arms, and she rubbed her hands up and down them but the cold did not go away. She put her hands back on her lap. "How concerned are you?"

"For myself? Not at all." But he did not turn away from the window.

"Then why don't you want me to go with you?"

He turned around at last. He straightened his shoulders. His military bearing was all too obvious. "I would like some day to have the link between the families be peaceable. I will be giving them a lot to take in all at once, and I do not know how they will react. I should do this alone."

He walked toward the door, but stopped at her side. His hand came down on her shoulder, a soft touch. Warmth seeped into her skin. "I believe this is for the best. You have a nurse to help get settled. I promise you, I will be sure to tell you how things went."

Verbena felt his unease, and reached up, catching his hand before he could pull it away. "Take care."

"Always, my dear." Then he moved toward the door, taking the warmth with him.

23

The streets were sloppy with the promise of spring soon to come. Melting snow splashed up the horse's legs and onto his freshly polished boots and newly pressed trousers. He knew the way to his parents' house, so other than dodging horses and carriages, his mind was free to wander toward the upcoming conversation.

Roderick. The first grandchild and Andrew's flesh and blood. And, of course, his marriage, Verbena and the children.

He rode neatly between two carriages and turned the corner onto his parent's street. The stable was open. He dismounted and tossed the reins to the nearest groom.

"Sir Damon!" The man smiled broadly. "It has been a while. Good to see you, sir."

"Thank you."

The groom led his horse away as Damon turned toward the house.

"Sir Damon!" The housekeeper was coming down the stairs when he walked through the door. "What brings you here? How lovely to see you." She scurried down the last few steps. ""Can I get you some tea?"

He shook his head. "Thank you for the offer, Mrs. Nordly, but save it for when my parents ring. I expect you will be bringing plenty then."

Her eyes filled with rare emotion. "It does my heart good to see you so healthy. I don't know if I will ever get the sight of you back from the war out of my mind. You looked like death then, you did."

He grinned at her. "Then I must come more often." And with Roderick, he would be a frequent visitor.

The parlor was empty, pristine as always, not a chair or a candle out of place, so he hurried through it and into his mother's morning room. Sure enough, there she was. He stood in the doorway, watching her as she sat at her desk, her quill in her hand, writing. There were unhappy lines on her face, the same lines he had seen after Andrew's funeral. Her hair showed more grey than it had before he left on his momentous journey.

He smiled as he tapped on the doorframe, and stepped into the room. "Mother."

She looked up, startled. "Damon. Where on earth have you been?"

Damon crossed the room to kiss her cheek. "Out of town. Checking on a report, one that you should find most interesting." He plucked the quill out of her hand and pulled her, protesting, to her feet. "Come, Mother, let us find Father and I will tell both of you what I discovered."

"Your father is in his study, and you know how much he hates being disturbed."

He tucked her hand through his arm, drew her out of the room and continued down the hallway. "Some things are worth the interruption."

At his father's study door, Damon knocked two sharp raps and waited with ingrained courtesy until he heard the "Come" before entering. "Hello, Father. I hope you have a few minutes free."

He seated his mother in one of the chairs that faced Edward's desk. Dark, impressive and heavily carved with elongated deer loping up the legs and across the front, it sat in the middle of the room, almost a duplicate of the study in Thernwood.

"Damon. How good of you to bother to come and let us know that you are alive." His father relaxed in the chair, its impressive back rising far above his greying head, and frowned at Damon. "I have been making excuses for your absence all over town for almost two weeks now."

"Good morning to you, too, Father." Damon walked over to the side of his father's desk and pulled himself straight, looking from one puzzled and annoyed face to the other. "I come with remarkable news. When I rushed out of London, there was a very good reason. I ran into one of the guests from the funeral. She had a report that shocked me. I had not heard a single hint of what she said until that moment, and before she spread the tale I had to see if it was true. I could not tell you until I was certain either way."

Father gave a grunt, disgust put to sound. "If you run after every rumor, you will never have a chance to catch your breath. Really, Damon, surely you know that. There are more important things in life than chasing stupid remarks."

Damon looked at his father. Best to just say it. "Edeline and Andrew were expecting a child."

A strange sound came from his mother. Damon glanced over. Her eyes were wide and shocked, her hands clasped so tightly her knuckles were white.

"So Edeline was pregnant." Edward shrugged. "What does that have to do with us?"

"He's Andrew's son," Damon said with asperity. "That makes *him* your heir, not me."

"Who told you this fairy tale?" There was such certainty in Edward's voice, such coolness in his manner.

"I have seen the child, Father." Damon did not move, just stood there and fixed his father in his gaze. "I assure you he does exist."

"Oh, I don't doubt that for a moment."

"Edeline slipped out the very morning Andrew died," his mother said, her voice shrill. "Who else would she have gone to meet but a lover? Your father is right, the child cannot be your brother's. Do you not think we would have given anything for a grandchild?"

"I know exactly where Edeline went that morning." Damon looked at his parents. This was uglier than he could possibly have expected. What a good thing he had insisted his wife remain at home! "She sent a message for her sister Verbena. They met in the gazebo."

"Honestly, Damon!" His mother was slightly pale. "Who told you that tale?"

Damon felt his fingers clench on a shelf. "I caught her sister on the route back home. I spoke to her. There was no illicit tryst. The morning Andrew died, Edeline merely went out to meet her sister."

The room was quiet for a sudden moment. "You spoke to the sister? You are certain it was that same morning?" The color seemed to have drained from Imogene's face.

"Quite certain, Mother. And there is more proof. Edeline wrote a will before she died, begging Verbena to care for their son. She was very clear in it that the babe was her husband's."

Edward's eyebrows rose in surprise. "What is this you say?" He exchanged a quick glance with his wife. "Edeline is dead?"

"Yes. She died birthing her son two weeks ago." Damon's gaze went from one to the other.

"You are certain the child is Andrew's?" Imogene was on the edge of her chair, her hands tight on the chair's ornate arms.

"Now, my dear," Edward said in a rush, "you know it cannot be. Do not let your wishes override your good sense."

"But what if it is?" Imogene turned her attention to her husband. "Do you know what I did? That very morning I accused her of rushing off to meet a stableboy! I said that to her very face! No wonder she would not tell us anything about the babe. We must get our grandson." She turned back to Damon. "You said you have seen him? Is he well? He did survive?"

His mother had said such vile things to a new young widow?

And the very morning of her husband's death? The more he heard, the more he understood why Verbena could hardly stand his family. "Yes, he survived. He is well and healthy. I took the babe, he is at my house here in London now. His name is Roderick, by the way."

Imogene sagged back into her chair, the color seeping back into her cheeks even though white spots remained on her forehead. "A boy. Andrew's child." Wonder filled her voice. "And safe in the family." She tried to rise, but her legs did not seem to want to hold her and she remained perched on the edge of her chair. "We must go see him. Right away. Today. There is no time to waste."

It was time for his second piece of news. "Before you go charging over to my house, I have a second bit of news."

"Oh, Damon, now is not the time." Imogene smiled at her husband. "Edward, can you believe it? We have a grandchild! I must go see him. The other news can wait." She managed to get to her feet.

Damon held up his hand. "No, Mother, it cannot. This second news is all of a piece with the first. Mother, Father," he looked between the two of them, "One of the reasons I was away so long is that I am married."

"*Married!*" Edward's voice exploded in the room.

"Married?" Imogene echoed him, and sank back down into the chair. "You are wed? Oh, Damon." The words were rich with shock and reproach. "When? Where? To whom? Why did you not tell us? We should have been there! How could you get married without us? Do we even know the woman?"

Damon looked between his parents. "No, in all truth, I think you do not. I see now how very lucky I was to succeed at all. It took all my powers of persuasion, not to mention subtle threats, to convince Verbena to marry me." He felt himself stand straighter, proud to claim her.

"What?" Edward gasped out the word, and rose slowly from his chair, like a thundercloud building on the horizon. "Tell me it is not true. What have you done?" His father's face went pale, as pale as his mother's had been.

That look stabbed as harsh as a knife. "Yes, you heard what I said." He had expected it to be difficult, otherwise he would have brought Verbena along, but this? He had made his choice and he would not change it even if he could. "I am married to Edeline's sister. Her name is Verbena." It seemed incomplete, so he added, "Verbena Thern."

"You would not do such a thing to your family and our name." Edward slammed a fist on the desk. "I told you not to marry into that . . . *family*! Did I not tell you that her father is a drunk? You would link us to them *again*?"

"Edward!" Imogene bolted to her feet. "All that matters now is Andrew's child!"

"If having a drunkard in the family were a sign of bad blood, no one would dare claim our prince," Damon said in a dry voice. He felt his fingers relax. At least he had one parent on his side. Although if Verbena had been told of his mother's cruel words, finding forgiveness might be a challenge at best. "I was lucky to get her to marry me. You know nothing of her. Of how hard she has worked to raise her brothers and sisters. She is the linchpin of that family, a woman of rare courage and devotion and loyalty. She is ferocious in defending those she loves, and I cannot think of a safer place for Roderick to be."

Damon took the few steps over to the desk, and bracing himself on his fists, leaned close to his father. "Just in case you ever try to cast aspersions against her character, she was pure when we wed, and I am certainly with enough experience to know. If I hear anything against her that I even suspect might have started with you, I will call you out, father or not."

Twin gasps fairly sucked the air out of the room. "You would never!"

"I recommend you not test me on that." He straightened. "We were wed in Bath, and it is duly recorded. Just as Roderick's birth is recorded there. Verbena has a paper in Edeline's writing bequeathing the baby to her care."

A sob burst out of his mother's throat. "My foolish tongue! If I could only take my words back."

But Damon had to wonder, even as he hated himself for doing so, how much of her grief was for Edeline's hurt and how much was for herself, and the possibility of ensuring a visit to see Andrew's son.

Andrew, always his mother's golden boy.

24

Thomas Barnes jumped off the farmer's wagon as it slowed before the inn, the iron wheels splashing through the mud left by the melting snow, doffed his hat at the man, and stretched the kinks out of his back. His stomach twisted from hunger, setting up aches deep inside. He looked at the familiar place where he had spent many an hour away from the squabbles of his children and sighed. Ah, the sweet smell of drink, wafting off the first breezes of spring. He took another deep breath, his nose quivering after so many months at sea, alcohol a thing of dreams. He jingled the coins in his pocket, and chuckled. His second daughter was a gorgon when it came to a man having a draught or two. Well, she was not here, and he had coin, and the scent of ale teased his nose, fairly making his eyes water from longing.

He strode across, shoved the door open, stepping inside and breathing in the cooking food, meat pies, the fresh bread coming from the oven in back.

And best of all, the drink. He jingled the coins faster as he walked to the counter and leaned against its high top. The innkeeper, round from eating too much of his own food and bald headed, with a wild fringe of hair about the ears, had his back turned as he loaded a plate. Thomas smiled. "An ale, Robbie me man, and a plate of meat pie and pudding, if you would."

Robbie swung around, and blinked when he realized who it was. For an old friend, the man did not seem all that happy to see him, but then he never did. Well, Thomas had money this time, and he would make sure Robbie knew just how much. He might even toss the innkeeper a tip, just to rub the man's nose into it.

"So, Tom Barnes," Robbie said with a sigh that made Thomas clench his teeth, "ye're back from the sea then? This last trip was a long one. I hear your coins rattling."

"That it was, Robbie, that it was. You got no worries on that score." Thomas slapped a shilling onto the counter and looked up just to watch the innkeeper's face. "See, I can pay."

"You always can when you first come back," Robbie said in a bland voice. "You always can."

A sharp clap on his back sent Thomas into the counter with a 'whoof.' He whirled around with a scowl, only to yell with glee, "Jemmy! Ah, Jemmy!" He pulled the man against him and thumped him in return, then shoved him backward and grinned. Jemmy, about Thomas's age but with fewer streaks of grey in his tawny hair, was nearly half his size, but wiry from years of plowing and chopping on the Thern land and strong as an ox. "You are here?" Thomas hooted with laughter, only to wince from the stomach pain in his side. He'd gotten good at ignoring it, but today it was sharper than usual. He had to eat soon. He concentrated on his friend. "And at this hour of the day? I would have thought your wife would have something to say about that."

"It is too early to plant, Tommy. You have been away too long. You have forgotten the seasons." Jemmy looked up at Thomas, all the laughter washed from his face, and a strange prickle ran down Barnes' spine. "You'll not have heard, then, have you, Tom?" His friend's eyes were sad, his face filled with concern.

The room seemed suddenly quiet, all conversation from the tables behind him muted and far away. Even the sounds from the kitchen had gone still, the crackling of the meat on the skillet of a moment ago seemed to have faded as well. Thomas looked over at Robbie, but the man's face was just as somber.

"What?" He looked around the room, but everyone seemed to be either engrossed in the mug in front of them or giving none-too-subtle prods at their companion, as if urging the other to speak. "What?"

"Your daughter Edeline died in childbirth, what would it be, a few weeks ago now," Robbie said quietly. "She gave an heir to the Therns, but did not live to see him. A boy, it was."

Thomas looked at Robbie, then Jemmy, then around the room at the other faces, none of whom wanted to meet his eyes. "When did this happen? How can the child be a Thern? She was not with child when that worthless husband of hers died."

Robbie's slow shake of the head stopped him. "Ah, so everyone thought. She hid it well. After the young Mr. Thern was buried, your daughter fled to your wife's sister and hid there until the babe was about to be born. One day this winter, deep in a snowstorm, an old carriage rattled up and a liveried coachman got out to ask the way to your house. The next day the same carriage left, Mrs. Downs told us. Miss Verbena left with the carriage, and was gone for several weeks. Next thing we know, the other young Mr. Thern was in and gone like 'is tale was afire, to come back one week later with your second daughter as his wife, and the babe in his possession. He dismissed Mrs. Downs and brought the rest of your children up to the big house. They stayed only a couple days, from the reports out of Thernwood, and then the big fancy carriage rolled down toward London, and we ain't seen hide nor hair from them since. All the servants told the same story, that he took your whole family off to London."

"London? All of them?" Red blurred Barnes's vision, anger that boiled up from a deep well in the pit of his stomach. His skin prickled with the rage seeping out from every pore, years of resentment toward the Therns trying to find some way out, some release. Those Therns had stabbed him again! Would their perfidy never end? First his land, and then his daughter. Six whole years they had kept Edeline away from him, six years, and now their rutting son had killed her with his seed.

And they had taken Verbena, too!

Fear whispered through his brain, cold fear that beat against the hot rage boiling there. Verbena. Gone. He depended on her. She cooked and cleaned for him, and kept the other children out of his sight.

It did not matter that the children were a constant nuisance, they were *his*. He had fathered them, and no one had the right to steal them away. No one! Especially the Therns, those scourges on the countryside, trotting around stealing land away from decent hard-working people and not caring if their victims lived or died.

How was he going to survive without his children's help, a little voice whispered from deep in his mind. He could not cook for himself, and he certainly could not come here every day. He did not know how long his wages from this latest trading journey would last.

Who did those high-and-mighty Therns think they were? There had to be some way he could force them to pay for everything they did. Killing his daughter, kidnapping his children, running off with Verbena. Well, the Therns could just think again. He would get something out of them for all the misery they had caused him if it was the last thing he did.

And now they had stolen his grandchild, his own heir that he had not even seen yet. A cold chill prickled down his spine as he remembered how quickly this last sea trip had come up. Had Thern planned this all along, hoping he would die at sea?

Well, he was going to go to London and drag his children back, that he would. He just needed to come up with a good idea. "Give me an ale," he snapped at Robbie, and pushed the shilling closer to him. Once he got some ale, he would be able to come up with a plan. He always had good plans with a drink or two in him.

25

Verbena walked with Mrs. Smythe to the front door, where the two footmen waited to hand the new wet nurse into Damon's carriage. They were to go back with her and help collect her belongings.

She looked at this woman with whom she would be sharing Edeline's son. "Don't hesitate to ask the men for whatever help you need. They will load what you want to bring with you, and lock up your house." *Hurry back,* she thought, the urgent wish springing from some unknown part of her brain. She could be feeling jealousy at Mrs. Smythe for intruding on what should be Verbena's place alone, yet she liked this woman. "I look forward to having you here." And it was true, strangely, happily true.

Mrs. Smythe looked up at her and Verbena saw unease flicker in her eyes. "Mrs. Thern, I just wanted you to know that I will do my very best for your son. I don't want you to worry that I might try to usurp your place."

It seemed neither of them was entirely comfortable with the sudden turn their life had taken. A smile slipped free. "I know you will. I admit, before you came I was worried about what kind of woman you would be, but I see how much you love your own son. I hope we can be friends." She suddenly remembered her husband was at that very moment exposing Roderick to a danger not even this woman could help her with. Her smile threatened to waver. She held it in place with sheer determination.

Mrs. Smythe gave one last tug to make certain the gloves were secure, or maybe to expend some nerves. The anxiety in her eyes seemed to increase, as if she was afraid something would go wrong before she could come back and get settled in. "Mrs. Thern, I am not a nurse, I am just a mother. Your son will need me for a short while. I will have to make my own way then."

"Perhaps you will remarry," Verbena said, and immediately wished she had not. Mrs. Smythe was not over her husband yet, how could she be so crass as to mention finding another?

The other woman just smiled sadly. "Perhaps. It would be the best solution. I would like more children." Then she turned and walked down the stairs and out into the winter chill. At least for a while, she would have some income and could gain a measure of independence.

How strange. Mrs. Smythe was gaining independence, while she was losing it. Which one had made the better choice?

Verbena caught herself scanning the street for Damon's horse. How long could his meeting take? Would he come back alone, or would his parents' carriage follow him?

A chill colder than the air wafting through the door made her shiver. Verbena quickly shut the door, but the chill followed her inside.

She turned and looked down the hall into the house in which she now lived. Damon had enough servants to handle all the chores that previously had been hers. The children were upstairs. He had given the boys some kind of school exercise to do, a way, he said, of knowing what to look for in a tutor. Just one more evidence of his efforts for them.

There was work waiting, but it was so different from her usual occupations of cooking and cleaning and mending. She could not start without someone else to show her how and where. Mrs. Thompson was to take her about the house after the noon meal. Counting sheets and towels instead of washing them, learning where the plates and silverware were instead of laying them out.

She was not used to having so much time on her hands. There was one useful skill that she could use right now, this moment, though, something much more important than household accounts.

Verbena went deliberately up the stairs to the next floor. For a while at least, she could dismiss the maid, hold Roderick and feel like she was keeping her promise to her sister.

The house was so quiet. She had never been in a house this quiet. It made her uneasy and gave her too much time to think. Her thoughts were poor company, filled with pain. Memories of her sister, her own longing for a house where she felt needed.

As Verbena reached the top of the stairs, her steps lagged. No one was nearby, no one to watch. She leaned against the rough brick wall and pressed her arms against her chest, holding back the pain. She and Damon had come together for so many wrong reasons that had seemed right at the time.

The only right reason, she now knew, was love.

Would they, could they, ever have that? If they could not, how would she survive? Because, fool that she was, she thought she might be falling in love with him, if love meant being transfixed by his beautiful eyes, longing for the nighttime with him, enjoying his touch, feeling pride at his courage in walking and even riding a horse with his injuries, marveling at his keeping his word with her brothers and sisters.

Was that love?

What kind of revenge would that be, to have Damon force her into marriage and then to fall in love with the only man who could never accept her?

She shuddered against the clench of her heart, holding it in with her inadequate arms until she could breathe, then straightened and stood there until she thought her face might be calm again.

Only then did she continue down the hallway, push open the door and walk into the nursery.

DAMON STOOD outside the front door and handed over the reins to the groom. He needed these few minutes to gather his thoughts before he went in and broke his news to Verbena.

His mother was coming whether the answer was yea or nay. His father was coming to make certain his wife did not get swept away by emotion and wishes.

It was reassuring to have been right when he told Verbena that his mother would love Andrew's child. He had hopes for his father as well, once Edward saw his lost son in the babe.

Damon had asked for time to get Roderick fed, but highly doubted he would get it. What he had meant was that he needed time calm Verbena and coach the children. They would want the confidence of knowing proprieties, and he wanted them to have that first sense of pride at fitting in to this new world.

His parents, Damon was certain, had heard what he had not said, hence he expected them to arrive at any minute.

His mother had accused Edeline of running off to the stable to have an affair with a stableboy! On the very day of Andrew's death! If his mother could do that while Edeline was numb with grief, he wondered very much what else had gone on. Verbena had tried to tell him, but he had squelched her every argument.

Where had Andrew been all that time? If he knew his brother, Andrew had undoubtedly been hiding in his books or off at the club where he could read without anyone thrusting his responsibilities in his face.

Damon winced when he remembered how he had bullied and threatened Verbena to get her to marry him. She had tried to warn him what to expect, but he had run roughshod over everything she said, had even thrown her father's own drunkenness into her face.

And now his mother was going to descend on them. The only one she was really interested in seeing was Roderick.

He hoped his mother truly had learned from her mistake because, unlike Andrew, he intended to be in the room every minute they were together and he would not tolerate insults.

He nodded at Samuels as he went past.

"Your wife is in the nursery with the babe, Sir."

"Thank you." Damon stopped and turned around. "My parents are expected shortly."

"Very good, sir. I will see that refreshments are ready."

Damon headed up the stairs. He did not hear the four children, which was surprising. How could four children manage to be completely unnoticed?

The nursery door was ajar, a sliver of sunlight reflecting into the hall. He stood by the doorway and listened. Soft singing drifted out, a mother crooning to her child. Verbena's voice.

Damon knocked, then pushed the door completely open. Verbena sat alone in the rocking chair, cradling a sleeping Roderick. He wondered if she had put him down for a single moment. "Where is Mrs. Smythe?"

She looked up at him. "She is at her old home, packing. Her son is with the girls in their schoolroom, and one of the maids is there as well, watching over them. So far no one has screamed, and nothing has been broken, so I believe everyone is fine." She stroked her hand over Roderick's little head, possessiveness in every touch. "Are your parents not with you? What did they say?"

"Well, therein lies a tale." Damon pulled over a chair and sank down into it with a groan of relief. "It seemed I underestimated my father's . . . dislike, shall we say, of your sister." He leaned forward and touched her knee, claiming her as she just had Roderick. "I owe you an apology, my dear." This was not something that could be said at a distance. He rested his hand on her cheek, and hoped it was not still too cool from his ride. "You were absolutely right about Edeline and her stories. I believe her life with my family must have been miserable."

Verbena opened her mouth, and then closed it again. She did not have to say anything, the *I told you so* hung on the air.

"I fear that my father might be well-nigh intolerable." He made himself lift his hand, and leaned back. "But now that my mother is convinced that Roderick is Andrew's, she at least seems ready to make amends."

"It is a little – "

"Late for Edeline," Damon interrupted her. "Yes, I know. And again, I can only apologize. And do my best to make atonement."

A strange look crossed Verbena's face. Damon could not begin to decipher it, and was not certain he wanted to.

He leaned forward to stare straight into her eyes. "I am not Andrew. I will not leave you to my family's less than tender mercies. I have already warned my father that if he says anything against you, I will call him out."

Verbena's eyes grew round as saucers. "You would never!"

He felt his mouth lift. "Probably not. Almost certainly not. But it does not hurt to leave him wondering."

Someone cleared their throat at the door.

"Sir? Er, my lord?" Samuels stood in the doorway.

"Yes?"

"Sir Edward and Mrs. Thern have arrived."

They had not wasted any time. He did not dare turn and look at Verbena. At least he had given her a bit of warning. "How close behind you?"

Samuels stiffened as if he had been insulted. "I asked them to wait in the front parlor."

Damon rose and turned to Verbena. "Brace yourself, Verbena. You are about to meet my parents."

Then he strode out the door behind Samuels.

VERBENA WATCHED DAMON LEAVE, and listened to his footsteps as he hurried down the hallway.

His mother was willing to make amends. Verbena looked down at Roderick, sleeping in her arms. Did that mean she had to allow Mrs. Thern to hold him?

Because she feared the woman might snatch him and run away. Foolish thought. The house was full of servants ready to block any escape.

Mrs. Smythe would be here soon. Verbena did not want the poor woman to be caught in anything uncomfortable. What was she thinking? *She* did not want to be caught in anything uncomfortable, either!

A soft knock came at the door. Verbena swiveled to look. Did she stand? Could she remain seated?

It was too late to decide. Mrs. Thern and her husband stood at the door. Verbena recognized them from about the village. She stood and clutched Roderick closer. The rocking chair creaked behind her, bumping the back of her legs through her skirt.

"Hello –"

"Is that – "

They looked at each other from across the room. Mrs. Thern's face was stark with grief. Her dark hair was striped with grey, and the corners of her eyes drooped with new lines. More lines pleated the space between her eyebrows. She wore a black dress, not so much a sign to the outside of mourning as a mirror of her sorrow.

Her mouth pursed in instantaneous reaction, and Verbena stiffened her spine. Then, even as she drew herself up for a battle, Mrs. Thern's face, her whole bearing, slowly lit with hope. Her eyes met Verbena's. "Is that Andrew's son?"

She had expected those words, expected that Edeline would be left out of Roderick's existence. Looking at the sadness that had etched those new lines on the other woman's face, though, Verbena could not summon even a sliver of offense. "Yes. Yes, it is. Please, come in," she said.

The other woman stepped inside. Verbena moved away from the rocker, and motioned toward it. "Please, sit."

Mrs. Thern met Verbena's gaze again. "I know you would much rather I not be here. I realize we do not meet under ideal circumstances, but Andrew was my son and I never thought I would see a child of his." The lines on her face deepened, hope overlaid with suspicion. "You are certain this is his child?"

Behind her, still in the doorway, Damon shook his head at the same time the thought slipped through, *I will not take offense.* "Absolutely certain. Come look for yourself." But she did not hold Roderick out. If Damon's mother wanted to see her grandson, she had to make some move.

And Mrs. Thern did. With slow steps, she crossed the big room, empty except for the rocker and a couple of chairs. Her head swiveled to take in the barrenness. Verbena knew what she thought, it was obvious in the curl of her lip. "I see you have not made much effort to settle him."

Verbena felt her jaw tighten. "We've only just arrived. We do have a wet nurse coming, however, and want her to furnish it to her own taste. She has her own child, so Roderick will have an instant playmate."

"Hmph. I hope you have checked her over carefully." Mrs. Thern reached her at last, and Verbena could see, beneath the defensive exterior, the aching hope beneath. While her face showed disapproval, her true feelings were in her eyes.

"Please, sit in the rocker if you will." Verbena invited a second time, and took another backward step to give the woman room.

Looking between Verbena and the chair, Mrs. Thern must have decided the chair would yield first, so she eased past, trying hard not to get too close, and seated herself with much rustling of petticoats and skirts.

Taking a breath, trying to hide the trembling inside, Verbena leaned over and placed Roderick in his grandmother's arms.

"It is hardly the first child I have ever held," Mrs. Thern grumbled, but her eyes never left that little, sleeping face. And then, "Oh! Oh. Oh, my baby."

Verbena wanted to snatch Roderick back. He was not Mrs. Thern's baby, he was her own. Damon must have slipped inside the room because his hand came down on her shoulder and held her in place.

"Does he look like Andrew?" Damon asked quietly.

"His hair is a bit darker." Mrs. Thern's voice broke. "But so much. So very much." Her hand came down over Roderick's tiny head, stroking it with a feather touch. "So much."

She gazed across the room to where her husband still stood rigid and disapproving in the doorway. "Edward." A single drop slid down her cheek. Her voice quavered. "Edward, come see. Come see our grandson. He is the virtual image of our Andrew."

Verbena held her breath as she watched the man in the doorway. It seemed like an eternity before he moved, each step slow, but finally he was at the rocker. No one spoke, not even Mrs. Thern, as he looked down at Roderick. Finally his hand came up and one finger traced the dark hair on the tiny head. Edeline's hair, Verbena knew.

"Remember . . ." it was Sir Edward's turn to quaver. He cleared his voice and started again. "Remember how dark Andrew's hair –" He stopped again, and this time it seemed it was for good.

Mrs. Thern was openly crying now. "I thought that very thing." She lifted him up and pressed her lips to his forehead. "My little Andrew."

The words might as well have been shouted, they resonated so hard. Verbena took a breath to protest, but Damon gave her shoulder a warning squeeze. He said the words Verbena had feared all along. "Would you two like a few moments alone with him?"

She gasped but Damon turned her around and started walking toward the door. Verbena dug in her heels. "I am not leaving," she whispered in fury.

"Yes, you are." His hands came around her waist and he actually lifted her off her feet, walked to the door and out, then set her down. He winced and rubbed his leg but Verbena was not in a mood to be sympathetic.

The door to the nursery shut behind her with a solid thump. Verbena whirled around, to see Samuels with his hand still on the handle.

"Why did you do that? I am not going to leave them alone with him! Open that door back up."

Damon's arm caught her in an unbreakable grip, pinning her back against him. Over her head, he said, "Thank you, Samuels. You may go now."

Verbena squirmed in his hold, and tried to pry his hand off her waist. "I need to be in there! Did you hear her call him Andrew? She is trying to claim him!"

Damon's arm just held tighter. "She is his grandmother. As such, she does have a claim on him. He is her grandson, and he is Andrew's son. It is only natural to look for pieces of Andrew in him. You should be glad that she has verified your sister's faithfulness."

Verbena stilled for a moment. He was right on that at least. "But what if she wants to take him with her? I promised Edeline I would keep him safe." She managed to stop the last few words. *From them.*

Damon seemed to hear them anyway. He turned her around to face himself. One hand came up to capture her chin. The other held her in place, strong around her back. "I realize you would rather none in my family even lay eyes on Roderick, but that was never going to happen. He needs both sides of his family, and I intend to see he has that. Now, leave my parents alone with him. Roderick will wake soon enough and need to eat, and I promise you, they will be only too happy to turn him back over."

"Mrs. Smythe!" Verbena grabbed at the reminder with relief. Anything to guarantee that Damon's mother would be forced to relinquish Roderick. "She should be here by now. I wonder if anything went wrong."

"She is already here. The foyer is full of her possessions. I asked her to give us a few minutes. Her son is running about in the kitchen, keeping Mrs. Thompson and the staff so busy we will be lucky to have anything to eat tonight." He seemed to want to smile, his mouth crooked on one side, but it did not reach his eyes. "I apologize for my mother's words. Give her a chance, Verbena. Your grief is new and fresh, but hers is painful, too. Roderick has given both my parents new hope. You were not there when she found out about him. I promise you, she knows what she did to your sister. In her own way, I believe she regrets it."

Verbena remembered Mrs. Thern's face as she came in. Letting go of the resentment was hard, but she had to admit that he might be right. The constant snapping could be so ingrained Damon's mother did not know how to get rid of it.

She stepped back and out of his reach anyway. She had given much, it was his turn to yield on a point. "Don't you dare let her remove him from this house. Anyone who wants to see him can come here."

He raised his hands. "Understood. And agreed. I hope that with enough visits, my family can come to a whole new appreciation of your family. Perhaps with Roderick, someday the animosity will be put to rest. Now, come with me and greet Mrs. Smythe."

"No." His brows came down. "I am sorry, Damon. I know she is your mother. You tell me to wait outside, so I promise I will not go back into the room, but I *will* wait here."

They stared at each other. Neither said a word for a long, long breath.

"Some day you will let go of your sister's prejudices." Damon turned around and walked away, leaving her there.

But he did not make her come with him. Verbena gazed down the empty hallway where he had so recently been. He might be angry with her – very well, he *was* angry with her – but he had respected her fears.

Edeline had not been defended by Andrew or she would not have been abused by his family and staff. Verbena realized she was still gazing at where her husband had been. Could it be that her own marriage, started so inauspiciously, had more than her sister had managed in six years?

Somewhere nearby a clock ticked. It was her only company. That, and her thoughts, and a strange feeling, like a warm bubble, building behind the fichu in her neckline.

Damon was growing in her heart.

The thought kept her company as she stood, alone, too distracted to watch the door.

26

Thomas Barnes stood on the street and stared up at the impressive house before him. Pillars marked the entrance, and the steps leading to the door were washed so clean they looked polished. On either side of the door, the windows were nearly as wide as one wall of his house.

Four stories tall and big enough for several sizeable rooms per floor. Large windows lined every wall, rich curtains behind the glass only hinted at the wealth within.

So this was where the Therns lived. They could certainly afford such a grand place, what with all the money they got now from their land, rents that were squeezing the life out of the villagers.

He himself was a working man, he earned his own money, rather than living off the sweat and backs of others. No leech, him, no sir!

Thomas strode up the walk and stomped across the portico, telling himself that the thumping of his heart was rage, not nerves. He was going to make a claim on his grandson, and they were going to finally pay!

He raised the heavy knocker and slammed it down. The sound reverberated into the bowels of the house. It opened as though reluctant to let anything outside pollute the perfection. He caught a quick glimpse of a polished table just inside, probably for cards when the family could not be bothered to invite the people in. Just leave the card and they will get back to you when they had the spare time, he thought sourly.

The door opened. He puffed out his chest. "I'm here to see the master of the house, an' you can tell him I won't be fobbed off with excuses." He tried looking down his nose at the man behind the door, but it was hard to do from a step below.

The man, clearly some kind of servant from the spit-and-polish uniform, did it much better than he had. In fact, the man's lip curled. "Servants to the back," he said with revulsion, and slammed the door shut.

Slammed the door! In his face, him, the legal grandfather of their only grandchild? Thomas stepped forward and grabbed for the knocker, but the door opened so quickly that he almost fell inside.

He talked fast. "I know my children are in this house. Now let me in to see them or I will spread the word all over London that the Therns stole them. See how that sits with all their high and mighty friends!"

"A likely story! I said, servants in the back, and don't think you will get any more attention. Now get away."

And he slammed the door again. Harder.

They would not open it again, even if he kicked it. And it was so heavy and so thick he would only hurt his foot.

Something moved at the side of the house. Thomas stopped staring at the door and watched the corner, one hand on the railing for a quick vault and escape, half afraid the Therns were about to send their staff after him. But it was nothing so threatening, he saw with relief. Instead, a scruffy young boy carrying some letters in one hand and a small box in the other fairly pranced along the graveled drive. Thomas walked back down the steps, keeping his eye on the child as a plan took shape.

Was the youngster a member of the household staff who would

feel obligated to report anything that happened? Or was he just one of the boys who roamed London, one who would do anything for a coin?

He still had small pouches of his wages hidden on his person. Thomas reached the sidewalk and watched the boy walk along the street. The boy's clothes certainly did not have the stamp of a household servant, with ragged bottoms on the legs and a coat too thin and too small. His shoes looked a bit too big but sturdy, no doubt the one piece of his attire he dared spend any of his earned cash on.

Up closer, Thomas noticed the boy was dirty, and his hair so greasy it was impossible to guess its color. If this boy was a street urchin with access to the house, nothing could be better. If a family with children had moved in, no doubt the servants would be nattering about it in the kitchen, and the kitchen was about the furthest into the house such a ragged little person would be allowed.

Thomas caught up with the boy at the end of the block while a carriage rattled past and they had to stop anyway.

"Boy! You looking to earn some coin, or you already work for someone?"

"Me?" Bright blue eyes looked up at him. The kid did not even look surprised at being stopped by a stranger. That was a good sign. "Naw, I just carry letters an t'like around. Ain't nobody better'n me at gettin round London. I jest try to know all the servants in the better 'ouses, an' they allus send for me when they gots stuff to get delivered." He looked Thomas up and down with mercenary intent. "Why, you got a package you wants delivered som'eres?"

"How'd you like to make money just for finding out something?"

"Like what?" The boy's eyes went wary, but Thomas saw the gleam of greed was still there.

"Is there a family of children staying there, in that house you just left?"

"Why you want to know?" The carriage was gone, and Thomas figured the boy wanted to get this errand done so he would be able to take on another.

Thomas spoke fast. "Those children are mine. They were taken away while I was off on a ship and I'm back to collect them."

Sure enough, the boy started across the street, taking for granted that Thomas would follow. He did. "'Ow am I s'posed to know they be yours? Iffen they are there, that is."

"I can tell you their names." Thomas hoped the boy would not be cagey enough to ask for their ages, because he could not remember.

"Don't matter," the boy said. "There ain't no kids there 'cept them two girls."

Two girls? But if it was his family, there should be three girls. And where were the boys?

"I hear they aim to marry one of them off soon. That worth anythin to you?" The boy gave him a sideways look but did not slow.

The pain that was making Thomas's life miserable lately flared up, one sharp push that presaged more. "No, but if you stop for just a moment, I will tell you what help you can be."

The boy stopped with obvious reluctance. "Talk fast, then, mister, because I earn more iffen I'm quick. So what you wanna know and how much you willin to pay?"

"I want to find my children, and I know that family knows where they are. I want to know if a man with a limp ever comes and if anyone mentions a baby. And if you can tell me that, I will pay you," Thomas did some quick calculations, "a pound."

The boy's eyes widened, but his wary nature surfaced. "An' what if I can't find out where 'e lives? You gonna back out?"

Thomas knew then they had a deal. "You are a bright lad. I'm sure you can find out something. Here." Thomas fished a shilling out of his pocket and flipped it into the air. The boy caught it with a skill that indicated he had had to get most of his wages that way. "You find out about the man who limps and I will give you a whole pound in addition to that. But you need to find out where that man lives. That is the bargain, a pound for the address."

"You got a deal! How'm I s'posed to find you?"

"You know The Ram's Ear? In Cheapside? Send a message there. The name's Barnes. Repeat it."

"Barns. I got it. Now, Barns, I gotta go. I hear anythin, I send word." He lifted a hand and took off running.

Thomas rubbed his hands together. *Just you see,* he thought to Thern, *just you see. I will get my grandson and if you want him back, you will fork over every penny you have.*

He rubbed his side. He needed something to eat, and some ale to wash it down.

27

CONCEALED BY DARKNESS AND HORSES, THOMAS STARED ACROSS THE span at the house, trying to see. His stomach churned. He had spotted servants moving about the back, probably the kitchen, while he had sat here waiting.

Thomas rubbed the painful spot on his right side, and frowned. The children were most likely asleep now, which was all to the good. They did not like him much, he knew that, they were not going to help him.

The house at last went dark, the servants all seemed to be off to bed. The fewer awake, the better. Thomas eased out from the nest he had made in the stable and bent and stretched until his aching bones began to move. He had kept his eye on one tree that brushed against a window on the second floor. That room had been dark since his disloyal daughter and her husband had left in the big carriage. They even had a coachman to drive the thing.

Now was the time. He slung the duffle with everything he could possibly need over his shoulder, and slipped across the courtyard to the tree. He had spent most of his life climbing masts and hanging onto sails, he was as at home shimmying up anything tall and straight as he was walking across the road. And a tree, with all its branches? It was made for him.

The window was latched, a mere inconvenience. He had planned for that. He took the thin pick out of his bag and eased it into the seam. It squeaked as it slid against the metal latch, but with a little more pressure – ah ha! The latch popped out of the holder and the window sighed open a crack.

Not a sound came from the other side of the heavy drapes. Thomas pushed himself off the branch and landed in the room with a soft thud. He had hoped to make less noise than that, but his body had not moved so easily lately.

He was in. The room was big, a massive bed and matching armoire, a chair, even a little prissy table with a mirror that his daughter probably used, and empty of any people, not even a maid sleeping in a chair waiting for his daughter to come back. Better and better.

He listened at the hallway door, but not a sound came from outside. Placing every foot with care, he crept down the hallway, peeking in one door after another. In the faint light from the banked fires he recognized Julius in one room, Matthew in another, their breathing slow and regular.

The child was not on this floor. Thomas knew he was in the right house, the other children were here, the babe had to be here as well. He had seen another floor above this this one, and staring at the door at the hallway's end, knew another set of stairs had to be hidden there. The servants' stairs, no doubt, and better than retracing his steps.

Thomas eased it open and listened, just in case a servant was wandering around in the dark. It was silent. He slipped through it and edged it shut, then quiet as a cat climbed to the next floor.

Another door, and another silent entry. Another hallway, but this one had fewer rooms. Only one door on this side, and two on the other.

He started with the single door, opening it as carefully as he had done on the floor below.

Aha. At last. He had found his quarry. The rocking chair and the cradle barely visible gave it away.

Thomas slipped inside and eased the door closed except for a crack. Soft breathing, the sound of deep sleep, whispered through the stillness. He waited until his eyes adjusted to the play of shadow. This room, too, boasted a fireplace, faint red glowing along its base and softening the shadows, the scent of smoke drifting past as he breathed. A big room, a table and chairs for meals away from the Mighty Therns, two tall armoires, several padded chairs, a bookshelf, small side tables – what had they done, emptied a whole house into this one room? – and most important, a bed. Solid but not overly impressive, covers in a fluffy mound, it sat pushed against the wall where it would stay warm but not too hot. A nightcap poked out one side of the bundle.

Ranged in a small "L" by that head sat not one, but two small child-sized beds, one the cradle he had seen on first glance, the other a low miniature bed nearly hidden in the shadows.

"Who are you?" A woman's voice, breathless but shrill, cut the air like a whistle. Beneath the nightcap wide alarmed eyes stared at him, the fire's glow leaving pinpricks of light on their surface. The woman flung off the covers, and vaulted from the bed. Arms outstretched as if that would stop him, she moved in front of the two small baby beds, trying to block them with her body, and opened her mouth to scream.

His hand shot out and caught her on the chin without conscious thought. The woman did not make a sound, she just crumpled like an empty gown. Thomas grabbed her before she landed on the cradle.

The woman was a tidy armful, but he managed to get her back onto the bed. The pain in his side lanced through him again, and he bent double, fighting for breath. His knees trembled, and for a muddled moment he feared he would faint.

Finally his legs stopped shaking, and he was able to breathe again. The woman was still out. What he could see of her body showed a woman ripe and curvy, with heavy breasts. Milk leaked through her nightgown.

So that was who she was. The wet nurse.

He turned to the cradle and looked at the infant. Lord, it was a little one! On the rare occasions he was home from the sea when the children were this size, he had left most of the work to his wife. All they seemed to do was eat, puke and foul themselves.

He stared at the tiny mite, at the pushed-up nose starting to find a shape, and the brows that framed new-moon lashes, the miniature bow of a mouth. He saw pieces of each of his children in the little face. Time slipped back. *His wife smiled across a bundle at him. "Don't you see your eyes in her face, darling? She's going to be a beautiful girl." Her own eyes twinkled. "I've always loved your eyes."*

Another time, another smile. "You're back! Oh, Thomas, see." His wife's belly had been the sweetest bump when the ship had sailed, but Rosaline still smiled at him across the table covered with dough and flour, no blame in her eyes. Her hands were sticky from kneading. "Go look, my love. You missed this one's birth. I called for you." From the basket on the floor, big eyes stared up at him, the color of spring leaves, identical to the eyes alight with joy on the other side of the table. "It is a girl. Such a pretty baby, see the white curls all over her head?" She came around, wiping the flour onto her apron, and wrapped him with love. Lips as sweet as ripe fruit touched his, and his heart swelled. "We make the most beautiful children, don't we, dear?"

He heard himself say, "I will be here the next time."

A day of rich joy, he felt himself laugh while he held the baby the midwife handed him. On the bed, the same smile, tired but happy. Her face was pale, dark circles rested under those smiling eyes. "A son, Thomas. We did it. We have a son now."

More years, time rushing by. The eyes that smiled at him had lines around them now, gentle creases from endless smiles, and her brown hair was snowed with grey. "See our family? Two girls and two boys, how perfect."

The babies kept coming, with no way to stop them except leaving their marriage bed, something he could not do. Rosaline's hair went more white than brown, her smile was slower to come, her body became thin with work. The older girls helped, he knew they stepped in while he was away at sea.

Laws changed each time he came back, laws that demanded more money and took away more land. The world he knew was slipping away, only the sea remained constant. Rosaline begged him to stay, but as much as he needed her, the unending sea called and he had to go. She never understood that sailing was as much a part of him as breathing. She tried to understand, he knew she tried, but she never fully realized it, or she would have stopped asking.

And then that awful day when he came home and she was not there. Verbena stood by the fireplace stirring the stew, and when she turned around, there was grief in her eyes. "Mother is dead," she said.

That day his life lost all meaning. He could not stay in that house with six pairs of eyes staring at him. Her eyes, her hair, occasionally her smile, but never her. The sea called again and again, stronger and harder, and only with the ship beneath his feet and salt wind in his face could he forget.

Somewhere deep in the house a clock chimed the hour, and the world snapped back, the past vanishing like smoke, leaving only endless grief and burning anger. He was in a Thern house, where they had stolen his life, his land and his children. Now, finally he would get something back from them.

A boy, they had told him. A son. No, not a son, a grandson. The Therns did not have time for it, but if young Mr. Damon had gone to all the effort of hiring a wet nurse, clearly he would pay plenty to get it back.

It did not matter which Thern paid.

Another stab of pain twisted him, wrapping around his side. He knew something was wrong inside his body, time was slipping away, but vengeance still burned in him. All those years alone, empty. If the Therns had not kept taking the land, buying it up for the cash Verbena kept saying they needed for those cursed fences, those barriers between the Therns and nobodies like himself, maybe Rosaline would still be alive.

They had everything and he had nothing. First his wife gone, then his eldest daughter dead, and now that rakehell younger son had taken the others. Right out of his own house!

The Therns owed him a life, and he would make them pay.

Reaching down, he unhooked his sailor's bag and spread it wide. He looked down at the pile of blankets surrounding the babe. The coverings would certainly fit in his duffle bag easily. They would have to, it was cold outside, and it would never do to let the child catch a chill.

He grabbed the corners of the fluffy blankets and lifted the bundle like a knapsack. His grandson mewled as he rolled into the middle, a tiny fist flailed out, but he did not wake. Thomas glanced over at the woman, but she had not moved. Panic formed sickly in his stomach as he stood there and stared at her, holding his grandson in the sling of blankets.

He could almost feel the noose around his neck. It would be hanging for sure if the woman was dead.

He heard a breath from her limp form, and was able to breathe himself. He had not hit her that hard. Thomas tucked the babe into his duffle and hooked the catches.

Then he slipped out of the room and down the hall, through the stairway's doors, and out on the family's level, placing every step with care. The baby was small, but with all those blankets, it felt heavier than it should.

Back at the window, he tucked one handle over each shoulder to keep his arms free and eased himself out onto the branch. It should have been easy, it was so easy to get in, but his body felt shaky and he was afraid he would fall.

Him? A sailor? Fall? But every grasp was uncertain and each foot placement felt slippery.

The baby started to whimper, and he forced himself to move faster. At last his feet felt solid ground.

Thomas ran.

28

THE THEATRE WAS EVEN LARGER UP CLOSE, THE FRONT MARKED WITH tall pillars. It blazed in the darkness like a beacon.

London time was still so strange, people up at all hours. Back in Thernbury she would have been asleep long ago, and here the night's entertainment had not even begun.

She would not have come, she was after all in mourning, but Damon had insisted that she be seen. "It is not as frivolous as a ball," he had assured her. "I can hardly wait the entire three months mourning – "

"Six," she interrupted.

He pretended not to hear. " – before I introduce you. Now that our families are being mended, it is best that any rumors be stopped. One evening at the insistence of your husband will be forgiven. After tonight, you may live within the rules as strictly as you wish, but we *will* take this one night."

So here they were. Damon's hand, resting in the middle of her back ever since they alighted from the carriage, gave Verbena a gentle push. Her new gown, stitched with speed and additional seamstresses to make the deadline, was black silk bombazine, high-waisted, with sleeves of the softest matching black crepe, and it rustled under the equally new pelisse that had been finished at the same time. The crisp night air should have chilled her, but both gown and coat were warm. She had not been cold in days.

Seemingly endless groups of people funneled toward the impressive building like ants moving toward their anthill, London in miniature, from all levels of Society, those dressed much like herself and Damon, in rich capes and greatcoats, down to rowdy clumps of men and women in clothes patched from top to bottom. Scattered among the moving mass, children held out bouquets of hand-made flowers and called, "Gifts for your ladies? Gifts for your ladies? A penny each."

Verbena's heart ached as she watched them. They were about Annabelle's age, so young, with dirty faces and ragged clothes.

"No," Damon ordered. She turned and looked at him. "No, Verbena, we can't take in all the poor children in London." He winced. "I agree, it is a blight on the conscience of England." He looked down at her face. "Oh, very well, my dear." Damon lifted her hand and pressed a quick kiss on it. "Stand right here and do not move."

He went up to the nearest ragged little girl, younger even than Annabelle and plucked her entire supply of tiny bouquets from her dirty hand. Verbena could not see the coin he gave her, but the little girl's eyes went wide. "Oooh, thankee, sir!" The girl whirled around, grabbed the hand of another girl slightly older, and they dashed off. Safe for the night, at least.

He came back and gave an elegant bow as he presented his handful of posies to her. "Your flowers, my lady." Damon's eyes twinkled as she took them.

Verbena stared into those dark eyes that held such compassion. "That was very kind of you, Damon. You saved two small girls, did you see that?" She tucked her free hand into his arm. "Odd, how little it takes to make such a big difference."

The huge doors of their goal were held open by ushers. Light beckoned from deep inside.

She waved a hand at the crowd around them. "Damon, are you

certain this is not the Season yet? There are so many people here." If it was like this and the Season had not yet begun, what would it be like later? Edeline had told her a bit about London's merry whirl.

He chuckled, the sound vibrating the cold air. "Some have already returned from the country, waiting for Parliament to open. It is not going to be as crowded inside as you think. The season will get under way shortly after Easter, so enjoy what space we have while we have it." His hand slid up and down where it rested on her back in a subtle movement, sending strength and support through her layers of clothing. She lifted her chin and stepped forward with paper-thin confidence she hoped no one could see through.

They swept through the doors and into Covent Garden Theater. Verbena gasped, her sound swallowed up by the pound of voices and the vibrations of laughter on the air. Stairs reached up floor after floor, chandeliers hung from the ceiling, prisms casting rainbows all over the walls. The crowds outside had been jammed into the foyer, and odors assaulted her: perfume layered upon perfume, unwashed bodies, a faint tinge of horse. She was jolted from side to side with people pushing past, and only Damon's arm firmly around her waist kept her from losing her footing. She doubted she would have landed on the floor, there was no room to fall.

"Follow me," Damon shouted over the roar around them. "I have a box."

"Your own?" She had a hard time keeping up with him despite his solid support as they climbed a stunning staircase leading to the floors above. She noticed everyone on the stairs with them was dressed as elegantly as herself. All those in more everyday garb spilled through the doors on the main level. "Why did you not tell me you had your own box?"

"I could say I meant it as a surprise." Damon did not give the main floor swarming with shouting, swearing theatre-goers so much as a glance. It was quieter up here. He looked back. "The truth is, I did not think to mention it. I purchased it before I left for the war, and my friends used it until this past summer when I came back well enough to use it again. It is just where I go to watch the opera."

Last summer was still a delicate subject, fraught as it was with pain. They both turned their attention to the openings at their side and pretended to be absorbed in finding the right one.

Partway down the hall, dotted with curtained alcoves that had to be the boxes he referred to, Damon pulled aside a velvet hanging and waved her inside. "Get yourself settled, my dear, and let the curious come to us. I doubt we will have long to wait."

Verbena was surprised how high up they were. She pulled her chair away from the box's edge, tucking it into as much of a corner as she could make, and sank down. The wall on her left separating her partially from the neighboring box gave the illusion of security. She unfastened her pelisse and slipped it off. Despite the sharp chill of the night, warmth from all the bodies in the building left her arms just pleasantly cool.

She smoothed the wrinkles out of the gown, and reached up to make sure the jet earrings were still tied to her ears. On her left hand, her wide gold wedding ring shimmered warmly, announcing to all her honored status. She loved the feel of it.

The ceiling arched high above her, and another row above their own with more boxes just like theirs ringed the walls. How could anyone enjoy the performance if they were hanging so high above the floor? She was glad Damon had not chosen a box up there.

Down below them, the auditorium floor was a moving sea of people. A fistfight broke out beneath them just as Damon lowered himself into the chair beside her. She pointed at the fight. "I have the strangest urge to go down and knock heads together. If people don't know how to behave so everyone can enjoy the performance, then they should not come."

He reached over and took her hand, patting it just as he would have patted one of the girls' heads. "That is part of the performance." His eyes twinkled. "You will see soon enough."

A male voice boomed out behind them, making her jump. "Damon, old chap!"

Her husband's eyes closed for the barest second before he rose and turned slowly to the uninvited guest. "Fitz."

They shook hands. What might have been a smile bent Damon's mouth.

"Thing is, man, there is a rumor going around that you are wed." Fitz stepped closer, as if he thought their conversation could be overheard. Verbena was positive he had not seen her yet. "The report is that there are children old enough to be out of the nursery and into the schoolroom, and a babe."

With a subtle move, Damon suddenly blocked her view of Fitz, and his view of her. "Take care, Fitz."

Fitz's voice became more urgent. "I don't remember you having children. The babe makes sense, you were out of Town for Andrew's funeral, I can see grabbing comfort from the village doxies, but you don't have to marry them. Just pay them off! A little cash, a pretty brooch, and get out of there. No one will challenge you if you ever deny it."

Damon's shoulders were rigid. "You have been misinformed. It is true, I am recently wed, to a lady in every sense of the word. The child is my late brother and sister-in-law's child. The younger children are my wife's siblings. You should know better than to listen to useless gossip, Fitz. It can only get you into trouble."

Verbena had heard enough. She stood and stepped around Damon, ignoring his restraining hand. "How do you do?" Her voice was cool. It was not solely this man's fault, she had to remind herself. He was merely spouting what the men of his class thought. She contented herself with resting her left hand on Damon's arm, making certain the wedding ring caught the light. "I don't believe we have been properly introduced."

She saw Damon sigh, watched his coat move with the heavy breath, then he turned around and drew her forward. "Verbena, I would like to present an old friend of mine, Mr. Fitzgerald. Fitz, my wife, Mrs. Thern."

Fitz's mouth sagged. She knew he wanted to look her over, but manners, arriving a little late, prevented him. "Beg your pardon, ma'am, er, Mrs. Thern. I did not start the rumors, you know, I just wanted to know the truth."

"I have two brothers and two sisters, as Damon said," she said, "and they adore my husband." Her breath caught as she realized what she had said.

They adore my husband.

Not just them. No, not just them at all.

Adore. The word whispered in her mind, and floated like a feather down to her heart. *I adore my husband. I do.* She wanted to laugh, and sing, and throw her arms around Damon, standing there with his polite look on his face and a hint of pride in his eyes.

I am one of the lucky ones. I love my husband. And how worthy he is.

Somewhere between that early injury and his solicitous care, the walk down the drive and the gifts he had rescued for Edeline, all so carefully chosen, somewhere between finding clothes for her brothers and sisters and rescuing Mrs. Smythe, even giving a little girl enough money to keep herself and her sister safe for one night, she had fallen in love with her husband.

She wished she had the time to relish in the moment, sit and absorb it, take his hand in hers and tell him. How surprised he would be. The laugh softened into a whisper of tears. She forced them back. There would be time later. There would *have* to be time later. The floating feather of contentment and joy turned into the first brushes of unease.

How was she going to tell Damon?

And how did he feel? Did he feel even a portion of what she did? The wedding ring felt warm on her finger. He had said he valued her when he gave her his grandmother's ring. Did value equal love?

The box was abruptly quiet, and she realized they were waiting for her to answer. She had not even heard the question. "Beg pardon?"

"No, my dear, Fitz was begging yours." Damon smiled, but it was grim and humorless.

She could not help it, she beamed at Fitz. "Of course I accept your apology." How could she not, when talking to him had finally opened her mind to what her heart had been trying to tell her?

Fitz blinked, and bowed, a bow worthy of a queen. "I shall help you straighten out the story. I assure you, not another untoward word about you will ever pass my lips. You are indeed a prize, and I envy Damon."

She smiled at him, and curtsied. "Thank you."

The box was chilly after Fitz left. She turned toward Damon, nervous about meeting his gaze. She was so full of emotion she felt it must flow out from her like sunbeams. Would he see her love in her eyes? Would it embarrass him if he did?

"You did not need to be so flowery about it," Damon muttered, his brows still furrowed and fierce. "The man just insulted you and your entire family. I was ready to call him out."

"At least he had the courage to come to you about the tale, rather than spreading it behind your back." She waved a hand toward the milling, teeming mass around them. "How many others have come to find out the truth?"

"Don't look now, my love, but you will have plenty more chances, starting just about now. Another set of old friends is coming." He nodded to a nearby box, where a group of four gentlemen all were rising. One of them caught her eye and winked.

Damon the Demon.

"Prepare yourself for some more explanations." He glared over at the now-empty box. "When I said I wanted to introduce you, these were not the friends I had in mind. If you would, this time please allow me to do the talking."

Her wedding ring still felt warm on her finger. She looked down at it, and it glowed gold and proud.

THE BEGINNING of the opera came as a relief. She was tired of meeting people. Somehow she had imagined, after their brief time last summer, that Damon's social whirl had been totally blown away by the injuries of war. Based on the number of friends who insisted on finding out if 'the tale' was true, and said tale seemed to grow with every new collection of guests to their box, he could spend every day with a different person and still not have made the circuit before the month's end.

At least there was the small comfort that, between Fitz and their own efforts, the news of Damon's marriage was well known among all his friends and acquaintances in town.

He said little after the performance began, but he held her hand. A memory came back, sweet now, of him holding her hand just like this at their wedding. There had not been much hand-holding since then, and her fingers curled around his as they had not that day.

If she had known this emotion was in store for her then, she would have clung to his hand with all her might. There was no going back, but the going forward – ah, what fun they would have together.

She hoped.

She still did not know what he thought of her, but if this evening's quiet contentment was any indication, telling him how she felt would not be so very hard.

One of them had to speak first. Cowardice did not suit her.

The music swelled, carrying her to a place she had never known existed before, rich, complex, filled with subtle shades that could never come out of the church piano. Voices filled the huge room, soaring above the swelling notes. In the carriage on the way here, Damon had said, "You have not heard music or singing until you have been to the opera. It can't be described, it has to be experienced." How right he was. Verbena felt goosepimples rise on her arms, and she shivered with delight.

Damon turned around, she noticed his movement out of the corner of her eye, but could not take her gaze from the stage. He rose and slipped from the box, his sudden absence breaking the spell around her.

She turned to see him whispering to an attendant through the curtain opening. She could not hear their words, but felt his alarm. He took a small scrap of paper from the man and read it, and his face lost color.

Verbena rose. He turned to look at her. She had never seen him like this, not even the day Andrew died.

Without being told, she grabbed her fur cloak and his great-coat. Damon flung her cloak over her shoulders, and headed down the stairs, putting his own coat on as they went.

"What is it? What happened?"

"Roderick is gone. Stolen. Someone came in and took him from his crib."

"No! Please, no!" Verbena grabbed at his arm, clinging tight. A name pushed at her lips, but she dared not say it.

His jaw was tight, and his shoulders tense even through the layers of his coat.

Would they go this far?

29

Where was Roderick?

The horses' hooves pounded on the dark cobbled streets, a frantic rhythm that matched the beat of Verbena's heart. *Hurry up, hurry up, hurry up.* The wheels slipped as they turned a corner, then caught and the carriage rattled on. Damon's eyes were grim and cold.

The carriage stopped, rocking as it settled into place, and Damon did not wait for the coachman to lower the steps, just vaulted out, stumbling as his bad leg hit the sidewalk. He reached back for Verbena. Her skirts got in the way, tangling around her legs, but finally she kicked herself free and, holding Damon's hand, raced with him up to the door.

Samuels had it open. The house was ablaze with light, it streamed through the windows, and out the opened door. It seemed the entire household staff stood there, and behind them Julius, Matthew, Lizabeth and Annabelle. The boys had their arms around their sisters. They were all crying.

Off to one side, she saw Mrs. Smythe holding a cloth to her face. Little Alice stood by her, patting her awkwardly on the shoulder. Verbena did not have a chance to go over and see what had happened, the group was pressed so close together, like a wall of concern.

Everyone had red-rimmed eyes, or fists clenched in impotent rage. Voices rang out around them. "We found the window he got in." "He took everything out of the cradle." "Mrs. Smythe is hurt!" "There are tracks beneath the window."

The villain had not come through the door, but the window. *Their* window. Damon and Verbena exchanged glances.

They had not been home.

Mrs. Smythe had been asleep. She spoke around the snow-filled cloth, but more than pain muffled her words. Verbena knew how much her every heartbeat must hurt, and how the screams were locked in her throat.

Across the hallway, she and Mrs. Smythe locked gazes, seeing their own despair in the other's eyes.

Little Roderick.

Who could do such a thing?

They needed answers, and the questions had to be asked. No, Mrs. Smythe said, she did not know what had awakened her. A shape, definitely a man, but it had been dark. She did not remember the blow.

"I could not have been insensible long." Her eyes begged for belief. "As soon as I was aware, I sounded the alarm."

Samuels' skin was grey. Lines Verbena had never seen before etched his face. "I had to send for you." His eyes filled. "Someone got into a house under my care."

Damon put a hand on the man's shoulder. "This is not your fault." His voice was calm, but she knew her husband's fear was as great as her own. "Whoever did this would have found a way in. He planned well."

Damon gestured to the other men, down to the lowest footman, Julius and Matthew included. They clustered in a group by the foyer wall, talking urgently in low tones.

Lizabeth and Annabelle ran across the foyer to Verbena. She wrapped them in her arms even as she wanted to go over and find out every step the men planned to take, but her legs had gone weak and she looked around for a chair. One appeared beside her, she did not know who put it there.

Ringing began in her ears. Perhaps Damon could hear it, too, because he suddenly broke off talking and looked over at her. Faster than she thought he could move, he was at her side, and knelt on the floor to look into her eyes. Warmth flowed into her icy hands from his large ones.

"Verbena? Are you all right?" His dark eyes held hers, and with a sudden cry, she fell forward onto his broad chest. He caught her with a muffled "oof," and she felt him steady himself, wrapping his arms around her and holding her tight. She did not care if the whole house saw, she could not bear it without his strength. Whatever happened tomorrow or the next day, right now he held her, and she wept her fear and pain onto his shoulder.

Warm lips touched her ear, her eyelids, her cheeks, her mouth, whisper touches, each kiss a gift, balm on her crushed heart. Finally he eased her back onto the chair, and cradled her face in his big hands. "Verbena, listen to me."

She nodded, and sniffed the tears back, drawing the girls into her arms again. Which of them needed the hold more, she did not know.

"I'm taking one of the footmen. Julius and Samuels will stay here with you and the girls." He stood up, but something in that expression, the same one she had seen on his face all night, told her where he planned to start.

He was going to question his parents. Verbena ached for him. They had not fought over his family for days, but Mrs. Thern's visits had become more frequent since that first time.

My Andrew, Mrs. Thern had said. Had she learned they would be at the theater tonight?

Nothing had alarmed Verbena for the last few visits. Mrs. Thern had even met the other children. Not happily, but at least with courtesy. Had the Therns been biding their time?

But what would be the point? Where would they go? Would

they dare risk the scandal when they could see him whenever they wished? It made no sense. They loved Roderick. They would never consider anything that would hurt him.

But if not them, who?

Damon was going to question them, she was certain. He rose and Verbena stood up with him as if they were connected. Movement behind him caught her eye. Mrs. Smythe lowered the cloth she had held on her face. Verbena gasped at the swelling there, the color that was already starting down her cheek.

Her legs suddenly remembered how to move and she rushed over to the wet nurse's side. "Oh, my goodness! How are you? Is anything broken?"

Mrs. Smythe tried to smile. "Not broken, but it hurts." The words were barely audible.

"More snow, please, Alice," Verbena ordered, glad for something to keep her busy. She felt Damon's gaze on her, and turned. He gave her a nod before he and the footman left, shutting the door tightly behind them.

The house felt empty, despite the people still clustered in the foyer, all because Damon was gone.

He had smiled at her, nodded to her in perfect understanding, kissed her. How different from her actions all along toward his family. She had not been able to separate Edeline's difficult life from Damon. He was a Thern, and therefore unworthy.

She was a Barnes, and he had not given, by word or deed, any blame to her. To any of them.

When Damon came back, with or – God forbid – without Roderick, she would tell him she loved him. He had 'valued' her, she would take the leap and expose her heart. The words had been building, the feeling growing unknown, unacknowledged. Now in this time of fear and pain, they had to come together.

Who else did they have to lean on?

Damon looked out the carriage window as they pulled up in front of the family home. Candles flickered against the draperies upstairs in his sisters' bedrooms. Downstairs, shadows moved behind the parlor curtains. He climbed out of the carriage and strode firmly up to the door, his greatcoat swirling around him. The door was opened to his pounding by the butler, awake and at his post despite the time of night.

"Sir Damon. What a surprise," Adams said, but Damon, for the first time in his life, ignored him, marched toward the parlor and flung the door open. It slammed back against the wall.

"Where is Roderick?" His voice thundered in the room. His father stood by the fireplace, a beautiful cut crystal glass in his hand. The liquid sloshed as Edward jerked in surprise at his loud entrance.

"What is this about Roderick? What is going on?" His mother whirled around in the tufted chair that faced the fireplace. Her hand pressed against her heart. Damon could see the pulse beating in her neck from where he stood. "What has happened?"

"Someone stole Roderick from his crib tonight. He is gone and his nurse was injured. I want to know if you had anything to do with this!" Damon stood there, his legs braced, fury heating his body, and glared from one parent to the other. "Is he here? Did you take him?"

His parents exchanged alarmed glances. His mother covered her mouth with a shaking hand, and her eyes filled with tears. She looked from Damon to his father, just as Edward dropped down into the nearest chair. Her voice wavered. "Edward?" Not blame, but a cry for help.

It was no act. Damon saw his own terror reflected in his mother's face and felt his rage drain away.

His father's face was suddenly haggard. "Son, tell us everything. *Everything.*"

Damon felt his own legs shake. "I hardly know where to start. Someone opened a window and got into our house tonight. Our wet nurse was attacked. All she remembers is seeing a man in the room. Verbena and I were summoned from the theatre. The whole house is in an uproar. Mrs. Smythe does not think she was insensible long but we still do not know how much time passed before the kidnapping was discovered."

If not his family, then who?

Damon ran a shaking hand over his face. "I owe you both my deepest apologies. I know how attached you are to Roderick."

"Oh, Damon." The hurt in his mother's eyes was reproach in itself. "How could you have thought that? We would never, *never* do anything to hurt Roderick."

"Mother, I do apologize." He braced his hands on the wooden frame of his mother's chair back and locked his knees. "Where do we go now? Who did this? How did he find us? What does he want from us?"

"Nothing else was taken?" His mother's voice was soft, breathless, as if there was no air to fill her lungs.

"No. Just Roderick and his blankets."

"Who would want him? He is so little, just a baby." Shudders shook her breath, sobs held in the barest check. "I must go there. I must be there." She twisted to look up at Damon. "You will find whoever did this! Pay whatever he wants! If you need more, come to us."

"There was no note?" His father's eyes were hollow with fear.

"Nothing." His hands clenched on the wood beneath them. Odd that he did not dent it, his grip was so tight.

"Sir?" A respectful voice came from the doorway. Adams stood there. A worried frown pleated his forehead.

Damon did not wait for his father. "Yes, what is it?"

"If you will forgive me for overhearing, I think I might know a possible suspect."

Three pairs of eyes fixed on him. Edward found his voice first. "Well, who, man? Speak!"

"A rather rough-looking elderly man was here days ago."

His mother interrupted, her voice going shrill, "What help is that? That could be anyone, a beggar from the street."

"Except he demanded to see his daughter. He tried to get in twice, pounding on the door, but at the time I thought him . . . confused and I sent him off. Although," Adams seemed to be searching his memory, "he did know your name, and he did mention his children. I believe he was the late Mrs. Thern's father."

"Did anyone else see him? Might he have talked to any of the other servants?" Damon knew if he himself had been the one turned away, if Verbena and the children had been kept from him, he would have found another way in, even if it meant climbing through a window. Barnes was a sailor, and if Adams was right, newly returned from the sea.

"Not that I have heard, but I will ask."

"*Now*, Adams." Edward took back the responsibility of giving orders. "Wake them all. Immediately."

With a single nod, the butler turned and left.

Damon wanted to follow Adams and shake the poor servants awake himself. Under normal circumstances he would show more compassion, but this was not a normal circumstance and the life of a tiny baby was at stake. That was worth a few hours of lost sleep.

The room went quiet, only the sound of harsh breathing.

"I am sorry I suspected you."

Edward shook his head. "I'm glad you came. Now there are twice as many on the trail. Between us we will move heaven and earth to find him."

The room went quiet again. An eternity later, when his skin was crawling with the need to do something, *anything*, Adams came back with a small maid blinking sleep from her eyes. Damon did not know her name, she must be new to the house.

"Lily says she saw the letter boy talking to an old man a few days ago. I might venture a guess that it was the very day I sent the man away. She says they talked for several minutes and the man tossed the boy a coin."

Damon turned to Lily. "Can you describe him?"

"'Is hair was pulled back in a queue, like, down his neck, and it was grey. 'E was all thin, but tough, and 'is skin was all dark and tanned an' yellow, like. 'E looked like a farmer, kind of. 'E weren't too tall, but 'e weren't short, neither. 'E looked shaky-like, though, an 'e kept rubbin 'is side liken it hurt 'im."

Tanned skin, not like a farmer but a sailor, Damon thought. And tough from months, years out at sea in the biting salt winds. Tanned and yellow and rubbing his side – was the man ill?

A footman skidded to a halt in the doorway. "We just got a note!"

Damon held out his hand, hope and rage in equal parts. "Let me see it." He unfolded the paper and read aloud, "Bring $1000 pounds to the Cock and Bull in Cheapside tomorrow at noon, and I will return the babe." Roderick's tiny life reduced to cold coin. It was unsigned, but Damon knew they must be right, it had to be Barnes. "When did this come?"

"Just now," the footman said. "A little boy brought it to the back door."

What would Verbena think when she found out it was her very own father? "At least we know Roderick is still alive. We are not going to wait for tomorrow. He no doubt is not at the Cock and Bull, but I am going to wager everything that he will be some-where close."

"But this late? And in Cheapside? It is not safe!" Imogene put one hand on his where it still held the chair back. "No doubt that is why he set the time for noon. He knows it is too dangerous a trip for anyone to take across London." She cleared her throat, and said almost under her breath, "I have lost one son, I do not intend to lose another."

"Why did he send it to us?" Edward rose at last. "Why not to you, since he knows where you live?"

Damon shook his head. "I don't know. I believe he holds your wealth against you. He would have no reason to blame me. But why so little? A thousand pounds? Why not five? If he really wanted to hurt us, why not ten thousand?"

"I doubt the man can think so high," Edward said with the

scorn that had been missing until now. "To him a thousand pounds must seem like a lifetime's wages."

A lifetime's wages. His father might be right.

Edward rested his hand on Damon's shoulder. In an almost soundless voice, he said, "This is against me."

Damon bent his head closer. "Why do you say that?"

His father drew him to one side. "Think, Damon. He only went to your house to get the child. The threat came to me. He hates *me*. He wants to meet you tomorrow for the ransom. I believe he will come here tonight. Take your mother to your home for safety. Gather the footmen and find that man as quickly as possible, before he comes back."

"I will. Are you certain you can spare your staff?"

"Adams and I will sit up a watch. Besides," his father nodded toward the wall where two dueling pistols hung, "we will be well protected."

Damon stared at the guns. A horrible image formed in his mind. "Promise me that you will not point that at anyone holding Roderick."

Edward grimaced. "Have some faith in me, son. But if you need it, I give you my word. I will take no chances. Just bring Andrew's son back."

Time was slipping by. Damon held out his hand. "Thank you, Father. Verbena needs to know the plan. I will not sleep until I have Roderick back."

Imogene rose. "I am coming, too. I won't wait here. I need to be where Roderick last was." She hesitated. "I should keep Verbena company. She needs me right now."

That was a surprising sentiment. Damon nodded. "Get ready quickly. I cannot delay." As his mother hurried out of the room, off to keep another servant from getting any more sleep, her words lingered *She needs me*. No doubt the truth was that his mother needed Verbena right now. He turned to his father. "May I take some of your footmen? I think two or three will be enough. Too many descending on Cheapside this hour of the night will spook Barnes and give him time to slip away."

"Take whoever you wish. Just bring back my grandson."

THE PARLOR WAS CROWDED. None of the adults could sleep, but they did not want to talk either so while the chairs were full, the room was silent. Little Alice had stood by Mrs. Smythe like a child to her mother, running out for more snow whenever needed until Verbena feared the girl would collapse, so she currently slept curled up on one of the soft wing chairs. Annabelle and Lizabeth dozed together on the settee. Julius and Matthew, after standing by the wall on guard, had finally dropped down on some straight-backed chairs in matching slumped positions, arms draped over their legs as they stared at the floor.

Samuels had taken the door as his post. "I'll keep watch for the master, Mrs. Thern. You and the children rest."

As if that was possible.

Verbena had forced herself to sit after her worried pacing had begun to alarm the others, and they were worried enough. Sitting had been the hardest thing she had ever done.

The boys suddenly rose as one.

She heard a sound now, too, the closing of the front door. Verbena leapt to her feet, picked up her skirts and ran. The boys reached the parlor door first and nearly clipped her jerking it open. They all but fell into the foyer.

She saw only Damon. "Did you find him?"

By the grim lines around his mouth, his face gave the answer before he spoke. "No." He stepped aside.

Mrs. Thern stood behind him. On her face was the same terror Verbena felt. The last suspicious doubts vanished. She took the first uncertain step, Mrs. Thern moved forward as well, until step by step they gained speed and ran into each other's arms. A cry from the depths burst out of the other woman. Verbena felt it in herself, a rising wave of anguish, building and building. She had the children to think of and had to hold her own screams in.

But it was a relief to finally hear it.

"What did you find out? Anything?"

Damon handed her a scrap of paper. Verbena took it with one hand, while the other still supported Mrs. Thern. She recognized the writing before she even saw the words. "My father? My own father?"

"Father?" Julius had overheard, not that she had made any attempt to speak quietly. It was too much of a shock.

"Father took Roderick?" Red rushed up Matthew's face, and he turned and slammed his fist against the wall. "I hate him! I hate him, I hate him, I hate him!"

Verbena could not scold him. How could Damon stand to look at any of them now?

Julius took the paper from her hands. "He's in Cheapside." He looked over at Damon. "That's not so far. We can go tonight and get Roderick back!"

"Not so fast." Damon's voice was calm. What would they have done without his calmness? How could he manage to think with all this fear churning around him? Only the grim line of his mouth gave away his feelings now. "I talked it over with my father. Barnes would hardly lead us directly to him. But I do not think he would dare travel far with an infant. I believe he is near there, close enough I trust we can find him tonight."

"One thousand pounds?" Verbena had just spent that much on her new wardrobe. Roderick was worth no more than a single shopping trip? She did not know what to feel, insult that Roderick's life was worth so little, fury at her father, humiliation that she had brought such a man into Damon's life.

And fear. Utter, overwhelming fear.

THOMAS SHOVED a corner of the rag of sugar-water into the baby's mouth again, and gritted his teeth against the endless wailing. Nothing he had tried had satisfied the babe. Not a stick of dried bread, not his finger, and now not even the sugar water the innkeeper's wife had brought up, along with her complaints that if he could not keep the baby quiet, he would have to find another place to stay. They had other guests who paid for a night of *sleep*, she had told him, stressing the last word.

He stood and paced the room, jouncing the baby in the crook of his arm. He remembered doing that with his own children, all of whom were sleeping the night away in Thern's house.

Anger simmered again. His children had left his house, his own house, the one his hard work had kept for them, the house that had been handed down for generations, all for fancy curtains and a raft of servants.

What did the rich know about work?

Edeline's babe belched up a belly full of air, and for a breath the room was quiet.

SHOPS LINED THE STREET, shirt makers, tailors, jewelers, their wares proudly displayed in the store windows, but they were closed now for the night. Few lights shone in the windows of the residences above the shops. Small wonder, considering the time. Still, men of all classes strolled along the streets, young bucks looking for a thrill, others shabbily dressed, looking like they had no permanent home, little boys playing too obviously, pushing each other into the passersby, on the lookout for an easy mark. Even as he watched, Damon saw one group scatter. Someone would discover their money purse missing in a minute, but the light-fingered children would be long gone.

He was glad the doors of the carriage were locked, because in the darkness of the mews he saw deeper shadows. Footpads, waiting for someone careless enough to cross their paths. Damon slid his hand into his greatcoat and felt the small revolver in the pocket. In addition, his cane had an interesting surprise in the tip. All around the tightly packed carriage, the footmen felt for their own weapons. Damon had taken just two of his father's most imposing men, and he was glad to have them.

The coachman was armed, too. Riding outside, it would be folly not to be.

The Cock and Bull came into view at the end of a street cluttered with inns. The King's Staff, the Lady Fair – which Damon suspected had ladies but not so fair – the Bull's Horn, the Ram's Ear.

"Just as I suspected," he said in low tones to the footman beside him, and pointed to the line of inns. "It will take us all night to search, if he's even here."

Reggie the footman returned, equally quietly, "How many people would miss an old man with a babe? People here watch, and they notice. And for a coin, they talk."

Reggie would probably know. "I don't want Roderick to endure another minute of suffering, but a crying baby will suit our purposes right now." Damon tapped on the box. The coachman dutifully pulled the carriage up. The horses tossed their heads as they obeyed. The metal bridle rings jingled, but the soft sound blended into the noise of the nighttime street.

Damon looked around, taking the measure of the street before they stepped out into it. If the roles were reversed, only three of the inns would suit his purposes, the ones with the dogs waiting to bark and seemingly little activity. Just the place for strangers to catch the attention of someone watching from an upper room.

He had the same itchy feeling he had had during the war watching for snipers and scouts. Back then, when the whole company relied on him to get them through safely, his instincts had been good. Those trusted instincts had only failed him once, and he would bear the scars of that mistake for the rest of his life.

It taught a man caution.

"Two whistles if you have anything." Damon looked around the box. "And be on guard."

The men nodded and split up, each with his own weapon and a supply of coins to ease a reticent tongue. Three inns, one on either side of the Cock and Bull, and the one across the street. The Ram's Ear. That was the one that interested Damon, the old instinct whispering insistently. He slipped around bins and barrels, weaving his way silently through the jumble toward the inn door. The dogs were quiet, gnawing on some bones he had not been able to see from the carriage.

The common room was smoky and smelled of spilled ale, burned meat and boiled potatoes. In the far corner, two men in rough worker's clothes were slumped against the wall. Tankards sat in front of them, leaving dull dark circles on the table. One of the men was snoring.

Someone had made an effort to clean the place before going off to bed because the floor was free of bones and the manure carried in from the stables, although a faint memory lingered on the air.

Head down on the long counter by the guest book, a young man dozed. Probably the owner's son, Damon thought.

Catching him groggy and off guard would be ideal. Amazing what people divulged before their defenses came up. "I'm looking for an old man with a newborn babe," he said softly in the boy's ear.

"Upstairs, last room on the left," the boy mumbled without lifting his head. But he was not asleep because he kept talking. "We thought summat was up with him. The babe's been cryin all night. Some of our guests threatened ta leave. E's yours, iffen ya want 'im."

"Thank you. I do." Damon set two gold coins down on the counter. "There is more if it is the right man and baby."

The boy lifted his head. His eyes were surprisingly clear, and interested now as he looked Damon over. "Is the babe yers? Was it a kidnappin?"

"Yes to both. Go outside and whistle twice. A man will be

nearby waiting for the signal." Damon walked around the end of the counter and up the stairs along the wall. He thought he could take Thomas alone, he had the strength of his fury, but Thomas was a sailor, and undoubtedly quick on his feet, where Damon had to remember his weak leg.

At the top of the stairs, he turned left, and just as he did, he heard a baby's piercing scream. The anguished cry stopped him in his tracks for only a second. Shouts came from the rooms behind him. "Take 'im away!" "We're tryin to sleep 'ere!" "Not agin!"

He ran down the hall toward the sound, and pounded on the solid wood door with the head of the cane.

The heavy door popped open abruptly. "Shuddup – " Thomas gaped at Damon. "You! How did you find me?"

Damon shoved him hard enough to make Thomas stumble backward, and held him off with the knife tip of his cane. "Come near me, man, and I will use this. I doubt Verbena would blame me."

Footsteps thundered up the stairs. Reggie burst in, and after one single look at Damon's face, just stood there, blocking the exit.

With another quick twist, the knife disappeared. Damon did not think Thomas was a serious threat anyway. He had noticed something about Thomas when he first saw him, and as the man found his balance, still blustering empty threats, Damon saw it again.

Yellow eyes.

30

The parlor was still lit when the carriage pulled up an hour before sunrise. The upper floors were dark. Damon hoped Verbena had gotten the girls to sleep, but he understood how hard it would be for them to drop off with all the tension and fear in the house.

Roderick whimpered in the basket beside him. Damon rubbed the little one's empty stomach and hoped the movement kept the hunger pains away. Once Roderick got onto the breast and that essential task was done, he would have to take Verbena aside and tell her that her father was dying.

Together they would have to settle on a solution for the man's final days. It would be wrong to let the man die alone, however tempting that was. Barnes had been nothing but a burden on her and the children, but family ties were awkward things and his wife had a loyal, loving heart.

No matter how hard she pleaded, though, Barnes would not be allowed into this house, not even to die. Damon would have to hire a strong man to nurse him through, but Thomas was not going to stay with them, however short the days left. He could not be trusted. Anyone who had put them through what they had endured this night forfeited all rights to the children.

Damon refused to pass Roderick over to anyone for the whole ride. He intended to be the one to bring him home.

The door swung wide before he reached it. Mrs. Thompson took one look at the bundle in his arms and burst into tears. "Ye found 'im! Oh, praise the Lord, e's safe, the little mite!" She beckoned him in. "Get 'im out of the cold." She dabbed at her eyes with her apron with one hand while she shut the door behind him with the other.

The house was quiet. No one came rushing out to meet him. "Has everyone gone to bed?"

Samuels was on his way down the stairs, possibly the only time he had missed catching the door before Damon reached it. "Mrs. Verbena got the girls to sleep shortly after two, but I think the boys are still awake. Your wife has been packing Mrs. Smythe's face in snow all night."

Mrs. Thompson interrupted. "That poor, poor woman has quite a bruise."

Damon stopped at the foot of the stairs and looked at her sharply. "Is anything broken?" The anger he had been able to hold at bay on the way home since he had Roderick safe in his arms rose again, hot and urgent. "She might need a doctor."

"Well, I can't say 'bout broken, but she can open her mouth, and I gave her some tea. She did not have any problems swallowing. She can see out of that eye, too, so I'm thinkin she'll be all right."

Damon released a relieved breath. "I am glad for that. Where will I find my wife and my mother?"

"Mrs. Verbena is probably in the nursery with Mrs. Smythe at the moment. She 'as been pacin like to wear the floor clean away."

Damon chuckled. "That sounds like her. And my mother?"

"I made up a room for her so she could get some rest." She shook her head like a scolding mother. The frill on her mobcap bobbed as if in agreement. "A lady her age, beggin yer pardon, sir, oughten not be awake that late."

"She should know immediately. Will you wake her up? I will have their footmen wait and take her home. I think my parents should be together." He started for the stairs, with her right behind. "Oh, and Mrs. Thompson? Can you prepare us some tea, and bring it up? I think we need to settle our nerves."

She stopped on the stair and turned around. "Land, yes. I'll bring it in as soon as it's brewed. An' I'll wake your mother."

He walked up the angled flight of stairs toward the next floor. He was only halfway down the hall when Verbena burst out of the nursery, her eyes wide and anxious.

She looked at him, then her eyes went to the bundle in his arms. "You found him." Her voice was hushed, almost reverent, but piercingly clear in the quiet house. Gathering her skirts, she ran to him and slid to a halt. She reached out her hands, and he did not know for an instant which of them she meant to touch, himself or Roderick. Luminous green eyes, swimming in tears of joy, looked up at him. "You found him. Oh, Damon, you found him. How did you manage? Where were they?" Verbena slipped her hand under the little head and kissed Roderick on the forehead, only to stop abruptly and look up at Damon. "He is warm. Is he sick?"

"He has been crying, not surprisingly, but I think he will be fine. Hungry, certainly not happy, but he has not been abused."

He thought he heard a dainty snort. "I have been so worried." To his amazement, she rested her hand lightly on his arm, and went up on tiptoes, and then she brushed his mouth with lips as soft as rose petals.

In full view of any servants or family who might be watching.

When he lifted his head, he saw Julius and Matthew standing in the doorways of their rooms, grinning hugely. For all he knew, the whole staff had followed him up and was behind him in the hall, but he refused to care.

Verbena's radiant face looked up at him, her eyes only on his face even as one hand cupped Roderick's little head. The other hand still rested on his arm.

She turned to see the boys. "Everyone is home safe. Back to

bed." They obeyed. While they were fond of Roderick, neither of them needed to come and check him out for themselves.

"We have to get Roderick to Mrs. Smythe immediately," Verbena said. "He must be starving, poor sweeting, and she needs to feed him."

Damon shifted Roderick and prepared to hand him over. Instead of taking Roderick from his arms, though, she turned around and walked back to the nursery's open door, leaving him standing there in the hallway.

He remembered the long trip from her aunt's house, when Verbena did not want him so much as to sit on the same side of the carriage as the babe. She had not even worried that he would drop Roderick now, if she trusted him to finish the last walk to the nursery.

How things had changed.

He found himself smiling as he followed her down the hall.

———

NERVES TINGLED down her arms as Verbena slipped away from the nursery. She was not needed right now, and for the first time since she felt her position was being taken over, she was glad.

Everything was as good as they could hope for. Damon had examined Mrs. Smythe's bruised cheek and pronounced it no more than a very bad bruise, then had discreetly left so Roderick could get a much needed feeding. Alice was helping Mrs. Smythe with her own son, who had decided since the rest of the house was up and about, it must be time to play.

Lastly, Mrs. Thern had reassured herself that every inch of her grandson was unmarred, kissed Roderick's head, and took Samuels' arm to be led out to the waiting carriage and her husband.

Verbena had spent these last hours, whenever her mind was calm enough, rehearsing how to apologize to Damon. All those months of resentment had to be wiped away, if an apology was sufficient for such a task. She had been so worried about the dangers from his family, and all the while, her family's sins were the worst.

She owed him so much more than the apology. She had to tell him she loved him. It could not be put off any longer. He had gone into the dangerous London night to find Roderick, and had succeeded.

She pushed the bedroom door open, and stopped short. Damon stood before the fireplace, jabbing at the logs with the poker. He met her eyes. Now that the time was here, her stomach knotted.

"I have something to say," she blurted out before her courage could desert her.

One eyebrow lifted. Damon set the poker into the rest, and leaned against the mantel. He lifted a hand in encouragement.

"I love you." This was not how she meant to tell him! She meant to do it right, not just blurt it out, and especially not until she had done the apology. "I mean – "

He raised his hand, and turned his head away. "You don't owe me anything for finding Roderick."

He thought that was gratitude? Her heart had just popped out of her mouth, and he could not believe it. She guessed she could understand why. Verbena gathered her courage, shut the door, and walked slowly over to him. Her rich black opera gown, which she had not thought to remove, rustled in counterpoint with the fire's crackles.

She stopped in front of him. The fire scented the air with a rich woodsy aroma, and cast Damon's face into sharp relief. She reached a hand up to that beloved face, those strong features. "It is not gratitude, although I *am* grateful. For Roderick, for how you took on all the children, for not caring who I am. Your friend Fitz, at the theatre? When I told him the children adored you, I realized it was not just them. It was me, too. I wanted to tell you as soon as we were alone, but the news came about Roderick and there was no time to even think of it. I could hardly – "

Before she could finish, Damon's strong arms pulled her close.

Just before his lips captured hers, she saw his black eyes were glowing with a heat that blazed as warm as the fire at his back. His lips, warm and firm, merged with hers, compelling a response. She had to return that kiss, to feel his mouth. His hands roved over her, holding her close, sliding around her curves.

She did not want to move, did not want him to ever stop, but finally they both needed air.

He rested his forehead against hers, and kissed the tip of her nose. "You only realized this today? Why did this not happen last summer when I was trying so hard to court you?"

She leaned back far enough to meet his eyes. The heat had faded, but a softer warmth still glowed there. "You were courting me?"

He gave a muffled laugh. "Clearly I was not doing a very good job of it, if you could not tell."

"I knew you wanted something," Verbena said, settling back against Damon's solid chest, his steady heartbeat sending little pulses through her, "but I did not think I could love you and remain true to Edeline. You took such good care of us, but I had that terrible secret to keep. I could not even stop to wonder what I felt. I remember how much it hurt when you left last summer. Maybe it started back then. All those lonely months – I kept waiting and waiting for you to come back. Everywhere I looked, there were memories, so many things you had done to help."

Beneath her cheek, she felt him let out a long breath, a sigh felt but not heard.

She wanted to see him when she said the rest. Verbena leaned back just far enough to look up at his face, so dear, a beauty far beyond the surface. His dark eyes looked down at her, as warm as a chocolate drink. "That day when you came to Aunt Mabel's, I was so relieved."

He chuckled. "You hid it very well."

"I had been carrying the load all alone for so long, and when Edeline died, I thought I would break under the strain. And then you were there. Breathing fire, but you were there." Verbena reached up to touch his face. It was bristly with whiskers, and she did not care. "But I had to take a stand for Edeline. Without Roderick to smooth the way, I do not think this blending of our two families would have been so easy. Do you understand?"

"Of course I understand. You will remember how patient I was when you would not share Roderick with me. You sat on one side of the carriage with Roderick, and I sat on the other." He lifted her chin with one gentle finger, leaned down and kissed her, quick and hard. "I shall not let you take those words back. I have waited nearly eight years for them."

"Eight years?" Her mouth dropped open and she stared at him, stunned. Eight years? "Why eight years?"

"That is my secret. We have better things to do now than talk, don't you agree?" He pressed a kiss against her mouth, starting gently, but gaining intensity as the tension of the day found release in the merging of their mouths. The kiss ended, his hands cradled her face as his dark gaze fixed on her face. "I wish I could pick you up and carry you to that bed, but we both know that can never happen. I wish I were whole for you." Deep regret filled his eyes.

She could not bear to see that expression, could not bear that he thought anything about him disappointed her. Verbena pressed one hand over his mouth. "Shush. I would not change a single thing about you. Those scars are badges of courage and honor. They show me how strong you are inside, the power of your will. Your shoulders are broad enough to carry all my burdens. Look what you have taken on! You have won over the boys. They want to be just like you – and I can't think of anyone finer to emulate. Annabelle and Lizabeth fairly worship you. Do you think they care about your limp?" She wanted to shake him. "You are perfect to me. You have defied your family for mine, you have rescued Roderick. I shudder to think what dangers you risked. And you worry about a few marks on your body?"

He kissed her softly this time, his lips caresses on hers. "Very well, then, my dear. I would not wish to argue with you." His fingers worked busily along her back, finding hooks and undoing them. "I love you," he whispered as each little fastening gave way. "I love you, my sweet." The words were balm, washing away all the months, all the worry, all the fear, her burdens taken away by this man, her husband.

Her heart overflowed with happiness. He loved her. In spite of everything, he loved her.

THEY LAY THERE IN SILENCE, the only movement Verbena's hands stroking up and down Damon's back. She relished the peace that filled her. For the first time since he came into her life last summer, she knew exactly where she belonged. No confusion, no uncertainty, no tangled loyalties, just Damon and her in their marital bed, relishing the touch and scent of each other.

His words of earlier came back, but without urgency, just curiosity. He had said they were a secret, but somehow she thought, after what they had just shared, that he would tell her. "Why eight years?" she asked as she toyed idly with the crisp hairs on his chest.

"What?" He lifted his head and looked at her, the blankets making a tent over his shoulders.

"You said you waited eight years." Verbena held her breath.

"You want the truth?"

She nodded, and smiled at the rueful expression on his face.

"Very well." He rolled to his back, sinking into the soft down mattress, and tucked her into the crook of his arm before he pulled the blankets over her. "Eight years ago – the day in the woods, my dear, when you were but a girl. You and that basket of bread, on the path through the trees, and your hair as bright as sunshine. You kept me alive, my sweet, during the war. Remember when I saw you in those same woods last summer, when Andrew died? We both remembered that first day those years ago, but you could not know what a shock it was to see you, my vision in the flesh. During all the blood and the death, I would dream of you. You were so bright and wholesome, so untouched, and I needed some-thing clean to hold onto. I had a vague thought of trying to find out if you still lived in the village, but I hardly dared believe you were unwed. To find out that I could have you – " He broke off and his mouth captured hers again.

"You were so huge on that horse," she said softly when their lips parted, "so high above me. I was very intimidated."

'You did not show it," he said, and shifted to press a kiss into her hair.

"Father had always warned us about men, how we must always beware when they are being nicest because they only want one thing."

Damon chuckled. "It is a very nice thing, don't you agree?"

She found she could laugh, too, now. "Yes, I guess I do." But serpents had a way of sneaking in where they were not wanted, and the mention of her father had left its poison.

Damon must have felt something because his arm tightened. "What is it?"

Verbena shook her head, feeling it rub against the strong shoulder underneath her cheek. "Nothing." But he had shared his deepest secret, and she could not betray this new trust. "Just – Father." She sighed. "I cannot believe he did such a horrible thing. I never thought he loved us, but I never would have expected him to do such a thing as kidnapping a baby."

Damon sighed, too, matching sighs for the identical reason. He closed his eyes, and Verbena felt tension slip back into him, too. "Don't worry about your father causing any more problems."

"How can you be so sure? If he could do this, I don't want to think what else he has planned. This is so embarrassing to talk about." Verbena tried to get a hand free, to cover her face, but their bodies were so wrapped together that her hands were trapped under his muscular arms.

Just the mention of her father made her feel low. She forced herself to continue. "I think it would be worth it to hire a guard and transport him back to the village, if he would stay, or even somewhere further. Scotland, or Australia?" Damon pulled away to look at her, and she slipped from under his arm and rolled onto her side. "Would that be too expensive, Damon?"

He tucked her back where she had been, and rested his chin on her head. "No. I had the same idea. I don't think Australia is necessary, though." He took a deep breath. "I need to tell you something, about him. Your father is dying, Verbena."

The words just hung there on the air. Verbena did not move, she could not react. She should be sad, should she not? But the words brought no answering emotion. She should say something. Her father was dying. "How do you know?" Even the question came out flat, just like her insides. Underneath the dullness, though, there was a strange sensation, a tiny bubble, like something was beginning to brew.

Whatever that something was, she did not want it. She would rather have the nothingness.

"It is the drink," Damon answered in a quiet voice. "I saw it in the war. His eyes were yellow."

Damon let go of her, and rolled onto his back. They lay there, the two of them, in silence.

She stared up at the ceiling, the rich crown molding around the edge, the top of the curtains. Someone had not been able to dust all the way up, because a cobweb glistened in the flickering firelight. "Father did not use to be like this," she said softly, "but after Mother died, he lost the will to live. Not even the children were enough for him."

Her husband did not say anything, just waited.

"I should be crying. He is my father," she said, and it hurt that her voice did not even show a hint of tears beneath it. "Why am I not crying?"

His hand found hers under the covers, and squeezed. "Give it time," he said. He rolled his head so he could see her. "Get some sleep. Everyone here is safe, and he won't be able to get back in. I don't think he will try again, anyway." One more soft kiss, and he turned on his side and settled into the mattress. Those strong arms pulled her close, and cradled her head under his chin.

Sleep did not come. Thoughts chased themselves around her head.

Father was dying. Whatever he had done to them, he was still her father. Even if she did not really want to, she needed to see him.

What did Damon plan to do with him? Whatever time he had left, if he went home alone, he would be going to an empty house.

She rolled over carefully, and watched Damon sleep. What thoughts went through his dreams?

Life was hardly fair. She did not want her father in their lives, did not want to worry about his madness, or fear another threat against them, but she did not want him to suffer needlessly, either.

Her father was somewhere in London, ill and alone.

And the coachman knew where that was.

31

JUST AFTER DAWN, VERBENA SLIPPED OUT OF THE HOUSE AND RACED across the yard to the stables. She hoped her movements had not awakened Damon. The coachman did indeed know where her father was staying but refused to take her unless several footmen went along.

It was a well-protected carriage that headed out for Cheapside.

The stable yard was bustling with early risers. The inn smelled heavily of fresh bacon, onions and stale ale as she trouped upstairs following Reggie. He led her down the hallway to a door at the far end, and pounded on it. Several footmen stood behind her, crowding the narrow space.

On the second attempt, a familiar voice from inside yelled an obscenity in slurred tones, followed by a growled, "Go 'way!"

She pushed Reggie away from the door, and pressed her face close to the crack. "It is me, Father. I need to talk to you."

The room went quiet. Then she heard the bed creak, and a low, "Oh, hell."

They all stood in the cramped hallway while rustles came from inside, and then the door jerked open. "What are you doing here?"

She could only gape, shocked, at his appearance. His skin was sallow, his hair thin and brittle, his hands shook as they hung onto the doorframe, and the whites of his eyes were indeed yellow.

"What happened to you?" she whispered, as she stood there and stared at him.

"Well, if it ain't the little traitor." He swayed on his feet, and she almost reached out to steady him. "What made you think you could take my children away from me? And to a Thern, no less."

"What were we supposed to do?" Verbena tried not to wrinkle her nose at the stench of unwashed body and drink that draped him like fog across the field. She knew better than to argue with him in this condition, but the footmen behind her gave her confidence. "You did not even leave us enough money to survive!"

He spit onto the floor, and Verbena flinched away from the foul spot. "And so you married into that family? Is that all it takes, to dangle a bit of gold in front of your nose? You and your sister, all you do is look after yourself. You think nothing of your pa."

"You think nothing of the children!" She took a breath, and reined in her fury. "You kidnapped Edeline's baby, Father. He is so tiny, he could have been injured, or gotten sick. What got into you?"

He glared at her through those unnerving eyes. "Both you and Edeline betrayed your responsibilities to me. And *you*! You are the worst. What right had you to take away my children? Have children of your own, but leave mine alone! I will expect them ready and waiting when I show up at your bleedin fancy door."

The threat somehow had no teeth. Verbena looked at him as he was now, sick and smelly. A deep sadness weighed her heart. "Oh, Father, you missed so much. You could have had the children as memories of Mother, there are bits of her in each one of them, but instead you ran away. You ran to the sea, and you ran to the bottle, and you missed their whole childhoods."

His eyes were unfocused, and she fought the sudden surge of anger that he was not even listening to her. She hated anger, it had eaten up too much of this past year. She and the villagers had suffered under Parliament and blamed the Therns. Roderick had suffered because her father was angry at the Therns. Edeline had died because the Therns were angry with her.

She was done with it. "I adored you when I was young. You were my hero, so big and brave and strong. You could hold me over your head like I was a feather. And how you loved Mother. Yet that love destroyed you. Love should make you strong. The father I adored would never have sunk so low. I don't want to spend the rest of my life filled with bitterness and anger. I can forgive the father you once were, and when I think of you, I will try to remember who you used to be. But I can never trust you again. And I wish I could."

Verbena took a breath, and smelled the familiar stench of drink. "Go home, Father. Go home to your memories. There are letters there, she left them for you. You can find her there in her words. She would not want you to live like this. Go home, and find her again. Maybe someday you will have peace again." *Before you die, which I can see will indeed be soon.* "I hope you do. I want you to have that much."

The words were hard, but something released inside her. It was not this simple, Verbena knew there would be hours when memories would come back and the battle for peace would have to be fought again, but at that moment a little bit of pain and hurt let go.

Thomas's eyes were suddenly watery. She did not know if it was genuine emotion or the remnants of drink. Her struggle for peace and a measure of forgiveness might as well start now, Verbena told herself. She would choose to think his old self was in there, grieving.

But they would still have to send him away.

She turned around to leave. Behind the bodies of the footmen, Damon stood there in the hallway, waiting for her.

The door slammed shut. Her father's way of expressing his opinion of her husband, no doubt. "How did you know I was here?"

"I expected this. It is so like you." They walked silently back through the inn, past the doors and the smells, out into the brittle

March sunshine. Damon helped her into the carriage. His stallion was tied to the rear.

He sat down beside her, but made no move to touch her. "You went to see how sick he really was, did you not? Even now, I suspect you are trying to come up with some remedy that will heal him."

Verbena shifted on the seat to face him. "Perhaps. A little. I just could not leave him there alone." She lifted her shoulders in a helpless gesture, and looked into Damon's rich dark eyes. "It was all for naught, though, was it not? He won't accept anything. It has been so many years of hurt and struggle and poverty, all of it so unnecessary. So terribly unnecessary. Where would we have been, if not for you?"

Damon tucked a curl back under her bonnet, his fingers gentle. "I would have come and found you. I was looking for you, all that time, even from across the sea, I was looking for you."

She smiled. "Yes, you were." She leaned against his shoulder as the carriage rattled down the bumpy London streets. "I am so glad. We will be happy now, won't we, Damon? All of us."

He smiled at her, and bent down to steal a kiss. "In spite of everything, yes, I believe we will."

ABOUT THE AUTHOR

Mary Ellen Boyd is a romance author whose passions are in Regency and most important to herself, Biblical fiction, although if the muse strikes, she will happily branch into other genres. Her special passion is building a fictional story around a factual account. She is always on the lookout for another tidbit that begs to become a novel.

She lives in the beautiful state of Minnesota (and yes, it does get hot there in the summer). She and her husband have been happily married since 1982, in May, the prettiest month of the year. They have one son.

ALSO BY MARY ELLEN BOYD

Temper the Wind

His Brother's Wife

Warrior of the Heart

Regency Romances - Available in paperback and on Amazon Kindle

The Thief's Daughter

This Time Love

To find out what books are coming and to receive the FREE prequel to "Temper the Wind" :

https://maryellenboyd.com/newsletter/